THE EDGE OF LOST

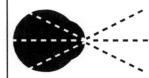

THE EDGE OF LOST

KRISTINA MCMORRIS

KENNEBEC LARGE PRINT
A part of Gale, Cengage Learning

GALE
CENGAGE Learning·

Farmington Hills, Mich • San Francisco • New York • Waterville, Maine
Meriden, Conn • Mason, Ohio • Chicago

Copyright © 2015 by Kristina McMorris.
Kennebec Large Print, a part of Gale, Cengage Learning.

ALL RIGHTS RESERVED
Kennebec Large Print® Superior Collection.
The text of this Large Print edition is unabridged.
Other aspects of the book may vary from the original edition.
Set in 16 pt. Plantin.

LIBRARY OF CONGRESS CATALOGING-IN-PUBLICATION DATA

Names: McMorris, Kristina.
Title: The edge of lost / Kristina McMorris.
Description: Large print edition. | Waterville, Maine : Kennebec Large Print, 2015.
| ©2015 | Series: Kennebec Large Print superior collection
Identifiers: LCCN 2015038112| ISBN 9781410485076 (paperback) | ISBN 1410485072
(softcover)
Subjects: | BISAC: FICTION / Historical.
Classification: LCC PS3613.C585453 E34 2016 | DDC 813/.6—dc23
LC record available at http://lccn.loc.gov/2015038112

Published in 2015 by arrangement with Kensington Books, an imprint
of Kensington Publishing Corp.

Printed in the United States of America
1 2 3 4 5 6 7 19 18 17 16 15

ACKNOWLEDGMENTS

First and foremost, I'm enormously grateful to two people who were essential in paving the path of this story while keeping me from panicking en route: my husband, Danny, and my mother, Linda Yoshida. Our countless brainstorming sessions, research excursions, and daily status updates were invaluable, but more than that their belief in me always.

Likewise, I'm thankful for my beloved friend Tracy Callan, who somehow never fails to make me feel worthy of the Most Amazing Author in the Universe Award. Also for my father, Junki Yoshida, an immigrant whose deep love of America, family, and sense of home largely inspired this book.

I'm grateful to Brianna Gelow and Madison Elmer for the million ways they helped my family survive another deadline intact; Sue McMorris, Kathy Huston, and Sharon

Shuman for their eagle-eye proofreading and ongoing support; Aimee Long for contributing input on everything from plotting and cover copy to the finished draft; and all of the incredible bloggers, reviewers, and readers who have not only allowed my stories into their lives, but also spread the word to others.

For keeping me sane and always assuring me I'm not alone, I'm indebted to my dear and talented friends Erika Robuck (one brain!) and Alyson "Twinsie" Richman. The same goes for the brilliant Therese Walsh, whose support and story insight have proven priceless yet again.

Tackling such a research-heavy novel would have been infinitely more daunting without the generous help of many people. I'm thankful to Sharon Haller, an "Alcatraz kid" and daughter of former associate warden Robert Weir, for painting a vivid picture of civilian life on the Rock; Alcatraz Gardens program manager Shelagh Fritz for providing a trove of essential details and photographs; Alcatraz park ranger Jim Nelson for enduring my endless list of questions; and author Michael Esslinger, whose feedback and thorough documentation of Alcatraz served as my gateway across the bay.

I send my sincere appreciation to author and U.S.P. Leavenworth historian Kenneth LaMaster for sharing hours of fascinating stories about prison life and jailbreaks; Claire Organ for ensuring the authenticity of my Irish characters and settings; and Florence Fois for doing the same with my Italian cast and language. I'm also thankful to Joan Swan for again guiding me through medical specifics; Steven Burke for details of courtroom proceedings and legalities; Derick Callan for help with plumbing logistics; and Jay Farrell for historical information about Navy recruiting stations. Of course, any errors are mine alone.

I'm convinced librarians are the saints of the literary world. Of them, I'm especially thankful to the Multnomah County research librarians for answering question after question on topics ranging from New York racetracks to 1930s military equipment; and to the research librarians at Leavenworth Public Library and Kansas State Library, who were also generous with their time and assistance.

As always, I thank my editor, John Scognamiglio, for his support and faith in my work from the beginning; superstar publicist Vida Engstrand for her unyielding enthusiasm; and the rest of the wonderful team at Kensington who work tirelessly behind the scenes.

Last, though far from least, my love and gratitude overflow for my sons, Tristan and Kiernan, who continue to be my most fearsome cheerleaders and the source of my deepest pride. Our family, above all, truly gives meaning to every page, milestone, and moment in my life.

PROLOGUE

Alcatraz Island
October 1937
Fog encircled the island, a strangling grip, as search efforts mounted. In the moonless sky, dark clouds forged a dome over the icy currents of San Francisco Bay.

"You two check the docks," shouted Warden Johnston, his voice muffled by rain and howling wind. "We'll take the lighthouse. The rest of you spread out."

More people traded directives, divvying up territory. They were off-duty guards and teenage sons who called Alcatraz their home, an odd place where a maze of fencing and concrete kept families of the prison staff safe from the country's most notorious criminals.

At least in theory.

From inside the warden's greenhouse, inmate 257 strained to listen — that was his number. Even his coveralls bore a stamp of

9

his designation, branded like cattle. The beam of a searchlight brushed past the glass-lined walls.

Over and over in the dankness of his cell he had envisioned this very scene. Had seen it as clear as the picture shows he grew up watching in Brooklyn. *The Mark of Zorro,* he recalled. It was the first swashbuckler he'd ever viewed on the silver screen. The film was silent, long before talkies became all the rage, but the action and suspense had quickened his pulse, gripped his lungs. Same as now.

He drew a breath, let it out. Raindrops grew insistent. They tapped the ceiling like fifty anxious fingers. Seventy. A hundred.

"Eh! Capello!"

His heart jolted. Normally he stayed keenly aware of sounds behind him, a survival tool in the pen, but somehow he'd missed the creak of the door.

He tightened his hold on the garden trowel before turning around. It was Finley, a guard with the look and nose twitch of an oversize ferret.

"Yeah, boss?"

"You seen a little girl pass by? Ten years old, light brown hair. About so high?"

The answer needed to sound natural, eased out like fishing line. "No, sir. I'm afraid I haven't."

Atop the single entry step, Finley surveyed the room with an air of discomfort. He wasn't a proponent of the rare freedoms afforded to passmen, the few trusted inmates assigned to work at the warden's house.

"Aren't you about done here?" Finley asked.

"Sure am. Then I'll be heading to the lower greenhouse to finish up."

Finley hesitated, an endless moment — of gauging? Of suspicion? At last he gave a partial nod and turned to exit.

The door swung closed.

Adrenaline rushed with the force of the pounding rain. The risks and consequences gained new clarity. Doubt invaded his thoughts.

It wasn't too late to turn back. He could serve out his time by sticking to the grind, sleeping and eating and pissing when told, and one day walk out a free man . . .

But, no. No, it wasn't that simple. Not anymore. He recalled just how much lay at stake, and any chance of reneging crumbled.

Through the fog, lightning cracked the sky. The air brightened with an eerie blue glow, and from it came a boost of certainty.

He could do this.

The plan could work.
So long as they didn't find the girl.

■ ■ ■ ■

1919

■ ■ ■ ■

1

Dublin, Ireland
March 1919
The foul haze of whiskey and cigarettes was lighter tonight than usual — a shame the same couldn't be said of the mood. Not that this surprised Shanley Keagan. At nearly twelve, he'd performed in enough pubs to understand the patterns in a calendar.

Fridays were a sure bet for nice crowds, men eager to spend their fresh wages. They would sing and laugh with old pals, toasting God's grace shining down upon them. If in an especially generous mood, they'd even buy a round for strangers. And when they were hushed down enough to welcome Shan to the "stage" — sometimes a solid platform, more often a crate from the kitchen — they might mumble over the disruption, trading dirty looks, but by the delivery of his second joke, third at most, they were roaring with laughter, as attentive as parish-

15

ioners at Easter Mass.

Mondays were the worst of the lot. Even Uncle Will, who was far from choosy when scheduling Shan's shows, knew Mondays were to be avoided. If there was a crowd at all, it was mostly customers addicted to the drink, or veterans just back from the Great War hoping to drown their memories. The few others were brooders in search of refuge from their wives, having no more interest in being nagged about finding a job than in actually doing just that.

Wednesdays, on the other hand — now, those were tough to predict. They could resemble Fridays as easily as Mondays, or fall somewhere in between. And on this particular Wednesday, as Shan stepped onto a splintered crate, he sensed precisely which it was.

Of the dozen patrons seated about, two were passed out at their tables. Up in front a pair of scabby fellows looked deep in conversation with no mind for anything more. The rest stared at Shan, their eyes right quick to judge.

"Hoi, now! Get on with it," ordered a grizzled man from his seat. "Or be Jaysus, bring on the dancing girls!"

Another shot back: " 'Tis the closest you'd ever get to seeing a lady in her knickers.

Aside from that ugly sister of yours."

Several customers chuckled, egging on a retort.

Shan needed to regain the spotlight before sneers could turn to punches and squelch any chance of a show. Of this he was well aware, even before catching a glimpse of his uncle.

Across the room William O'Mara stood at the bar, scowling between sips of his pint. The freckled skin of his bony face, normally pale next to Shan's dark features, was reddening to the shade of his patchy beard. *Perform well,* his firm eyes said, *or I'll be wise to drop you at an orphanage, where you'll be sleepin' with rats on a dingy floor and eatin' rotten cabbage soup.*

The man had spoken these words often enough that Shan could hear them in his mind. And he knew better than to ignore the warning.

With a loud clearing of his throat, Shan straightened to feel grander than his average build, ignoring the hollow ache in his stomach. "Good evening, ladies and gents. I'm Shan Keagan."

He had learned early on not to use his proper christened name unless he wanted to be heckled — "Shanley" being traditionally reserved for a surname. He'd change it

17

altogether if it weren't among the few things left from his mam.

"I'll be entertaining you tonight while you enjoy your pints." Now that he'd gained their attention, he started with a reliable joke. "There's such a chill out, it brings to mind a tale of a terrible snowstorm. The drifts were so high one night, a priest and a nun found themselves stuck in a church alone. When the sister complained of being cold, the kindly father searched about and fetched her a blanket. Again and again this happened, but the heap of blankets failed to help. At last, desperately freezing, the sister insisted the Lord would surely forgive them for acting as a married couple to keep warm for a single night. Full of joy, the father agreed. 'Aye,' he cried, 'from now on, you'll fetch the blankets on your own!' "

Shan paused to read the audience. Only tepid smiles, but not to fret. Experience had taught him to skip to his impressions, normally the second part of his act.

From endless practice, he proceeded to reshape his voice into a colorful range of characters. Fists on his hips, he transformed into a harping Irish mother. A lick of the lips and he was a whistling Yankee, his new favorite for many a reason. With shoulders hunched, he became a dumber-than-ox

Englishman.

Still, for all of this, he earned only a sprinkling of snickers.

His palms slickened with sweat. Insulting the Brits usually endeared even the hardest Irish crowd. Since late January, when the War of Independence began, sentiments against the Crown had ratcheted to a higher level — if that were even possible. Perhaps this explained why Shan sensed a swelling desire in the room to take aim at a target. And that was just what he'd become if he didn't switch course. A silly song would hopefully do.

In the warbling style of folk singer Eugene Fitzpatrick, he belted out " 'Twas Sure I Fell in Love When I Fell into Me Ale." Nerves magnified cracks in Shan's voice, a growing curse of his age, and he found relief at finishing the tune — though none from the room's intensity.

The few sounds from the audience came from an old man being repeatedly woken by his own nasally snores, and from a lady giggling at a far table, where a scruffy man in a flannel shirt tickled her sides. She wore a dress as bold as her red lips, the sort of woman who, according to Uncle Will, charged for the pleasure of her company. When she leaned forward, her bosoms rose in large white mounds, resembling loaves from the baker.

Shan fought the urge to stare. He mined his memory for material and remembered Murphy, a made-up fool of a drunk. If nothing else, the tales could fill enough time to secure a free supper, his personal reward from the pubs.

His stomach growled as he launched into a story. He was halfway through when a burly man pushed back from his table and shot to his feet.

"What's that you're sayin' about me, boy?"

"Ah, Murphy," hollered an older man. "The lad wasn't talking about *you.* Sit down on your arse."

Murphy swayed, as if riding the internal waves of his liquor.

Shan forced a swallow. "Did I say 'Murphy,' sir? What I meant, of course, was 'Mickey.' My apologies for the error."

The man held a stern face but slowly reclaimed his seat. Shan sighed to himself before praying to the good Lord that no one in the room was a Mickey.

"Now, then," he tried again. "I believe I was describing the day *Mickey* awoke covered in mud and feathers, head to toe."

No one spoke out, a fortunate thing. Shan was about to continue when, once more, his belly grumbled. This time it brought a hunger so strong it jellied his knees. He tightened his legs to keep his balance, but the shift of weight caused a loud crack beneath his boots. Before he could adjust, the crate gave way and he landed hard on his rear. Laughter broke out in the room. He hurried to rise from the wooden floor, brushing grime and spilled ale from his clothes.

"What's that you were singing about?" a man called to him. "Something about fallin', was it?" The laughter spread, but Shan didn't rejoice. Embarrassment and anger formed a bitter reply on his tongue. The words churned and expanded, preparing to spew free. Just in time, he gulped them down, remembering Uncle Will.

Shan dared to look over. Beside the bar, his uncle and the pub owner were engaged in a chat. A welcome discovery, until Shan noted the sharpness of their eyes. Uncle Will shook something — a coin — in his right fist. The owner stood a good foot shorter, but in the manner of one not intimidated by height. As if to prove as much, he crossed his arms and jutted his chin. The challenge wasn't missed by Uncle Will, whose clenched jaw signaled a rage in the making.

Shan bristled, a reflex. His body was well

aware of where those rages led. The scars on his neck and hip throbbed as a reminder, urging him to take cover. Alas, he had no choice. The last thing an orphan needed was for his only relative to be carted off and locked in a cell.

"You heard me, all right," Uncle Will said as Shan approached to intervene. "I called you a cheatin' bastard, because that's what ye are. The deal was for a shilling, not a goddamn sixpence."

The owner's nostrils flared as if swiped with smelling salts. "You're lucky to get *that* much. The boy would bring in a crowd, ye said. Would make me more money, ye said."

"And he bloody would have, if this place weren't such a hellhole. I've taken a shite in privies better than this."

"Uncle Will, *please,*" Shan implored. But his uncle ignored him and spat at the owner, who burst into a fit.

"That's it! Get out. Right this minute, or I'll thump ye in the —"

The threat stopped short. Uncle Will's knuckles made sure of it by plowing into the man's face.

Shan reached for his uncle to coax him away but a bartender and another man moved in, pushing Shan aside. A whirl of punches flew. Barstools toppled and a pint glass shattered.

Two hands grasped Shan's shoulders. He started to wrench free, but a woman's voice entered his ear. "Shh, 'twill be all right," she said, drawing him away from the scuffle and shards. She was the lady with red lips and loaves for a chest.

The owner swung hard at Uncle Will's gut before ordering his helpers to put the rubbish where it belonged. Dutifully the men dragged Uncle Will, short of breath and doubled over, out to the street.

Shan just stood there, already dreading the long walk home. He wasn't dim enough to think a free bowl of corned beef remained an option. Around him, people returned to their lives as if nothing had happened.

Except for the woman. She swept past Shan, picked up the dropped coin, and tenderly curled it into his hand. "You've got real talent, sweet lad. Don't let it go to waste." She gave him a smile that seemed heavy to wear before returning to the man in flannel, a fresh giggle in her voice.

That was when it dawned on Shan that he wasn't the only actor in the room.

2

Murmurs drifted up from the alley. They lured Shan to the window of his uncle's one-room flat, as they often did this time of night. Every sound was amplified in those dark, empty hours before Dublin settled in for sleep. Or most of it, rather. A few times a week the husband next door would drink through wages meant for food and rent, and he'd stumble home bellowing songs, promptly cut short by his wife's furious shrills.

Then there were the rats. They'd scratch and scamper well into dawn, between the walls, in nooks and crannies. They were nomads on a constant hunt for food, shelter, and safety. Same as Shan and Uncle Will. And those in the alley below.

The pane too dingy for a decent view, Shan tugged the window upward. Cold air shot through his thinning cotton shirt. The paraffin lamp flickered on the table by the bed. He rubbed his arms against the chill. His wool coat and sweater sagged on a rope strung over the coal stove. The garments, damp after his walk from the pub, released a musty smell.

Shan gazed down the back side of the building, a shabby stack of four bricked floors. A web of laundry linked them to the next set of flats. Each line drooped vacantly in the rain but for one. A widow from the second story had a habit of leaving her sheets out on rainy days, which was most of the year in Ireland. She would drape them like a canopy, attracting a small herd of vagrants, mainly young, from the shadows.

Shan would hear tenants in the halls and stairwell exchanging their disapproval, blaming the widow's friendship with the landlord — on the word "friendship" they would raise a brow — for leaving them unable to state a complaint. "We're doing these children no favors," they would say, "by encouraging a life on the streets. Many are there by choice, you know. They'll be tinkers and knackers for good, expecting the government to support them forever."

Their expressions matched the harshness of their words. But Shan was a listener, a studier of more than pitches and accents. And what he heard, as faint as a whisper, was the truth behind their unease: the fear, and the guilt.

No man wants a daily reminder of the hardships that in a blink could be his own, nor to carry the shame of being unable, or unwilling, to help those in need. Such burdens were easier to discard when not planted outside your window.

All the same, Shan couldn't help but look.

Beneath a roof of linen, the strangers huddled around a fire set in a metal barrel. They held their gloved hands over flames that glowed orange across their faces. All appeared to be boys, Shan's age or older. Orphanages favored infants and toddlers, as did parents willing to adopt — unless they were seeking free labor. The overflow went to local churches, where girls were given priority for meals and beds. Even in the house of the Almighty, beggars had a pecking order.

Already Shan knew this. He also knew very little prevented him from standing in that queue. The money left from his parents — no doubt the reason his mam's brother first took him in — had been spent long ago. And when it came to the government's weekly charitable dole, the few extra shillings his uncle received for fostering Shan hardly made him essential, as Uncle Will told him on a regular basis. One wrong step and he'd be out on the street, his future far more grim. Sure, he could read and write at a level beyond his age, but now, without schooling, without parents . . .

At the thought of them, Shan felt the weight of their absence, as heavy as stone on his chest. More and more they were fading from his mind. Like people he'd only imagined.

He closed his eyes now and strained to summon his mam: her long auburn curls, her angelic skin. He could almost smell her talcum powder, a sweet lavender scent, and hear the rhythmic creak of her rocker. In their old house in Dunmore, on the coast of County Waterford, she would sway there for hours and read her books — a love she passed down to Shan — and she would send him a wink as he played on the floor with his jacks and marbles and wooden train.

Meanwhile in the evenings, his father — a doctor with silvered temples and a forehead lined with wisdom — would flip through articles in the *Irish Independent* and puff on a hand-carved pipe —

Well. Not his father precisely. Rather, the man Shan had known as his da. Back before the façade had been yanked clean away with the discovery of a letter.

"Jaysus, Mary, Mother o' God. Are you heatin' the bloody neighborhood?"

Shan twisted around to find his uncle glaring from the doorway. "Sorry, Uncle Will," he spouted, and rushed to shut the window. He braced for a verbal lashing, not unlike those he'd received from his teachers, back before his performing schedule replaced schooling altogether.

But Uncle Will simply tossed a paper sack onto the kitchen table. "Open it," he said with a trace of a slur.

Shan held in place, knowing better than to trust a glimmer of his uncle's kindness. Same as the fairies from his childhood tales, it could vanish as quick as a snap.

"Go on," Uncle Will said. "Eat."

Shan had briefly forgotten how famished he was. He hurried to the table and emptied a U-shaped sausage from the bag. Half as thick as his wrist, it had a greasy sheen and light black crust. One flight up, the butcher's wife must have retired for the night, unable to stop her husband from trading the last of their supper for a jelly jar of moonshine.

It was one of Uncle Will's rare talents, brewing the concoction himself with ingredients bought with the dole. He called the drink "liquid gold." To be used only for bartering, he'd said.

From the current reddening of his eyes, however, it was clear yet again that no rules applied to Uncle Will. Not that this concerned Shan. His sole interest lay with the meat before him, worlds better than the weak broth he'd expected. Only from his proper upbringing did he find the willpower to fetch a plate, utensils, and a glass of water.

As Uncle Will hung his cap and coat over the stove, Shan took a seat at the table. To savor every ounce of flavor, he sliced up small bites and forced himself to chew slowly.

"Would you look at yourself." Uncle Will reclined in the chair across from him. He mockingly waved around a match and hand-rolled cigarette. "Eatin' like British royalty, ye are."

Shan kept his gaze low. Mealtime together was like wading through a swamp: one wrong step could pull you under.

Fortunately a distraction arrived in the form of a cry. The new tenants upstairs had a newborn girl who wailed, according to her mam, whenever hungry or tired or just plain fussy.

"They'd better shut that gob of hers," Uncle Will muttered. His eyelids sagged as he lit his cigarette, the first deep puff triggering a hacking fit. The cough came from years of factory jobs, every sort imaginable, made worse by his frequent smoking. Shan was to warn him against the habit — Doc O'Halloran had instructed as much during his last visit to the flat.

Before Shan could do so, the coughing subsided. He held out his glass of water, but Uncle Will waved it off, wanting only a draw from his cigarette. The tip glowed orange, like the flames in the alley, and he exhaled a swirl of gray.

As Shan continued to eat, his uncle slogged from the table and dropped onto their creaky bed. The lit cigarette dangled from his lips as he started to doze off.

A fire would do them no favors. Nor, for that matter, would more dirt on their coverlet.

Shan hastened over to crush out the cigarette in an ashtray made of a tin can. Then he yanked off his uncle's crusty boots. He cringed from the odor, as ripe as sewage on a summer day. Through the ceiling, the baby's crying grew.

Anxious to finish his meal, Shan went to close the privacy curtain. It was a quilt turned rattier from hot scrubs in the sink, his endless fight against fleas.

"Come back," Uncle Will mumbled, suddenly roused. He waggled a hand in sloppy movements.

Shan inched forward, but stayed out of reach. He'd first learned his lesson the day he delivered broth to help his uncle's cold; when Uncle Will burned his tongue, he'd flung the soup at Shan's legs to show it had been too hot. "Yes, sir?"

"A song. I be wantin' a song."

"What sort of —"

"Anything, for Christ's sake. Just drown out that goddamn babe."

Until his parents died, Shan had barely known his uncle, making the man's requests that much harder to fill. A funny tune could amuse him to the point of hearty laughter, but only if the mood was right. Tonight, Shan's gut said to go with a gentler choice, a song praising Ireland for its soft rolling hills and stony strength.

Halfway through the first verse, his uncle cut in.

"Not that. Another."

"I . . . yes, sir . . ."

Taking a guess, Shan switched to a tune about seeing a girl on the banks of the river Shannon, but again the man interrupted. "Anything ye haven't bloody sang a hundred times already."

Just as panic loomed from coming up

31

blank, Shan recalled an old favorite from his mam: a Gaelic lullaby she would sing at bedtime. If he gave it much thought, the lyrics would escape him. He simply opened his mouth, and as if by magic, the song flowed out, transporting Shan to a happier time, a better place.

He was so lost in the moment he didn't spare a glance at his uncle until the last note. Only then did he catch the upward curve of the man's mouth, a wisp of a smile. Even the infant upstairs had gone quiet.

"Our gram," Uncle Will said. "She'd sing that to us as children. And your mother, och, she'd ask for it over and over, she would." A mix of care and sadness enwrapped his voice, and he released a sigh that seemed to have been held for years.

Shan stared, motionless, shocked by the stranger before him, nearly as much as by the mention of his mam. It was a topic Uncle Will never broached on his own. Silently Shan pleaded with him to continue. But the man said nothing else, and his eyes began to close.

A wave of questions surged in Shan's mind. There could be consequences to voicing them, as proven just weeks ago, the day he found the letter.

He had been sweeping the floor mindlessly

when he knocked over the books inherited from his mam, stacked in the corner. A folded paper slipped from the depths of *Sense and Sensibility.* A novel for ladies, it was among the few Shan had yet to read, despite its being his mam's favorite. He otherwise would have much earlier found the missive penned by an American sailor.

My dearest Moira,

If my letters have managed to reach you, I can only assume you no longer wish to hear from me. Whether you've moved on with another beau or simply don't feel the same as I do for you, perhaps I'll never know.

Nevertheless, let me express once more that I miss you beyond words — the beauty of your hair and eyes, the softness of your skin. I shall continue to pray that one day soon I will receive word in return. Until then, sweet Moira, please know I love you with all of my heart.

John

Shan's urgency to learn more had led him to ask the sole living person he knew with ties to his mam. Uncle Will, taken by surprise after indulging at a pub, replied in stammering bits: damning the Yank sailor who'd taken advantage of his sister, just a poor teenage girl with no sense to know better.

Uncle Will had paced as he spoke, the speed increasing with his words. "Off on a church mission, she was, making the state he'd left her in all the more unholy. You can't tell me the shock of it didn't have a hand in our parents' demise — God rest their souls. If the good doctor hadn't found it in his heart to marry Moira, hiding the shame of it all, our family name would surely have been tarnished till the end of time!"

Shan's world had spun, a torrent of thoughts. Among them was the date on the letter: a month before his own birth. Overwhelmed by what it all might mean, he struggled to find his voice. "Are you saying . . . my mam and . . . that they only married because —"

Uncle Will had halted and his glossy eyes widened, as if Shan had interrupted a private talk. Not a second later, the man's face hardened with fury. "You want to beckon the banshee, do ye!"

Some believed merely speaking of the dead would invite death to the door. Regardless of whether Uncle Will ascribed to such a thing, he ensured an end to the discussion with a fierce slap to Shan's face. Before Shan could recover, Uncle Will snatched and wadded the letter and threw it into the stove. Had there been enough money for coal that day, the page would have been burned to ashes, instead of rescued by Shan in the wee hours of the night — though perhaps he shouldn't have bothered. His parents were gone, almost two years past.

"On account of the consumption," the nurse had explained. A female patient of Shan's da had died from the sickness in the lungs, but not before spreading it about. Revenge for not finding the girl a cure, some would claim. Whatever the case, it left Shan's parents in a terrible state, too terrible to even say good-bye. "Best to remember them as they were," the nurse had said. "Let bygones be bygones."

It wouldn't be as easy as that, but what choice did Shan have? Determined to try, he'd prepared to burn the letter himself. And yet, when the moment came, so did an unshakable thought: that somehow his mam had guided him to that letter, that she indeed wanted him to know the truth.

He considered this again now. In seconds at most, Uncle Will would be lost to sleep, taking his willingness to share with him.

Given the man's grogginess, Shan stood a decent chance of pressing the issue without earning a slap or worse. Or so he hoped.

"Uncle Will?" Absent a reply, Shan hurried to retain his nerve. "My father — the one by blood. Could you tell me anything about him?"

Uncle Will grunted. Likely a warning, but Shan persisted.

"Please tell me, is there something more you know?"

His uncle murmured, producing a recognizable word.

"Music. Is that what you said?" Shan was sure of it, and his mind raced. Maybe the sailor had a knack for singing, or played an instrument. All at once it made sense that he himself was drawn to performing. "He was a musician, then. In America."

Uncle Will yawned and more sounds tumbled out. Shan leaned closer, enduring the man's sour breath. What he caught were snippets of information — about the sailor's being from New York and the name . . . John . . . Lewis.

Lewis. A surname.

"What happened between them? Was there something that tore them apart?"

Uncle Will was drifting away.

With little choice, Shan gave him a gentle

shake, attempting to stir his uncle without waking an angry giant. But a rattling snore rose from the man's nose, confirming his drunken slumber. There would be no more shared tonight.

Frustrated, helpless, Shan relented. He returned to his chair and poked at the remaining meat. He'd lost all appetite.

But why? Now he had hope.

The man's name was John Lewis. A musician from New York. While the details were few, they made the sailor more real. Which meant Shan wasn't an orphan.

Was it possible the sailor, too, was alone?

Right then, Shan's purpose became clear, the reason he'd found that letter.

One day he would go to America and find this John Lewis. Surely, with such devotion in his writing, the man would embrace his child with open arms. They would reunite, Shan and his father, in the glamorous city of New York, and embark on a splendid life together.

It was just a matter of time.

3

Over the next several days, whenever speaking to his uncle, Shan would drop casual mentions of America. How he'd heard that the wives of the Doherty and Gallagher families were busy packing to move, now that their husbands had earned enough in New York to buy passage for them all. And my, how it must be nice to see a brand-new film at the pictures in America so many months before they reached the likes of Ireland. Oh, and did he know what people have been saying about the fine quality of Yankee cigarettes and liquor?

This last one caught Uncle Will's attention, but only in the way of a stern warning for Shan: to steer clear of such depravity, if he knew what was good for him.

Though the rest of Shan's hints were brushed away or ignored, he wasn't about to give up. Even now, plenty more highlights were flitting around in his head as he and

38

Uncle Will waited to be seen at the Labour Exchange. The thoughts were like birds in a cage, desperate for release, but trapped for the time being.

After a restless night of coughing fits, Uncle Will had no tolerance for yapping. The fact that smoking in the queue was frowned upon, as it displayed a vulgar waste of spending, only worsened his uncle's mood. Soon, though, they would receive their weekly dole — the free funds always cheered Uncle Will — and Shan would again plod toward his goal.

"O'Mara!" The mustached clerk stood in the hall. "William O'Mara!"

"Aye." Uncle Will rose, clutching his cap.

Shan followed as usual, eager to flee the area that smelled of sweat and nerves and stale breath over yellowed teeth. He grabbed hold of his uncle's free hand, as was expected. It was dry and rough with calluses, his grip rather awkward, but deep down Shan couldn't deny craving the comfort in it, even if logic said he shouldn't.

In silence, they passed the wooden benches packed with men in hats and dark suits, many with stitched-up holes, all with eyes lowered. A charity line was one of the few places where even the proudest men sank to a slouch.

At the open doorway, the clerk directed Uncle Will toward the center of the room, where he and Shan would stand before the table of three to be judged.

"I'm well aware what to do," Uncle Will muttered.

One would think the clerk would recognize them by now and deem the instructions unneeded. Then again, his ambivalence made it clear that the men who filed past him each week were all but a faceless mob.

The committee leader, on the other hand, seemed to keep mental notes on every man on the dole. Or at least on Uncle Will.

"Ah, yes," sighed the suited gentleman with a ring of gray hair. "Mr. O'Mara . . ." He paused then and traded knowing looks with the men seated to his sides. This was typical of the routine, but Shan sensed a change coming on, even before the next words: "We're very pleased to see you today."

Uncle Will's bushy brows dipped. His hand tightened around Shan's. "Are ye?"

"Indeed we are. We've heard some troubling news, you see. And we're all hoping you might be able to clear it up."

The other men nodded, signaling the leader to continue.

"As it so happens," he explained, "we have

it on good authority that a man by the name of William O'Mara has been using a portion of his funds to create a drink meant to lure fine Catholic men into a shameful life of sin. A temptation as poisonous as Eve with that juicy red apple. And we want to be sure this isn't the case."

Of course, Shan could see they wanted just the opposite.

"Clearly," Uncle Will said, "I have the misfortune of sharing a name with a grave sinner." His indignant tone was almost impressive. "To make me wee poor nephew here suffer as a result would be an unthinkable tragedy."

Shan recognized his cue to look up with desperate eyes, which in truth took no effort. For he well knew the consequences of going without a meal and, more than that, of Uncle Will's displeasure when he viewed Shan as not doing his part to aid in their struggles.

From the committee's sympathetic nods, there seemed to be hope. But then the leader of the group asked Uncle Will about his failure to keep a job for any reasonable length of time. The inquiry was a standard one — it was the rages, of course, to blame — but at that particular moment William O'Mara had reached his limit for being

41

challenged. Suddenly he exploded, like a spark to gunpowder, sending his own accusations flying, of the board being full of thieves and dictators and surely Protestants at that.

The last one caused the greatest offense. In a blink, Shan and Uncle Will were escorted to the street, banned from ever returning.

Shan's performances in filthy pubs would now be their only source of income. But this wasn't what caused the twisting of Shan's gut. It was the realization that a trip to America would be that much further away. Absorbing this blow, he only vaguely caught his uncle's parting words: about needing a pint to ease the injustice before meeting Shan at home. Then Uncle Will ambled away while scouring his pockets for change.

Reminded by the sight, Shan reached into his coat to retrieve his sixpence. He had taken a great risk, keeping the money a secret, with hopes of saving up for their tickets. What an eejit he was for thinking it would make a difference. He should have spent it all on himself by now.

Indeed that was exactly what he'd do. On chocolates or toffees or anything he pleased. And he knew just where to buy them. It was a minor rebellion at best, but better than nothing. Out of spite, he would gobble the sweets in a single sitting, simply because he could. Even if it meant a bellyache for the night, he would relish the fact that Uncle Will would never know.

4

Beneath the overcast sky, bloated with coming rain, Shan marched toward Kerry Street. Every sound grated on his ears: motorcars rattling and honking, horses clacking the cobblestones, vendors shouting the prices of their goods in open carts. Just after noon, hordes of people bustled about, the smug upper class most of all.

Even aside from their fashion and cleanliness, it was easy to tell the rich from the poor. The rich were always in a hurry: walking and shopping and traveling with purpose. Quite backward, in Shan's eyes. If anyone should be enjoying a leisurely stroll, it ought to be the wealthy.

Soon he arrived at Maguire & Co. The familiar fragrance of tea and sweets filled his nose and lungs. He felt his bitterness waning. Determined to keep hold of it, he reminded himself why he'd come.

Among the customers sprinkled about,

two ladies were admiring trinkets in a glass case, a display of Celtic crosses and pendants devoted to saints. Others sifted through the wall of books, shelved in rows as straight and orderly as King George's guards. While most stores had a particular specialty, this one offered a bit of this and that, linked by a simple goal of bringing people joy.

Out of the storage room stepped Mr. Maguire. He carried a pair of winged figurines to the register counter. His buttoned vest wrapped tautly over his belly and his scalp peeked through his black hair. "Well, well, now," he said after a glance at the entry. "If it isn't the world-famous Shanley Keagan. Right under me very own roof."

"Hello, Mr. Maguire."

"Come let me look at ye." A sparkle lit the man's eyes as he waved Shan over, making it a great deal harder for Shan to retain his rightfully sour mood. "Growing like a weed, ye are. Won't be long before your hair's caught fire on the sun."

Only a few weeks had passed since Shan's last visit. Still, from the flattery, he couldn't help standing straighter, feeling older and more . . . important. As he always did around Mr. Maguire.

"Ah, I nearly forgot!" The man pointed

emphatically, then bent down and opened a cupboard behind the counter. "Now, where did my Nora put it?"

His wife, as the shop's bookkeeper, organized so well that Mr. Maguire often couldn't find a thing.

"Ah, yes, there it is." He rose with a gramophone record, and not one of his usual. Shan knew each and every disc in Mr. Maguire's personal collection. "I hear it's a belter," he said with a grin.

"You're saying . . . you haven't listened yet?"

"Brand-new in the case. Been waiting for you to come by before putting the needle to it."

Bridling his eagerness, Shan accepted the offering as if handling fine crystal. He read the label: *Billy Murray and Steve Porter.* He wasn't familiar with the second performer, but the first was far and away his favorite. Though Shan had acquired most of his accents from the funny recordings of Ralph Bingham, no one delivered jokes and silly songs better than Billy Murray.

Plus, there were personal reasons for the preference. More than a year ago, when Shan first came into the store to buy sweets with a halfpenny he'd found on the street, he saw a younger lad, poor and scrawny, sneaking toffee into his pocket. Mrs. Maguire caught him red-handed, and the boy blubbered with pleas for her not to tell his da. *Never do we take what doesn't belong to us,* Shan's da had ingrained in him since birth, deeming the act worthy of consequence. Even so, the sheer panic in the lad's eyes said the punishment at home would far outweigh the crime, spurring Shan to volunteer his halfpenny as pay for the boy's toffee. Mrs. Maguire accepted, despite her reluctance, and shooed the lad out with a warning.

Weeks later, Shan had wandered back in, seeking refuge from the rain and his uncle's wrath. He leafed through the records, though he had no money to buy such a thing and doubted he ever would. It had been a terribly low day. His heart was aching for his parents and the life he'd once had, and Mrs. Maguire happened to notice. From the warmth in her eyes, it was clear she remembered him. The roundish woman with light hair in a soft bun did something quite unusual. "Follow me," she said, and led Shan to the back room. Between the shelves of supplies, she invited her husband to show off his latest gadget, a beautiful oak gramophone, which the man kindly did.

He'd placed the needle on a record featuring Billy Murray, and what emerged was a fanciful tune called "Foolish Questions." The lyrics put such a smile on Shan's face that Mr. Maguire asked if he'd like to hear it again. The second time through, Shan softly chuckled. By the end of the third, he laughed out loud, something he hadn't done since his parents had passed.

"Come back anytime," Mr. Maguire had said, to which his wife winked in agreement. And so Shan began his regular visits after school, losing himself in every record the shopkeeper owned. With little to offer in return, Shan would sometimes help with dusting the shelves or counting inventory or unloading boxes — becoming easily distracted when those boxes included new books. Yet as long as he used care and scrubbed his hands clean, Mrs. Maguire allowed him to peruse the pages. On occasion Mr. Maguire would even share a handful of toffees while he and Shan listened to records, ranking their favorites. Certainly, Shan enjoyed the likes of Marion Harris's "I Ain't Got Nobody" and John McCormack's "It's a Long, Long Way to Tipperary." But not half as much as Billy Murray's "I'm the Guy" and "Under the Anheuser Bush."

Shan wound up visiting so many times he

could recite the recordings on his own, entertaining the Maguires — often until their cheeks were red and sore from laughter — and sometimes the customers too. Eventually, a friend of Mr. Maguire suggested the act was quite fitting for a local pub. Uncle Will, upon hearing the news, called the idea bloody rubbish — until learning there would be pay.

A fortunate thing for them both. As of today, how else would they live?

The reality of this would press down on Shan later, but not now.

"This Steve Porter fellow, is he a comedian too?" he asked.

Mr. Maguire nodded. "A real amusing one, at that. I'm not sure he's a vaudevillian, like your Billy Murray. But he's also a Yank, and making quite a name for himself, I hear."

"I can hardly wait to hear it." The fact that the record had never been played made it all the more enticing.

"Sir? Pardon me." A woman at the trinket case raised her gloved hand. "I wish to purchase this claddagh pin, if you please."

" 'Tis a grand choice." Mr. Maguire turned to Shan. "Back in a bit."

While waiting, Shan ran his fingers over the record label. He imagined what it would be like to watch the performers in person. The velvet curtains and brightly lit stages. The orchestra and balconies and ushers. Each of their theaters was surely elaborate, as was everything in America.

The vision of the scene played through Shan's mind, and from it came a thought. A solution to all their troubles. An idea that should have come to him long ago.

Uncle Will would take some convincing, of course, but all the evidence needed to make a strong case was literally in Shan's hands.

5

"Where the hell've ye been?" Uncle Will yelled from the bed. Shan had just walked through the door, expecting the room to be vacant, and the shock loosened his grip. Too late, he felt the record slip from inside his coat. He scrambled to save it, but Mr. Maguire's brand-new purchase toppled to the rough wooden floor. "Ah, Jaysus, no!"

He dropped to his knees. Hands damp from the rain, he used his fingertips to slide the disc from its flimsy casing. Distantly he heard his uncle scolding him for the use of foul language. But Shan continued to examine the record as best he could. The table lamp and afternoon grayness seeping through the window provided the only light.

Not shattered. Not cracked. No scratches he could see.

"You'll answer me now, boy, if you know what's good for ye."

Shan's awareness returned. "I-I'm sorry,

Uncle Will." He returned the record to its cover. "I didn't expect you back from the pub this early."

"Plainly so. Or you'd have gone straight home as I told —" Uncle Will broke off into raspy coughs. He muffled them with a yellowish handkerchief that might have been white when originally sewn.

Shan rose to explain himself, but was detoured by the clacking of shoes. Doc O'Halloran appeared from behind the half-closed privacy curtain, dropping his stethoscope into a medical bag. He was as slender as he was tall, and looked even more so under the flat's low ceiling.

"Good day, Shanley."

"Dr. O'Halloran. I didn't realize we'd be seeing you."

"Your uncle's had a terrible coughing fit. Ended in a fainting spell at Callaghan's. I happened to be across the way, sending a wire at the post office."

"How lucky that you were nearby."

"Indeed." Doc O'Halloran smiled. The combination of his peppered temples, proper suit, and leather case reminded Shan of his da. Of course there were differences too. While Doc O'Halloran had a warmth about him, Shan's da had been more of the logical, scientific sort.

Uninterested in the pleasantries, Uncle Will narrowed his eyes at Shan. "You might not feel so lucky, boy, when I find out what you're tryin' to hide from me."

Shan glanced down at his hand, recalling his mission. "It's only a record. But I wasn't hiding it. Just protecting it from the rain."

"Is that so? And how would you be affording a thing like that?"

"He lent it to me — Mr. Maguire did. For the night."

"With no way to play it," Uncle Will scoffed.

"Well, yes. But it wasn't to play —"

"Bring it here. Now." The command was firm but less harsh than usual. This was typically the case around Doc O'Halloran. Maybe it was on account of the doctor's kindness, but more likely it was due to his skillful service. When a person had something you needed, it was best to show you were worthy.

As the doctor put on his long wool coat, readying to leave, Shan made his way toward the bed. Footsteps upstairs rattled the ceiling, and again a baby cried.

Shan displayed the record by holding it up, but his uncle demanded he hand it over. With dread, Shan obeyed, trying not to picture the disc snapped in two.

"If I find out you stole this, I'll tan your hide, I will."

"I only borrowed it to show you, I swear."

"Oh? And tell me why I'd have any interest in a bloody record."

Shan strained to recall the words he'd rehearsed on the way home. "I've heard . . . that is, Mr. Maguire said . . . the performers on the record have become famous for telling jokes . . . and singing songs in different voices."

"And you think you're going to be some grand star. Is that it?"

Shan wanted to clarify — to merely convey that his talents could prove more lucrative across the sea — but his focus was fixed on his uncle's hands, in dire need of a wash, gripping the record too tight.

Doc O'Halloran stepped closer. "Is that a recording of Billy Murray you have? Ah, what a funny one he is. May I?" He held out a palm, and with only brief hesitation Uncle Will gave up the disc.

Breathing easier, Shan said to the doctor, "He's my favorite."

"As right he should be."

Shan started to remember the points of his speech. Though not smooth and connected, they were at least within reach. "He's a vaudevillian. Travels about with a

54

troupe. They perform all over America. Singing and dancing and storytelling. Even some magic too."

"Sounds exciting," Doc said. "And not altogether different than the shows you do yourself."

"Aye," Shan said simply.

"Good money too, I'd bet. Over there in America."

Shan felt a smile spreading from the inside out. Yet under his uncle's heavy gaze, he aimed for an even face, not wanting to appear scheming. The seed of an idea would have no chance of sprouting if stomped out by suspicion.

"You know, Shanley. Before I go, I do have a private matter to discuss with Mr. O'Mara. If you could wait in the hall, I won't be but a minute."

The request was a surprise, but of course Shan agreed and found a seat on the floor in the hallway.

Before long, the temptation to eavesdrop became too much to resist. He pressed his ear to the door, yet heard only mumbles. Neighbors' voices made the task all the more challenging. From behind thin walls Mr. Boyle ranted as usual about his support of the IRA and the Sinn Féin party, but not seeing Michael Collins as the savior every

Irishman was making him out to be. Mrs. Boyle's urgings that he hush down were nearly as loud as his objections to doing any such thing.

Suddenly, the knob of the apartment door creaked above Shan, and he scurried to his feet. Doc O'Halloran emerged with his bag in one hand and a jelly jar in the other. While he was more of the sherry-drinking type, he always accepted the moonshine with grace, not one to insult a man's form of payment.

"You take care of your uncle, now."

"I'll do my best."

"Good lad." The doctor gave a thoughtful look before continuing on his way.

Shan never did learn what was said behind that door. Yet two nights later, after returning home from a pub show that paid a shilling, Uncle Will stared out the window in silence. He finished two cigarettes, one right after the other, filling the air with as much smoke as tension. Then without turning from his reflection, he said to Shan, "We'll be going to America."

6

The weeks following Uncle Will's decision to move halfway across the world passed like a ride on a runaway horse. A bewildering blur of thrills and uncertainty. A forward charge with no time to rest. And if given a chance, you'd find yourself asking: *What in God's holy name have I done?*

For Shan, that feeling came as clear as day on the morning of their departure. He had just entered Mr. Maguire's shop when the realization that the visit would be his last struck with the force of a broad-knuckled punch. While the store's sweets and records had initially lured him in, it was the Maguires who had truly drawn him back time and again. Although his conversations with the couple rarely surpassed light chatter, a sense of deep care had grown beneath their words, even in the quiet that lay between them. Maybe there most of all.

In light of this, he anticipated a heartfelt

parting. On the contrary, in a level tone Mr. Maguire simply wished him a blessed journey, then without so much as a handshake he hurried off to handle inventory.

Shan stood there in silence.

"Now, now, don't be taking that to heart." Mrs. Maguire gently smiled. "Just needs a moment to himself."

When understanding set in, that Shan wasn't the only one feeling the blow of parting ways, he nodded.

"Truth be told, we couldn't be happier for you, Shanley Keagan. And we know you'll make us proud." Mrs. Maguire's eyes grew watery above her rounded cheeks. "Off you go now, or you'll miss your grand adventure."

The couple had never had children, which likely explained why her hug right then had a genuine but unpracticed feel. Then again, Shan's memory of his mam's made all others fall short.

He gratefully accepted a small bundle from Mrs. Maguire — biscuits, tea, and toffees for the trip — and left to meet his uncle. Shan refrained from taking a backward glance at the store for fear of changing his mind, as if that were an option. Their flat had been rented out, and every belonging he and Uncle Will could spare had been sold to help pay for their fare. The rest had been raised from Shan's daily shows, on streets and in pubs all over town, sometimes four a day, and from sales of his uncle's moonshine. The result was an extra bit of savings to be used for resettlement, to give them a decent start. Unfortunately, without a drop to drink Uncle Will's mood soured further.

Once they'd boarded the ship, this was just one reason Shan avoided their assigned room. A greater deterrent was the stench of sweat, feces, and vomit on the third-class level, now beyond overcrowded. A steamer from Italy on its way to New York had a pipe burst, and a chunk of its travelers were moved onto Shan's passenger ship. The buckets of waste were dumped out on a regular basis, yet there was no keeping up when seasickness hit from the rolling and rocking of the waves.

Thanks perhaps to his childhood days of fishing — the only hobby he'd shared with his da, who had appreciated the ruling quiet — Shan adjusted fairly well. There were many who'd been ill from the first day till now, almost twelve days later. Uncle Will among them.

A better person than Shan might feel pity for the man, being stuck in his berth, unable to keep anything down. To Shan, it seemed a class of justice.

Of course, if he ever said so in confession, it would surely require penance. Ten Hail Marys and a heap of Our Fathers. But at the moment, he would enjoy the satisfaction. Besides, the sea was mercifully calm tonight and just one day remained before they would be back on soil. Lovely American soil.

The sheer excitement of it left Shan too restless to sleep. In the quiet, he crept down the hall and around the corner to reach a crew supply room. Passengers were prohibited from the area in order to prevent thievery. At this late hour, Shan had no worry of being discovered.

He settled in a back corner, away from the door and the dim entry light. The air was musty and thick with salt, but he didn't mind a bit. The space had become his nightly cave. No babies fussing or couples bickering — the result of boredom in cramped quarters — just a song formed by small creaks from the gently shifting supplies.

Shan fastened the top button of his wool coat to keep warm. He borrowed a flashlight from a shelf, tucked among linens, towels, and such, and over his lap he opened a book. It was one of the few he'd been allowed to keep, having convinced Uncle Will the bindings were too tattered to make the sales worthwhile.

On this day in particular, Shan was grateful for *The Prince and the Pauper.* Fittingly, the story centered on choosing a new life. A far better one, with opportunities rarely found back at home. Turning the pages now, Shan envisioned himself as Tom Canty, the character known as the pauper. From the dregs of London he was raised by a mean-hearted father, turned even meaner from the drink. Shan was so deep into the tale it took him a second to notice the squeak of a door handle, and his heart jumped. He raced to turn off the flashlight and held it close.

Across the room footsteps made their way inside and the door clicked closed. Shan sat as still as a rock, trying not to breathe. The ship had originated in England, same for the crew. Who knew what punishment they would hand down to some Irish kid breaking the rules? A toss over the side seemed extreme, but history said they'd do worse.

The steps proceeded, moving ever closer, then paused. Shan felt a hammering in his chest, a throbbing in his ears, before he caught a giggle. Light and airy, the sound of a girl. There was also a boy, speaking just above a whisper. The snippets of words suggested Italian. A second giggle was muted by the rustling of fabric and the moist sounds of kissing.

Shan quietly sighed. He had wondered in recent days if the sixpence in his pocket, the coin he'd yet to spend, was the reason for his luck, and now he had the answer.

The couple continued with their flirting, and Shan worried how long he'd be stuck in this spot. He craned his neck to see if sneaking out was an option. A gap in the shelves offered a view of the teenage pair. The girl's back was pressed to a wall, the boy's face buried in her neck, where the motion of his kisses sent her head to the side and a moan from her throat.

Shan's mind flashed back to the woman at the pub, the way her bosoms rose and fell. This time he wasn't forced to turn away.

Again the Italian boy murmured; then he covered the girl's mouth with his. Shan rose onto his knees — drawn by the devil's magnet, as the nuns at school would say — enabling a better look. He was almost at full kneeling height when something dropped from his lap.

The book.

Oh, God. Had they heard?

Shan shrank against the wall. He braced himself for the boy to come charging over, for the girl to blush with embarrassment. But in a split second he heard the door swing open and immediately shut. The couple must have taken the noise for that of a crewman, or maybe a ghost, causing them to flee.

That was Shan's assumption until more voices entered the air. No one had left; rather, more had joined, and all were speaking Italian. Shan was familiar with the accent when used in English, but not the language itself.

Soon, talk turned to laughter, a threatening sort, followed by a thud.

Far more careful this time, Shan raised his head for a peek through the shelves. There were three more Italian boys in their late teenage years. Two of them had pinned the original fellow against a wall, his face now in view as he struggled to break free. He was fourteen at most. Shan had seen him on board from a distance, gambling with dice under the stairs and smoking on the lower deck, a sooty area reserved for steerage. He had a grand charm about him, clearly not missed by the girls. Perhaps not even by those who were already spoken for.

Shan discounted this as the issue, however,

when the girl held out her palm and the fourth fellow filled it with coins.

"Ciao, Niccolò," she said, and blew a kiss toward the boy she had baited. His eyes, even in the low light, flared with betrayal. As soon as she slipped out, the leader of the gang fisted his hands. He gave a snarling smile before pounding away on Niccolò. Twice to the face, the same to the gut.

Shan yearned to help, but what could he do? From the handful of times he'd defended himself against scrappers in Dublin, along with the dozens of pub brawls he'd witnessed, he knew how to throw a punch. But there were three here to take on and he was the smallest of the group.

Then the leader pulled a knife. He moved closer to Niccolò and held it between their faces. Niccolò took in a sharp breath, but then pushed out his square chin, a dare — even as the blade hovered over his throat.

Panicking, Shan scoured his thoughts for a plan. He tightened his grasp on the flashlight.

The flashlight . . . meant for the crew . . .

His gaze shot to a box at the end of the row. It was the size of a small crate. Like so many stages he had performed upon. Could it really work?

Among the shadowed shelves before him,

he found a kitchen worker's hat. No time to search for something better. Donning the cap, he prayed his scheme wouldn't fail, or he might be tossed off the ship after all. In quick succession he stepped onto the box, flicked on the flashlight, pointed at the Italians' faces, and ordered in a low British tone, "You there! Stop what you're doing."

All eyes snapped toward the beam, squinting. It was clear the fellows were puzzled by the presence of a stranger suddenly in the room. From another door perhaps?

At the possibility that they might investigate, Shan's nerves rose like a rash. He hastened to add, "This area is strictly prohibited! Give me your names this instant."

They appeared to understand. One of them nudged the leader, who threw Niccolò to the floor, and the trio scrambled into the hall.

Thank heavens.

Niccolò coughed as he pushed himself to rise, trying to scurry out.

"Wait, don't go." Shan switched to his natural brogue, but with a tremble from his jitters. "You're safe now. Don't you see?" He shined the flashlight straight up under his chin, wishing he could say it in Italian.

Niccolò watched as Shan hopped off the

box and added, "I thought you could use some help." He slowed down and exaggerated his speech. "You understand what I'm saying? *Help.*"

The start of a smile stretched Niccolò's lips, the bottom one swelling. He used the back of his hand to wipe blood from the corner of his mouth. "Oh, I got that part. Just a little shocked how you pulled that off."

Shan looked at him, stunned. After all, the fellow's olive skin and brown deep-set eyes were typical of an Italian immigrant. "You speak English."

"Well, I'd hope so. I was born and bred in the States. It's my Italian that needs work."

Shan shook his head, feeling ridiculous. "Sorry about that."

"For what? You just saved my ass." An Italian accent did actually dip his words, though it was faint enough for many to miss. "I'm Nick, by the way."

"Shan."

They shook hands. Then the fellow stretched his jaw and gave it a rub, no doubt stiffening from the hits. Shan knew the sensation.

"Are you all right? Took quite a beating there."

"Ahh, that was nothin'." Nick shrugged,

but the movement caused a slight wince. "Girls, huh?" He rolled his eyes, as if recognizing his failure to see it coming.

"Might want to rest here a bit. In case them fellas are still hanging around."

It was truthful advice, but not Shan's sole motivation. Aside from the relief of pleasant company, Nick was a real Yank, a member of a group Shan was eager to join.

"Sure. I suppose," Nick said. "For a minute."

Shan quickly pulled over a second box, keeping the flashlight angled downward, and they took their seats. Nick's dark hair was close-cropped like Shan's, a common tactic to fend off the lice that often plagued the ships.

"You wouldn't have a cigarette, would ya?" Nick asked.

"I'm . . . afraid I don't." Shan regretted not having one of his uncle's. But he did have something else. He grabbed two pieces from his coat pocket. "Toffee?"

Nick grinned. "Why not."

They were soon sucking on sweets, filling the air with the heavenly scent of caramel. The smell was straight from Mr. Maguire's store. One of the many things Shan was leaving behind.

He pushed away the thought. "So, you're

from the States, you said."

"New Jersey. But we're moving to Brooklyn." Shan's puzzlement must have shown because Nick added, "It's a borough in New York. A lot of Italian Americans there."

It was hard to believe the ship would be arriving in a matter of hours. Shan felt heady from the thrill of it.

Nick shifted on his box, perhaps antsy to leave. Not wanting him to go yet, Shan stammered to form a question. "Where did — or how long, I mean — have you been away?"

"About three years." Nick used his tongue to move the toffee from one cheek to the other, where it clicked against his straight white teeth. "My parents took us back to Italy when my grandfather got sick, so my dad could run his business. It's a shoe shop in Siena. And now we're finally going back."

"Oh, I see. I'm sorry about your grandda."

"Don't be. The cranky old bastard got better, which we should've expected. He'll probably outlive us all."

The corners of Nick's mouth rose. It was only a partial smile, as though something were holding it down.

Shan sensed not to ask. In the quiet, he recalled his kitchen worker's cap and tugged it off, a reminder of the confrontation.

"Those fellas from earlier, I take it they weren't pals from Siena."

"Didn't know 'em till last night. We played a few hours of poker. Guess they held a grudge over thinking I cheated."

"Because you won?"

"Well — yeah. Also 'cause I cheated." Nick's eyes gained a glimmer. "I just figured they'd had too much wine to notice."

They both laughed, and Nick paused to hold his right side, a flash of discomfort in his face. As he relaxed, Shan chewed his toffee into tiny pieces, almost missing the murmurs echoing from the hall. The door hadn't fully closed. They were men's voices, growing closer.

Maybe crewmen were headed here for supplies. Or worse yet, if the Italians had somehow uncovered the trick, they could be returning, and in greater number. Shan went still, his sudden worry mirrored in Nick's eyes.

But then the voices became clearer, with the guttural consonants of German, and faded when the strangers continued past.

Shan and Nick traded smiles of relief.

After a moment, Nick geared up with a breath. "Well, I guess we'd better get some shut-eye. Big day tomorrow."

"Aye. Big day."

Nick pushed on his legs to rise. "Thanks again, Shan. I owe you one."

" 'Twas no bother."

Nick tipped his head before exiting the room, leaving Shan suddenly drained.

Tomorrow would be the start of a new life, and he would need all the energy he could muster. With his book in hand, he returned to his berth, where the stench was as horrid as ever. Uncle Will slept in the lower bunk. Thankfully he wasn't hacking away, and Shan managed to doze off.

That bit of peace, mind you, didn't last for long.

7

It seemed only minutes had passed when chatter and bustling roused Shan from sleep. Through the fog of his mind came a child chirping, "It's her, Mama! The statue. You have to come and see!"

Slowly Shan realized which statue it had to be. Jolted awake, he scrambled down from his berth, still in yesterday's clothes. He had barely found his footing when he was swept into the stream of immigrants eager for a peek at paradise.

He shuffled up the stairs in a never-ending queue until emerging on the deck. Fresh sea air washed over him and the chill raised the hairs on his scalp.

Then he saw her. That beautiful green lady of liberty. She looked like royalty in her crown and robe, but also welcoming, holding a torch to guide in their ship. To Shan's surprise, emotions swelled inside him and tears wet his eyes. How odd that the sight of sculpted metal could cause a squeezing in his chest.

People around him were waving to no one in particular. Somehow he didn't feel foolish doing the same. For once, even the English and Irish seemed united.

After a time, word spread that they were close to docking. Shan followed the group down the way he'd come. First class would be let off, they said, then second class, then third. A good thing for Shan, since it took quite some time to weave through the commotion. Folks were crisscrossing while rounding up their families. Arranged brides were nervously primping for the grooms they would meet.

In the middle of it all, a young lass stood alone, tears rolling down her freckled skin. Frayed ribbons hung from her red puckered braids. Shan wanted to pass by, like everyone else, but he couldn't. He knew how it felt to cry for help and not be heard.

He bent down to meet her gaze. "Gotten yourself lost, have you?"

She didn't answer, but paused her weeping and took in a small gulp of air.

"Come on, now. Let's find your family."

Though wavering with uncertainty, she accepted his hand.

"You just tell me when you see someone

you know."

After he'd towed her around for a stretch, voices in all languages swirling about, the girl released her grip and shot straight into the arms of a mother whose face was twisted with worry. "Ah, thank the Lord! I'm grateful, very grateful," she said to Shan. "With four little ones, and me husband not here, it took time to notice the youngest gone . . ."

Shan offered reassurance and wished them well, anxious to get back. By now, the greeting that waited at his berth would not be quite as warm. Hopefully seasickness had left Uncle Will too weak to shout.

As luck would have it, the man wasn't even up to standing. He was sleeping the day away, as he often did following rough nights at home.

"Uncle Will, we're here." Shan rushed to collect any belongings that had escaped his satchel and shoved them back inside. A stray sock, a shirt, his book from last night. The other passengers in their room had already headed out.

All the while Uncle Will refused to rise.

"We need to hurry now. It'll be our turn to get off soon enough."

Still nothing. No gripe. No movement.

Not even, Shan realized, the rasp of his breathing.

Shan dropped his bag. He stared at the back of his uncle, layered in his clothes and the scratchy wool blanket provided by the ship.

"Uncle Will?" The name came out strained.

Shan's fingers trembled as he reached out to poke his uncle's arm — to no response. He moved in for a closer view. Uncle Will appeared to be asleep, his body curled and eyes shut. But a handkerchief lay wadded in his calloused hand. Large spots of blood wilted the cloth like a rose.

The shake in Shan's hands traveled to his knees. Breath held, he grabbed hold of Uncle Will's shoulder and rolled him onto his back. His skin looked paler than usual above his reddish beard. As waxy as a candle. Lifeless.

Shan forced himself to touch the man's cheek, in order to be certain. It was so cold Shan's hand reflexively pulled away. His stomach curdled. His brain went dizzy. More than ever on the ship, he feared he might be sick.

When inspected upon boarding, his uncle had provided a note from Doc O'Halloran. It explained his cough as the result of years spent in factories, nothing more. The Spanish flu was still so prevalent; Uncle Will wanted to avoid any concerns.

Shan wondered now what had truly ailed the man. Not that it mattered. Whatever the illness, Uncle Will was gone.

Weighted by this fact, Shan lowered onto the floor. He was starved for air, for reason. Despite the hardships, he had grown dependent on this person to survive. There were times he'd despised his uncle so much, he wished the man would die in his sleep. And now that he had, Shan was confused about how he should feel.

There was relief and guilt, spite and grief. But mostly, he felt alone. At the entry to a foreign world, what was he to do?

Empty beds and scraps surrounded him, the remnants of old lives, shed like a used cocoon. Again tears rose to his eyes, but for an entirely different reason. No longer the beginning, it was now the end. During the trip over, he'd heard of immigrants being turned away, sent back for many a reason. What would they do to a boy with no guardian?

"But my father is American," he could tell them. "A sailor named John Lewis. No, I don't know where he lives. And no, he doesn't know I'm coming. Nor, perhaps, that I exist."

Even if Shan were allowed to stay, placed

in an orphanage, who was to say the conditions wouldn't be just as foul as the ones Uncle Will had described. "Act up the smallest bit," he'd warned, "and they'll lock you in a cage, starve ye for a week. And if you're hopin' good wholesome parents will show up one day to add you to their family, you'd better think twice. Any stranger willin' to adopt the likes of *you* isn't looking for a sweet child to raise. They only want free labor to work to the bone before they toss you out on your arse. Either that, or because the man of the house wants a nice young lad for *other* reasons."

Sure, Uncle Will might have stretched the truth. But Shan remembered how boys lived in the alley, some of them homeless by choice, and he couldn't rule out the claims.

On the floor his satchel had fallen open. A corner of his book peeked out in mockery. The story of Tom and Edward. Just hours ago, Shan had imagined himself as the pauper, slipping into the role of a prince.

He envied that fellow Nick. Moving to New York with his family, raised in a community with the same culture and traditions, even this far from Italy. They probably all shared similar looks, with olive skin, dark hair, and dark eyes. Everything to make a person feel he belonged.

Not like Shan. Next to Uncle Will's fair features, the same for Shan's mam, one wouldn't have guessed Shan was even related. More than one person had re-marked that his dark Irish features could easily be taken for . . .

Italian.

Shan turned back to the book. When the characters changed places, they managed to fit in only because they looked so much alike. Granted, it was a made-up story and happy endings were harder to come by in real life. But at this point, what did he have to lose?

I owe you one, Nick had said. He might not have truly meant it, not in the literal sense and surely not this soon.

Nevertheless, Shan was determined to collect on the favor.

8

In the Great Hall on Ellis Island, iron railings funneled passengers into winding queues like cattle in an endless maze. Most had fled their homelands to escape the lingering effects of war, yet after the two-week voyage every immigrant, from young to old, appeared to have served on the front. The stained clothes, the dirty faces. Worst of all, the smell.

But not even the stink bothered Shan now. All of his thoughts, along with his hopes, hung on a person he'd yet to find. He adjusted his grip on the handles of his bags. As a courtesy after being ferried over on a barge, folks were invited to check in their luggage. Although Shan wasn't the only one to keep his belongings close, his reasons were likely darker.

Before rushing off the ship, he'd covered Uncle Will with a blanket. He was picking up his own satchel when he remembered his uncle's belongings in the corner. It could take longer to identify a body, he figured, without the passenger's documentation. And so, adding to his infinite list of sins, Shan snatched the second bag and embarked on a search for Nick.

Unfortunately, a series of medical exams had hindered the mission. Stoic in their blue uniforms, inspectors performed separate duties to decide who continued on. They observed fingernails and skin, the ability to walk and raise both arms. Eyelids were lifted, teeth were viewed, as if purchasing a horse at market. The verdicts were displayed on passengers' clothing in a secret code of chalked letters.

Now that Shan had finally made it through, he hoped he wasn't too late. He surveyed the massive hall, teeming with restless strangers. Their suits and shawls peppered the area in an endless quilt. Brimmed hats covered the head of nearly every man; same for the women except for those wrapped in scarves. Rigid expressions reflected Shan's own fear of still being turned away.

"Stay calm," he told himself. A bead of sweat slid from under his tweed cap. Could he trust his memory to locate a face he knew only in shadows?

Uniformed officials shouted instructions in an impressive number of languages. The sharp clicks of their knee-high boots echoed off the floor and up to the vaulted ceiling. People should have their documents ready, they said, to be identified and registered in the most efficient manner.

Shan moved about, carefully scanning as panic gnawed inside. He was halfway through the room when he spied a familiar face. Yes. It was Nick. He and his family had almost reached the front of the final line. To have any chance, Shan would have to hurry.

"My family, they're right up there." He repeated this over and over to glaring immigrants as he wormed his way past.

"Nick," he said, approaching, and the fellow turned. After a moment of recognition, Nick looked pleasantly surprised. Shan wasted no time quietly explaining the situation. He'd barely finished when Nick went straight to his father, standing several feet ahead. They spoke in hushed tones, and once again Shan wished he knew Italian.

He studied Nick's mother, who stood close enough to hear the conversation. She was a petite woman with high cheekbones and full lips, her brown hair pulled into a low, graceful roll befitting her demeanor.

With the faintest nod or smile, she could dispel Shan's worries, assure him that her husband would be willing to help. Instead, her face was drawn into an unreadable expression. All the while, her daughter, a few years younger than Shan, stared back with deep, curious eyes. Her nose and chin were as round and dainty as buttons. She swung a foot, brushing the floor, while clinging to her mother's side.

Down the rows, people jaggedly moved forward, taking their places before the long series of desks. The seated immigration officers wore the hardened faces of magistrates. They brought their stamps down like gavels.

It was almost time for Nick's family to take the stand.

Inspectors continued to work through the room. Before long, Uncle Will's death would be discovered and an investigation would lead to Shan.

He swung back toward Nick's father. In a charcoal gray suit, the man stood with his arms crossed and his square jaw set, as still as the statue that had greeted their ship, but not as congenial. He was of medium height and average build, just like his son, though his presence made him larger. This didn't stop Nick from attempting another plea. But then his father turned gruff on a single word, a verbal stomp. The discussion was over.

There was no time for Shan to make a case for himself. He needed an alternative. The mother he had helped on the ship — she might be grateful enough to claim him. Plus, she was Irish and in need of an extra hand. But how could he weave back through the room without drawing attention?

Just then, Nick's mother held her husband's arm. She whispered inches from his ear and connected with his eyes. A long beat passed between them before his face softened, and he talked to his son. Then Nick faced Shan, and he nodded.

They'd agreed. Ah, thank goodness, they'd agreed.

For the moment, Shan had a family.

He nearly burst into a grin but pressed it down. It was no place to celebrate and far too early. He slid over to wait by Nick, who spoke under his breath. "Just keep your head down, and don't talk unless you got to."

By no means were those a challenge for Shan.

"You're my brother, all right? And you were born in Jersey, same as me and Lina."

Nick's brother, Jersey . . . Lina? Of course. His sister. Shan nodded, absorbing it all.

"Oh, and listen. If they ask —"

"Next!" The closest officer flicked a hand, an order to approach.

The people in front of them had been processed much too fast. Shan stayed at the rear of the family, beside Nick, as they gathered their belongings. At the desk, they set down a suitcase and a black steamer trunk. Shan did the same with his satchels, freeing his hands to tilt his hat lower.

"Italiano, signore?" the official asked.

"Si, si." The father nodded. *"Buongiorno."*

The officer went straight to business, no warmth in his words. It was clear Italian wasn't his native tongue. Nick's father produced documents from his coat. He flashed an envelope of cash, which he then put away. Proof they had enough funds, apparently, to be respectable members of society.

"I speak English, if that is helpful," the father offered.

"Oh. Yes, good."

The two continued in English, back and forth, with basic questions and answers. Between each, the officer referred to a form, scribbling notes. He was confirming details, Shan realized, based on information the father had provided before departure. Just as Uncle Will had.

The officer paused and surveyed the family, puzzled.

Shan's body tightened. Bloody hell, he knew where this was going.

"I see on the manifest that you traveled with only two children."

"No, no. Three," the father insisted. "There are three."

"But I have two written here, clear in black and white. Why didn't you formally declare all three children at your point of embarkation?"

"Maybe, eh . . . maybe the man who writes this down did not hear correct." Nick's father sounded perplexed, though Shan detected a current of nerves.

"Sir, your son could not have boarded without being accounted for."

"Yes, but — mistakes, they happen, *si*?"

Lina tugged on her mother's skirt. "Mama, *perché* —"

Her mother furtively shushed her, a stern message in her eyes.

The idea had seemed simple. Shan had assumed a family with American-born children would enter with ease. It wasn't meant to cause them trouble. Could they actually be denied entry, thrown back on a boat? Could the consequences be worse, all because of him?

Before it was too late, Shan whispered, "Nick."

Nick shook his head, gaze locked forward.

Once more the officer flipped through the documents. He looked weary and agitated from issues of this kind. "Now, which of these children are" — he read from the paper — "Niccolò and Angelina?"

"That's me," Nick jumped in, "and my sister here. And this is my brother, Tomasso."

The officer eyed Nick skeptically before switching his focus to Shan. "Tell me, young man. In Italy, did someone check you in upon boarding?"

Shan froze, unsure how to answer. Not just regarding content. Back in Dublin, he'd earned many raves over his Yankee accent, but all by the Irish. Standing before an American now, one with raised suspicions, Shan suddenly doubted his ability to mimic.

"Son, do you speak English?"

Shan hesitated before nodding, aware more difficult questions would follow.

"Allora." The mother's interruption turned the officer. She clapped her hands once and clucked her tongue at a thought. "*Un momento, per favore.* I show you, okay?" She gestured to the steamer trunk.

The officer blew out a sigh. He waved his

hand for her to proceed but not to dawdle.

Nick unlocked the case and opened it. His mother knelt and scrounged around, searching under garments and shoes.

Shan felt stares from every direction burrowing into his skin. Would someone remember him traveling with his uncle? He pulled his neck inward, a tortoise desperate for a shell.

Finally the mother found a picture frame embroidered with grapes and ivy. In the photograph, among a group of Italians posed before a house, a younger version of the mother stood with a little girl and two boys, one of them propped on her hip.

She rose and tapped the picture while handing it over. "You see? It is my children. Niccolò, Angelina, and Tomasso. All born in America. We take them to Siena to visit family, all of us together. You check, you see is true."

Her husband supported this with a close-lipped smile that seemed to be covering a scowl.

The officer looked at Shan, then the picture, then Shan. The whole plan felt ridiculous and bound to fail. Under close scrutiny, surely a leprechaun couldn't look more Irish.

But the mother spoke again, more firmly.

"What you do? Take a boy from his family, send him to Italy alone? *Che pazzo!* You believe a paper or a mother?"

Challenging an officer with such boldness had further heightened the stakes. This much was clear from the man's silence. They had gone too far.

Shan gauged the area. Three staircases just ahead were marked with different signs. Three destinations. He could take off running, hope to choose the right one. If caught, he could explain it was all his doing, that the family wasn't to blame.

The officer returned the photograph. Without a word, he inked his stamp, marked the papers — *thunk, thunk* — and added their names to a ledger, ending with Tomasso.

"Welcome home," the man mumbled, and directed them to the proper stairway.

It was official. They had passed.

Still, Shan didn't relax until the family was a good way down the steps, headed for the ferry. Behind the group, he helped Nick carry the trunk. When Shan had insisted it was the least he could do, Mr. Capello had sniffed his agreement.

"Nick, I didn't mean to cause trouble," Shan offered.

"I told you I owed ya. A fella's word is

everything. Right?"

The past few years Shan had spent plenty of time with people who gave no weight to promises.

"Anyway," Nick said, "you're welcome to stay with us a while if you like."

The surprise of this almost caused Shan to miss a step. "Are you sure?" Not that he had anywhere else to go at the moment.

"Eh. We're Italian. The more, the better."

As they continued their descent, Shan's mind flashed back to the portrait. He wondered about the child whose image had proved a savior. "The boy in the picture — Tommy, was it?"

"Tomasso," Nick corrected, his attention on the stairs. "He always went by his real name."

The uncanny similarity occurred to Shan only now, of the pauper's moniker being Tom in the story. It was a decidedly good omen. "And he's a relation of yours?"

"He's — was my brother." There was no emotion in Nick's face, but the soft catch in his voice betrayed him.

All at once, it made sense why Nick's father had been reluctant to call a stranger his son, even for show. Worries over being caught had been merely part of the dilemma. Shan thought of Nick's mother, what it must have taken for her to hand over that photograph.

At the bottom of the stairs, Shan turned to Nick. "I truly hope I'm not putting your family out."

"Stop it, would ya? You're comin'." It was delivered as a command, but with deliberate lightness. "Besides, we're brothers now, right?"

The truth was, as an only child, Shan had always longed for a sibling. Yet under the odd circumstances, he wasn't sure how to reply. "I suppose . . ."

"Good. 'Cause I ain't about to lug this dang trunk to Brooklyn by myself."

When Nick smiled, Shan couldn't help but do the same. Hopefully, before long he would find his American father and reclaim a family of his own.

Until then, there would be little harm in playing the role of a Capello.

9

As it turned out, New York wasn't paradise at all. In fact, even calling it a city was a stretch. It was a wide range of countries clustered on an island, almost as if a series of tornados had swooped from Europe to the Orient, picked up entire neighborhoods — a good many of them poor — and dropped them into the boroughs of New York.

There were no signs declaring *Welcome to Ireland,* or *Entering Russia,* or *Leaving Poland, Come Back Soon.* And yet, excluding some tenements, the borders indeed were there. It took but a few days of roaming for Shan to discover which streets bounded each territory. While many spent what money they could spare on typical American clothing, their efforts to blend appeared to stop there. Shan would cross a street and find himself in a different world. The language would change, both spoken and printed in newspapers, directly matching scents in the air. Chinese spices would give way to baking German dough, or fermenting wine from the basements of Italians.

Now, though, as he wove through Times Square, he smelled only the tang of gasoline from motorcars. Contrary to legend, American streets weren't paved in gold, just rutted, grimy pavement. All around him people were walking and shouting; carts and delivery trucks rattled and veered. The city itself was a living creature that could swallow a person whole.

Shan glanced at the hulking buildings that for once didn't make him feel small, not on this wondrous April morning. A day that could change everything.

In his coat pocket he fingered the blessed photograph, just to confirm it was there. Anticipation propelled him around the corner, past a paperboy touting headlines.

No different than in Ireland, here politics abounded from an excess of wants. Unions wanted better pay and conditions. Women wanted the vote. Protestants wanted alcohol banned from the country, of which they were making great strides. Given that reason alone, Uncle Will's mortal end had come in a timely fashion.

Shan, on the other hand, had only a single desire: to find John Lewis. Yet in the two weeks since arriving, he had made little progress. "Might as well be John Doe," scoffed a bartender in Manhattan. Shan had been lured into the club by a posted sign, a list of entertainers performing that week. But like in a dozen other places that featured musicians, no workers there were familiar with his father.

The reality that Shan could inquire at a thousand similar spots and still come up short had threatened to overwhelm him. Then last night, to salvage any resettlement funds, he'd emptied his uncle's satchel. For many days prior, he had waffled over whether or not he should. Aside from the bag being tainted by death, it seemed a test of morals. That was before he recalled that much of the money he'd earned himself, lessening the intrusion.

What he discovered inside came as a shock. For in the paper sack of meager savings was a portrait: a Yank sailor in uniform. And on the back, written in the same hand as the letter to Shan's mam, was the name *John Lewis.*

The fellow had a slight wave in his hair, which looked to be black. From his dark downturned eyes to rather thin lips, he mirrored Shan a decade older. His ears, too, made for a striking match, with one top rounded and the other more pointed. His skin, however, bore a deeper tone. Hinting to Italian, of all things. Or perhaps Shan's view had been influenced by time spent with the Capellos.

Whatever the case, Shan now had proof of a father. He was equally thrilled and befuddled that his uncle had not only kept the photo — presumably from the belongings of Shan's mam — but also packed it for the trip. Until yesterday, it seemed the fame and riches of vaudeville alone had enticed Uncle Will to cross the Atlantic.

But maybe that wasn't so. Maybe, with Doc O'Halloran's guidance, Uncle Will had recognized the chance at one act of decency before departing this world.

"May I help you?" the secretary said, a second before lifting her gaze from the paperwork on her desk. At seeing Shan, weariness flickered in her eyes.

"Yes, ma'am. I was hoping Chief Madison might be available."

"I see . . ." The woman wore her flaxen hair tight in a twist. It was her signature style, Shan guessed, based on his prior visits to the Navy recruiting office. Her blouse also was similar to before, with its pearly buttons and petal collar, but this time in dusty blue. "Unfortunately, I'm not sure that will be possible. Chief Madison is rather busy today."

"But it won't take more than a few minutes."

"Yes. I'm sure that's true, but —"

A hammering rattled the room. The woman glowered at the wall that was being pounded from the other side. Posters featuring drawings of battleships and sailors rippled where they hung, and a wooden chair scooted as if nudged by a ghost. In the second chair a teenage boy continued to flip through *The Saturday Evening Post.* The secretary, troubled by the nuisance, cursed under her breath — just as the noise stopped.

She snapped a glance at the chief petty officer's closed door, as if to confirm he hadn't heard. Then she returned to Shan, explaining, "A legal firm is preparing to move in next month. That is, if I don't burn the place down first." She smiled without humor, and Shan nodded politely.

"As I was trying to say," she went on. "I'd be happy to pass along a message for you." She held a pencil over paper, ready to jot a note.

Ten days ago, Shan had been exploring Broadway, in awe of its playhouses, when the sight of *U.S. Navy* painted on a window reeled him onto a side street. The recruiter on duty had been kind enough to listen to Shan's case; he suggested checking in after a couple of weeks for any updates on tracking down the right John Lewis.

Today marked Shan's second visit since.

"I was being hasty, I know, coming back last week," he admitted. "But I really do need to speak to him in person. You see, I have a photograph this time."

The woman exhaled as though stifling a sigh. "You do understand this is a recruiting station?"

"Yes, ma'am. I do."

She set down her pencil. "I'm sure Chief Madison would like to help. But given your situation, I think you'd get further at the Navy Yard. If you just go —"

"But I've tried that. They said no one there could help me. That's why, when I first saw your office, I thought maybe someone here could, and I was right." Shan smiled to reinforce that he was referring not just to her boss, but to her as well.

The secretary went to reply but held back, and her expression softened. She ignored another burst of hammering, this time resembling a bird tapping a tree. "You say you have a picture?"

Shan tamped his enthusiasm and reached into his pocket.

Holding out her hand, she said, "The chief really does have meetings most of the day. But if you'd care to leave it with me, I'll be sure to pass it along."

Shan peered at the photo. He hadn't been aware of its existence until the night before, but already he considered it a prized possession. Though he'd memorized the sailor's features — an easy task, given their similarity to Shan's — he still feared losing his only record of the man.

"I promise to keep it safe," she said in understanding. "Or . . . if you'd like to come back with it, you're welcome to. I just can't guarantee when Chief Madison will be available. Recruits and Navy business take priority, as you can imagine."

The phone rang on her desk.

Shan resented the insistence of its metal bell but welcomed the opportunity to think. He weighed his choices as the secretary handled the call.

The sooner the chief received the photo, the faster he could act. Shan struggled to trust anyone, let alone a stranger. But if he wanted to find his father, any such worries couldn't block the way.

"Yes, three o'clock on Tuesday," she said to the caller, and wrote something down. "Thank you, Lieutenant. Enjoy your day, as well."

She hung up the phone and finished her notes. By the time she looked up, Shan had brought himself to relinquish the photograph. She accepted the offering only by its edges, a display of care, fulfilling her word.

"When you hear of anything," he began.

"You'll be the first to know," she said. "And if I can personally help, I certainly will."

10

Of all the things the Irish had in common, their knowledge of rain — and by relation, clouds — ranked near the top. Among the most favored were light wispy ones that feathered a summer sky, and billowy puffs the color of milk. You had to enjoy them while they lasted, because inevitably they would darken into a wall of gray, dense and cold and ripe for a storm.

It was that type of cloud Shan now imagined hovering over the dining room, where tension saturated the air. Any moment it would reach its limit, unleashing a downpour on them all. Until then, Shan would quietly eat his supper in the guarded manner he had long ago mastered. And he would try not to dwell on thoughts of the recruiting station — even though three days had passed without a word.

"*Allora,* I forget," Mrs. Capello said, breaking the silence. "We have bread." She rose and scurried to the kitchen for what must have been the twentieth time since the meal began, either a motherly habit or an excuse to flee.

A minute later, she offered the small basket of rolls directly to Shan, suggesting she had noticed his trepidation over to-night's oddities: eggplant fried in oil from olives, paper-thin slices of salty ham, and a grain called "polenta." On the upside, they were something other than the family's staple of noodles covered in sauce made of stewed tomatoes, referred to as "macaroni and gravy." The latter, mind you, bore no resemblance to the gravy Shan knew from Ireland. But Mrs. Capello showed such pride in her menus — supposedly diverse, thanks to a southern Italian grandmother — he always did his best to clean his plate. Besides, food was food.

He accepted a roll with gratitude, then passed the basket to Nick. Once it had made a full round, Mr. Capello picked up the decanter of red wine to refill his glass. Shan, in fact, was the only one at the table not indulging in the drink that appeared to be treated as water.

"Say, Pop," Nick said, and swallowed a bite of bread. "Since we got a guest, I was wondering if I could borrow a few bucks.

Thought I'd take Shan to Coney Island, show him the highlights."

"Borrow?" Mr. Capello repeated the word as though unfamiliar with the translation. Affording his son barely a glance, he set down the decanter with a little extra force. "Borrow means you pay back."

"Yeah, I know. And I will. Just need a chance to save up some dough."

"And you think this *dough* will appear from nothing."

Nick remarked just loud enough for Shan to hear, "I was hoping it would appear from your pocket, actually."

Shan dipped his chin to hide a smile as Mrs. Capello reminded her husband not to speak of finances at the table.

"This is not finance," Mr. Capello said. "This is life." Then toward Nick, he pinched invisible coins in the air, his hands strong and toughened from his trade as a plumber. "You want money? You work. For five generations, this is how Capello men survive. *Capisci?*"

Across from Shan, Lina observed the scene in her usual way — head tilted, an artist surveying her subjects — until Mrs. Capello scooped a heap of polenta on the girl's plate. "*Basta,* Mama. I'm full."

"Eat," Mrs. Capello said, then returned to

her own meal.

Nick slouched in his chair. "Look, Pop. I already talked to Mr. Sarentino. He said there might be an opening this summer to help out at the bowling alley."

Mr. Capello took a gulp of wine and nodded. "*Va bene.* Then soon you will have enough money for Coney Island."

Nick started to roll his eyes but apparently knew better. He poked his fork at his remaining food, and silence reclaimed the room. Not a single call rang out from the phone, set on a table near the entry. Though Mrs. Capello would grumble whenever customers interrupted supper — at which her husband would insist, "Pipes do not break on a schedule" — tonight she, too, might have welcomed the distraction.

Shan had once heard Italian family meals were as lively as a circus. But here, the majority of the sounds came from chewing, sipping, and the clinking of silverware, all magnified in the seclusion of a house.

On Maywood Place, in a modest neighborhood not far from Prospect Park, the rented home had two floors and three bedrooms: a small one for Lina, the largest for her parents, and one of moderate size for Nick — shared with Shan for now. A private bathroom and real bedroom doors were luxuries Shan would never again take for granted. There was a sitting room for guests, complete with furniture, and a kitchen with cabinets and drawers.

Shan could only hope that his own father's dwelling would be just as lovely.

Mrs. Capello caught Shan's eye and gestured to the last slice of eggplant. "You want more? Uh . . . yes?" She struggled, as they all did, to know what to call him. As if an immigration officer might be listening at the door.

"I'm just fine. Thank you."

"Prosciutto?" She lifted the plate of salty ham.

"Really, no, but thanks. My stomach couldn't fit another bite."

Shan could feel Mr. Capello watching. The intensity of his eyes could eliminate the heartiest of appetites. *How long will this go on?* the man wanted to know. Or more aptly, with all this talk of money and earning one's way: *How much longer must I support a stranger's child?*

"Mr. Capello," Shan said finally, "I've been meaning to tell you. I found a bit of money from my uncle. If it's all right, I'd like to contribute in some way."

Mrs. Capello waved this off. "Nonsense. You will need money until you are living with your father. Mm?" Her gaze dodged that of her husband, who simply finished off his wine.

It went without saying that the predicament was more burdensome than what the couple had agreed upon. If Shan could do anything to speed up the process, by all means he would.

"I should be hearing from the Navy office any day, now that they've got the photograph to help."

Mrs. Capello smiled, but not without effort.

"Say, Ma," Nick chimed in. "Anything for dessert?"

"Certo," she said with an air of relief. Rising again, she directed Lina to gather the plates.

Soon every person had a piece of cake. To Shan's dismay, it was soaked with bitter coffee. He worked through it in nibbles, his efforts as strained as Mrs. Capello's attempts at light chatter.

She spoke about her shock that, in the brief years they'd been gone, the price of steak had shot up to forty-four cents a pound. And about news of a niece in Genoa expecting twin girls. She also discussed her preparation list for the religious feasts in the coming months. From there, in an almost-casual segue, she went on to inform her husband that Shan was well aware of the saints the community would celebrate — as if a Catholic upbringing alone made him welcome beneath their roof.

Unfortunately, her need to make that clear only confirmed the opposite.

11

Later that night, as Shan readied for sleep, the issue of his presence clung like threads of a spiderweb needing to be brushed away. At the wardrobe closet, he buttoned flannel pajamas borrowed from Nick, who preferred sleeping in an undershirt and drawers.

"Shut the door, will ya?" Nick was the first to slide into bed, parked near the window. His nightstand lamp produced an amber glow.

As soon as Shan fulfilled the request, Nick pulled a magazine from beneath his mattress and propped his head with a folded pillow. The cover advertised articles on the fishing trade, disguising its contents of nude bosomy figures drawn in suggestive poses. Admiring one of them, he let out a low whistle. "Boy, I'd love to see a real gal bend like *that*."

Shan could visualize the legs-over-her-head pretzel position without looking; he'd secretly perused the magazine when no one else was around. "I think she'd have to be made of rubber."

"I could live with that." Nick grinned and proceeded to leaf through the pages.

Shan settled into the blankets on his mattress, which lay on the floor next to the small oak desk. Mrs. Capello had again apologized today for not yet scrounging up a bed frame. He'd insisted he was fully comfortable — the honest truth after two years on a lumpy mattress with metal springs against his spine. Plus, why bother when he planned to leave before long?

The sooner, perhaps, the better.

"Nick, I've been thinking . . ."

Nick mumbled in reply, only half listening.

Although Shan would have no place to live until connecting with his father, he had to at least offer the family a way out. A courtesy he'd been avoiding.

"Nick," he tried again. Gathering his courage, he pushed out the rest: "Maybe it's time I go."

Nick turned with a crinkled brow. "Go where?" After a pause, he appeared to comprehend.

"You've truly been grand, letting me tag along. But I'm sure you all must be wanting to get on with your lives."

Nick took this in and rested his magazine on his chest. "Look, don't worry about Pop. He's just been like that. Even before . . ." The sentence trailed off, but Shan recognized the reference to Tomasso. A boy no one had spoken of since Ellis Island. Shan had respectfully done the same. It wasn't as if he himself blathered about loved ones he'd lost. But now that the conversation had led to the subject, it seemed appropriate to ask.

"Was it an illness he had — your brother?"

Nick shrugged lightly, despite his sudden graveness. "It was his heart. Kept him from running around like other kids. He had to stay inside most the time."

"I see." While Shan wasn't one to pry, his want to understand the family pressed him on. "Did he . . . pass away in Italy? After you went to see your grandda?"

Nick issued a nod, supporting his mother's claim about all three children traveling to Siena. "We stayed for a few years afterward. Then, like I said, my grandfather got better and it was time to leave. To start fresh."

Shan could relate. As could most immigrants, he supposed, who'd dared make the crossing. But he sensed there was more to the story than Nick was sharing, unspo-

107

ken words still hanging like threads.

"Well," Nick said. "Better get some rest."

Shan considered saying more, but thought better of it. The message was clear that Nick was done. He affirmed this by returning his magazine to hiding and turning off the lamp with a tug of its chain.

For several minutes, they lay there in silence. From a small gap in the curtains, a slant of moonlight sliced the room. Shan rolled away from the window. He closed his eyes, nestling in. The grayness of sleep was just taking hold when Nick's voice snagged him back.

"So, whaddya think you'll do?"

Shan strained to follow the question through his grogginess. "About?"

"If it turns out you don't find him — you know, the sailor."

Although Nick had used the word "if," somehow it felt like "when."

Shan's vision sharpened, gaining focus on the wall beyond the desk. Sure, the search could fail. He'd be demented not to know that. But he refused to give up.

"Really, I ain't trying to borrow trouble," Nick went on. "But it's been a long time since he was with your mom, right? For all you know, the fella could have his own family by now."

The suggestion delivered a sting that brought Shan to full consciousness. True, he should have considered it before: how the shocking appearance of a bastard son could disrupt a happy family. But to him the letter was new, the man's loving words seeming fresh on the page.

A rustling indicated Nick had shifted on his pillow. "Sorry. That came out wrong. I'm just concerned, is all."

Part of Shan wanted to snipe back, spurred by a feeling of betrayal. But Nick's genuine tone managed to soften the offense.

"I guess what I'm saying is, aside from standing on the corner, shouting the guy's name like some newsie, seems to me you've tried about everything you can."

Shan wished he could argue the point. Indeed, he was running out of options. But the same could be said of his welcome.

He simply chose not to answer.

Soon Nick drifted off, leaving Shan wide-awake. He combed his mind for ideas, grasping for hope, worn thin over the years.

Outside, the moon rose and the borough went still. And suddenly Nick's comment circled back, about a newsie hollering a name. It floated through Shan's mind until merging with a detail the secretary had shared. Together, they formed an idea.

There would be risks involved, from trespassing and deception, and costs of a sizable sum. Yet none of that would matter if the plan managed to work.

12

Already it was Sunday.

Shan had scouted the place earlier in the week. The legal firm would move in soon, according to the naval secretary. From furtive glances through windows, Shan had confirmed the renovations were almost done. He would have preferred more than five days for his ad in the papers to spread word, but there wasn't time.

"This is downright stupid," Nick said, crouching outside of the firm's back door, small metal picks in hand.

The gripe was loud enough to reach Shan at the corner of the building, a lookout spot several yards away. He wanted to tell Nick to shut his gob, growing tired of the complaint that raised unneeded doubts, but he restrained himself. Nick was, after all, helping him break the law.

A city clock chimed, marking half past ten. People were strolling here and there beneath the canopy of gray clouds. Though all appeared engrossed in their own lives, Shan's skin hummed with jitters.

He whispered to Nick, "Could you hurry it up?"

"Think you can do better, feel free." Nick shook his head and continued his efforts at the door.

When Shan had asked about anyone who could jimmy a lock, Nick named himself before learning the reason behind the question. Hopefully he hadn't overstated his ability. In less than thirty minutes, any John Lewis who had read or heard of the ad would surely be arriving. Not that there would be more than a few. The classified listing in various New York papers, costing Shan most of his savings, had been very specific.

DECLARATION OF INHERITANCE: Seeking a member or veteran of the U.S. Navy based in England in 1906, a musician known as John Lewis, for the receipt of a great valuable bequeathed by an acquaintance now deceased. Claim upon verification of identity at law office.

Shan had crafted the words with care. He'd included the office address with the time and date. Sunday had guaranteed the absence of construction workers and employees at surrounding offices, allowing Shan a better chance of slipping in unseen. If he ever got past the lock.

"How about that?" With a laugh, Nick rose and pushed open the door. "Thing was unlocked the whole time."

The laborers must have forgotten, or figured there wasn't a need for caution. Either way, Shan was grateful.

Nick gestured to the doorway. "Your show."

It was only right for Shan to go first, as the mission belonged to him, but a curse of conscience gave him pause. He had been raised to adhere to rules. To mind his parents, priests, nuns, teachers, doctors, elders, and more.

"Second thoughts?" Nick said, clearly hopeful.

Shan took it as a challenge. He strode inside, and Nick trailed him with a sigh.

They wound their way through an L-shaped hall, sprinkled with sawdust, tools, and ladders. The air smelled of fresh wood and paint. Plenty of daylight shone through the lobby windows. There were no proper desks, cabinets, or couches to be found, but the worktable and chairs would do.

Shan immediately went to work, spouting out directions. Nick helped carry and move as needed, though not without muttering. When the stage was set, Shan used his coat sleeves to dust the tabletop and wipe down the chairs. From a coat pocket he unfolded a paper sign and propped it on the table.

ATTENTION: JOHN LEWIS
BE BACK SHORTLY!
PLEASE WAIT HERE.

At last Shan unlocked the entrance and retreated to an office with the most strategic view, located just off the hallway. Inside, Nick was seated against the wall on the tile floor. He was flinging cards one at a time, from the deck he always toted, using an upturned hard hat as the target.

Shan kept the door open a crack. Too nervous to sit, he peeked out at least once every minute. It had to be ten o'clock by now. "Please, someone come," he said under his breath.

"Oh, don't worry," Nick said. "They're coming, all right. Suddenly, every bum without two nickels to rub together will be named John Lewis."

Shan wasn't a dimwit. He understood the possibility. But he was also aware that this particular office, known for housing experts of the law, would help as a deterrent.

"It'll work," Shan contended. "You'll see."

"If you say so." Another flick of a card.

Shan clenched his jaw, resentment growing. Yes, this whole plan was a gamble, but considering Shan's life so far, by all counts he was due for a blessing.

Finally a noise sounded from the entry. Shan raised a hand to halt Nick's movements, but Nick had already gone still. Peering through the door's gap, Shan spied a man in a suit. A brown bowler hid his face as he gazed down, reading the sign Shan had posted. An eternity passed until he raised his head and Shan could see it wasn't his father.

The man had a beak-like nose and terribly pale skin. He sniffed, raising his upper lip above a line of crooked teeth, yellowed from cigarettes.

Shan had barely registered his disappointment when another figure entered. He had a promising build, dressed in a pea coat. The common coat of a sailor. And he wore a tweed cap, like Shan's.

Shan strained to see his face, but the first man blocked the view. Then the new arrival stepped toward the sign, revealing his features — none of them familiar. Grizzled and worn, he had the look of a dockworker. He removed his cap and swiped a hand over his balding head.

Nick whispered, "Well?"

Shan shook his head. Again, he homed in on the front door, envisioning the sailor from the photograph walking through.

Ten minutes must have passed before a third fellow shuffled in. Right away, Shan's hopes dropped another notch. Even past the walrus moustache, the man bore no resemblance to Shan.

The dockworker leaned against a wall, folding his burly arms. The other two sat in chairs, the first with legs primly crossed and tapping an impatient tune on his bowler.

Over the next half hour, maybe more, no one else arrived. Nick played several rounds of solitaire. Now and then, the group traded questions regarding the ad, and eventually about one another. A challenge of who was there under false pretenses colored their tones, though the accusations went unsaid.

At one point, the dockworker surveyed the hallway in a suspicious manner, and Shan jerked his head back from the door. He held his breath.

There was a window in the office, but no way of exiting without being detected. What would happen if the men decided to snoop?

Then Shan heard voices.

With caution, he returned to the door. The three were discussing their surroundings, agreeing that something was fishy. Before long, to Shan's relief, they donned their hats, buttoned their coats, and went their separate ways.

But the relief was short-lived. Because left behind was a cavernous space that echoed with a harsh reality.

No one else was coming.

They rode the trolley in silence, the aisle separating their seats. Shan stared out the window, unseeing. He didn't dare meet Nick's eyes, dreading a gleam of smugness. It was enough to sense its presence, and that certainty stoked the frustration and anger simmering deep in Shan's chest.

They were nearly at their stop when Nick spoke. "Hey, about today . . . I'm sorry it didn't work out."

After days of mocking and muttering, was Shan really supposed to believe him?

"I doubt that," he replied under his breath.

After a moment, Nick said, "Look, I just thought —"

Shan turned to him. "I know what you bloody thought. I'm stupid. You said it a hundred times."

"Now, hold on. I wasn't saying you were — it was the idea . . ."

The trolley was slowing. Shan didn't wait. He rose and hopped off while it was still in motion. After a block of walking, he heard Nick's steps in his wake but continued his determined strides. He refused to listen to one more word about the futility of his search, how any effort was doomed from the start. How he should have known better.

Shan entered the house and tugged off his coat. He flung it onto a chair in the sitting room, where Lina lay on the floor, propped on her elbows. Her black braids dangled as she looked up from her journal. "Mama said she needs more flour from the market."

Leaving the duty to Nick, Shan sped up to their bedroom and shut the door. He fisted his hands, wanting to strike something down. To make someone feel as low and beaten as he did himself.

He sat on the desk chair in an effort to rein in his temper, and took several deep breaths. What he inhaled were smells of garlic and stewing tomatoes, a stark reminder that this wasn't his home. Not his family. Not even his room. He was an outsider, borrowing a life, just as he'd borrowed that office.

The door swung open. Nick hitched his hands low on his hips. "Now, listen," he said with forced patience, as if Shan might otherwise not understand. "I was just worried you were gonna get conned. That's all I meant."

"Ah, so you were worried for me." Shan laughed spitefully, surprising even himself. "Because I thought it was about your need to be right and for everyone else to be wrong."

Nick's mouth became a hard line. When he replied, he barely moved his lips. "You know what? I'm gonna do you a favor and walk away." He started to turn, but Shan couldn't hold back.

He shot to his feet. "Don't do me any damn favors."

Now Nick was the one who laughed with spite. "I see. So you don't need my help. That's what you're saying? 'Cause it sure as hell didn't seem like that when you got off the boat. You remember — back when nobody else was there to save your ass." Nick gasped, tight with sarcasm. "Oh, wait. That's right. You got a father you're *supposed* to meet up with. The hero who made it through the war and isn't some lousy bum on the street."

The words struck straight at Shan's gut. It

felt like Uncle Will taking swings all over again, only worse. At least with his uncle, he was prepared for what was coming.

"Niccolò?" Mrs. Capello's voice floated up the stairs. "*Sbrigati.* I need flour for the supper. Niccolò?"

Hesitant, Nick turned toward the hall. "I'm coming, Ma." He slowly angled back to Shan, regrouping, and raised his hands in a truce. His fingers held a slight tremble. "It's been a long day. Let's just . . . take a break. All right?"

When Shan didn't respond, Nick went to speak again but stopped. He shook his head before heading downstairs, leaving Shan all alone. The way he wanted to be. The way, in truth, he always was.

Suddenly the ceiling seemed lower and the walls closer. They cinched around him. He pressed his fists to his temples, desperate for escape, tired of feeling unwelcome.

Why delay the inevitable?

He crossed the room and pulled open the wardrobe closet on a hunt for his satchels.

Nick was right about one thing. It was time for a break.

13

By his fourth day on the streets, the money had run out.

Shan recalled the war veterans back in Ireland. How he'd seen them on the streets or in pubs, looking lost, without purpose, harboring the worst of their wounds far beneath the surface. How they would hunch their shoulders as if hauling a sack they couldn't put down.

Only now was it evident that what filled their bags was regret. At least, that was the case for Shan. He was anything but proud of the things he'd said to Nick. But then, there was no sense in looking back. Not when survival took priority.

On the day he'd left the Capellos, he found a line of children needing food and shelter on the back side of St. Peter's Church. Joining them could have helped stretch his funds, meager as they were, but a sign on the door read: *Children's Aid Soci-*

ety. In Shan's short time in the country, he'd already heard about the group that fed and tidied young orphans before handing them off to any willing taker.

Truth or not, he couldn't take the chance.

He had chosen instead to spend that night on a bench in Prospect Park, until a policeman shooed him off. For every night since, he'd hunkered down in a warehouse, where nibbling rats assaulted his sleep. Some were so large he could mistake them for cats. They were the same kind of scavengers he'd competed with for scraps in trash cans behind restaurants, most of them all but picked over.

Now, on the tenth morning, aching from hunger and exhaustion in every way, he felt the darkness of desperation. Yesterday was his twelfth birthday, but it had come to mean nothing. He refused to dwell on memories of his mam sewing him a shirt or baking him a pie. Especially the pie. What he needed was real food, like that being sold across the street. Colorful fruit and vegetables were piled in baskets on a horse-drawn cart. Shan's mouth watered as he moved closer, clutching his satchels, telling himself he only wanted to look.

But with the vendor distracted by a customer, a tomato drew Shan's hand like a moth to a flame. Once it was in his grasp, the compulsion to take a bite sent him scurrying away with the morsel. His parents had raised a son who would never stoop to thievery, yet shame was the least of his concerns as he squatted in an alley, gobbling up the tomato, its juice streaming down his chin. When he was done, he wished he'd taken two.

That didn't make him a thief, not to his core. He wished he could buy them outright. He'd tried panhandling and street performing, the weather making them pointless. For six days straight, relentless drizzle had drenched the city and planted a shiver in his bones. His throat had gone raw, made worse with every cough and sneeze.

To survive, he needed a job. He had already inquired at countless saloons and pubs, offering to put on an act — if only for a meal. But few folks spared him a word, aside from voicing their disgust over filthy Irish beggars.

Much like orphans, immigrants in America were ranked by order. It was best, Shan had learned, to hide his brogue.

Putting on his best Yankee accent, he now approached the owner of another saloon. A flick of the man's hand, as if batting away a fly, provided his answer. The bar mistress at least passed Shan a stale slice of bread.

At the pub next door, the bartender told him, "Sorry, kid. New York's got more than enough free entertainment to go around. But who knows, maybe someday you could star in a variety show on Broadway."

The comment, riding a chuckle, was meant to mock, though Shan had nothing to lose for trying. He smoothed his hair into his tweed cap, using rain and spit to clean his face, and set out on the legendary street. He would hit every playhouse if needed.

Less than an hour later, he discovered he just might have to. Ticket clerks were even less hospitable. When the urge arose, Shan knew better than to ask for the use of a washroom.

Around Forty-third Street, he could no longer hold his bladder. He crept behind the Fitzgerald Building and relieved himself on a wall. Light rain tapped old playbills curled and wet in the gutter. Shan was just buttoning his trousers when the stage door of a theater flew open.

Two suited men emerged in overcoats and brimmed hats, grumbling over the weather. The taller one, with a slightly hooked nose, opened an umbrella with ease. He snickered at his friend struggling to do the same.

"Would you look at this. Fella runs half of

Broadway but can't open an umbrella without a butler. C'mon, hand it over."

"Nah, I got it," the other replied, persisting. His neck muscles strained above his bow tie. "Lousy thing keeps getting stuck."

"Hey, kid!" The taller man looked over at Shan. "You want to show Mr. Cohan here how to work this fancy contraption? Apparently it's too complicated."

Mind in a haze, Shan needed a second to digest the name. Once he did, he stared in disbelief. It was George M. Cohan, his sketched likeness widely known from ads, fliers, and magazines. He was an Irish Catholic, like Shan, and a famed vaudevillian who became a hit producer, songwriter, and everything in between. In Dublin, Shan had even sung a few of his popular tunes, "Over There" and "Yankee Doodle Dandy."

And here the man was, mere steps away. This meeting couldn't be coincidence.

Shan adjusted his cap and the satchels on his shoulder. He walked over, aiming to look stronger than he felt, and extended a hand in greeting. "Mr. Cohan —"

"All right, all right. I give up." Mr. Cohan surrendered his umbrella.

Shan hedged a moment but swiftly recognized how earning the man's gratitude could warrant a return favor.

Taking on the challenge, Shan pulled and pushed and tugged. He persisted, unwilling to yield, until Mr. Cohan said, "Hey, hey. You gave it your best shot, kid."

Right then, Shan's grip slid forward, ripping a gash in the fabric. "Ah, Jaysus, no," he said, a whisper lost to a burst of laughter from the taller man.

"You were right after all, Cohan. That umbrella's definitely the problem." Another bout of laughter.

"Sir, I — I'm so sorry. I didn't mean to," Shan said, handing it back.

Mr. Cohan examined the damage and sighed. "I suppose it was time for a new one anyhow."

"But, sir, I . . ."

"Don't worry about it, kid." Mr. Cohan winked. "See, here? A peace offering." He held out a gray handkerchief from his chest pocket, gave it a small wave. "Now, get yourself out of this weather, huh?"

Shan accepted, confounded by the gift. That was when he realized the moisture on his lip wasn't just rain, but snot. Had it been there the whole time? He rushed to wipe his nose. When he looked up, the men were halfway to the corner, sharing the good umbrella.

Shan was losing his big chance. Quite possibly his only one.

"Mr. Cohan," he called out, and a jagged pain gripped his throat.

"It's okay, kid," the man hollered through the rain. "You keep it!" Then he vanished around the building.

Shan clenched the fancy monogrammed handkerchief. The man probably owned a dozen others like it. Fighting a swell of tears, Shan shoved the cloth into his pocket and forced a swallow that burned all the way down.

A roar of thunder shook the sky.

As Shan turned to leave, he noted the theater door was open a crack. A theater . . . where heat enveloped the air. He imagined rows and rows of real chairs enclosed by solid walls and a high ceiling.

If only he could rest in a place such as this, a haven free of rats and rain, he could revive his strength, his will.

The open door practically seemed an invitation, not unlike that at the legal firm. He remembered how he and Nick had walked in and out, with nobody the wiser.

Shan scanned the alley and found no one around.

Get yourself out of this weather, Mr. Cohan had said.

So that was precisely what Shan did.

A pair of offices and a zigzag of dressing rooms lined the back hall of the playhouse. Some doors boasted names and gold stars. Shan considered finding a vacant corner behind any one of them, but then music entered the air. He perked at the sound of chimes and a flute, an Oriental melody.

If he was careful, he could blend into the audience. While thawing himself, he could enjoy part of a show. It would be a good while before he could afford a ticket of any kind.

Following the notes, he climbed a spiral staircase that wound up to the next level. A manager's passageway, he guessed. From there he continued onto another set of twisting metal steps, up and up, until he reached the uppermost balcony.

A weekend picture show flickered through the darkness, projecting enough light to confirm that the seats on this floor were vacant. Shan surveyed the theater in awe. The plain exterior of the building gave little indication of the extravagance inside, with columns and box seats and a lush arch that framed the screen. All around, murals adorned the walls, though Shan couldn't quite make them out.

He took a seat in the center of the balcony and melted into the cushion. He'd almost forgotten the luxury of sitting on something soft.

In the film, a white actor in Chinese clothing moved his mouth in conversation. Words of explanation flashed on the screen: *The Yellow Man in the Temple of Buddha, before his contemplated journey to a foreign land.*

Aside from its brownish tint, Shan had never seen a film look so real. *Broken Blossoms* was the title. He recalled it from the marquee.

He continued to watch as the monk realized the fruitlessness of his mission to bring peace to the West. For years, the man plunged into a pit of sin and opium, until crossing paths with Lucy, a fellow outcast who found splendor in simple flowers. And yet, her drunken prizefighting father made a habit of taking out his aggressions on the young girl.

The obvious similarities to Shan's life should have caused him to look away. Instead, he was captivated by a glimpse of where his own journey might lead. He craved the promise of a joyous life in the end.

But that wasn't what waited in the show.

Shan learned this when the boxer used a hatchet to chop his way into a closet, where Lucy had sought safety. Though there were no voices, Shan could hear her screams. The audience on the main floor seemed to hear them too, for they shifted in their seats and whispered their discomfort. A few ladies walked out, looking sickened, followed by a couple more when Lucy forced a smile around a trickle of blood as she died.

As a moderate consolation, the Yellow Man shot the father with a gun before taking his own life with a blade, a sacrifice of love to his innocent White Blossom. There was no applause when the screen declared *The End.* The remaining audience had become statues in their seats, stunned and horrified. Robbed of true justice.

Shan knew this because he felt the same. He sank farther into his seat, weighted by knowledge that his own destiny would more likely resemble Lucy's than that of the pauper. He would not become an adviser to a prince and live out his days in the lavishness of a royal court.

It was this thought, this acceptance of his fate, that dragged him down the dark tunnel of sleep — only to be jolted by a firm grip on his collar.

14

Shan couldn't say how long it had been since he'd drifted off. He had no knowledge of anything save the panic that now seized him while being yanked into the air and onto his feet. Squinting against the glare, he recognized the man's uniform. An usher . . .

Shan was still in the theater, but the lights had been raised. The audience was gone.

"This ain't a flophouse." The usher gave him a shove. "It ain't a free show neither."

Shan stumbled into the aisle. He hurried from the balcony, vision clearing, and toward the main staircase. The occasional poke of a flashlight indicated he'd be escorted all the way out. When he made it through the lobby and onto the sidewalk, he heard the man's voice over the thrum of the rain.

"Now, beat it or I'll put the cops on ya!"

The door slammed shut, but eyes watched from inside.

Thick droplets ran down Shan's face. He shuddered from the chill he had hoped to leave back in Ireland. Before the usher could make good on his threat, Shan left without thought of destination.

He raised his coat collar and rubbed at his sleeves. The evening sky remained just as gray as it had been that morning, only darker.

An automobile honked. Dapper couples traversed the avenue beneath umbrellas, clutching their tickets for the latest shows.

Several blocks passed before Shan registered something missing from his shoulder: his satchels! He'd forgotten them in the balcony. The clothes weren't worth a shilling, but the books . . . his mam's precious books . . .

Yet what was he to do?

In no position to recover them, he bridled the pang of loss, for he couldn't bear to absorb it now. He trudged onward until a coughing fit, similar to those of Uncle Will, brought him to a halt. When it passed, Shan remained hunched, hands on his legs for support.

"Pal, you okay?"

Shan raised his eyes to find a man in a weathered hat and threadbare coat. No fewer than three buttons were missing, the same for his teeth.

"You got a home?"

Lacking energy for a front, Shan shook his head.

"Figured." The fellow sighed. "Well, come on, then."

Following him would be foolish; even decent people weren't kind enough to take in a street urchin for nothing.

Aside, that was, from the Capellos.

The man peeked over his shoulder and shrugged. "No skin off my nose. Breadline's a few blocks over if you're wanting some soup."

Faint memories of broth and chowder and stew caused Shan's stomach to gurgle. When the man trekked away, Shan trailed at a distance. Even if he wanted to catch up, he wasn't sure he could. He was so very tired, and the dampness of his trousers hampered every step.

It seemed an eternity before they traveled past several buildings and around the corner, into an open lot sprinkled with gravel. Downtrodden men stood in a line that led to a large canopy. There, three women in peaked white hats ladled steaming liquid into tin cups.

The man who'd led Shan here had disappeared into the crowd.

Shan tacked onto the end of the line, his hands in his pockets. His left fingers found his sixpence. He pulled it out and fiddled with the coin; the friction created a trace of warmth.

Gradually the line shuffled forward and Shan with it. A whiff of roasted chicken breezed past. Given Shan's congested nose, perhaps he only imagined it, but it struck as the aroma of a king's feast.

"Ah, now! Would ye look at that."

A male brogue caught Shan's ear. Its familiar comfort beckoned like rays of a summer sun. He swung around to find a teenager in stained knickers, a smudge on his nose, speaking to boys his age. He held up a coin for them to see.

"Richer than the Rockefellers, I am. Wouldn't ye say?"

A stocky red-haired one sneered. "Maybe now you can afford a feckin' brain."

The others laughed, and suddenly Shan noticed his own hand was empty. The sixpence — it must have fallen to the ground, his fingers too numb to notice.

"I dropped that" — the group snapped to face him — "it belongs to me."

The boy with the sixpence bit off a laugh. "Aye, sure it does."

"I'm telling the truth."

"Let me guess." The same boy widened his eyes in exaggerated shock. "You're a leprechaun and it fell out of your pot o' gold."

More snide laughter.

Its monetary worth didn't matter to Shan; a sixpence bought nothing in America. And clearly it was proving a failure in all levels of luck. Rather, the true value lay in its connection to his past, a final tie that if severed might forever set him adrift.

In some way, the boy would understand this. Surely he couldn't deny their common ground. "Please, I'm from Ireland, like you. Just trying to get by."

The boy drew his head back. He surveyed Shan from head to toe. "Can you believe it, lads? All this time, I've dreamt of meeting me long-lost brother. I had no idea this Yank was part of our clan."

Shan was becoming so accustomed to suppressing his brogue, to revive it now carried the odd feeling of putting on a show.

Regardless, it was clear the thief wasn't going to budge. Shan had nothing to offer in trade. And without the coin, Shan himself had nothing at all. There was only one way to reclaim it.

Before the group could react, he lunged for the money. The boy managed to stretch it out of reach and pushed back with his free hand. Shan tried to maintain his footing but landed on the ground. An icy puddle flooded his trousers. The group broke into jeers. Shan's arms and legs quivered. Not from the cold, but from anger rising like mercury, boiling through his veins. A primal instinct took hold. Like a madman, he shot to his feet and charged back with a bellow that came from deep within. It sounded of something barbaric and raw.

There was a glint in the teenager's eyes, of surprise and fear, a split second before Shan's fist slammed into his jaw. On another day Shan would have paused to measure the effect, but a mounting blackness had been uncaged. Every ounce of it sent his arms swinging and pummeling, powered by fury, unwilling to stop until the enemy was reduced to a sack of meat and bones.

Shan faintly registered the other boys hitting his back. But then a punch connected to his kidneys, paralyzing him enough to be flung to the ground. His chin and palms scraped gravel. Clamoring shouts echoed in his ears. In a blink he was flipped over and a sea of fists descended. His forearms flew into an X, an old reflex, absorbing blows that came in sloppy succession.

"Enough, I said!" At the man's booming voice, the din fell away as if dropped off a cliff. "Clear out, the bunch of you hoodlums!"

Shan saw the scuttling of feet through the gap beneath his arms, still raised as a shield. His heart thrashed in his chest.

"Goddamned micks," the man muttered. "Hey, kid. Let's go. You hurt or what?"

From the outskirts of Shan's mind came a lyric from Billy Murray's "Foolish Questions." How a person could fall twenty-seven floors down an elevator shaft, and while he's lying there inert, the first thing he'd be asked was: *Oh, are you hurt?*

"Come on. On your feet." Rain dripped from the bill of the man's hat as he hefted Shan upright. He was a policeman. Surprisingly, based on his dark features and disparaging remark, not an Irish one.

"What's your name?"

Though out of sorts, Shan realized advertising his heritage wouldn't improve the situation. He mumbled the first alternative that came to mind. "Capello."

"What's that you say?"

"Tommy Capello," Shan repeated, but not too loudly.

The officer's face softened a fraction. "Your family around here?"

Shan answered honestly with a shake of his head.

"Where do they live?"

"In . . . Brooklyn."

"Whereabouts?"

The officer had beady eyes and a bulbous nose, features certain to sniff out lies. But after all of Shan's struggles, he couldn't just surrender to an orphanage. Not when all he needed was a plausible address to be sent on his way.

"Maywood Place. Number eleven."

The officer went quiet, the discrepancy obvious. The neighborhood was a nice one. If this kid had a family and a home there, why was he in a gravel lot in the rain, alone?

But then he replied, "I'd say it's about time you headed back. Don't you?"

The interrogation was over.

Shan nodded in earnest. "Yes. Yes, sir." Despite his soreness, he scrambled to pick up his cap from the ground, then his coin, which he glimpsed in a shallow puddle. As he turned to leave, he felt a tinge of relief until the officer stopped him.

"This way," he said. "My car's over here."

15

The soothing rumble of the motor would have lulled Shan to sleep if not for being jostled by bumps in the road. Each one alerted him which body parts had taken the hardest hits. While he had no desire to move from this seat, he still hoped a police emergency would force the officer to let Shan out.

That hope evaporated when they parked before the house.

Shan clambered out, realizing how groggy he'd become. The officer escorted him up the short walkway, as close as a shadow. It took concerted effort for Shan not to trip on the handful of steps to reach the porch.

No doubt, the Capellos would be less than delighted by a reunion with the ungrateful mick they barely knew, filthy from a fight and delivered by a cop. He was also now as broke as could be, with nothing to offer, including his pride. If they denied ever knowing him, he wouldn't blame them a bit.

The policeman rapped on the door. Soon it opened to Mr. Capello, whose face swiftly clouded.

"Sir, I'm Officer Barsetti. I believe this boy is your son."

Mr. Capello's gaze cut to Shan. Before the man could respond, his wife rushed to the door in a floral apron. She layered her hands over her chest. "*Mio Dio.* Where have you been? We are so worried. And your face?"

She looked to the officer, wrought with concern.

"Your kid got a little scuffed up by some boys in the breadline. Nothing to fret about."

Mrs. Capello knotted her brow, disagreeing with the assessment. She reached for Shan's chin with a gentle touch, but still the pain caused him to wince. "You are so hot," she exclaimed. "And thin." Then over her shoulder: "Lina! Fill a bowl of *ribollita. Pronto.*"

Officer Barsetti crossed his arms with authority. His eyes returned to Mr. Capello, who had yet to utter a word. It was evident the policeman had more to say, perhaps aware Shan had taken the first swing, or detecting dishonesty.

"Sir," he said, "I don't mean to make assumptions. But from the looks of things . . . it doesn't appear your family's in need of much charity. That food is for folks down on their luck, not kids looking for a free snack."

At this, Mr. Capello straightened. He was a man who believed in accepting only what he earned. If ever there were cause to reject Shan's claim to the Capello bloodline, this would be it.

Without so much as a glance at Shan, he replied in an even tone. "Of course, Officer. It will not happen again." To solidify the deal, he extended his hand.

The policeman accepted, but added, "Let's hope you're right."

"Grazie, signore," Mrs. Capello interjected, an edge to her gratitude. She ushered Shan inside as the officer tipped his hat. The instant he turned to depart, Mr. Capello closed the door.

This was the second time the father had protected Shan from a questioning official. An unexpected gesture. Then again, given the family's fibs at Ellis Island, maybe he felt obligated to remain consistent. Now that the officer was gone, he could send Shan on his way.

"Go and sit," Mrs. Capello said. "I will get a cold cloth." She hurried to the kitchen as heat from the potbelly stove transformed the room into an oven.

Mr. Capello appeared to be contemplating his next words.

Shan fumbled to remove his cap, sweat pooling on his scalp. He stepped toward the davenport, but sapped of adrenaline, his muscles weakened. The air went hazy and the floor began to tilt. A relentless drumbeat grew in his head. He vaguely made out Nick entering the room. Shan reached for the wall, but his hand seemed to pass right through.

"Niccolò, *aiutami,*" he heard Mr. Capello say with urgency.

Then everything turned black.

16

When Shan was a young boy, his mam sent him to the cellar. He was retrieving a jar of peaches for her when a mouse skittered across the floor. Despite a diligent hunt, Shan never located the rodent, but he did find its home: bits of food and paper and leaves harvested in the corner of a crate. After he excitedly told his parents, his da marched down with a broom and dustpan, and in a couple of sweeps the nest was gone.

Shan supposed, in many ways, memory was the same: a collection of scraps, pieced together one by one. Whether useful or comforting, rough or sharp edged, combined as a whole they provided a semblance of security. Identity, even. Until wiped away.

This was never more apparent than now, as the odds and ends of his life fluttered through his mind. Lying in the dimness, he stared at the ceiling, determining dreams from reality. He remembered Mr. Capello standing in the doorway, gazing in. Then there was Mrs. Capello seated nearby, praying with a rosary, and later sewing needlepoint. She was there again, feeding him soup, then speaking to a doctor in another language.

Of course, mixed into the visions was Shan's own family, namely his mam and da, and Mr. and Mrs. Maguire. But their faces, unlike the Capellos', lacked the details they'd once had. Their features were like wax left too long in the sun, melting into figures he barely recognized.

"*Allora!* You are awake."

Shan turned toward Mrs. Capello, who entered the room with a tray. She set it on the bedside table and opened the curtains with a flourish. At the shaft of light, Shan blinked repeatedly, fighting the bleariness of hibernation.

"Your fever, finally it is gone." Leaning over him, she touched his forehead with the back of her fingers. *"Bene,"* she said, and smiled.

Shan realized he wasn't on a mattress on the floor, but in the bed belonging to Nick.

With an apron over her light yellow housedress, Mrs. Capello twittered about like a hummingbird, zipping from one task to another: refolding clothes at the wardrobe closet, shaking out the blanket at the foot of the bed. And her words kept similar pace.

"We are worrying so much. But the doctor, he says you are only needing food and sleep." She propped Shan's head with an extra pillow. "Niccolò and Lina are gone to the market. They will be very glad to see you."

There was good reason to doubt that, at least where Nick was concerned. Shan swallowed against the dryness of his throat. "How long . . ."

She pulled the desk chair over. "It is four days. You are waking and sleeping many times." Once seated, she picked up the bowl and spoon from the tray. "Now? You eat."

In a practiced manner, she brought the broth to his lips. The warm liquid soothed his throat and continued into his chest.

He suddenly pictured his mam, how she would feed him soup — a brew of onion and pepper boiled in milk — to ward off any cold. Yet as quickly as the memory arrived, it drifted into the distance, a scrap of paper carried by the wind.

Again Mrs. Capello fed him a spoonful. Then she dabbed his chin with a napkin, preventing a drip from soiling his undershirt. She must have cared for Tomasso in much the same way.

The difference was Shan didn't deserve it.

The family had dared to lie to Immigration, provided food and shelter and, above all, use of their late son's name. And Shan had repaid them by running off without a word — except to unload on Nick for stating the truth. But that wasn't the worst of it.

During the fight in the breadline, deep inside Shan had found pleasure in releasing his fury. If it weren't for being outnumbered or the officer's intervention, he couldn't say he would have stopped until the boy had taken his final breath.

That darkness scared Shan now. He feared the same vileness behind his uncle's rages could run in his blood like the plague. An illness destined to infect others. Although he dreaded returning to the streets, he had to speak up.

"Mrs. Capello . . ." His voice came out raspy from disuse. When she tried to feed him more, he gently held off the spoon. "I want you to know, I can leave as soon as I'm stronger."

She tsked. "Come, eat," she said. But Shan needed to explain, to make clear he wasn't ungrateful.

"I know it's been hard . . . and I'm only making things worse."

Mrs. Capello reclined slightly in her chair. Her sudden solemnness confirmed she understood the reference to the son she had lost.

She set aside the spoon and bowl. Mindlessly she wiped her hands on her apron.

Shan suspected she might depart, in need of privacy, until she replied. "If you wish, you may go. First, you will listen." The order was gentle but an order all the same.

Working to concentrate, Shan nodded. After a moment, Mrs. Capello's unseeing gaze settled on the window.

"For so long, Tomasso's heart, it is not well. He is getting worse, but nothing we can do. Then one night, a dream comes to me. It is so clear I wonder if I am awake. I see my mother. She is a beautiful angel." Mrs. Capello made the sign of the cross, clarifying that her mother, too, had passed on. "She is smiling at Tomasso. She warms him with light, and he is well again and so happy. The next day a telegram comes. My father-in-law is sick, it says. And I know this is a sign. My heart tells me we must go there and God and the angels will heal our boy.

"Benicio says he will return to Siena to see his father. But I tell him we go together, *come una famiglia* — as a family. The children, they have never seen our home country, I say. I do not tell him the dream. It will sound foolish. And my faith must be strong. *Pero* . . . on the ship, another dream comes to me. My mother, again she smiles at Tomasso and there is much light. But now he is taking her hand, and I see they are going to heaven. I reach out and call to them, but they are too far. I beg them, *please do not go.* Then the light grows so bright, I cannot see. And then they are gone. I wake up screaming. I want to go back, away from Italy. But it is too late . . ."

During the tense pause that followed, Shan barely dared breathe. It was a mistake, bringing up the topic; he hadn't intended to open an old wound. He was about to say as much when she resumed her story, sunlight glinting off the moisture in her amber eyes.

"In Siena, my sisters say we must go to *il duomo* to pray to the Madonna. They say she will give miracles if we pray very hard. Lina and Niccolò, they do this. But it is Benicio who goes two times every day. He prays for his father, but even more for Tomasso. Finally I go to the church, but not to pray. I will bring Tomasso to show Madonna that my mother, she is wrong."

At this, Mrs. Capello's tone intensified and a tear rolled down her cheek. "God will see he is too young, that he needs to live many more years. But Tomasso, he is in my arms and he looks up in *il duomo.* His eyes are so big. He sees something I do not see. He smiles at me and says, '*Va bene,* Mama.' It is good, he tells me. And he holds me close. I feel so much peace, so much love."

The sudden awe in Mrs. Capello's voice matched the glow in her face, shedding layers of sorrow and years. It seemed as if speaking of her son was less a hardship than a keepsake in a trunk sealed for too long. Shan saw this in her eyes when they finally connected with his.

"It is ten more days when Tomasso dies. I am sad, yes, but also happy. I know he is in a beautiful place with my mother. Benicio, though, he feels only anger. He curses Madonna, and also God. Even more, he curses Benicio. He is Tomasso's father and he cannot fix this. But then . . . then you come to us in New York, and it is a sign to me. We can save this boy, I say. But Benicio, he does not agree."

Shan lowered his gaze to the coverlet. Mr. Capello's resistance had been clear from the start. Now at least Shan knew the reason.

"I understand," he offered, and truly he did. "Using his son's name — it was too much to ask."

"No." She tilted her head at Shan, correcting him. "He does not want to fail again. When you are gone, he is so worried we will not find you. He blames himself. Niccolò and Benicio, they search and search."

Shan tried to hide his surprise at this. All the time he was away, he hadn't imagined the family feeling anything but relief.

As if to emphasize the contrary, Mrs. Capello reached out and clasped his hand. "One night I wake up and Benicio is gone. I am going down the stairs, and I see him. He is on his knees praying. He is praying for *you.* The next day you come to our door, and I know you are sent by our sweet angel Tomasso. I know this," she said, "because already you bring faith back to us."

Where a terrible soreness had plagued Shan's throat, a lump of emotion now took its place. Or maybe it was something else. Maybe it was hope, something he had considered long gone.

It was an idea he'd love to believe, anyhow, that a guardian was looking out for them. If so, perhaps his mam, too, had guided him here, to this home, this family.

Yet with the thought also came a weight, the responsibility of proving himself worthy of such a blessing.

Footsteps sounded down the hall, brisk

taps that brought Lina bursting into the room. "Oh, goody. You're up!"

Releasing Shan's hand, Mrs. Capello smiled and stealthily brushed tears from her face. Meanwhile, Lina launched into a list of items they'd bought just for Shan at the market. He tried to keep up, switching tracks, until a second figure appeared in the doorway.

Lina halted her rambling and stepped aside to make room for Nick.

"Hey," he said.

"Hi." Shan managed a wavering smile. He searched for something to say, to ease the awkwardness.

But Nick rested his hands in his trouser pockets and said, "Does this mean I get my bed back?" His mouth slid into a grin.

Relieved, Shan replied, "Anytime you want."

Nick pondered this. "I don't know. I kinda like yours better," he said with a shrug.

"I suppose we're okay, then."

"Yeah, we're okay."

The exchange was as simple as that. No explanations or apologies, for they were all there in the unspoken.

Then Lina jumped back in, recounting the trip to the market. As Nick inserted wisecracks about the quirks of other customers,

Mrs. Capello picked up the bowl, returning to her task.

And somewhere in the middle of it all, Shan made a choice. Once well enough, he would return to the Navy recruiting station. Not for an update, but to let the kind secretary know there was no reason to search any longer.

17

The bell dinged as the trolley approached another stop. Shan had chosen a seat by a rear window to take in the midmorning air, somehow forgetting the fumes and industrial smoke that clung to the city. It was his first outing since recovering. In contrast to the serenity of the house, every sound and movement seemed magnified, almost to an overwhelming level. After his visit to the recruiting station, a nap might be in order.

Mrs. Capello had insisted Lina and Nick help her at the community garden today but would have preferred Shan stay at home. "You must not do too much," she'd told him with a sigh of worry. It was a far cry from the warnings Nick often received from his father to avoid being viewed as a lazy Italian: "Always we must show pride, that we are good, hardworking Americans."

This was the reason, no matter the occasion, for shined shoes and tucked shirts and trousers smartly pressed. It also explained Mr. Capello's constant drive to improve his English by reading the nightly paper and practicing words over and over that were difficult to pronounce. And it was certainly why Nick had been given an ultimatum, as his father saw no purpose in waiting until summer for his son to earn a wage.

"You have two weeks, or I find a job for you," Mr. Capello had declared during supper the night before. It went without saying that the latter would involve ice deliveries or garbage collection, common work among Italian boys their age. Mrs. Capello concurred, so long as the job wasn't dangerous and would not interfere with school in the fall.

The trolley rolled to another stop. Outside of a café, a newsie peddled the latest headlines. Another boy across the street polished the shoes of a businessman puffing on a cigar. Despite no demand that Shan do so, it seemed only appropriate for him to seek similar work.

As he contemplated his options, passengers rose to exit before others climbed on. In the midst of the shuffle, Shan noticed a gentleman seated near the front. He was wearing a brimmed hat and reading the paper, like most men on board, but a partial turn of his head revealed Mr. Capello's profile. An odd surprise.

"I will be working on Staten Island all day," he'd said to his wife over breakfast. While he did usually wear suits for consultation appointments, he was now traveling in the opposite direction. Suddenly he broke from his reading and glanced around, as if suspicious of being watched.

Shan sank into his seat, cap lowered. Mr. Capello didn't seem the type to sneak off with another lady. And not when he had such a lovely wife.

After a cautious stretch, Shan stole another peek. Mr. Capello's attention had returned to his paper. Shan was due to change lines at the next stop. He knew he ought to leave well enough alone, but curiosity won out and he continued to ride until Mr. Capello finally stepped off — in Ozone Park.

What would he be doing in Queens?

The streetcar was about to depart when Shan hustled from his seat and hopped out. At an inconspicuous distance, he followed Mr. Capello into a stream of people toward an entrance of some sort. Chatter and bells grew with each step, a commotion explained by a sign overhead: *Aqueduct Racetrack*.

The possibility of Mr. Capello gambling

with even a penny was enough to freeze Shan in place. He realized it had done just that when a boisterous man excused himself, bypassing Shan with a woman on his arm. Nearby a uniformed guard eyed the crowd. Shan turned his face away, unsure of rules pertaining to age, and stuck close to the couple as they continued at a snail's pace through the gate.

The fellow, in a blatant attempt to woo his date, rattled off tidbits about various horses scheduled to race. The gal's obvious disinterest did nothing to dampen his efforts. Once safely inside, Shan broke away in search of Mr. Capello. Huddles of gamblers, mostly men, dotted the area. Shan wove through clouds of pretention and cigarette smoke. He found relief in the open air of the grandstand, where breaks of sunlight brightened the sky. Attendees talked and laughed and shook hands while awaiting the next race, no different than guests at a church picnic.

Come to think of it, the purpose of Mr. Capello's visit could be no less moral. He might have come here to simply meet a friend who enjoyed the sport.

Shan had just ruled this the most probable explanation when he turned and found himself face-to-face with Mr. Capello. The man stood there alone. Shock was etched into his features, deepened by a reprimanding look for finding Shan in such a place.

Shan tried to explain. "I . . . saw you on the trolley . . ."

There was a paper in Mr. Capello's hand. It was no longer a newspaper but rather a small white note. The receipt from a bet. Mr. Capello traced Shan's gaze, and his neck reddened. More from embarrassment, it seemed, than anger.

Unsure what to say, Shan blurted, "I promise not to tell."

The silence stretched between them until a corner of Mr. Capello's mouth lifted. It was a ghost of a smile. Only then did Shan comprehend the amusement of the scene, as if a child had been caught sneaking sweets before supper. A grown child, at that.

Just then, a bell rang and the race began. Many in the crowd moved toward the rails. Mr. Capello glanced at the horses, a swift debate in his eyes, then gave a nod toward the track. "Come," he said.

Shan gladly obliged.

Jockeys in colorful clothes and helmets clung to their horses. They yelled commands and swatted with short black whips. As the animals rounded the first turn, folks became more vocal. Based on Mr. Capello's murmuring, he had bet on the one marked Number 5. It was three horses behind but making reasonable headway. By the time it reached the second spot, Mr. Capello was moving his hand in short jerks, as if wielding an invisible whip. It appeared to be working when Number 5 caught up to the first horse.

Shan gripped the top rail, swept into the excitement. "Come on, you can do it." The two horses competed for the win. Their necks bobbed and legs stretched, dirt spraying from their hooves. On the final stint, Number 5 lurched into the lead. Mr. Capello's encouragement gained momentum. "Let's go, let's go! *Andiamo!*"

Though Shan had nothing personally invested, his thrill as Number 5 crossed the finish line verged on electric. He and Mr. Capello simultaneously threw their arms into the air. For that instant, in a strange twist of events, they were united as a team.

When the cheers died down, Mr. Capello led them toward a betting window. In line to collect his winnings, he reviewed a list of horses and odds for the next race.

Soon they reached the clerk, who counted out a calculated sum. "Care to make another bet?"

Mr. Capello proceeded with an air of

confidence, this time with his hopes on Dusty Moon. Shan recognized the name. The man in the entry had shared news regarding that horse. Shan wracked his memory, trying to remember, not wanting to be wrong. Then it came to him. "Don't do it."

Mr. Capello turned his head, puzzled.

Shan kept his voice low in the event it wasn't supposed to be common knowledge. "I heard a man say Dusty Moon prefers grass. That he doesn't run well on dirt tracks."

Mr. Capello deliberated the information. The men behind them were growing impatient, shifting their stances and narrowing their eyes.

"Well?" the clerk pressed.

Mr. Capello returned to his list and drew out his words, deciding as he spoke. "Instead I will bet on . . . Wild Shamrock. The Irish, they are lucky, yes?"

The clerk barked a laugh. "Whatever you say, pal."

Shan remained silent as the bet was finalized.

Once away from the booth, Mr. Capello stopped and held the ticket before Shan's face. "You must never," he said, "risk more than you are ready to lose. *Capisci?*"

In this way, the man's vice still befitted his ethics. More or less.

"Yes, sir," Shan said.

As the start of the race closed in, Shan's enthusiasm gave way to apprehension. What if the man with the racing tips was wrong? The newfound pleasantness from Mr. Capello could very well end if Dusty Moon, in fact, took the win. What's more, he could now lose money on a horse representing Shan's heritage. Potential for double the blame.

But it was too late to reverse. The horses were lined up at the starting gate.

Spectators again crowded the rails. They raised binoculars and fanned their hats. In a matter of minutes, the race was on.

Along with Mr. Capello, Shan cheered openly for Wild Shamrock, though internally he was also rooting *against* Dusty Moon. A track never seemed so large, nor a competition so fierce. The hooves thumped as wildly as Shan's pulse. By the final stretch, Dusty Moon and Wild Shamrock were battling two other horses for the lead. Shan was now screaming for Wild Shamrock, feeling as though he were the jockey himself. But then Number 2 tore away as if spurred by a jolt, leaving all his competition behind.

Dusty Moon came in fourth, and Wild

Shamrock in second. Shan expected Mr. Capello to be disappointed; instead the man kissed the ticket with gusto. "We win!"

The bet was merely to place, he explained. Apparently his faith in the Irish only went so far.

By late afternoon, from a combination of luck, calculations, and more overheard tips, Mr. Capello had won far more than he'd lost. The grandest time, however, came from the exchanges between races as they rested in the stands.

Mr. Capello spoke about weighing the odds, tempered by trusting your gut. By way of example, he cited the brave feats of Christopher Columbus — "Cristoforo Colombo," more accurately — which led him to list great contributions from other Italians over the centuries: from the Roman Empire and the pope to Dante and Michelangelo.

Still, his zeal was no stronger than when he landed on the subject of baseball, the feats of "Ping" Bodie in particular. The Yankee centerfielder was said to be one of the most feared sluggers in the game, his skills naturally owing to his Italian descent.

"He was born Francesco Pezzolo," Mr. Capello said. "And do you know what I hear? Last week he challenged an ostrich to a duel of eating."

Surely the man's accent had altered the correct word. "An *ostrich*?" Shan repeated.

"Eleven bowls of macaroni, and only Ping is standing. This is how you know he is a true Italian." The accomplishment was delivered with such reverence that Shan aimed for a straight face, but a laugh slipped out.

Thankfully Mr. Capello also chuckled, adding, "Even before going to the Yankees, always he is Tomasso's favorite."

There was his name again. Tomasso Capello.

Variants of it had saved Shan on more than one occasion. And yet, while he'd learned a good deal about how the boy had died, he knew nothing of how Tomasso had lived.

Mr. Capello's lingering smile suggested an opportunity to ask.

"What was he like?" Shan ventured gently. "Your son, that is."

Like a plummeting pop-up, the man's face shut down. He appeared to have briefly forgotten that his son was gone, but now remembered.

"I'm sorry, sir. I shouldn't have asked."

The day was going so well. Shan cursed himself for ruining it all.

Mr. Capello gazed distantly toward the track. He inhaled as if to speak, surely to announce it was time to leave. Instead, he gave an answer. "He was a kind boy . . . always curious." The words carried a hint of a rasp. "He had questions, so many questions. He wants to know why this, why that, Papa. How does this work, Papa." Mr. Capello shook his head, softening from images Shan couldn't see. "Every day he would make me laugh. He was a good boy, my Tomasso. A very good boy."

Shan was tempted to touch the man's shoulder, yet feared he might overstep. He simply offered, "I miss my parents too. My mam especially."

Mr. Capello absorbed this, an admission Shan rarely voiced, then he gave a look of understanding. Shan sensed the start of a tenuous bond as they sat in quiet — a moment soon broken by the boom of a lady's voice.

"Signore! Signore Capello!"

Mr. Capello hesitated, shifting gears, before coming to his feet. He pinned on a smile. "Signora Allegri."

Che cosa fai?" The woman appeared in her sixties and somewhat plump. Her facial features differed from how Shan pictured Italians, with her fair skin, blue eyes, and blond curls straying from her cloche.

"How nice to see you." Mr. Capello exchanged a peck on each cheek.

"My husband is over there, placing a bet." She wriggled her gloved fingers toward the entry area. "He will be so pleased to find you. We have heard you are back, but we have not seen your family at Mass."

"Yes . . . we have been busy. With work and children. Settling in."

"*Si, si.* Of course." She nodded, though Shan could see she didn't entirely believe the reasons. After all, not all immigrants strove to leave their pasts in another country. For some, Shan realized, the past lay just across the river.

"And who is this?" The woman noticed Shan seated in the background but looked uncertain. "You are . . . the oldest son?"

Shan slowly rose, not knowing how to respond. He barely had a chance to shake his head when the woman gasped and clasped her hands together.

"You are the one we hear of. The small one, who is doing so well after going to Italia." She made the sign of the cross before holding Shan's face in awe. Her hands were like a baker's, strong from shaping dough. "My goodness, has it been so many years? You have grown so tall."

She turned back to Mr. Capello. "It is a miracle. A gift of God, no?"

The man's mouth moved in a subtle twitch, as if choosing between answers.

Perhaps it was the common ground he'd found with Shan, and the suggestion that Tomasso had brought them together. Maybe it was the hope flickering in the signora's eyes, or because, quite plainly, it was easier to agree.

But for one reason or another, Mr. Capello replied with a smile, "*Veramente.* A true gift."

18

For once, Shan appreciated the noise and bustle of the streetcar, relieving any pressure to talk the whole ride home. At the racetrack, he and Mr. Capello had already said so much.

When finally they entered the house, where Italian spices fragranced the air, Shan breathed in the new scent of home.

Nick was reclined on the davenport. "That errand sure took a while." His casualness as he flipped through a magazine — this one appropriate for family viewing — suggested nothing buried in the comment.

Shan shrugged. "I ran into your father." An honest answer without specifics. A harmless secret to keep.

In the entry, Mr. Capello removed his hat and pointed for emphasis. "And now he knows why Italians have made this world great. Without them, we would not have the ceiling of the Sistine Chapel. We would not have democracy, or even America for that matter —"

"Papa, not again," Lina groaned from the sitting room rug, where she stopped in the midst of dressing a doll. "We've heard all of this a thousand times."

"Oh? A thousand, eh? Then you must only listen to it one thousand more."

It was difficult to judge from his expression if he was teasing. Before Shan could decide, Mrs. Capello emerged from the kitchen, wiping her hands on her apron. "*Bene,* you are both here. Supper will be ready in twenty minutes. I will put out olives and nuts —"

"No," her husband cut in.

"But . . . I am keeping the prosciutto for supper."

"No," he repeated. "You are not making supper."

Shan's confusion was reflected in the faces of the others until Mr. Capello clarified. "I am taking my family out to dine."

From the stillness pervading the room one would think he had announced plans to jump from the Tower of Pisa.

He flicked his hat upward. "What are you waiting for? *Andiamo.* Get ready, we go."

Breaking into a grin, Nick tossed his magazine aside. "Sounds dandy to me," he said, and started for the entry as Lina sprang to her feet.

"Wait! I want to wear my favorite blue dress," she said, already sprinting for the stairs.

"But — we cannot go," Mrs. Capello insisted. "The food, it is cooking —"

"And we will eat it tomorrow," her husband declared.

Not since childhood had Shan dined in an actual restaurant. The excitement of choosing from a full menu made his mouth water.

"I don't know about you," Nick said, pulling his coat from a wall hook, "but I could go for a big juicy steak tonight."

Shan agreed, relishing the thought of his old favorites. "So long as it's with a large heap of potatoes."

Clearly outnumbered, Mrs. Capello marched back into the kitchen, muttering in Italian. Something about her terrible appearance and putting the food away and — if Shan understood correctly — money not growing on trees.

Shan and Mr. Capello traded a look, acknowledgment that the extra funds had come from elsewhere.

Twenty minutes later, the family arrived at

the small but lively restaurant. The irony of Mr. Capello's choice was not lost on Shan, nor on the rest of the family.

"But, Papa," Lina pleaded as they were guided to their table, "we eat Italian food all the time."

"This is not Italian," he said. "This is Sicilian."

Over the wall murals of Italy hung decorative strings of garlic and peppers. The ingredients, like the aroma, matched those in the Capellos' kitchen, just three blocks away.

Shan quietly asked Nick, "Is there a difference?"

"What do *you* think?"

The waitress left them at a red-and-white-checkered table in the corner, a white candle aglow at its center. Opera music played faintly in the background.

Still standing, Nick said, "Pop, why can't we just go out for a hamburger? You want us to be seen as good Americans, right?"

Shan caught the glimmer in Nick's eyes, an awareness of using the man's theories in the rest of the family's favor. Hopefully it would work.

"But you are not just Americans," Mr. Capello said, taking his seat. "You are Italian Americans. Now, sit."

Shan obeyed, still grateful for the luxury of the outing, and the others followed. Though Mrs. Capello proceeded without complaint, over her face passed a message that at home they'd have been eating similar food by now at a lower price. Her husband's claims that Palermo Ristorante was rumored to be one of the finest eateries around did nothing to alter her stance.

Before long they all placed their orders, and soon the meals arrived. Only then did Shan recognize the true value of the outing: Mrs. Capello was able to eat without delivering dishes, clearing the table, or tidying the kitchen. Aside from a brief remark about her own sauce being better than the one on her ordered ravioli — likely rooted more in pride than in taste — she wound up looking as pleased as the rest of the family.

Even Shan had to admit his "tomato pie," made of thick, rectangular bread covered in sauce, anchovies, and cheese, was rather delicious. He just wished the same could be said of the grappa.

At Nick's urging, Shan had accepted the after-supper drink, which appeared as clear as water. Unimpressed by the smell, he'd decided that downing the small glassful, as he would cod liver oil, would be wiser than drawing it out. Yet when he gulped it down, the liquor caused his chest to flame and his face to scrunch as if he'd bitten into a lemon.

Lina and Nick snickered, and their father couldn't help but smile. Mrs. Capello chided Nick for not giving Shan a proper warning. But then she promptly tucked her chin and used a napkin to wipe her mouth, long enough to suggest a grin.

Once Shan recovered, his delight at seeing the family this way increased the lightness in his head caused by the grappa. It had been a good while since he'd been the source of people's laughter. He had forgotten the satisfaction of entertaining a crowd, knowing he was directly responsible for the smile in their eyes.

Perhaps he had more to offer the Capellos than he'd thought.

He straightened in his seat and puffed his chest. From weeks of observing Mr. Capello, Shan lowered his voice to mimic the man's accent and declared, "Why are you laughing this way? Always Capello men are serious. For five generations, this is how we survive."

The family halted as they registered the likeness.

"Papa, it's you!" Lina suddenly laughed, as did Nick, who pressed for more.

Relying on details he had collected, both consciously and not, Shan continued the impersonation. "Just look at the success of the Romans, eh?" He pinched invisible coins. "You think they build a great empire by laughing all day? No. And what of Michelangelo? He would be hired to paint only the . . . the pope's bathroom ceiling if he sat around, listening to silly jokes. *Capisci?*"

Mrs. Capello covered her mouth while giggling, this time her amusement clear — unlike her husband, who gave no hint of a reaction. For a second, Shan worried he might have offended the man. But then a glimmer entered Mr. Capello's eyes, and Shan knew he was safe.

"Do that again," Nick demanded through his laughter.

Shan had no issue proceeding, but would sensibly vary his target. He leaned back in his chair, hands laced behind his neck, taking up space. "Pop, it's like I told ya," he said, shifting to Nick's tone. "If you'd have just let me borrow some dough, I could've bought the paint to decorate that, uh, Sistine Chapel joint myself."

Finally Mr. Capello's lips crept into a smile. Lina was pointing at Nick, saying Shan had captured him perfectly, despite her brother's weak protests that it hadn't come close.

The waitress delivered their desserts while Mr. Capello finished off his grappa. He ordered another as Shan presented warm-hearted portrayals of Mrs. Capello, then Lina. The candle on the table was melting into thin white streaks. Its flame accentuated the glow in Mrs. Capello's face.

"Do something else now," Lina said following a brief quiet, not wanting the evening to end. And really, neither did Shan.

He glanced behind him to view the restaurant from their corner table. The opera music had ended, and many of the diners had cleared out after their meals. He supposed he could pull out a song or two.

Boosted by the old buzz of performing, Shan started with "Foolish Questions" in the style of Billy Murray. He stood up now and again, when action enhanced the humor. Mrs. Capello was in the midst of eating her cannoli when Shan reached the line about falling down the elevator shaft. Her resulting giggles sent the confectioner's sugar from her dessert straight into Lina's hair, and the whole family burst into laughter.

Once they were settled again, Shan moved on to a slew of jokes. Some he had forgotten about until they all came rushing back.

Of course, he tailored the show for his audience, skipping the more unsavory parts as well as impressions only Irishmen would appreciate.

This concluded the act, and Shan took an exaggerated bow. But the Capellos weren't the only ones who applauded. He twisted toward the tables behind him, where strangers were clapping and raising wineglasses. Cheeks warming, he offered a few bows with his head and swiftly slid back into his chair, facing the other way.

In a flash, a man appeared at their table and introduced himself as the owner. Above his low apron, he wore a white long-sleeved shirt with a black bow tie and vest. His personal attention would have seemed a compliment if not for his tight-lipped expression.

A song request was surely not in the cards. Shan lowered his eyes, preparing to be ushered out.

But then the owner gestured across the room. "Signore Trevino said he would be very pleased to meet the young boy." In the opposite corner, three men sat at a table in pinstriped suits. At the center of the trio, a fellow smoking a cigar lifted his ample chin in greeting. Everything about him projected importance.

The owner waited for approval from Mr. Capello, who looked uneasy with the invite.

"I'm sure it will only take a moment, signore," the owner contended. "In the meantime, I will be happy to prepare your check if you would like. The grappa, of course, is free of charge."

"Free?" Mr. Capello said.

"*Si.* For the boy's entertainment." Even as he said this, the owner did not smile.

At Mr. Capello's reluctance, Nick scooted his chair back and stood. "Ah, Pop, don't worry. I'll go with him. Like he said, it'll just take a minute. What's the harm?"

Shan waited for the go-ahead, his mind still reeling.

Under the pressure of the owner's gaze, Mr. Capello nodded. "Only until payment is done."

Nick gave a slap to Shan's shoulder. "Well, come on," he said, and Shan rose to follow him over. The two men flanking Signore Trevino were focused on their meals, one eating a layered pie — called lasagna, Shan had learned — and the other twisting long noodles with a fork.

Shan and Nick hadn't quite reached the table when Signore Trevino reclined in his chair, away from his bowl of clamshells. He wiped his thick fingers one at a time with a napkin. "So, kid. You like to put on shows, huh?"

Despite the amiable tone, Shan felt like a horse from the track being sized up for its odds.

"Sometimes, I guess." He'd made a habit of suppressing his brogue, but now, without intention, he caught himself sounding a bit like Nick.

"Yeah? Well, I got a supper club in the Bronx, just off Third. Called the Royal. Ever heard of it?"

When Shan hesitated, Nick jumped in. "Who hasn't?" He said this with such confidence that Shan knew he was fibbing. And so did Signore Trevino, based on his smirk.

The man drew from his cigar and exhaled a cloud of earthy smoke. "So, whaddya think?"

Somehow Shan had missed the question. "Sir?"

"About making some dough with that stuff. Becoming a regular act."

A week ago, when Shan was out on the street begging for an audition, he would have answered with a resounding yes. But now, fed and housed and free of desperation, he reminded himself there was a vast difference between amusing a family over supper and performing on demand, as he'd done in a hundred seedy pubs.

"I'm not really sure," he said in truth.

Slight surprise betrayed the man's even expression, but not the offended kind. He tapped his cigar on an ashtray. "Well, when you make up your mind, you come see me at the club. I'm around most weekends. Just tell them Max sent ya."

Shan nodded. "Thank you, sir."

"Oh, and kid. This is for you." Max sent a look to one of his companions, who promptly stopped eating.

The slender fellow had to be in his early twenties, his pockmarked cheeks suggesting scars from smallpox. From the inside pocket of his suit jacket he produced a leather billfold and pulled out five one-dollar bills. He tossed them onto the edge of the table with the ease of emptying lint from a pocket.

"For the laughs," Signore Trevino explained.

Shan just stared at the cash, as if waiting for a punch line. Workers at the docks, or any number of factories, probably took weeks to earn that much.

"What, you don't want it?"

Nick stepped in. He scooped up the money and shoved the cash into Shan's pocket in one fluid motion. "Of course he does. And he's real grateful too." He shot Shan a glance.

Max drew his head back, his brow furrowed as if to say, *Who the hell is this guy?*

"I'm Nick Capello. And this here's my younger brother, Tommy. It's a real pleasure." He offered his hand, but before the man could shake it, Mr. Capello interjected.

"Niccolò," he called over, an edge in his tone. *"Andiamo."*

It was time to leave.

19

A dim alley in the Bronx was no place to be on a Friday night. Standing in line with dolled-up patrons, Shan tugged at his collar. His borrowed black tie felt like a noose.

Ever since Nick had suggested the outing three days ago, Shan had wavered on the idea. Being here now only solidified his reservations. Not that he had a choice, really. If it weren't for Nick, he'd be out on the streets, or stuck in an orphanage in one country or another. The least Shan could do was tag along for an evening. He only wished it hadn't required being sneaky with Nick's parents.

"We're just gonna catch a show," Nick had called to his mother, before he and Shan slipped out the door. According to Nick, given his father's disapproval of Max Trevino's generosity, it was best to stay vague about the setting of that show.

"Tommy," Nick said now, urging Shan to

keep moving with the line. The impatience in his voice indicated that it had taken several attempts to catch Shan's attention.

"Sorry," Shan said in a hush, "I'm not used to answering to that."

"Yeah, well, that'd better change in the next five minutes. Last thing I need is a guy like Max Trevino thinking I'm a liar."

The Royal was on the second floor of a large brick building, atop a drugstore and barbershop, with its entrance on the side. Shan glanced up the narrow stairwell that led to a doorman, a hulking Italian with arms like cannons, making Shan even less excited about the excursion. Again he pulled his collar from his neck.

"Now, remember." Nick spoke just above a whisper. "If you're still gonna be a dummy and not take the offer, give me a chance to land a job first. And stop fidgeting, will ya?"

Shan forced his hands to his sides, but wriggled a shoulder in search of comfort. "I can't help it. The bloody shirt's too small, and the suit's too big." Even his fedora didn't feel right.

"Bloody?" Nick grumbled and shook his head. "You can't be using words like that. Jesus."

It had been a while since Shan's old life had slipped into his words. He needed to focus. The faster Nick completed his mission, the sooner they could go home.

At last they made their way up the stairs. In front of them, a pair of couples — two men in tuxedos, their dates wrapped in fur stoles — were granted entry and sauntered into the club.

"Here we go," Nick said. Together they stepped forward on the landing.

The doorman gave Shan a once-over. "What are you — in grade school? Beat it." He waved his hand to summon the next people in line.

But Nick didn't budge. He stood taller in his black suit, one that actually fit. "We were invited."

The man laughed. "Yeah? By who?"

"By Max," Nick replied, as if nothing could be more obvious. Daring to press further, he added, "Don't believe me? Go ask him yourself."

The doorman looked unfazed. He cocked his head, surveying them for truth. Or more likely, weighing potential repercussions from wrongfully turning them away.

Annoyed, he jerked his thumb toward the entrance. "Go."

"Appreciate it," Nick said, and led Shan through the door. Once it shut behind them, Nick rolled his eyes. "What a chump."

Music gained volume as they continued down a hall lit by a series of sconces. Nick removed his hat and smoothed his hair. Same as Shan's, it had grown a good inch since the ship's arrival almost two months earlier. A lifetime ago.

"Now, just act like we belong here," Nick reminded him, "and we'll fit right in. Oh, and whatever you do, don't get the suit dirty. I gotta get 'em back by midnight, before anyone notices they're gone."

When the words sank in, Shan pulled him to a stop. "You said you borrowed them."

Nick looked defensive. "Yeah, and I did." But then he explained, "Got a pal who works at his gramp's cleaners. Owed me a favor."

"What about the shoes and hats?"

Nick shrugged. "From a pawnshop. Those are keepers."

Shan felt a headache setting in.

"Come on, already." Nick guided them around the corner, where a gal at a counter stood before racks of overcoats and shawls. She blinked, presumably due to their age — or perhaps just Shan's, as she couldn't have been more than a year or two older than Nick.

"May I help you?" she said to Nick. Then a moment later: "You got coats to check?"

Nick had forgotten how to speak. His reaction was understandable. The girl had ivory skin and piercing green eyes, accentuated by the matching ribbon in her platinum curls.

Shan answered for him. "Not tonight."

She gave a shrug of indifference before moving on to guests who appeared behind them.

Shan nudged Nick to break the spell, and they plodded onward.

Regaining his voice, Nick murmured, "Next time we bring coats. Lots and lots of coats."

Next time he would be on his own. Shan intended to say this, but the thought splintered and fell away the instant they stepped through the doorway framed in burgundy velvet drapes, entering a world he had never seen.

All the motion and lights and excitement of a city were contained in a single room. Floral perfumes and woodsy colognes mingled with smoke from men's cigars. Women, too, puffed on long black filters while clutching cocktails and flutes of champagne. They clinked them high in festive toasts.

Prohibition was coming, the newspapers had declared. By year's end the party would be over. Until then, it seemed the people here would enjoy every last drop.

"Now, this," Nick said, "is what I call livin'."

Shan couldn't disagree as he watched the colored musicians onstage. They wore white tuxedos with black bow ties while playing trumpets and trombones, saxes and a piano. Couples danced in the center of the room, corralled by a U-shaped arrangement of tables and chairs. The way they hopped about reminded Shan of old jigs from the pubs.

"Would you care for a smoke, sir?" A woman wearing a tiny, feathered hat and a sparkly dress, brazenly cut above the knees, approached Nick. She carried a tray full of cigars and cigarettes.

"Not right now, doll," Nick said, a line he'd clearly practiced. "But maybe you can help me find somebody."

"There's a whole lotta somebodies here. You got a particular one in mind?"

"Max told me and my brother to ask for him." Nick held out a folded dollar bill — which, in fact, had previously belonged to Mr. Trevino. "Just tell him Nick and Tommy are here, from Palermo's."

She glanced at Shan. Rather than disbelieving, she looked intrigued. Then she swiped the bill with the motion of a seasoned politician. "This way."

She guided them through the sea of linen-draped tables, each flickering with a candle domed in crystal. Waiters delivered meals on fine china. Nearby, a man embraced a woman from behind, guiding her to push a cork from a bottle. She timidly turned away, eyes closed, and the cork shot toward the ceiling. Her friends roared with giddiness as a stream of bubbles spilled onto the checkered tiles.

"Wait here," the cigarette girl said. She proceeded on her own to one of the booths along the wall. A partial curtain of white fabric obscured the person she was addressing. When finished, she returned to Nick and gestured toward the booth. "You got your wish."

Nick thanked her and headed over with Shan reluctantly trailing. He couldn't shake the feeling that beneath her words lay a warning.

"Well, look who it is," Mr. Trevino said when they approached. Shadows cast by stage lights gave his smile a menacing air. This time he accepted Nick's eager handshake.

Shan took off his hat and clutched the brim. "It's a pleasure to see you again, Mr. Trevino."

"Max," he corrected before puffing on his cigar. "I see you gave some thought to my offer."

"Actually, I" — Shan felt Nick's gaze sending a reminder — "I have, sir."

"Good, that's good. Here, have a seat." Max motioned to the vacancies on the white leather cushion.

The two had barely slid into the booth when Nick chimed in. "Max, I just want you to know, it'd be a real honor to work for you. So if there's any spot I could fill, I'd sure be grateful."

By any spot, of course, he meant outside of menial work, like garbage collecting and shoe shining. Something that required wearing nice suits and hats, accompanied by pay that would allow him to afford both.

Max raised his brows, as bristly as caterpillars. "You perform like your brother, huh? A duet." He nodded, imagining the act. "I like it."

"Well — no, sir. Not exactly." Nick's confidence faltered under Max's narrowed eyes; the man didn't like to be confused. "What I'm saying is, if there's anything else you can think of, I'd welcome the chance. I'm willing to do anything. Just name it."

Max leaned back in his seat, not agreeing but not opposing the idea. Then he angled to Shan. "How about you, kid?"

"Me?"

"You looking for a chance too?"

Shan swept his gaze over the room. There was no question how Mr. Capello would feel about their working in a place with cocktails and champagne and gals with dresses cut above the knees. Shan was debating how to decline when a realization stunned him.

The singer on the microphone — Shan knew his voice. He knew his face. To a small extent, he knew the man himself.

Shan looked at Max. "That's George Cohan."

Max glanced at the stage and released a long smoky exhale. "My pal Billy was supposed to be on tonight. But old Murray fell ill at the last minute. Cohan here was good enough to fill in."

The revelations competed in Shan's mind. "You're saying . . . *the* Billy Murray?"

"One and only. I figured you might be a fan of these fellas, what with your songs the other night. Maybe they'd even be willing to share the stage with you sometime. How'd that be?"

Shan could hardly imagine it. Performing with Mr. Murray himself, or lobbing jokes with the King of Broadway, George Cohan.

When they had last met, Shan was living on the streets, his nose runny, throat raspy, clothes filthy and drenched. He must have resembled a scrappy mutt in the alley, a world of difference from his appearance tonight.

Shan suddenly appreciated the suit from Nick, regardless of size.

Seconds later, a fellow — a waiter maybe — appeared near the table. Upon the flick of Max's hand, he leaned in and spoke in a whisper. Max listened closely. Darkness hooded his eyes as the waiter stepped away.

"Boys," he said, "got a little business to take care of. But you give the club a call this week and we'll work out details. Okay with you?"

"Absolutely." Nick beamed. "Sir, thank you very much."

The man left without saying good-bye. Nor did he wait for Shan's final decision.

To Max, the deal was cinched.

■ ■ ■ ■

1923

■ ■ ■ ■

20

It's fascinating, really, when you think about it. How a person can slip into a new life as one would a new pair of shoes. At first there's a keen awareness of the fit: a stiffness at the heel, the binding of the width, the curve pressed into the arch. But with time and enough steps, the feel becomes so natural you almost forget you're wearing them at all.

This was very much the way Shan's life transformed over the next several years.

Despite Mr. Capello's reservations, and with the help of his wife's deft coaxing, Nick and Shan accepted the job offers from Max Trevino. Or, in Nick's case, at least arranged by Max. Initially Nick wasn't elated over being a delivery boy for the drugstore below the club, far less glamorous work than Shan's comedic shows. But it did get Nick's foot in the door and also appeased his father with steady wages.

Thus, while Nick ran medications around town, Shan presented his acts at the Royal three times a week. Twice, he even performed with George Cohan himself — who thankfully didn't recognize him from the alley — and once with the legendary Billy Murray. Even Steve Porter came through on occasion. With events so surreal, part of Shan always feared the gig wouldn't last.

And it didn't.

At the tail end of that first summer, Mrs. Capello came to watch, having enjoyed the show a couple of times before. Already disconcerted by the brazen atmosphere influencing a boy his age, she was hardly pleased to discover a fan waiting in Shan's dressing room.

This alone might not have been detrimental if the teenage girl had been wearing a stitch of clothing. The awkward incident, combined with Mr. Capello's distrust of men like Max, brought Shan's stint at the club to a decisive end.

Shan's disappointment, however, was short-lived, as he had learned what to prize in life. Thereafter he earned money from random jobs: yard work or errands or painting fences for neighbors. And he joined Mr. Capello on plumbing appointments when an extra hand was needed — occasionally those "appointments" being secret jaunts to the tracks.

In short, Shanley Keagan — as Tommy Capello — became just another wop kid in Brooklyn, with few ties to his true past.

Never returning to the naval office, he chose to forever abandon his photo of John Lewis, along with delusions of a worthwhile search. When Nick amazed Shan by rescuing his satchels from the Cohan Theatre, Shan kept the sixpence and books but discarded the sailor's letter. Why save it when he'd already found his place in a real and loving family?

Although Mr. Capello wasn't the most affectionate sort, and remained unbending on a variety of topics, his care lay closer to the surface than that of many Italian fathers, whose quick tempers Shan was just fine to do without. In turn, while not inherently a baseball fan, Shan learned to enjoy the game that brought the man such joy, particularly since Nick had no interest. Shan even surprised Mr. Capello now and again with game tickets at Yankee Stadium. In the stands, the man would rattle off predictions before every batter's turn and always follow with praise or critiques. Once, when a pitcher threw a beanball too close to Ping Bodie's head, Shan had to all but hold Mr.

Capello back from charging the field.

Mrs. Capello, on the other hand, was quieter about her passions. The great pride she divided among her faith, cooking, home, and gardening went without question. As did the fact that each of them provided her little value without relation to her family. Shan wound up spending many weekends helping her in the community garden. He'd originally viewed his main role as being the puller of the wagon, toting all the fruit and vegetables she had picked for the week. But listening to her speak about plants she'd grown, here and in Italy — also sprouting other tales from her old country — was in truth his greater contribution.

For Nick, Shan was also a listener. The topics typically centered on the latest pretty girl or his big ideas for the future, his fears of failing often belying his words. But mostly Nick liked to play cards. This was how Shan came to learn strategies in canasta, bridge, pinochle, gin rummy, and at least a dozen versions of poker. In between rounds, while Nick shuffled the deck, Shan would toss out jokes he borrowed or created, and together they would laugh until the late hours of night — often when Mrs. Capello would appear, groggily ordering them to bed. On weekends, he and Nick would also find entertainment watching vaudeville acts on Broadway or silent pictures at a movie palace.

As for Lina — now, she was different. For she was an observer like Shan. She would gather what she saw in journals, telling stories through a sketch or a poem, a quote she overheard or a detail missed by most. Like the way a grizzled man at a diner would straighten all of his silverware before eating his meal, or how one button on the coat of a woman at the market didn't match the rest. As a collector of tales, she gradually made her way through all of Shan's books, which he would share and discuss with pleasure.

The rest of Shan's time was spent in school, mindful of good marks and keeping his nose clean. Nick would razz him at times, calling him "St. Thomas" for steering clear of smoking and booze, both being indulgences Nick came to relish — largely for the thrill of sneaking them. But for Shan, it wasn't a question of morality as much as an aversion to sharing his uncle's fate.

Perhaps this haunting possibility was the reason Shan never felt fully settled. Even now, a sophomore in high school, he kept his friendships at a distance. The same applied to courtships, all of them brief. Since many of the girls' families attended the same church as the Capellos, at times this created an awkward Mass, though never to the level faced by Nick.

On one particular Sunday, three girls from the congregation discovered Nick was secretly dating them at the same time. You could feel their glares, as sharp as saws, cutting across the pews. It was a miracle, Lina had said, that they refrained from throwing their communion wine right at his face. Unfortunately, not everyone who felt wronged by Nick Capello showed that much restraint.

Today was one of those cases.

Shan realized it now as he emerged from the Capellos' house, headed for the library. Scowls from the two guys waiting outside made it clear they hadn't come to discuss the unusually nice March weather.

"I got no gripe with you," the brawny one said, "but I'm gonna teach your brother not to try and steal another guy's girl."

Before Shan could reason with him, Nick strolled up with a casual smile. "Can I help you, fellas?"

There was no discussion after that. The brawny guy pounced on him with jabs and right hooks. In contrast to the night Shan and Nick had met on the ship, this time

Shan didn't think twice about jumping to Nick's defense. Predictably, the brawny guy's pal joined in, and the battle was on.

This wasn't Shan and Nick's first brawl as a team. Fights for any boys were inevitable, but especially in Brooklyn. The conflicts would start with insults, name-calling being the most convenient: Polacks, dagos, micks, kikes. If given the chance, Shan still preferred to walk away. But the same couldn't be said of Nick. Not that either of them had the option right then, when fending off a vengeful boyfriend and his crony.

In essence it resulted in a draw, though no one would have known from seeing Nick and Shan afterward, with their bruised jaws, split lips, and swollen eyes. Back in the house, Mrs. Capello told Lina to fetch rags and iodine, bandages and clean shirts, trying desperately to contain the damage before her husband came home from work.

But they could only do so much.

At the dinner table, Mr. Capello's glower shrank Nick and Shan down to the size of toddlers. Fittingly so, since Mr. Capello viewed their behavior as reflective of two-year-olds. His wife's attempts to help, emphasizing that the other boys had started the fight, went unheard.

The supper lasted an eternity. In place of

talking, they all drank more wine, Shan included. He had acquired the taste for it as an accompaniment to meals and was especially glad for it just then.

Eventually the trill of the telephone sliced through the room. Mr. Capello rose to answer, as he always did, bringing a dash of relief to the table. When the ringing halted, Shan could hear the man's greeting, then a lag of quiet.

"I see," Mr. Capello said repeatedly between pauses. His tone grew more clipped with each, and finally: "How long is this happening?"

Based on a single side of the conversation, it seemed a rare case of an unhappy customer. Such a thing would only worsen the mood. The family passed worried looks around, much as they would a bread basket.

Then Mr. Capello said, "This is for how many classes?"

Therein the topic became clear. Nick clutched the linen napkin on his lap.

"Yes, I understand," Mr. Capello said. "I will speak to my son. Thank you, Mr. Gelow, for calling."

The moment was inevitable, yet the ruse had gone without consequence for so long, Shan had started to believe, or at least to hope, otherwise.

With impossibly slow steps Mr. Capello returned to his seat. Audible exhales through his nose indicated plenty of words were mounting inside.

"Mama. Lina." He did not look up from the table. "Leave us."

His wife hesitated. But after a moment, she stood and quietly ushered her daughter up the stairs.

There had been plenty of lectures over the years at this table, occasionally directed at Shan or Lina, but mostly at Nick for his various antics: whether arriving late for supper, violating curfew, or ignoring his mother's requests for tidying one thing or another. Still, never had those reprimands involved anyone leaving the area.

Mr. Capello finally lifted his eyes, his voice tight and measured. "The principal says my son Nick Capello has been missing many days of school. He says several of his marks are not passing, and now he might not graduate in June. I am thinking this is not possible, because I have seen the cards with my own eyes. And this would mean my son has been *lying* to me."

"Pop, please," Nick reasoned, "if you'll just listen —"

"No! It is *you* who will listen." Mr. Capello's fists landed on the table's edge, rattling

199

the dishware. His gaze cut to Shan. "Did you know this? You will tell me the truth."

Shan tensed under the question. Yes, he had known. For the classes in which Nick wasn't able to sufficiently charm his teachers, the guy had honed the craft of altering his grades — with a razor blade, eraser, and pen — into ones that would satisfy his parents, preventing a lecture just like this.

But before Shan could voice the admission, Nick interjected. "He didn't know, Pop. All right? I did it on my own. Either way, I don't see the big issue."

The attention shifted from Shan, yet there was no cause for ease. Nick's flippancy widened Mr. Capello's eyes. "And you think lying to your father, this is not a big issue?"

"No — I just — I meant about school." Nick stumbled through his point, his own frustration growing, and not just from today. "Friends of mine quit a long time ago. They're making money for their families, same as me. Only difference is I'm doing both. Hell, I'm eighteen years old, but you still treat me like a kid, with curfews and even makin' my damn bed."

It seemed once the words flowed out, he couldn't dam the rest. "The teachers ain't no different. They act like we're in grade school. And what do they teach? Latin and chemistry. It's nothin' I'm gonna use. Truth is, the only reason I'm there is because Ma has some ridiculous idea it's important, even though it don't amount to a hill of beans in the real —"

"Enough!" Mr. Capello shot to his feet and swiped his hand at a wineglass. It flew across the room and shattered against a wall.

Shan scrambled to stand, as did Nick, who knocked over his chair.

"Benicio," Mrs. Capello urged, suddenly in the room. The word bordered on a plea.

But Mr. Capello gave no acknowledgment. He continued to stare at Nick, seething. Wine dripped red streaks down the cream wallpaper. When he spoke, his voice took the form of a deep rasp, a struggle to rein in his anger.

"You will *not* speak this way under my roof. You think you are too grown to be here? Too old for rules? That because you earn pay, you have a right to disrespect your parents? Maybe, then, it is time to see how a real man lives — on your own."

Shan caught the startled look in Nick's eyes and, more than that, the hurt. But Nick quickly concealed both. Through tightened lips he replied, "I'll get my stuff."

Nick had barely turned for his room when his father said, "Oh? And what *stuff* here do you own?"

In Mrs. Capello's face was an impulse to intercede, tamped by awareness that it wasn't her place.

Nick laughed darkly under his breath. "You're right. Keep it all."

"Niccolò, no," Mrs. Capello said. She stepped toward him with tears welling. Yet without a glance, he stormed from the house.

Seconds later, Lina scurried in, her gaze bouncing between her father and the open door. "He's coming back, isn't he? Papa? Isn't he?"

There was no answer.

Shan couldn't stand by without at least trying to help. "I'll talk to him," he told Lina, an assurance also for her mother. He started for the door, but Mr. Capello gripped his arm. The redness in the man's features began to slip away, replaced by a shadow of sadness.

"Let him go," he said.

"But Nick was just angry. I'm sure he didn't mean —"

"Tommy. No."

Shan had long grown accustomed to the name, from schoolmates and teachers and others who knew him as nothing else. He'd accepted it as a moniker of sorts, never truly

feeling he had taken someone's place.
Until that moment.

21

A slew of bitter words, a handful of minutes, and the Capello family was never the same. Three years had passed since Nick had moved out, first living with a friend, then later on his own. But even now, seated off in a corner of the sitting room, Shan could see the wine stain on the dining room wall. Faded from scrubbing and time, it resembled a scar left from a wound that might never heal.

"Save me."

The words snapped him back to the present as Lina slid into the chair beside him.

"It's absolutely maddening. That woman just won't give up."

"Who's that?"

"Mrs. Sarentino. Who else?"

Shan twisted around and spied Mrs. Capello. Amid the mingling crowd, she listened to her friend rattle away.

Lina flicked Shan's knee, almost knocking

over his plate of cake. "Don't look or he'll come over here."

But Shan kept looking until locating "him." For a celebration of Lina's sixteenth birthday, Mrs. Sarentino had brought a special gift: her gangly son, whose thick glasses were as prominent as his overbite.

"C'mon, he's not *that* bad." Shan returned to Lina, trying not to smile. "You know, one of these days he could inherit his father's whole bowling alley."

"I don't care if he inherited Woolworth's. His mother is *pazzo.*"

It wasn't difficult to see why any mother, sane or not, would aspire to pair her son with Angelina Capello. Her features, which had once been sweet and dainty, had gained her mother's elegance. The full lips, the defined cheekbones, the sleek black hair worn in finger waves down to her shoulders. Recently her figure, too, had grown more womanly, though part of Shan felt odd even noticing the change.

Lina went on, "Can you believe she actually complimented me on the width of my hips?"

Shan nearly stammered. "Your hips?"

Lina arched a brow. "For giving birth."

"Ahh, right," he said. "Well, that's understandable. They *are* pretty wide."

Lina's mouth dropped open. When Shan laughed, she shoved him in the chest, her smile barely suppressed. "Eat your dumb cake."

Her tone indicated a desire to stuff the piece into his face. And she likely would have if not for the need for propriety among their parents' friends. It was a typical festive gathering, abundant with food, wine, and kisses on cheeks. A guest's mandolin was leaned up against the davenport, awaiting a performance later in the night. "Tommy, a song," someone would call out, and he would indulge them with a repertoire of silly tunes and Italian folk favorites. But for now, the ladies would talk about recipes or gardening and the neighborhood's latest gossip. The men would speak of President Wilson and baseball and Mussolini's impact on Italy. And always there were stories. In that way, the Irish were no different.

From across the room Shan could hear Mr. Capello now, recounting one of his favorites: about a certain "unnamed customer" who hid his mistress's silk stocking by flushing it down the toilet, which then clogged the pipe, requiring a plumber's discretion. Shan had been present on that call; it was six months ago, just days after he'd received his diploma and started working with Mr. Capello full-time.

The men listening to the tale laughed heartily. They appeared oblivious to the glances Mr. Capello kept aiming at the front door.

Shan knew those looks well. They occurred during Sunday suppers when Nick neglected to join them, which was most Sundays now. It had taken Shan several months after the familial rift to persuade Nick to visit. The initial reunion made for a strained meal, in no way aided by the perfunctory nature of Nick's apology. But over time the family's interactions progressed from civil to pleasant. In fact, given Nick's extensive work hours, Mr. Capello didn't even demand anymore that he attend church with the family, despite Mrs. Capello's wishes to the contrary. Nor did he blow a gasket when Nick could stay only an hour for Thanksgiving dinner a week ago.

The extent of such latitude, however, had its limits. This much was clear from the current agitation in Mr. Capello's eyes; his son's absence from the party was not as easily dismissed.

"Any word from Nick?" Lina suddenly asked. She, too, must have noticed her father's displeasure. But then, she was always good at observations.

"I'm sure he'll be here soon. I know he planned to come."

She nodded and put on a smile bright enough to fool others.

"Oh, hey — I've got a little something for you." Shan reached over and grabbed the gift from the end table, a small distraction. He had kept it separate from her other presents piled on the coffee table, not wanting to miss when she opened it. "I was going to wait for the excitement to die down, but that might be a while."

"You know you didn't have to."

He shrugged. "It's just to hold you over, until you publish your own someday."

She quickly untied the bow and unwrapped the brown paper. At the hardback inside, she looked up in disbelief. "This was your mother's."

"And now it's yours. You'll see, the proof's inside."

Carefully she flipped open the cover, where Shan had inscribed *Angelina Capello* directly below the handwritten name of its original owner: *Moira Keagan.*

"But — I couldn't possibly. It was her favorite. You told me so."

"I don't think she'll be using it anytime soon."

"Well, yes, I know, but —"

"Lina, it's *Sense and Sensibility.* Trying to follow the insanity of how all those women think is enough to make my brain explode."

There was some truth in this, and they both laughed.

Then she gazed back at the cover and gently stroked the lettering of the well-worn title. "I'm really glad you're here," she said.

Something in her tone told him she wasn't referring only to tonight.

While he appreciated being valued, the comment also stressed the importance of her real brother's presence. On a Friday evening, Shan could guess what was keeping him. Nick had started working at the Royal a year ago in the capacity of host — a glorified waiter in Mr. Capello's view. Even so, the job held the key to his future, Nick claimed, and as such required long, late hours. A convenient excuse for rarely coming around.

"Here." Shan handed Lina his plate before rising. "I'm gonna call and check on Nick."

"You don't have to do that."

"Just eat my dumb cake. It's good for the hips."

She shot him a glare. But then a smile eased across her lips, warm with gratitude.

Shan threaded through the room, greeting guests as needed with hugs and pecks on cheeks. On the faces of fresh arrivals was a cold sheen from the early December night. Shoes glistened with slush.

He picked up the telephone on the entry table and held the receiver tight to his ear. Over the layered chatter of the party he asked the operator to connect him to the club. Shan had to repeat himself twice, and when he'd succeeded in placing the call, noise on the other end made it near impossible to communicate.

Just then, beside the phone, he glimpsed the small yellow pottery bowl made by Lina back in grade school. Shaped like a sunflower, it held the key to the Model T truck Mr. Capello had proudly purchased two years ago.

"You know what — never mind," Shan said into the mouthpiece, having no idea if the person could hear. "I'll be right there."

22

Swooped velvet drapes still framed the entry to the main hall at the Royal, where patrons basked in the glow of candlelight and a large crystal chandelier. Shan recalled how the place had looked through the lens of a twelve-year-old's eyes and figured it would be far less dazzling in reality and worsened by wear. But he was wrong. Max Trevino's supper club was just as striking as ever.

"Excuse me, pal. You mind?"

Shan realized he was blocking the entry for a man and his date and moved aside.

The couple was suitably dressed for the occasion, sharp and glitzy like the rest of the room. All about, ladies flaunted more feathers and rouge than in years prior. Their short hairdos with ruler-straight bangs made a statement, but the exclamation lay in the low roll of their stockings, exposing bare thighs below fringe-covered dresses.

Up onstage, jazz musicians blared a

snappy tune, and Shan's memories came flooding back. The laughter, the applause, the bubbling champagne.

"I *must* be seein' things." The woman's sultry voice registered instantly. "The Tommy Capello I know is too straitlaced for a joint like this."

He smiled at Josie, a far cry from the gal he'd first known as the "coat check girl." Her skin was still ivory and eyes halting green, but her platinum curls had been styled in a twist, save for a few escaping tendrils. She wore the long fitted dress of a hostess, purple satin with beaded trim and a slit up one leg. A dipped neckline outlined the shape of her breasts, accentuated by two straps over bare shoulders. He kept his gaze on her face.

"How've you been, Josie?"

"Can't complain."

"It's been a while."

"Four months. But who's countin'?"

The last time they'd crossed paths, coincidentally, it had been the night of Nick's birthday celebration thrown by his friends. Nick's pursuit of Josie Penaro had taken years to achieve a courtship — one with the standard ups and downs. This much was apparent when she'd left the party early with tear-streaked cheeks.

"I'm just here to see Nick," he told her.

She pouted her rosebud lips. "And here I thought you'd come to see me."

When Shan struggled with how to respond, she giggled.

"Oh, I'm only teasin'. Come on, I'll take ya." She clasped his hand, her slender fingers in long white satin gloves, and led the way.

Couples in the center of the room hopped about to "The Charleston," shimmying hips and hands and twirling strings of pearls. At the surrounding tables, guests toasted one another with teacups in place of glassware. Yet by the way they were swaying and tossing back their drinks, a façade of Lipton was clearly a precaution in the event of a raid.

As they passed the main bar, Shan noticed that the display lacked any evidence of liquor. Either the bartenders were hiding the bottles or patrons were bringing their own stashes. Neither one seemed practical.

"Where's everybody getting the booze?" he asked Josie.

"Now you're the one who's teasin'." A dimple formed on her cheek from the start of a smile, which disappeared when she realized he was serious. "From the drugstore downstairs, silly."

"The drugstore?"

"For the pure alcohol." His lack of knowledge clearly confounded her as they continued to walk. She lowered her voice only a touch. "They run it up the back stairs. It ain't the cat's pajamas, not like the bubbly stuff, but as you can see, no one out here seems to mind."

He surveyed the room and saw the waiters pouring. Suddenly he felt terribly naïve. All those years Nick was making deliveries for the drugstore — no doubt to numerous destinations — he was indirectly working for Max. And Nick had never said a word.

Shan tried not to dwell on the thought of not being trusted. "That's a lot of tea they're drinking. Don't the cops ask questions?"

"Not the smart ones," she said.

Such exceptions, he supposed, weren't confined to the Royal. While not all policemen ignored wine fermenting in Italian basements — Irish cops, in particular — those who understood it was part of the culture, like Officer Barsetti, had a habit of looking the other way.

"Max, darling." Josie paused at a booth where a man sat alone with his cigar. She leaned in to kiss his cheek. "Look who wandered in."

The last time Shan was here, Max Trevino had been parked at the same table. For an instant, it seemed only minutes had passed. But then a closer look revealed less hair on Max's head, more graying at the temples, his face a bit heftier than before. He squinted his eyes. "Well, I'll be. If it ain't the wonder boy."

Shan smiled and shook the man's hand.

"How the hell you been, Tommy?"

"I'm well, sir. Thank you."

"Sir? What's this 'sir' stuff? Known you since you was a kid and you act like we just met."

"Sorry, Max. Old habit."

Max sat back with a slanted grin. "So. You want to get back in the business, huh? Finally recovered from the backstage treat I sent ya?"

It took Shan a moment to comprehend the reference. When he did, he attempted to conceal his shock. He had never put it together.

The unclothed fan who had once surprised him — and Mrs. Capello — in his dressing room had evidently been a gift.

"I think . . . I'm set for now," Shan said, working to assemble his thoughts.

Max drew from his cigar and exhaled a breath of smoke. "Yeah, well. You always were smarter than the rest of us." Genuine approval shone in his eyes. "Here, have a seat. Tell me what I can do for you."

Shan suddenly remembered Lina, who still had hopes of seeing her brother by night's end. Remaining on his feet, he said, "Actually, I came looking for Nick. I was hoping to talk to him, if it's not too much trouble."

"Nick, huh? Pretty busy night here. Is it something important?"

"It's a family matter." Respect for family had always ranked high on Max's list.

Josie piped in, "Okay if I take him?" She tilted her head demurely, a nudge of persuasion.

Max puffed on his cigar some more. "Hell, I don't see why not. Got no reason not to trust Tommy here. Ain't that right, son?"

"Definitely, sir."

Shan questioned what he had just agreed to.

"Then, let's scoot." Josie hooked his arm and whisked him away.

Soon they were entering the kitchen. Chefs and waiters wove in a frenzied routine with plates, pots, and pans. Peppery filets sizzled and cream sauces boiled. Colorful vegetables were sautéing in butter. Shan had to duck to avoid a collision with an oversize serving tray.

He started to wonder if Nick really was a waiter, as Mr. Capello had remarked, when Josie led him into a storage room. Behind the barrels stamped as flour, they proceeded down a narrow flight of stairs, a light bulb dangling overhead.

"Shortcut," she explained as they landed before a metal wall. She gave it a knock and waved her fingers at a small hole. A scraping metal sound indicated the turn of a bolt and a portion of the wall slid open, a secret passageway.

"Thanks a million," Josie said to the hulking Italian. The fellow used to guard the main door. "You remember Tommy? Nicky's kid brother."

The guy lifted his chin in the start of a nod, as if dropping it took too much effort. Then he reset the lock and assumed his post at another door to the right.

Josie smiled at Shan. "Right this way." She towed him through a black curtain split down the center. What he found, down the rabbit hole, was a gambling hall in full action.

Flappers and men in pinstripes were huddled around tables of blackjack, craps, and roulette, the dealers in vests and bow ties. Cheers and laughter penetrated the haze from cigarettes. A far wall featured betting odds recorded in chalk, next to a table with several phones. Off to the side, a bartender prepared a tray of martinis and champagne for waitresses to distribute to patrons.

Patrons who were surely more appreciated than the ones in the front of the house.

"Not too shabby, huh?" Josie said, and laughed at his loss for words.

Gambling rooms and speakeasies had exploded since Prohibition. This much was common knowledge. He'd just never suspected both existed right here in this building.

"I guess Nicky didn't tell you" — some of Josie's words were lost in victorious squeals from a perky gal rolling craps — "he's managing the place now."

"Managing — the gambling?"

"Everything you see in here. Max offered him other spots before, at some of his smaller joints, but he held out. As you know, he always did want to be some bigwig around . . ."

When the sentence fell away, Shan followed her gaze to where Nick stood across the room. Dressed in a suit, hair smooth with tonic, he was speaking into the ear of a shapely brunette seated at a cocktail table in the corner. She tossed her head back in exaggerated laughter. Rolled stockings on her crossed legs advertised a lack of garters.

As though Nick could feel the heat of Josie's stare, he turned his head and startled at his find. He said something to the seated woman before breaking away and approaching with a questioning smile.

"Surprise," Josie said flatly.

Nick looked at Shan, tentative. "Max sent you back?"

"Yeah," Shan said, just as Josie interjected.

"Apparently, he knows who he can trust."

Nick expelled a sigh. "Josie. She's a customer."

"Of course she is. Which is why I'd better leave you to it. Wouldn't want to distract you from your work."

"Doll, c'mon. Don't be like that." He cupped her face to kiss her, but she pulled away and let his lips swipe her cheek.

"See you around, Tommy," she said, and strode back the way she came.

Nick rolled his eyes and smiled at Shan. "Well? Whaddya think?" He angled his body, allowing a full view of the bustling room, the flowing booze, the cash trading hands. The large bundles suggested a clientele of high rollers. "Didn't know the real party was back here, huh?"

Shan shook his head, feeling like "party" was an understatement.

"Took me years of working my way up. I'm managing the whole room, if you can believe it."

"Yeah — I heard. From Josie."

Nick appeared to recognize the implication of distrust. "I've wanted to tell you for a while, the rest of the family too. So you wouldn't think I just wait tables." He sounded so proud of the disclosure that Shan opted not to point out the obvious risks of the job.

"Congratulations. It's great, Nick."

"And to think, this all started when we snuck in the club way back when. You in that big ol' suit." Nick chuckled while tugging on his lapels, bringing attention to his current jacket of charcoal gray, no doubt silk and tailored to fit.

Just like back then, Shan suddenly felt inferior in comparison. Though they now stood eye to eye at five-nine, Nick still seemed taller somehow. Shan glimpsed his own fingernails, the grease he could never fully scrub away, and fisted his hands to hide them. Yet he sensed Nick had already noticed.

Shan cut to his purpose. "Any chance you could sneak out soon? Lina was hoping to see you tonight."

"Why? What's going on?"

"The party. Her birthday?"

Nick groaned. "Shit. It slipped my mind."

"It's not too late. You could still make an appearance."

"I wish I could. Really." Nick didn't sound quite sincere. Could he not imagine the hurt Lina would feel when Shan came back alone?

"Nick, it's her sixteenth birthday. You're supposed to be her older brother, for Christ's sake."

Nick's jaw noticeably firmed, along with his eyes. "Well, unfortunately, I don't have a schedule like yours. Can't just step away whenever I get the itch."

They both fell into silence, thick with tension that amassed too easily these days. But then Nick shook his head and lightened. "Ah, hell. You know me and these family things. I'm a disappointment whether I'm there or not." An awkwardness of truth belied his levity.

A dealer raised a hand, as if on cue, beckoning Nick over.

"Listen, I gotta go. Tell Lina I'll make it up to her, all right?" Not waiting for an answer, Nick started across the room. He didn't even ask Shan to keep tonight's revelations a secret. Evidently it was expected. After all, sharing such knowledge would compromise others.

And yet, only as Shan passed back through the curtain, where the doorman stared with unfeeling eyes, did he realize he hadn't prevented the same for himself.

23

"Fai attenzione," Mr. Capello said with clear impatience. Shan glanced down at the man, still lying under the kitchen sink, his hand outstretched. "Sorry, Pop. What did you need?"

Mr. Capello grumbled. "Pipe wrench."

Once again Shan had been gazing out the window, past the morning frost, debating how to broach the subject. He sifted through the metal toolbox on the counter and handed over the tool, which Mr. Capello took with a slight snap of his wrist.

"Why do you bother coming today?"

The question wasn't necessarily rhetorical. A kitchen sink simply needed replacing in the Rigonis' house over on Laurel Street. Nothing Mr. Capello couldn't have done on his own. But Shan had insisted on joining, even donned his coveralls — a match to Mr. Capello's — he just hadn't brought himself to say why.

"Thought you might want some company."

"You are not talking. How is this company?"

"Well . . . I didn't say I'd be good company."

Mr. Capello said nothing. He knew this typically wasn't the case. On most jobs together they would discuss the latest news, from President Coolidge's policies and rumors of coming strikes, to commentary on political races — less predictable now that women had the vote — and, as always, baseball. More aptly Tony Lazzeri. After Ping Bodie was traded, still a sore point for Mr. Capello, the rookie with the Yankees had become a beacon of hope.

Today, however, Shan's concerns lay elsewhere. Sure, he was troubled by the risks and realities of Nick's work, let alone his own predicament after a literal peek behind the curtain. But more than that, he was envious. Not over the riches and glamour, but over the self-sufficiency, the measurable achievements.

"I've been thinking," he said finally. "Now that I'm nineteen and done with school, maybe I ought to . . . move out on my own."

Mr. Capello ceased any movement. Then, in silence, he slowly resumed working on the new drain.

"I could still help the family, of course. I'd just get another job. Maybe find a roommate to split an apartment." He waited for a reaction. "What do you think?"

"So, you want a different job also."

Shan was referring to a second one, not a replacement, but now that the suggestion hung there, he couldn't deny its appeal. "I don't know. Maybe."

He had mixed feelings about performing for a living, but surely the wages would be higher, with so many customers paying Mr. Capello in trade. The homeowner today, for example, had offered a landscape painting of Genoa's coastline crafted by his wife. Since Mr. Capello knew an art-collecting winemaker originally from that region, he'd agreed to the deal, planning to exchange the painting for some nice bottles of red.

Mr. Capello again went quiet, his face still obscured by the sink. The day Nick moved out, the culminating argument had revolved around ingratitude. Shan hoped this wouldn't be viewed the same.

"I don't mean to seem ungrateful," he offered. "Everything you've done for me, it's incredible. Honest. I just think it's time, is all."

Mr. Capello slid out from under the

counter. He rose to his feet with a show of effort and wiped his hands on a rag. He drew a breath, turning to the sink. "You are right. It is time," he said. As simple as that. Then he went to work installing the faucet.

Shan would have been relieved if not for glimpsing the man's eyes. The light mist in them sent a wave of guilt over Shan, which logic told him to fight. Mr. Capello had to have seen this day coming. Shan couldn't live under the wings of the Capellos until he was middle-aged. Not with any amount of pride.

If he saved up, maybe he could start a business. A store of some kind in the city, where every day he would wear a dapper suit with wingtips polished as clean as his nails. And at night, he would stroll home to a wife and children — a boy and a girl who would never fear hunger or abandonment, or worse.

For now, though, he would keep those plans to himself.

With the job almost done, Shan collected tools from the floor of tiny white tiles. He was toweling up spots of water when Mr. Capello spoke in a level tone.

"I hear you have seen Nick."

The comment caught Shan off guard. "Yeah. I have."

Mr. Capello's attention remained on adjusting the spout. "I suppose he had a good reason for not coming to his sister's party?"

"It was the club — he just couldn't get away."

Mr. Capello didn't reply. He had heard the excuse too many times.

"Nick did say he really wanted to be there," Shan added, not knowing at first why he was bothering, as Mr. Capello's show of disappointment wasn't unusual. Rather, there was something beneath it. Deep down the man needed to know that his oldest son still yearned for his father's approval.

It was Shan's suspicion of this that sent out his next words: "He's really working hard, Pop. You'd be proud."

Mr. Capello glanced at Shan, taking this in. He gave an almost imperceptible nod before twisting the knobs to run the water. A successful test. The job was done.

Before leaving, they would need to discard the old cast-iron sink and drain, eroded by rust and wear. On opposite sides, they squatted and gripped the sink by its bottom corners. On the count of three, they heaved it up from the floor. They started toward the kitchen door, but after a few steps Mr.

Capello dropped down, causing the sink to list.

"Jesus," Shan said, pulling backward. He managed to bring the sink to the floor without its slamming into the tiles. Mr. Capello was on one knee, a hand pressed to his ribs.

"What happened? Are you all right?"

It was more than a strained muscle. The man's breathing sounded labored.

"Pop . . . Pop, what is it?" Shan moved closer. "Tell me what's wrong."

Mr. Capello's skin had gone pale. Sweat beaded along his hairline.

Shan looked around, seeking help. The homeowner's wife had run to the bakery. There was no phone in sight.

"I'll fetch a doctor." He started to rise, but Mr. Capello held his arm.

"No," he rasped, "I am okay."

"Pop, I swear I'll be right back."

Mr. Capello wouldn't release his grip. He took a deep, steadying breath and let it out, meeting Shan's gaze with resolve. "I do *not* need a doctor."

Shan had almost forgotten. Here was a man who'd endured countless visits to the hospital, all to help a boy with a heart that couldn't be saved.

"I lift up too fast. It makes me dizzy. That

is all. Already I am better."

Mr. Capello was indeed regaining his color. Nonetheless, it was startling to see him weaken so quickly and without warning. Shan hoped to God it wasn't the news of his intent to move out that had caused the problem. "I'll get you some water."

He filled a glass and knelt to deliver it. "You know Ma's gonna say she was right about you working too hard." A light remark, but also true.

"This is why," Mr. Capello said after a sip, "you will not tell her."

24

Airy snowflakes floated through the borough, a peaceful contrast to the inquisition at home. Shan and Mr. Capello had only just arrived in the entry when Mrs. Capello narrowed her eyes. She was bundled in her coat and scarf.

"What is wrong with you?" she asked her husband. "Are you sick?"

Mr. Capello turned away and stored his hat on a wall hook. "I am just tired."

"Your cheeks, they are pink."

"It is cold outside," he said, hanging up his overcoat. Shan did the same without a word.

She touched her husband's forehead with the back of her hand and appeared satisfied by his temperature, but not his answer. "Did you eat?"

"Yes," he insisted. "I ate. We ate."

"Then, what is it?"

"Basta, basta." He waved her off and

shuffled toward the stairs. "You are like an old hen, pecking, pecking."

Her gaze cut to Shan, who promptly grasped for a diversion. He gestured to her coat. "Were you going somewhere?"

She studied him, suspicious. "The market."

"I can go. You stay and relax." He grabbed his coat and put it right back on. "What do you need me to buy?"

Though with lingering reservations, she produced her shopping list. Shan accepted, and sidestepping an investigation, he headed out the door.

With the store just five blocks away, he decided not to drive and soon regretted the choice. The sidewalks were slick and grimy with slush, and the afternoon air had sharpened with a chill. A roadster swooshed past, leaving tracks that would freeze overnight.

He kept the collar of his overcoat hiked around his ears, his face lowered against the wind. Puffy white breaths rose from his mouth to the brim of his hat. He almost passed the market before realizing he'd arrived.

A bell on the door jingled when he stepped into Carducci's Market. An array of cans, jars, and boxes lined the walls of shelves and two aisles in the center of the room.

The air smelled of oak from clustered barrels full of various grains.

Behind the long wooden counter stood the owner in his black apron, the sleeves of his button-up shirt rolled to his elbows. He handed a woman a large paper sack and thanked her for coming in.

"Tommy," he declared, eyes alight, *"come stai?"*

"Bene, grazie. How about you, Mr. Carducci? You look well."

The man flexed an arm, as lean as his wrinkled face. "Fifty pushups a day now. Soon I will be strong as an ox."

Shan smiled. "In that case, I'd better arm wrestle you soon, or I won't stand a chance."

"Ahh. You think you have a chance?"

"You know . . . sad to say, probably not."

They both laughed.

Mr. Carducci said, "You are here to do your mama's shopping?"

Shan retrieved her scrawled list from his pocket, held it up in reply.

"Va bene. You have any trouble, you come ask."

Shan nodded and Mr. Carducci picked up a pencil. He leaned over to scribble in a ledger, humming a tune to himself.

The store offered ample protection from the cold, yet Shan would feel more comfortable after returning home and confirming that Mr. Capello had fully recovered. Grabbing a woven basket, Shan began at the top of the list.

Flour, salt, yeast . . .

He gathered the items, zipping from one area to the next. It helped when he became the lone customer in the store. For his final item, he squatted before the olives and set down the basket. Unsure which of two types Mrs. Capello would want, he grabbed both jars, hoping Mr. Carducci would know.

Behind him, the door jingled with a new arrival.

About to rise, Shan heard a man yell, as sharp as a bark: "Open the register — now!"

Shan dropped even lower. Twisting around with caution, he peeked past the aisle and the blockade of barrels. Two men stood at the counter with fedoras pulled low and black handkerchiefs hiding all but their eyes. The heavyset one pointed a pistol at Mr. Carducci's forehead. "I said, 'Open it!' Are you deaf?"

The taller guy, slimmer but still solid, held a gun in a more casual manner, as if toting a gin fizz. "Come on, old man, you heard him." He had the baritone pitch of a barbershop singer. "We don't wanna hurt you."

The stocky thug tossed a small canvas bag

onto the counter. "Give us the dough. Every last cent."

Shan tried not to move, not even to breathe. His pulse raced as Mr. Carducci stuffed the bag with cash from the register, his poor hands trembling. What else could anyone do? Only in picture shows did heroes save the day. Read any paper; when it came to robberies, the fellows trying to be noble were the ones who got themselves and others killed. These hoodlums just wanted the money — Shan hoped.

"Now for the safe," the tall one said. "Where is it?"

Mr. Carducci shook his head. "This is everything."

"You wouldn't be lying to us, would you?"

"No. We have no safe —"

The hefty one swung his pistol, backhanding Mr. Carducci, who stumbled onto the floor.

Shan could hear his own heartbeat pounding against his skull. He wanted to step in. He wanted to help. Suddenly, over to the left, a door started to open. Mr. Carducci's grandson, Henry, peeked out with an inquisitive look. The five-year-old had descended from the Carduccis' home upstairs, likely lured by the shouting.

In a panic, Shan gave a jerk of his head, a

signal for the kid to go back up. When Henry didn't respond, Shan made upward motions with his hands, forgetting his jars until one fell. It landed with a thud and rolled over the floor.

"Hey!" one of the guys boomed, and Henry vanished behind the door.

Shan held on to his remaining jar, his only defense, while being yanked up by the collar. He was thrown face forward into a wall of shelves. The right side of his forehead hit the outer frame. Boxes tumbled over him, knocking off his hat. His arms flew up in a reflex to cover his head, and his second jar slipped and shattered. Disoriented, he went to turn around but a shove to his chest pushed him back.

"You stay right there, you stupid son of a bitch." Cold metal pressed into Shan's neck. It was the pistol, held sideways by the stocky thug. His breath smelled of onions and cigarettes. "Whaddya think you're doin'? Waiting for the chance to pounce? That it?"

Shan stiffly shook his head, evading eye contact. He didn't want to appear to be memorizing the guy's eyes in the event of a lineup.

"Who the hell you think you are, huh? Who?"

Shan choked out the words: "I'm . . .

Tommy Capello."

The guy needled the gun harder. "Think I give a shit who you are?"

Shan squeezed his eyes closed, this time knowing not to answer. He remained quiet and heard a voice, dropped low, muffled. Too faint to hear. He risked taking a look and found the tall one whispering to his partner. The pistol was lowered onto Shan's collarbone, but a pudgy finger hovered over the trigger.

When the conversation ended, the stocky one gave Shan's face a once-over. He took a step back and raised his hands shoulder high, along with his weapon. "My apologies, all right? Didn't realize."

Shan nodded because it seemed he should.

The tall one swiveled back to Mr. Carducci, now upright with blood trickling from his mouth. "Next time, you have the safe ready for us, old man." Then he grabbed the bag of cash as the stocky thug peeked outside. Deciding the coast was clear, they charged out the door and into the snow.

Right then, Shan became aware of the quaking in his knees.

"Nonno?" A meek voice drifted from the doorway by Shan. Henry had dared to

return. "Are the bad men gone?"

But Mr. Carducci didn't respond. He looked out of sorts from the strike to his head.

"Mr. Carducci," Shan said. "Are you okay?"

The man turned toward Shan, then spotted his grandson. "Upstairs — go. *Pronto!*"

Henry scampered up the steps, leaving the door ajar. In mindless movements, Mr. Carducci closed the empty register.

Shan hoped the shop did indeed have extra funds stored in a safe. "Do you want me to stay? I'd be glad to talk to the cops if that'll help."

At this, Mr. Carducci's eyes shot up. "No. No police."

"But — they robbed you."

Mr. Carducci shook his head, adamant, his gaze looming heavily before looking away. "We have no robbery here," he murmured.

Bewildered, Shan stepped forward, crunching glass beneath his shoe. He had forgotten about the jar. "Could I at least help clean up?" A puddle of olive brine spread further over the floor. "Mr. Carducci?"

"Please," the man said with sudden firmness. "Just go."

25

Shan walked out of Carducci's in a blur of uncertainty. A block down, he slowed to a stop. He struggled to determine what had just happened and where to go from here. Left without even the shopping list, he was returning empty-handed. He could say the wind swept it away. The last thing he would do was burden Mr. Capello with more worries.

"Tommy!"

Shan turned to discover a woman standing below the awning of a café. She waved through the light veil of snowflakes. "Josie?"

"Jeez Louise," she called over. "I was right there knockin', you goof." She pointed to a table by the window only a few yards from Shan.

"Guess I didn't hear."

"So I gather." Smiling, she hugged the sleeves of her white cardigan, which layered a navy dress, flared to midcalf. Aside from a

white belt that flattered her slender waist-
line, the outfit was far more conservative
than her satiny numbers at the club.
"What're you doing out here?" she asked.

"I . . . had to go to the market. Ma needed
some things."

"Come closer, would ya? So I don't gotta
shout."

Shan wasn't in the most conversational
mood but politely approached. He had just
stepped under the awning when her eyes
went wide.

"My God, Tommy. What happened to
your head?"

Remembering his collision with the shelf,
he touched his forehead. A knot was form-
ing, which partly explained the ache behind
his eyes.

"That's a story I wanna hear," she said.
"Come inside where it's warm." Before he
could give it much thought, she grabbed his
hand and pulled him into the café, where
the scent of espresso filled the air.

"Heya, Josie," a bespectacled man called
from behind the counter as they passed.
"About ready for another pot?"

"That'd be dandy. Another cup and saucer
too."

"Coming right up."

In this place, Josie was clearly a regular

239

being catered to, not the other way around. At the far window table, she reclaimed her spot. A black winter coat with a fur collar hung on the back of her chair. A tea set and a book waited on the square wooden table.

Shan took a seat across from her. "You here alone?"

"Usually."

"I didn't know you came to this area much."

"Not till lately. I moved in with a girlfriend around the corner a few months back. Pretty decent apartment. When her sister moves here from Maryland, I'll have to find something else, but for now it'll do. Got lucky, really, since the move was last minute."

It took effort for Shan to follow the train of thought. "What happened?"

She lifted a shoulder. "Had an issue with the landlady — at my rooming house, you know, over by the club. She never really approved of my lifestyle anyway." Josie's expression made clear the judgments had grinded on her. "So, when she caught Nicky in my room late one night, she had all the excuse she needed to send me packin'."

Shan suddenly imagined the activity her landlady had walked in on. "Ah," he said.

Josie read his face. "Sheesh. Nothin' like

that." Her skin warmed to a dusty pink, marking the first time Shan could recall ever seeing her cheeks hint at a blush.

She went on to explain, "Nicky was on the warpath 'cause I told him it was over. He followed me inside and refused to leave till I took him back. Landlady woke up from all his blathering, and that was that."

The scenario certainly fit. Shan knew how determined Nick could be once he'd set a goal.

Just then, the bespectacled man swooped in with a cup and saucer and traded Josie's teapot for another. When she thanked him, he replied, "Anytime, Josie the Camel," presumably an allusion to the amount of tea she could drink.

She released a laugh that sounded different than usual. Perhaps it was a reflection of her appearance — with less makeup, her curls simply pinned at the sides — but something about her seemed more real. Like an actress caught offstage.

As the man walked away, Josie poured two steaming cups that smelled of mint.

"Looks like you come here a lot," Shan said, accepting the drink she slid over. "I'm surprised I haven't seen you. I pass by all the time."

"I usually sit in the corner over there. But

241

those halfwits have been parked for over an hour."

Following her eyes, Shan peeked over his shoulder at three prim women decked out with pearls and brooches. They didn't appear to be in a hurry.

"So, you gonna give me the scoop?" Josie dropped sugar cubes into her cup. "Or do I gotta pull it out of ya?"

Shan took a moment to reset his thoughts. He blew on his tea and drew a long sip. Recounting the event might help make sense of it.

With the scene fresh in his mind, he backed up to the beginning and shared as much as he knew. "I was shopping at Carducci's," he said, "when I heard the door." From there, the details flowed out and Josie listened intently.

In the midst of the story, a thought came to Shan. He had initially taken the shop owner's cool demeanor for trauma over the robbery, but it could have been more than that. Maybe he blamed Shan for not jumping in to help. In all truth, part of him felt ashamed of his inaction. But he was also aware that, in the face of a threat, a childhood instinct placed his own survival first.

"Sounds to me like Mr. Carducci was

right," Josie pointed out when he had finished.

"About?"

"That he wasn't robbed. He was warned."

"How do you mean?"

"You *have* heard of shops paying a special tax, right? For protection."

"Yeah. Of course." A kid couldn't grow up in Brooklyn without hearing tales about "protection" from the likes of Black Handers. Extortion notes threatening business owners were sometimes marked with a black hand as a signature. Word had it their methods could be pretty persuasive.

Given a chance to think, Shan did see how a robbery, for example, could demonstrate the necessity of proper security. A downright crummy scheme.

"It's not right," he said.

"No. But it's the way things are." She stirred her tea with a tiny spoon and took a sip.

"What about me, though? Why did those thugs let me off like that?"

"Who do you think protects this area?" She waited, forcing him to guess. Which didn't take long. There was only one connection to Shan with that kind of authority, a person he'd shared a friendly exchange with only days ago.

"Mr. Trevino."

Josie confirmed this with a long blink.

"Swell," Shan muttered. It was no secret Nick Capello had worked at the club for years, but like the rest of the family, Shan had been treated as a separate entity until now.

"I didn't ask for any special treatment."

"Who says you gotta ask?" She raised her cup to take another sip, but instead shook her head. "Good gracious. It's hard to believe you and Nicky are even related." Coupled with a slow smirk, something in her tone caused the words to hang there, as if they'd been chosen with purpose.

Unsure how to respond, Shan retreated to his tea, drinking it down. He'd never had reason to question it before, but now he wondered if Nick had ever spilled the secret of Shan's identity . . .

No. He wouldn't have. Despite the differences in their lifestyles, even their bloodlines, they were still brothers.

Shan recalled the book on Josie's side of the table, a fresh topic. "You like to read, huh?" He angled the worn green hardback to view the title, expecting a romantic novel popular among women. What he found was *The Man in the Iron Mask.* "This is yours?"

"You sound surprised."

"I just — didn't know you read these kinds of stories."

"You mean the ones without pictures?"

He opened his mouth, struggling to answer, when she broke into a giggle. "Relax. I'm razzin' ya."

Shan let out a small laugh. But still aware of an odd vibration, he kept the focus on the book. "Have you read it yet?"

"About a hundred times."

The tattered binding and bent corners told him she wasn't exaggerating. It had been a decade since Shan had read that novel, one of the many Uncle Will had forced him to sell.

"It's a good story," she said, pouring them both more tea. "There's an evil French king. He's got a twin brother who's been locked up and kept a secret. Well, some fellas betray the king and switch him with his brother, and that brother gets to live in the palace with a whole new fancy life. Except . . . well, I don't want to ruin it. You should just read it yourself."

Shan searched her eyes for a message, a sign of knowing. "Yeah, I have."

"Oh. Then you know what happens. Of course, it's not the happiest ending. But it's realistic, don't you think?"

"Meaning . . . it couldn't actually work

out better than that?" He didn't clarify whether he was referring to the entire tale or just the character's change of identity. But she shook her head and replied as if she'd fully considered it before.

"In real life, second chances and happy endings — they only come from fairy tales."

26

Three days had passed since Shan had run in to Josie, yet her words continued to haunt him, reinforced by every stop in his normal routine. The bakery for a snack, the newsstand for a paper, the deli for his lunch, the barber for a trim. From the stares aimed his way, it was painfully clear that the second life he had built, shiny and golden for so long, was being tarnished by rumors.

The vendors weren't unkind but offered nothing past courtesies. Shan had been a customer to many of them since he was twelve, but a distance suddenly divided them. A chasm formed of fear, suspicion, or disappointment.

In this moment, on the winemaker's front porch in Flatbush, Shan detected a similar feeling. Then again, perhaps it was normal for the man to act aloof when distributing alcohol, particularly to an unfamiliar customer.

Shan had volunteered to deliver the painting of Genoa, completing Mr. Capello's latest trade, not wanting the man bothered with lugging wine. And that was even before Shan knew the deal was for three boxes, not one.

He had barely said *"grazie"* when the winemaker closed the door, followed by a turn of the lock, a precaution residents rarely took unless they had something to hide.

A partial moon cast a glow on patchy day-old snow and cars retired for the night. The faint yips of a dog drifted from a neighbor's house, where an elderly man was ushering his pet inside. The street was otherwise vacant of people. Shan balanced the three boxes and descended the porch steps, careful not to slip in the slush.

He packed the wine in the flatbed of Mr. Capello's truck. As he finished concealing the boxes with a canvas tarp, a siren started to wail. His stomach cinched, twisting like a rag. On a side street in the distance, a police motorcar zoomed past and the noise waned.

Shan hurried to resume his place behind the steering wheel. Though anxious to return home, he drove with care to prevent unwanted attention. In a handful of minutes that felt much longer, he parked before the house, its windows aglow. At the rush of relief, he couldn't help but laugh. Most Italian folks transported wine on a regular basis. Likely the same went for the Irish and their bottles of whiskey. Yet here he was, feeling like a major smuggler working for Capone.

He reached for the door handle, but a noise jolted him. A tap on his window. The silhouette of a man stood just outside his door. Through the shadows, Shan made out the beady eyes and bulbous nose that comprised a face he knew. He willed his nerves to steady while rolling down the window. Just Officer Barsetti. No one to get riled up about. Plus, he looked to be off duty tonight in a civilian hat and overcoat.

"Tommy Capello. Thought that might be you."

"Officer. What a surprise."

"You know it's actually Agent now."

"Is that right?"

Barsetti shrugged. "With all the mess of Prohibition, figured the Bureau could use another hand. Made the switch last spring."

Shan felt pores open on his scalp. He resisted the urge to remove his hat. "I hadn't heard. I'm sure you'll be a great help."

"I appreciate that." Barsetti smiled. "Say, I was actually hoping you might have a minute. You mind?" He gestured to the passenger side, and the muscles in Shan's neck tightened.

"No. Of course not."

Barsetti circled around and climbed right in. When he shut the door, the bottles rattled ever so slightly.

As an officer — an Italian American living in Brooklyn — Barsetti was known, in general, as a friend to the neighborhood. But as a federal agent? Even if he remained one of the lenient ones, his opinion of sipping a glassful over supper might very well differ from his view of transporting three full boxes. A volume suggesting the wrong intent.

"Boy, it's cold as an iceberg out there, isn't it?" Barsetti blew on his hands and rubbed them together. "They say it'll be a long, brutal winter. I'm guessing they'd be right."

"Looks that way."

"You know what's funny? I was just thinking of you recently." Barsetti's lips slid into a smile, exhibiting a small gap between his lower front teeth.

"Oh?"

"Yeah. I was picturing the day I first found you in that breadline. You were in a scrap with some Irish kids. Remember that?"

Shan nodded through his discomfort, trying to grasp the point of the story. The point of this visit.

"Thought for sure you'd end up a no-good jail rat, like half those vagrants still running the streets. But look at you. Got your diploma now, working with your father. Earning a good, honest living. Your mother, she's got every right to be pleased as punch."

Headlights suddenly illuminated the agent's face. The beam swept through the truck like the hand of a ghost. Barsetti's gaze trailed it and settled on an unseen spot in the darkness. "I tell ya," he sighed. "For a guy in my field, there's nothing sadder than seeing promising young men throw their lives away. I'm talking about the ones who start thinking everything they've got, it just ain't enough. They see other fellas out there, a brother maybe, making dough the easy way. So they get curious. Can't blame 'em for that." He shook his head as if lamenting to himself. "But then they go and start hanging around questionable joints. Schmoozing with men who'll do *anything* to keep their rackets going."

Shan gripped the lower edge of the steering wheel, bracing, comprehending.

"See, it's real easy to get tricked, thinking it's important to impress these kinds of men. So it might be tempting to do things like, I don't know, help nab cash from stores that aren't very . . . cooperative. Or maybe it isn't about those men at all. Maybe it's to impress a pretty girl, one you might share long chats with at a café. You know the sort."

Dumbfounded that he was being watched, let alone by the implications, Shan struggled to respond. "Officer — Agent — I swear to you. I know how it could look, but I'm not part of any of that."

"Tommy, I honestly want to believe you." After a pause, Barsetti turned to him. "When it all goes down, I'd hate to see you and your brother caught in the middle. Truth of it is, my boss cares a whole lot more about who's supplying Trevino's joints than the man himself. But hell, sometimes you gotta take what you can get."

Barsetti's words, while perhaps meant as a warning, felt more like a threat.

Shan stared out the windshield. In Brooklyn, nothing good came of snitches.

"Anyhow," Barsetti said. "You're probably eager to get inside where it's warm. But I'm glad we had this chat. You ever feel like having another one, you come on down to the Bureau and see me."

At last the agent stepped out of the truck, a small relief until he angled back. "Oh, and

Tommy. Be sure not to leave anything valuable in your truck tonight. The low temperatures will be freezing, well . . . just about anything."

Then he tipped his hat and shut the door.

27

It was an unshakable feeling. For the next several days the sense of being followed loomed over Shan. He became acutely aware of anyone emitting the slightest air of suspicion, whether seated on the streetcar or at a shoeshine, or strolling nearby in the city.

"Something wrong?" Lina had whispered at Mass yesterday morning, having caught him sneaking glances over his shoulder. He'd noticed a man in dark glasses several pews back, one of the few people not reading a hymnal with the rest of the congregation.

"Thought I saw an old friend," Shan told her, and turned back around. He preferred not to worry the family any more than necessary. And he was especially glad he'd divulged nothing when the stranger in glasses rose with a blind man's cane to navigate the aisle for Communion. Proof

Shan was being paranoid. But how could he not be, with so many of his actions being tracked? No doubt the authorities were keeping an even closer watch on Nick.

Fearing an imminent takedown, Shan had twice attempted to call him, but without success. A good thing, really; it was wiser to speak in person, eliminating the chance of an operator listening in. Yet when he'd knocked at Nick's apartment, nobody had answered.

Shan now lowered onto the sofa chair at home and focused on the orchestra music from the RCA radio. Lacking an appetite, he'd eaten very little at supper, claiming to have had a late lunch, and drank extra wine to settle his nerves. Only marginally effective.

"What is bothering you?" Mrs. Capello lowered her needlepoint. She was seated on the davenport beside her husband, whose mouth was moving while he read the paper as he practiced words in his head.

"Not a thing, Ma. Why do you ask?"

"You are up, down, up, down. Always looking out the window."

In all honesty, Shan hadn't realized it. After all, what was the point? Little could be seen in the darkness. Winter made eight o'clock look like ten.

Mrs. Capello flicked her hand toward him. "Go out, do something fun."

She thought he felt cooped up. The problem was far from that simple, though it was a great excuse for his restlessness. He was about to borrow it when he recalled his discussion with Mr. Capello about the need to break away — an impulse that had fallen to the wayside.

"I'm happy right here. Anyway, it's freezing outside."

Mrs. Capello tsked. "This is New York, not the North Pole. Go to the city with a friend. It is almost Christmas. Even on a Monday there is much to do."

From this, a thought tugged at his mind. Nick worked at the club on Mondays. It would be less crowded than on the weekend. At this relatively early hour, odds were high Nick could sneak away for a private talk. A few minutes were all Shan needed.

Feigning casualness, he said, "I suppose you're right. I could go see who's around. Maybe catch a picture show." He rose to get his coat, and Mrs. Capello smiled. Satisfied by her feat, she returned to her needlepoint.

Mr. Capello looked up from his paper. "You should see that new film. The one with . . . Norma . . . eh, what is her name?"

"Shears," Mrs. Capello said.

"It's 'Shearer,' " Lina corrected, coming down the stairs with her schoolbooks.

"Shearer?" her mother said. "That cannot be right."

Shan was buttoning his coat as Lina said, "Mama, no actress in Hollywood would use 'Shears.' "

"Why not?"

"Because it's a word for scissors."

"How is 'Shearer' better? This is a person who takes wool off sheep."

Mr. Capello sighed and returned to his articles, appearing regretful of what he had started. This wasn't the first time his wife had battled over the logic of a film star's name: such as why Joan Crawfish might be wrong, but Craw-Ford sounded like an automobile.

Shan had just put on his hat when Lina shot him a weary look that said, *Please, take me with you.*

Before she could voice the plea, he hastened out the door.

As expected, the Royal had drawn fewer patrons tonight than on a typical Friday or Saturday. Still, more than half the tables on the main floor were filled. The same went for the dance floor, where couples waved, kicked, and winged their arms as the band played the "Black Bottom Stomp."

Shan glanced around for suspicious eyes. He hated that his coming here would only affirm Barsetti's assumptions.

"Door at the top," a waiter said after guiding Shan to stairs that led to the club office.

"Thanks for your help."

When the fellow lingered, Shan fished a dime out of his coat pocket and handed it over.

"Anytime, sir." A nod, and he sped away.

Shan proceeded up the narrow staircase to reach the lone office. With Max out for the evening, as per his usual on weeknights, Nick was said to be managing the paperwork. But as Shan neared the door, a woman's voice rang out over the music. It was Josie.

"My point," she was saying, as if through clenched teeth, "is you never put me first. Ever."

"God Almighty. I ain't got time for this shit tonight." Hearing Nick's reply, Shan waited to knock, not wanting to intrude.

"Oh, yeah? Fine, Mr. Big Shot. I'll get outta your way — for good."

"Damn it, Josie. Just stop."

Footsteps came closer, then halted, and her tone changed. "Let go of me."

"Josie —"

"I said, *let go!*"

The sound of a slap caused Shan to bristle, but just for an instant. He turned the knob, grateful it wasn't locked, and opened the door. The couple snapped their faces toward him. Though it was Nick's cheek that had flushed from a hit, Josie's eyes were the ones brimming with panic.

"Everything okay in here?"

Josie yanked her arm free as if burned by Nick's grip. An imprint of his fingers reddened her skin.

"We're fine," Nick told him. "Just a little disagreement."

"Josie?" Shan wanted to hear the answer from her.

She straightened in her sleek white dress, fists held stiffly at her sides. Thick black kohl lined her eyes. "Peachy," she said. Then she exited with her gaze straight ahead. Her heels clacked down the stairwell before the sound melded into a fresh, snappy jazz tune.

Nick moved toward the mahogany desk. He smoothed his disheveled hair and straightened his tie and vest, an effort to regroup. "She gets like that when she's had a few," he said, taking a seat. Before him lay a spread of documents, a stack of folders. Cigar stubs filled a crystal ashtray. The office could pass as a banker's, if not for the decanters of booze. "What do you need, Tommy?"

Recalling his purpose, Shan closed the door. It was clear Nick wouldn't be discussing the trials of his love life. Nor, at the moment, did Shan want to hear them.

"Well?" Nick pressed.

Shan removed his hat and held it atop a wingback chair facing the desk. "I need to talk to you. It's about the club and your involvement downstairs. And about Max, and his business deals."

Nick shook his head and sported a humorless smile. "If this is some kind of morality speech, I appreciate the effort but I really don't need —"

"It's not that." Shan heard the lack of conviction in own voice. When he pictured Mr. Carducci being slugged with a pistol, it was impossible to feel indifferent. But that discussion was for another time. "It's the police."

"Cops?" Nick said. "What about 'em?"

"You remember Barsetti? He's a federal agent now."

"So I hear."

"Yeah, well. The other night he wanted to talk. Made it sound like they're on to everything going on here. That it's just a matter of time before they shut it down."

"Let me guess. They want to know who's runnin' the rum and bourbon?"

Shan paused, admittedly surprised. "That's right."

"And . . . that's all you came to tell me?"

The use of "all" made Shan hesitate. "I suppose."

Nick snipped off a laugh, no friendlier than his previous smile. "Don't sweat it. Barsetti's a chump. They all are."

Shan picked up on the sense that he himself was included in that group, for being naïve at minimum. He felt his defenses rise. "I know Max probably has plenty of cops in his pocket, maybe even some politicians. But that doesn't mean it'll last."

"What're you saying? That I should rat 'em out?"

"No. Of course not." Ramifications aside, Shan couldn't argue that Max Trevino had been generous in many a way. "I just think now might be a good time to walk."

Nick dropped back in his chair, brow knotted. "To hell with that. I'm not about to hightail it because of some Prohi's empty threats."

"Nick, all it takes is a senator needing more votes. The mayor, even. And they'll want to take credit for something in the news. Places like this get raided all the time. Just read any paper."

"Yeah, and that's why Max has it all taken care of."

Now who was being naïve?

"I'm sure he does — for himself. What about guys like you?"

The air went still. A look of affront passed over Nick's face before he dropped his gaze. Sitting forward, he fixed his attention on his paperwork.

Shan hadn't meant to belittle Nick's position, in whatever strange hierarchy had been established in their line of work; he was only being honest. Nonetheless, he tried another tack.

"Just think about the family. What it would do if you got arrested. Pop isn't as young as he used to be —"

Nick slammed his hand on the desk. "I said not to worry about it. They ain't your problem!"

The sentence hung between them, as cutting as a blade. Surely he didn't intend to imply that Shan had no rightful place to be concerned.

With no words to follow, they simply stared until the phone rang.

Nick grabbed it with reluctance. "Yeah?" He waited, listening. "All right, all right.

I'm comin' down. You deaf? I told you I'll be right there. Jesus." He afforded Shan only a side glance. "Look, I got work to do, so . . ."

Shan issued a nod and replaced his hat. "I'll see myself out."

Weaving back through the main hall, Shan grew even more agitated from idiots too intoxicated from glee and booze to notice his need for passage. An oblivious woman turned with her teacup and spilled half her hooch on the lapels of Shan's coat. She apologized through her giggles, but Shan continued on his way, wishing he'd had the foresight to stay home. If Nick was too wrapped up in his own greed and arrogance to heed the warning, that was no one's problem but his own.

Once outside and down the entry stairs, Shan emerged onto the sidewalk and just stood for a spell. His breaths rose in foggy clouds and the cold air seeped over his skin. He was glad for the supper wine that defended against the chill.

A block down, motorcars zipped past on the main street. Remembering where he'd parked, he started toward the corner. There he spotted Josie. Her unfastened coat flapped over her flimsy dress as she waved for a taxicab before it passed her by. It seemed a repeated occurrence, the way she cursed after the driver in a voice steeped in anger and desperation. She stopped only when her heel slipped on an icy spot. She barely caught herself from falling, just as Shan arrived and grabbed her elbow from behind.

She recoiled in fear, dropping her pocketbook.

"Josie, it's me."

After seeing his face, she covered her mouth. Her hands visibly shook. The frosty air had tinged her nose pink, and tears laid tracks of black eye makeup down her cheeks. He had never pictured her in such a state.

"Come on, Josie," he said gently, as if coaxing a wounded animal from a trap. "Let's get you home."

28

Their drive passed in silence, except for the few directions Shan needed to reach Josie's apartment. The three-story brown-brick building was located only blocks from the Capellos' place, certainly not putting him out. Not that convenience was a deciding factor in escorting her home.

After parking, Shan hurried around to help her out. Once on her feet, she watched him shut the door. She appeared to search for words.

"You gonna be okay?" he asked.

"Oh, yeah. Just fine." Her half smile was even less convincing than her tone.

"You want me to walk you up?"

She gave a shrug. "If you like."

Shan nodded and accompanied her inside and up the stairs to reach the second floor. The place was fairly quiet, the hallway vacant. At her door, Josie located the key in her pocketbook, but struggled with the lock.

"Let me help," he said, and gingerly assumed the task. The instant he opened the door, she retreated into the apartment.

He battled a sense of impropriety, stepping only as far as the entry to relinquish her key on a small table. "Well, if you're really fine, I'll get going."

In the sitting room, she tugged the chain on a floor lamp, sending filtered light through its mosaic-glass shade. She halted before an oval mirror. "Mercy. Don't I look ghastly?" She touched the hollow of her neck, as if to verify it was her own skin.

"Not at all, Josie. You just look tired."

"Tired." She repeated it the way Mr. Capello often tried out a new word, her gaze still on her reflection. "You got that right." She wiped her cheeks, only spreading the smeared kohl further over her skin. She paused in weary frustration and angled toward Shan. "Give me a minute to clean up, will ya?"

"Sure," he replied without thought.

She turned to walk away and disappeared into the bathroom.

A faint voice from the building hallway reminded Shan of the open front door. He swiftly closed it, despite his awareness that they had nothing to hide. He removed his hat and scratched the back of his hair, overdue for a trim, while taking in the setting.

A rolltop desk hulked against a wall covered in powder-blue wallpaper, like the rest of the room. Centered beneath a large window was a velvet navy couch with doilies on the curled armrests. In the corner stood a quaint Christmas tree that scented the air with pine. The branches were decorated with strung popcorn and shiny bulbs, a hand-sewn angel at the top.

Shan was trying to imagine Josie actually threading the popcorn herself when an object captured his eye. A gramophone sat on a squat cabinet against the far left wall. He made his way over to inspect the contraption and ran a finger over its smooth oak horn. It so closely resembled that from Mr. Maguire's shop, he warmed from the familiar. He felt reunited with an old friend.

Putting down his hat, he opened the cabinet below and found two shelves of records. He flipped through them until stumbling across Marion Harris, one of the many singers he used to listen to in that old back room in Dublin.

"Put one on if you like," Josie said from behind.

Shan turned and paused at her appearance. The fact that she'd changed into a robe wasn't in and of itself a surprise; it was the bulkiness of the garment, the floral print faded from years of laundering, the shaggy slippers on her feet. With her unmade face and untamed curls hanging loose over her shoulders, she looked nothing like the glamour gal she portrayed at the club. No doubt her regulars imagined her lounging at home in silk and feathers, straight from boudoir scenes in the picture shows.

Of this, Shan realized, he was just as guilty.

"Records are all Doris's, but she don't mind," Josie said, and continued into the kitchen, not much larger than a ship galley.

Unable to resist, Shan set the record in place and cranked the handle until fully wound. A shimmer of light reflected off the spinning black grooves. Carefully he lowered the needle. He closed his eyes, savoring the crackle that always preceded a recording; then sweet musical notes entered the air and led to Marion Harris singing "After You've Gone." Lost in those bluesy tones, Shan startled at the touch to his elbow. It was a highball glass of amber booze, whiskey from the smell of it, an offering from Josie.

"One won't kill ya," she said at his hesitation. "Trust me, I'd be long gone."

He accepted, not because she looked in need of a drinking companion — which indeed she did — but because the accumulation of his week made the beverage's potency uniquely alluring. She walked away with her own glassful as Shan took a swig. A liquid burn sped down his throat and heated his chest, his gut. He was barely a teenager when he'd last experimented with the stuff, at Nick's insistence, naturally.

A second swallow went down smoother, as did a third, dissolving knots of tension.

Perched on the couch, Josie held out a pack of Lucky Strikes. In contrast to the booze, Shan had no qualms about declining the cigarettes; sometimes in his dreams, he still saw the bloodied handkerchief in his uncle's hand, still heard the merciless hacking.

After Josie lit one for herself, she said, "Ain't you gonna ask?"

"What's that?"

"What got me all hot and bothered."

He shook his head. "None of my business what goes on between you and Nick."

She drew from her cigarette and exhaled. "It wasn't his fault. Not really."

Shan downed his remaining gulp, not in the mood to help exonerate the guy.

Blue light from a sign across the street streamed through the lace curtains, casting soft speckles over Josie's face. She finished off her whiskey. If not for the cigarette poised between her fingers, Shan might have missed the slight tremble that remained.

He leaned back against the wall beside the gramophone, rubbing his thumb on the rim of his glass. On any other day, with anyone else, he wouldn't have pried, but he could see there was a story inside her, gnawing away, niggling to break free. "You can talk to me if you want, Josie. It'd stay in this room."

She nodded in a way that said she already knew as much. "You're one of the good ones, Tommy. Always have been." She tapped her cigarette on an ashtray set on the table. Elbow propped on her waist, she continued to smoke.

"What happened?" he asked, a gentle prod.

Her gaze lowered to a distant spot on the wood floor. She lifted a shoulder. "I was fourteen. Daddy didn't want me dating him — Albert, that is. Not just because he was eighteen, but because he was a Jew. So for months, I kept it a secret. Then I came home one night after sneaking out, and my parents had gotten back from their bridge party early. Saw me in my chiffon dress with the sleeve torn, my eye swellin' up. And Daddy filled in the blanks pretty fast."

Shan's thumb went still on his glass. He worried he shouldn't have asked for more, given the personal nature of the story, but Josie pressed on.

"I should've explained it right then. That Albert wasn't fully to blame. Hell, I'm the one who suggested we go to lovers' lane. But I'd waited too long to say no to him, and when he didn't stop, I panicked. I pushed like mad to get free and banged my eye on his elbow. When I scratched his face, he froze. I think he'd scared himself even more than me. He tried to apologize, but I just wanted to get clean away. He was probably just tryin' to keep me there to talk when he ripped my sleeve, but I rushed out of the car and ran all the way home."

Josie paused then, her eyes welling with tears. Her rare show of vulnerability at last drew Shan over to the couch, where he sat at a distance, allowing her space.

"Daddy was so angry," she said after another puff. "He was demanding who was responsible right when Albert showed up at the door. Me and Albert, we both tried to tell him it wasn't the way it looked. But there was no reasoning with him at that point. And suddenly Daddy had a baseball bat. I still haven't a clue where it came from — my brother always kept it in the closet.

But after it hit, the blood poured out and we just stood there. 'Cause we knew. Then the police came, and Daddy did most of the talkin', said I was in shock. Which I guess I was. He and the cop had been in the Elks Club together for years and shared the same opinion of Jews. Made it easy for him to believe that Albert chased me home and forced me to defend myself . . ."

As she trailed off, a single tear rolled down her face. Then her voice lowered, suggesting she'd formed a lump in her throat as thick as the one in Shan's. "The funeral was just days later. I watched from across the cemetery as Albert's father had to pry his mother from the casket. It's the same day I left home. And I never looked back."

In that moment, Shan was awed by the role Josie had played these many years, the costumes concealing her grief and guilt. It all made sense now. Her life here, her work at the club. This was to be her second chance. Yet part of her had never left that car, that house. That cemetery.

A long moment dragged out between them before Shan noticed the song had ended. The needle crackled along the inner grooves of the record. To stop the loop of static, he set down his glass and pushed on his legs to stand.

Josie looked up. "Please, don't go yet." Her voice came out raspy and small. Shan barely recognized it as hers.

"I won't," he said, and she nodded.

At the gramophone, not wanting the silence, but in no frame of mind to search for a song, Shan wound the crank and replayed the same record. He returned to his spot on the couch. Her cigarette, now more ash than tobacco, verged on crumbling. Gently he removed it from her fingers and stubbed it out in the ashtray. When he sat back, she finally met his eyes. In them was a yearning for comfort, a longing to not feel alone.

Sensing she wouldn't dare ask, he guided her to lean closer, and she readily laid her head on his shoulder. The notes of the song mixed with the rhythm of her breathing. Before long, as if deflated from releasing her confession, she sank further into Shan's arm, molding to his side.

Though briefly hesitant, he stroked her hair, all the while aware of his decent intent. "Everything's going to be all right, Josie. It truly will."

Neither of them was the type to make or believe in such promises, but in that instant it didn't seem to matter.

■ ■ ■ ■

The absence of music was Shan's first indicator that he had fallen asleep. His blinks were as heavy as the air around him. It took several seconds for him to determine his surroundings, and that the weight on his side was Josie.

Beneath his coat, her arm enwrapped his chest. Her head was nestled into the crook of his neck, her curls silken against his jaw. The smell of whiskey merged with the lemon scent of her hair. Parts of her robe had loosened, exposing the slope of her breasts beneath her brassiere. A slit up her leg drew his gaze to her bare upper thigh.

Josie must have felt him move because she lifted her head just then. Only inches separated their faces. She peered at him, a cloudy look of confusion, and touched his cheek, deciphering illusion from reality. But then her body relaxed and her fingers glided downward, landing on the inch-long scar on the side of his neck. She traced the mark from his childhood, seeming to understand the nature of its origin, though she couldn't possibly know.

As she continued over the angle of his collarbone, the sensation pulled his eyes closed.

His breathing grew strained. His muscles tightened.

He couldn't say precisely how it came about, but suddenly their lips met. The kiss started in tender motions that morphed into something sensual. When her mouth followed the trail down his neck paved by her fingers, a shiver traveled over his skin. He felt the soft fibers of her robe brush his hands, and his grip reflexively closed on the fabric. He cinched her waist, pulling her closer, sending an airy moan from her throat. At the sound, a primal urge coursed through him.

Shan drew her upward to again place his mouth on hers. As their kisses deepened, his right hand slid under her robe, exploring the length of her side. The sound of a second, lower moan dissolved any sense of control left inside him.

In a swift, single motion, he shifted her body to lie below him and parted her robe completely. His lips hungrily moved down her neck to the soft shelf of her breasts, causing her back to arch toward him . . .

And a sound trilled.

Once, twice . . .

The telephone.

Slowly they came to a stop, their breathing heavy and jagged. The metallic bell blared again and again. Each ring brought another splash of cold water. He looked into Josie's face. Josie Penaro. Nick's Josie.

Sobered by what they were doing, what they were about to do, Shan pulled himself off and sat upright. Josie withdrew in much the same way. With both hands, she clutched her robe closed.

"Josie, I . . . I didn't mean to . . ."

"I know," she said.

The ringing of the phone ended. Awkwardness and regret crammed the room in equal measure, leaving no room for words, only silence.

"Tommy," she said finally. "I think you ought to —"

"Yeah," he said. "I know." Then, as he should have done from the start, he left.

29

The sound of knocking seemed part of a dream until something jostled Shan's arm. He lifted his eyelids halfway.

"Rise and shine," Lina said, overly bright.

His mouth had turned to sludge. At a glance, he realized he was still wearing his clothes. "What time is it?"

"Half past noon."

"Noon?"

Lina thrust open the curtains, blasting him with light. He snapped his head from the glare.

"I came home for lunch and Mama told me to check on you. She said Pop took your appointment in Bedford Park."

Shan pressed on his temples to soothe the throbbing behind his eyes.

"They were certain you've come down with a cold, sleeping in this late," she said, then lowered her tone: "Even though you and I both know what really happened."

Through his clearing vision he noted her arms crossed, her expression reproachful. And with that, the whole night came flooding back. The drinks, the music . . . the couch.

Oh, God.

But how could Lina know?

Shan resorted to ignorance. "I don't know what you mean."

"Really? Because I'm pretty sure it wasn't a burglar who crept in at two in the morning. You're not as quiet as you think. And even if you were, I could smell the smoke and booze from a mile. Speaking of which — jiminy, your breath smells like something died." She turned her nose away and waved at the air.

A fitting comparison, given how he felt.

"I have to get back for class. There's soup on the stove for you." She started for the door. "If you want strong coffee, you'll have to brew it yourself."

He relaxed into the pillow with the smallest bit of relief. If he could, he'd never leave this bed.

"Oh, I almost forgot." She angled back at the doorway. "Nick called for you. He wants you to come by his apartment as soon as you're up."

Once she disappeared into the hall, the

words soaked in. Shan's throat tightened. He couldn't recall the last time Nick had extended an invite.

"Did he say why?" Shan called out, hoping for a clue. More than that, an assurance.

But Lina didn't answer.

All along as Shan prepared for the day, he treated the message like an archaeological find: pondering, analyzing, searching for meaning.

He had left Josie's apartment only hours ago. Why jump to a conclusion? He would simply go and see what Nick had to say.

The plan seemed sound enough until Shan put on his overcoat and a discovery halted him: he'd left his hat at Josie's.

A clue that revealed nothing. It was a hat, he told himself. And even if the thing could speak, it would say they had shared a kiss. Fine — a few kisses. But nothing more.

He concentrated on this reasoning for the entire ride on the streetcar, attempting to ignore the lie in it. The truth was, if not for the phone ringing, he couldn't say they'd have come to their senses before it was too late. But just as true was his regret that they had gone as far as they did.

At Nick's apartment door, Shan pulled in

a deep breath and let it out, a reliable routine before taking the stage. And then he knocked.

He knocked again.

From the lag of silence, he felt the dread and relief of stepping onto a scaffold in preparation to be hung, only to learn of a missing noose.

"Hold on a sec," Nick hollered from inside.

Shan battled his mounting nerves as the door opened.

"I was in the john," Nick said of the delay. No trace of a smile. "Come in." He turned just enough to permit Shan entry before shutting the door, then securing the lock.

"I heard you called." Shan aimed for light and inquisitive, a toe in the water. But Nick skipped to a command.

"Have a seat."

Shan nodded and proceeded into the sitting area. Since his last visit, additional décor had enhanced the room. A claw-footed table now divided two Victorian chairs, all set upon an Oriental rug. One still-life painting had expanded to three, despite Nick's usual disinterest in art, and peacock feathers filled a giant vase by a window.

Shan lowered onto the settee, which appeared freshly upholstered. He waited as Nick sat on one of the chairs directly facing him.

"Lina said you wanted to talk." Shan was anxious to move things along.

Nick propped his elbows on the armrests and laced his fingers. "It's about what happened last night," he said. "With Josie — and you."

The insinuation dangled between them, razor-sharp in the quiet. A reference to a five-minute interlude.

In that way, it seemed ridiculous that the effects could amount to anything significant. But Shan also recognized the offering before him: to come clean on his own. If afforded the same opportunity, Josie and her old beau might have thwarted an irreversible tragedy.

"Nick, I'm glad you asked me over." He straightened in his seat, girding himself. "Because I wanted to tell you —"

Nick flashed a palm. "Just hear me out, all right?"

Shan hedged, and nodded.

"Look, I know I was being a jackass. It's just, I'm under a lot of pressure and I don't wanna screw it up. I'm trying to make a good life for her, you know? So she can have everything she ever wants. I admit, sometimes I lose sight of that and don't give her the attention she deserves. But I'd never cheat on her. And I want you to know" — he pointed his finger for emphasis — "I'd never hurt her. Not ever."

The change of direction left Shan without a voice. Yet his silence was interpreted as a need to hear more.

"The thing is, last night you came to me trying to help, and I treated you like shit. I'm sorry for that. Really. About Lina's birthday, too."

Shan could count on two hands the number of times he'd ever heard Nick apologize, and of those the truly sincere ones tallied even less. There was a dark irony in the fact that, under the circumstances, it was Nick who deserved the apology.

"I guess I've gotten pretty wrapped up in this new job lately and all the responsibilities. It's taken so much to get here, I just don't want to lose it. And it doesn't help when G-men are breathing down our necks . . ."

Retrieving his thoughts, Shan tried again. "Nick —"

"You're right, you're right. Getting off track." Nick fluttered his hand and reclined a bit. "Anyhow, I just wanted to say this in person, with just the two of us. You know?

To make sure we're okay."

Shan's guilt had only gained mass from Nick's words. But realizing it could end as simply as this, he pushed himself to answer: "We're fine."

Nick smiled. "Swell." After an awkward pause, he said, "Well, that's it from me. Don't let me keep you. I'm sure you got work to do."

Shan smiled back, even managed to thank him for the chat, before taking the lead toward the entry. Nick unlocked and opened the door, but when it came time to exit, Shan's conscience grabbed hold.

If he explained the incident in the broadest of strokes, certainly it wouldn't sound so terrible. Nick of all guys knew how easy it was to misstep with a pretty girl — heck, that was just the sort of incident that had led to their own friendship. A relationship Shan shouldn't underestimate.

But just then, a man approached in the hallway. Tall in his suit, he had facial scars typical of smallpox. Shan had spotted him over the years as a business associate of Max.

"Sal," Nick said. "Wasn't expecting you till later."

The man responded in a low tone. "Nick."

"You remember my brother?"

Sal's gaze skimmed over Shan without interest. "Sure."

It became evident then, from the man's height and baritone pitch, that Shan also knew him from elsewhere. Sal had been the cool-headed robber at Carducci's, the one responsible for letting Shan go.

Shan smiled again to hide the revelation. The less he knew of Max Trevino's affairs, the better. "Well, I'll get out of your way."

"Yeah, okay," Nick said. "I'll see you around."

Sal entered the apartment as Shan headed into the hall. He was almost at the stairwell when Nick called after him.

"Hey, Tommy," he said. "Why don't you tell Ma I'll be at supper on Sunday? Probably long overdue. Besides, I still gotta give Lina her present."

"No problem," Shan said.

"Say, maybe I'll even bring Josie. It's been a while since I've brought her over." And with a wave, Nick headed back inside.

30

In five days Shan and Josie would be sharing a family meal. Already he knew their interactions — or, more likely, lack thereof — would feel utterly transparent.

As he rode the elevated train from Nick's apartment, he muscled down the thought. He would have ample time to dwell on the mess once he'd cleared his head. For now, he wanted only to be back in bed.

He had just transferred onto a streetcar when he recalled Mrs. Capello's request. Since he was well enough to be out, she'd said, would he mind swinging by Carducci's for tooth powder and laundry soap? He had gladly agreed, though planned to opt for another store. Now, however, he reconsidered. After his visit with Nick, the idea of righting any wrong suddenly held appeal.

Soon he stepped off and approached the market. Through the glass door, he saw Mr. Carducci and his grandson playing a game near the register. Seated on the counter, little Henry held out his palms, an inch below those of his grandfather. After a few intent seconds, the kid swung his hands in an attempt to slap Mr. Carducci's, but the man yanked them away too fast and Henry connected only with air. Mr. Carducci burst into laughter just as Shan opened the door.

The bell jingled as it had for all the years he'd been welcomed with warmth. As always, the place smelled of oak from open barrels.

Mr. Carducci glanced toward the door, and his amusement fell away.

"Nonno, do it again!" Henry held his palms out.

Mr. Carducci returned to the boy. "We do more later."

"Just one more. I almost got you."

"Basta, basta." He lowered Henry off the counter and gave him a green-apple candy stick. "Upstairs you go. Let Nonno work, eh?"

A woman with two jars arrived at the counter, and Mr. Carducci greeted her. Shan would wait to talk until he was ready to buy. He was partway down an aisle when Henry scampered past. Shan went to offer a smile, but the kid zipped straight to the stairs that led to the Carduccis' residence and shut the door.

By the time Shan collected the tin of tooth powder and box of Lux, the customer had departed. At the counter he set down his items. "Hello, Mr. Carducci."

"Buongiorno." The man directed all his focus on his ledger, denoting the purchases, then placed them in a paper sack. "Fifty-two cents, please."

Shan produced two quarters and a nickel from his trouser pocket. Mr. Carducci deposited them in the till and slid over three pennies.

"Mr. Carducci." Shan waited to go on until the man raised his eyes. "I realize how it must have looked, when those thugs came in last week, giving you a hard time." A jingle from the door rattled his thoughts, a brief distraction. "What I'm saying is, I want you to know —"

"Excuse me," a man called out. "Mr. Carducci?"

Shan's body stiffened. He knew it was Agent Barsetti without turning around.

"Could you tell me again where you keep the baking soda?"

Mr. Carducci gestured toward the far wall. "Three shelves down."

"Ah, that's right. Always good to have a reminder."

Out of the corner of his eye, Shan saw Barsetti stroll over to the shelves. The fact that the agent chose not to acknowledge him sent an unmistakable message. Barsetti had no intention of letting him be.

Mr. Carducci stood across the counter, waiting for Shan to resume, but the opportunity had withered.

"Merry Christmas," Shan said, and left the coins behind.

A voice drifted on a whisper. Shan would have dismissed it altogether, and continued up the Capellos' porch steps, if not for a second attempt.

"Tommy," she said, "over here."

He traced the words to a neighbor's overgrown shrubs. In her black cloche and fur-collared coat, Josie stepped into view. Shan glanced around to confirm the absence of an audience before ushering her to the side of the house, absent of windows.

"Your mother said you'd be back soon," Josie explained at a cautious volume. "I thought I'd wait around."

He blinked. "You talked to Ma?"

"I just told her you left your hat at the club, that I was in the area and wanted to bring it by. I asked her to give it to ya."

Shan sighed and nodded. His grip loosened on the sack from the store as Josie fidgeted with her gloved hands. He withheld the urge to still them.

She pressed, "Is it true you went to Nicky's? That's what your mother said, that you went to see him."

"He called this morning, asking me to come over."

"And?"

"And . . . I didn't tell him."

Josie smiled and patted her chest. "When I heard you were there, I was just so worried."

Her assumption became clear: she'd assumed guilt had propelled Shan to rush right over and absolve his sin — if that was even what they'd committed. She didn't realize they were still in a fix.

"Josie, he wants to bring you to supper this weekend. All together, with the family."

She considered this for a mere second before she shrugged. "Then we'll have supper. We'll move forward. No reason we can't do that."

Stunned by her certainty, he shook his head and looked away.

"What? You got a better idea?"

"I just don't want to regret that we should've told him first. I keep thinking" — he lowered to a hush, respecting her trust

— "about what happened with your father. How it was too late to set him straight."

"This ain't the same," she snapped, then caught herself.

Shan stole a glance at the walkway to make sure the area was still clear.

After a quiet moment, she edged closer and tilted her head until Shan connected with her eyes. "Look, Tommy. I can't go back and change things I've done. That includes last night. What I do know is I love your brother. In fact, I realize that now more than ever. I don't wanna lose him. I know Nicky and I got our trouble sometimes, like any couple. Especially down at the club. He can be different there — you've seen it. Tryin' to be some biggie, a real tough guy. But deep down he ain't like that, not when he's away from it all. He's got a soft heart. I know you know that."

Shan had to admit, today at the apartment Nick was again the friend he remembered. The person who stood by him when there was nobody else. Above all, he was the closest thing Shan would ever have to a brother, one he had no desire to hurt. As Shan had learned from his mam and her private past: there were times when caring for someone required the burden of a secret.

And so he conceded. "All right."

Josie squinted her eyes. "You'll . . . keep it under wraps, then?"

It went without saying that in addition to a courtship, her livelihood could be at stake. But Shan also knew she was a survivor. The plea in her eyes said this was about Nick.

"I won't say a peep," he promised.

She broke into a grin, brimming with appreciation — gratitude he didn't exactly deserve. "Tommy . . . I truly hope things won't be strange between us. We've been friends a long time. We haven't ruined that, have we?

"Not at all, Josie. We're just fine."

"Shake on it?" She pretended to spit on her glove before offering her hand, which Shan accepted with a smile. Before letting go, she said, "Thanks again for listenin' last night. It felt good to get it out."

He nodded in understanding, and Josie angled to leave. Shan trailed by a few steps on his way to the front door, but she turned to him with a final thought. "I meant what I said, you know. You're one of the good ones, Tommy. You really are." She leaned in and gave him a kiss on the cheek. When she pulled her head back, she looked at the spot and giggled. "Ah, rats. Don't move." She retrieved a hankie from her purse and worked to wipe away the lipstick mark —

but suddenly stopped. Directed past his shoulder, her eyes went dark.

Shan followed her gaze.

Mrs. Capello stared from the porch, a tote of empty milk bottles in her grasp.

"Ma . . ."

Ignoring his meek effort, she placed the bottles outside for the weekly delivery, the glass rattling upon landing. Then she went back inside, uttering not a word.

31

There was no explanation Shan could conjure that wouldn't sound downright pitiful. *It's not what it looked like. You've got the wrong idea. We're nothing more than friends.*

Still, that wasn't the primary issue keeping him from confronting Mrs. Capello. It was fear of facing the disappointment that surely waited in her eyes. And so they said nothing. They simply clung to their distractions, her with cooking in the kitchen, and Shan reading absently in his room.

Soon Mr. Capello arrived with enough boisterous verve to draw Shan out. The man had dragged in a Christmas tree he'd purchased in the city. Shan swooped to his aid, raising the tree to lean upright in the corner of the sitting room. Pine needles left a trail.

"Pop, you should've said something. I could've helped you."

"I hear you are sick."

Another scoop added to Shan's heap of

guilt. "Yeah, but I could've gone with you tomorrow."

"Why wait?"

"Because it's heavy, is why."

Mr. Capello grumbled about his being ridiculous. "Ah! *Guarda!*" He turned, alerting Shan to Mrs. Capello's presence. "It is beautiful, no?"

She sighed, hands on the hips of her apron. "Do not get sap on the floor," she said warily. "I will get the broom."

Only slightly daunted, Mr. Capello spoke with a wave of his hands. "Always she worries I will make a mess of things."

Shan managed to smile, not pointing out that as of today Mr. Capello wasn't alone.

Not long after, Lina returned from school. At the sight of the pine tree, now secured upright in a stand, she beamed with delight and hurried off to fetch the decorations.

Shan helped by topping the tree with a needlepoint star after Lina hung the ornaments. Most had been handmade by the two of them and Nick over the years, save for one fraying yarn angel from Tomasso. That one hung right at the center.

When it was time for supper, Shan obliged Lina by lighting the candles displayed on the branches, all of them safely placed. Mrs. Capello allowed the radio to play as they ate. Her reason for the exception was obvious to Shan: instrumental Christmas hymns filled any telling lulls. They also did well to distract from her and Shan's meager appetites. It was the first supper in a long while when he'd declined any wine.

As the family finished up, Shan prepared to excuse himself. "I'm feeling pretty tired," he said, which wasn't a lie.

Suddenly a heavy pounding shook the walls. The family froze, startled, before the front door flew open. Nick trudged inside and toward the dinner table. He had a hint of a stagger and no coat, his tie loose and crooked. His gaze cut to Shan. "We're gonna talk. Right goddamn now."

Shan rose from his chair. This time there was no misreading the topic.

"Niccolò," Mr. Capello demanded. "What is this?"

"Nick, please," Shan said. "Let's go somewhere else, just the two of us. Like we did earlier."

But he didn't budge. "I gotta know they're wrong. That what I heard ain't true."

Mrs. Capello placed a hand on Lina's arm, a signal to remain seated. Shan had brought this upon himself.

"See, last night after work" — Nick started to pace, his skin reddening — "I phoned

Josie to make sure she's all right. When nobody answered, I figured she's ignoring my call 'cause she's sore at me. So this morning, one of Sal's guys checked on her. She's nowhere to be found. Here I am, worried she might've meant what she said about leaving for good. Right away I start diggin' around. Turns out about the time I'd called, Josie and some guy were seen in her window. And all she's got on is a robe."

Nick's voice trembled, a fierce fight to remain calm. "Since Josie refuses to talk to me, I'm here to get the truth. 'Cause that slimy bastard just happens to fit *your* description."

"Enough!" Mr. Capello was now standing. "You are drunk. How dare you come into this house, accusing such a thing!"

Nick's attention veered to his father. "A neighbor saw him sneak away in the dark. In your truck, Pop. Yours!"

Shan had been so out of sorts, he'd made it halfway home before a motorcar honked, informing him that his headlights were off. An unintentional mistake — like all of this.

"Nick, wait," he tried again. He dared to move closer, hands lifted in a peaceful approach. "Hear me out. It's not what you think." He cringed at his own words, which sounded just as awful as he'd feared.

"Yeah?" Nick leveled his gaze at him. "Then look me in the eye. I want you to swear to me you didn't lay a hand on her."

Shan glimpsed Mr. Capello's expectant look; he was waiting for a denial.

If only Shan could give them one.

"Josie was upset — after your fight," he began. "I drove her home and we had some drinks. But we were just talking . . ." He faltered, with no easy way to phrase the rest. "We'd fallen asleep on the couch. We didn't mean for anything to happen."

"So you took advantage of her," Nick finished, clenching his jaw. "That's what you're tellin' me."

Shan wanted to denounce this, but given a split-second of thought, shame from the possibility barred him from arguing. "Nick, I'm sorry," he said simply. "I screwed up. I know this. But honest, it's not as bad as —"

The defense cracked in two and Shan found himself on the floor, his head knocked against a leg of the table. Only then did he fully register the slug to his jaw that had taken him down.

"Get up," Nick shouted with both hands in fists. "I said, get up!"

A mix of screams and hollers erupted in the room.

Clambering upward, Shan held out a hand

297

to hold Nick off, but it did nothing to stop another punch to his face, followed by the next. A glass distantly shattered.

Through the cavern of Shan's mind, an inner voice ordered him to curl up and endure the rightful punishment. Yet a darker part of him, a bitter anger born from an inability to fight back, swelled with an ancient fury. A raw instinct to survive.

With all the strength he could muster, he charged at Nick, rushing him backward, until they hit a wall in the next room. Nick tried to shove him off, but it was Shan's turn to unload a series of punches to the face, the gut. Furniture toppled and more screams sounded. Then the pendulum swayed and Nick pinned Shan on the coffee table. Gripping Shan's shirt collar, Nick drew back for another strike. When his fist plowed downward, Shan grabbed hold of it, preventing another swing. Nick was wrestling to break free when a flare of orange snagged Shan's focus.

Fire . . . the Christmas tree. It was in flames.

"My God," Shan said, right as Nick took notice.

Fallen candles had splattered wax on the wooden floor. The fire was spreading between branches. Mr. Capello swung a blanket at them, trying frantically to smother the blaze.

Nick and Shan split ways to help. Shan raced to the kitchen for water, past Lina already with a bowlful. At the sink Mrs. Capello was filling a large saucepan, which Shan grabbed half-filled, leaving her to prepare another. If they didn't work fast, their home would soon be engulfed.

Back in the sitting room, Nick was stomping out flames on the throw rug as Lina hurried back into the kitchen with her empty bowl. Shan flung his water at branches on the right while Mr. Capello attacked those on the left. Smoke crowded the room, causing them to cough.

Shan dropped his pan and yanked off his outer shirt, ripping the line of buttons. He joined Mr. Capello in swatting at the tree.

Lina reappeared and threw more water.

"Pop, I got it," Nick said, taking the blanket from his father, whose motions were slowing. The remnants of candles rolled over the floor.

Together Shan and Nick worked at extinguishing the flames, launching more smoke into the air. They circled the tree, their shoes crushing fallen ornaments. They didn't rest until every threat was reduced to cinders. The smallest spark was shaken loose and stomped upon, each branch left lifeless and bare.

Nick wiped the sweat from his ashen face. There was no denying the damage they had done, to the home, to each other. A shadow of soot blackened the wallpaper.

Shan squatted before a center branch. There, Tomasso's angel hung limp and charred. Of all Shan's regrets, this was his greatest.

"Mama, help!" Lina's cry turned them around. She was kneeling by Mr. Capello. He was slumped beside the davenport as if he'd fallen short of reaching the seat.

Shan hurried over with Nick, arriving as Mrs. Capello rushed from the kitchen carrying towels. Tossing them aside, she dropped down before him. "Benicio, what is wrong?" She touched his right hand, which was clutching his other arm.

His breaths had gone shallow and his eyes exuded pain.

"Rispondétemi," she pleaded, but still he didn't answer.

"I'll call a doctor." Lina started for the phone.

"No," Nick said. "We need a hospital."

Shan agreed. "I can drive. Lina, get the door." He bent down, releasing his singed rag of a shirt, and motioned to Nick. "I'll take this arm. You take the other." As they helped maneuver Mr. Capello to his feet, Mrs. Capello fetched several coats to layer over him during the drive.

"Don't worry, Pop," Nick said. "We're gonna get you help."

32

Time slowed to an excruciating pace at the Brooklyn Hospital. Infants' cries and a vibration of tension filled the air. Smells were ripe with disinfectant and the metallic scent of blood.

A nurse would update them soon. The Capellos were told this upon each inquiry until "soon" became a term Shan despised. Granted, they weren't the only ones waiting. Clustered through the check-in area were plenty of others with fear creasing their faces. Most were immigrant families, struggling to speak English, reliant on the volunteer hospital for any chance of a cure — whether for polio or scarlet fever or the wretched consumption.

Finally came the name: "Mrs. Benicio Capello?"

The family snapped to attention. They rushed toward the nurse who stood before the reception desk in a white hat and an apron that layered her seersucker dress, a pen and file in hand. Her height and broad shoulders gave an imposing air.

"My husband, Benicio — he is safe?" Mrs. Capello clenched the rosary she'd been using to pray.

"He does need rest, but he's going to be all right."

"Thank God," Shan murmured.

Mrs. Capello gasped and made the sign of the cross, exuding the same relief shown on Nick's face. Lina hugged the extra coats draping her arm. Not until then had she shed any tears, but now as she smiled, they came down in streams.

Nick asked the nurse, "What happened to him?"

"It appears Mr. Capello has suffered a heart attack."

They all fell silent.

Heart trouble, like Tomasso.

"Tell me," the nurse said, opening her file, "has he ever had heart problems in the past?"

Mrs. Capello shook her head. "No," she said, and Lina concurred.

As the nurse scribbled a note, Shan thought back to the last time Mr. Capello had collapsed, how his breaths had shortened in much the same way. And in that instant, he realized what he had missed.

"Actually," Shan said, and the group turned to him. "This might have happened before."

Lina blinked, astounded. "When?"

"Last week. We were at a plumbing job, and he nearly dropped the sink. He was out of breath and sweating. But he said it was just a dizzy spell."

"Why the hell didn't you say something?" Nick said. They were his only words to Shan since the family arrived at the hospital.

Shan wanted to explain, to justify — more to himself than anyone else. "Pop said not to. He was afraid Ma would worry."

Mrs. Capello lowered her eyes, making Shan wish he had chosen better wording. If any of them were to blame, it was Shan.

"Be that as it may," the nurse cut in. "The doctor has recommended he stay overnight for observation and follow-up tests. If those are clear, he may go home. In the meanwhile, should you care to see him, family members are welcome, but only for the next hour."

Lina stepped forward, cradling her mother's shoulder. "Yes, of course we would."

"Very well." The nurse shut her file. "This way." She pivoted, asserting a path through the room of strangers. Lina and Mrs.

Capello hastened to keep up.

Shan started to follow, but Nick halted him with a hand to the chest. The earlier heat in his eyes had since cooled to icy steel, now reflected in his voice.

"She said *family.*"

Shan just stood there. So shocking were the three words, they might well have been three thousand volts. He watched Nick disappear down the hall, wondering if Lina and her mother would even notice his absence.

Moreover, would they be relieved?

At this point, Shan felt no right to take a stand.

He felt gazes in the room upon him, most likely due to his bedraggled state. The tousled hair, the split lip, the splatter of blood on his undershirt dusted with soot. He closed his overcoat, grateful Mrs. Capello had brought it along, and realized the one way he could help was giving the family space.

Shan ambled through the darkness and soon found himself in Fort Greene Park. Fatigue setting in, from far more than the scuffle, he took a seat on a lone park bench. A lamppost glowed overhead, a spotlight on an empty stage. The frosty air caused his eyes to water and his nose to run, or perhaps emotion was the greater source.

From his coat pocket he retrieved the handkerchief he had carried for years. After wiping his nose and lip, he peered at the silken cloth. His thumb traced the elegant monogram, the embroidered initials of George M. Cohan, a reminder of the day they had first crossed paths.

In many ways, he still felt like the kid he'd been in that alley, no less cold and on his own. The Capellos had offered more generosity than any orphan deserved, but in the end, Nick was right: Shan wasn't truly part of the family. A fact he had allowed himself to forget.

It all began with a debt, long ago paid. The time had come to move on. Even before tonight's chaos, he had arrived at that truth. Scrutiny from the likes of Agent Barsetti and Mr. Carducci, and others just like them, only further confirmed the notion.

Shan squeezed the wadded handkerchief and thought of Mr. Cohan. A world-famous performer, he had grown up on the road, part of the Four Cohans, touring from town to town. It was a nomadic existence, allowing few ties, not meant for all types of folks.

But clearly it was a life intended for Shan.

■ ■ ■ ■

1935

■ ■ ■ ■

33

All things come into being through opposition, and all are in flux like a river. Put simply, nothing stays the same.

Shan had memorized the philosophy — from Plato, was it? — for an exam during his high school years. Even so, he hadn't afforded the concept much thought. Now proof of it glared in all things, and not just in his reflection — although the years of touring, booze, and girls had certainly left their marks.

The old philosopher had been right, too, about the tendency of humans to battle that change. He'd merely failed to mention that vaudevillians, more than anyone, would be leading the front lines.

"It's just a slump," performers asserted when ticket sales started to drop. "Folks out there still love a good variety act." And to an extent they were right. But what did they love more?

Breasts.

Fellows all over the country just couldn't get enough. No matter how rich or poor, educated or dim, once the curtains opened and the chorus girls appeared, every man in the theater traded his life's worries for a glimpse of those heavenly melons. Some patrons would hoot and whistle; others sat glued to their seats, entranced by the jiggling and bouncing. And when it came to the twirling of tassels, even the ladies in the audience couldn't hide their awe.

Shan had to admit, for his first few weeks as a comic in burlesque, it took fierce concentration to prevent his own arousal. A two-gal striptease had preceded his act, and Shan was, after all, a man. Who could fault him? But in time, the sexual luster faded — during the show, that was — and his focus returned to the crowd.

Performance-wise, the gig differed little from vaudeville, which he had first broken into with Mr. Cohan's help. That was when Shan learned how unglamorous it all was. The grueling rehearsals and constant shows, up to eight a day in "small time," left barely a moment to breathe. Each week folded into the next, same for the months, and ultimately the years. After traveling through snowstorms and rainstorms, he would slog into another hotel bearing no resemblance to the Plaza and find industrious ways to cook in his room and wash laundry in the sink.

But hell, it was a living. And there was no taking any job for granted after the stock market crashed in the fall of '29. That was just over two years after Shan joined his first circuit. Back when he was willing to play the straight man in a two-man sketch with a gagman who'd hog the laughs. The one benefit was it drove Shan to diversify his skills, allowing him to stand on his own.

Then, after six years in the business, it became clear that the usual wheels, or tours, were dying. The fact was, most unemployed men had the good sense not to spend their last nickel to watch a terrier do the cha-cha, or a dwarf yodel while riding a unicycle; but given a chance to see a bare-skinned beauty, they would empty their pockets down to the lint.

When Shan first announced his decision to switch course, he was scorned — mainly by the vaudevillian ladies — for being lured by the carnal appeal. They were wrong. It was the dough he was after, nothing else. A hefty bankroll ensured he'd never have to rely on anyone again.

Which made his surprise act tonight that

much more of a risk.

No doubt there would be a price to pay, in spite of his working for the famed Minsky brothers for the past two years. But there would also be consequences if Shan didn't put Paddy O'Hooligan back in his place.

The recently added comic, the son of a Hungarian Jew, had adopted his stage name to match his role of an immigrant from Limerick, fresh off the boat. For a month Shan had suppressed his irritation. As if the guy's ego alone wasn't enough, his exaggerated brogue sounded more suited to a Scot in the Highlands. It was understandable that his attempts at Hollywood stardom had gained little traction.

Still, Shan had felt no personal affront until today.

Late this morning, "Paddy" had knocked on his hotel door, delivering news that the rehearsal for the censors had been delayed by an hour. In every city, Pittsburgh in this case, all of the acts required approval to perform for the public. Nothing lewd enough to warrant a raid was permitted. A typical list banned full nudity and vulgar movements, the use of "damns" and "hells."

Of course, as went everything in life, there were ways around every rule. For cities that outlawed stripping onstage, for example, the gals would just step behind the curtain each time they shed a garment before coming back into view. What's more, after passing the censors, most obscenities were simply slipped back into the show. This made the approval process a pitiful farce, but still participation was vital.

It was not well received, then, when Shan arrived at the tail end of the run-through today, which had been moved to an hour sooner, not later, than planned.

"I could've sworn I'd said 'earlier,' " Paddy later told Shan, though a faint gleam in his eyes said otherwise.

The short, prune-faced director, Mr. Bagley, not one for excuses, blustered his displeasure, then moved Shan up in the order of acts, thereby shifting Paddy to a loftier slot. As billing went, the farther down, the more prestigious the performer. The one exception was the final number, reserved for a dreadful musical piece — such as a harpist who plucked away while tooting a kazoo — to help clear out the audience in time for the next show. "Playing to the haircuts," they called it, since that was about all the entertainer would see.

Shan's ranking certainly wasn't that low. But it soon could be if he didn't send a clear message, one that told Paddy he wasn't as cunning as he thought.

Now, waiting offstage, Shan wiggled his feet and straightened the vest of his tux. Kitty Lovely was in the middle of her signature bath number, requiring a pair of chorus line girls to hide in the tub and blow Ivory bubbles for ten minutes straight — or till one or both passed out.

Shan knew how Kitty would view his plan. Always even-keeled, about her job most of all, she'd think it was a hotheaded mistake, and tonight in bed she would tell him so. Assuming the powers that be hadn't ordered him to clear out . . .

The real possibility of this suddenly gave Shan pause.

Was he truly ready to leave, to go hunting for another wheel? Would his idea backfire and spread word that he wasn't worth the trouble? Sabotaging another comic could label him petty and spiteful. Most important, a risk to ticket sales. In many eyes, burlesque was a step down from vaudeville. If washed up here, he could wind up scrounging for change in seedy pubs full of drunks.

The full circle of life — in all the worst ways.

Shan reached into his trouser pocket

where he always stored his sixpence. *You've got real talent,* the woman had told him. *Don't let it go to waste.* He'd kept the coin as a reminder. Yet was he about to waste it all?

"Capello," whispered Carl, perched on a stool in the wings. Wearing a plaid scarf, the stage manager — resembling a basset hound despite his young age — waved Shan closer, a final cue.

The pit orchestra was wrapping up Kitty's number. Seductively she snuggled herself in a towel, finishing the act with no less clothing than the robe she started with — another pointless law. She tossed back her long sandy-blond mane before blowing a kiss to the audience. Amid the applause, men groaned, begging for more.

Shan did his best to ignore his resentment over their drooling and ogling. On the subway, minus the dolled-up face and done-up hair, Kitty would barely rate a second glance. But shine a spotlight on her sculpted assets, watch the masterful way she moved them, and there was no questioning her popularity.

As the song came to an end, Kitty sauntered off stage left without looking back at Shan. After four months of casual courting — for lack of a better word — he knew better than to expect even a wink of assurance that his attention was the only one of import.

And yet, its absence now firmed his resolve.

If the likes of Mr. Bagley and old Paddy had come to consider him a two-bit to brush aside, Shan was well on his way to washing up regardless. The least he could do was maintain his pride. He dropped his coin back into his pocket and retrieved the tin whistle he'd borrowed from a house musician. On Carl's signal, he headed for the microphone.

A heckler hollered some reference to the Pied Piper, but Shan stayed on track, not bothering to respond. For full impact, he couldn't just steal Paddy's routine, slated two acts from now; he would perform it better, earn noticeably more laughs. To do this, he would listen, as he always did, to the audience. Without saying a word, they would tell him when to pause, when to mug, how to deliver punch lines for full effect.

The room quieted, and Shan began.

"Top o' the morning to ye," he said with a flourish. Bagley would be blowing his toupee right about now.

Shan charged on, reciting Paddy's jokes about leprechauns and ale and stories of "the Old Country." A couple of minutes in, his accent regained a naturalness part of him missed, as he'd resurrected his brogue for only an occasional sketch over the years.

Through the crowd's laughter, he heard Paddy's voice before seeing him. Offstage and red-faced, the guy was ranting with large hand movements to poor, flustered Carl. The dilemma was clear: how could they give Shan the hook when he was slaying the audience?

Shan resisted a smile of satisfaction; there was still more to be done. Back while touring with the famous hoofing Nicholas Brothers, he had gained some modest tapping skills. He'd also played a flute here and there, but he had never performed both at once. It was a unique combination Paddy took great pride in. Or had, rather, until this moment. Based on his expression, that confidence was plummeting as Shan's imitation earned another wave of laughs.

Now Paddy looked downright panicked. As he should be, Shan supposed, with an entire slot to fill after the next act, a contortionist number of three women in G-strings. Unlike Shan, who'd honed a diverse range of reliable routines to protect his career, Paddy appeared to have polished only one bit. The guy might want to rethink that after tonight.

Shan finished by striking a dramatic pose. Applause filled the theater, topped with whistles and gleeful shouts. He stood there a little longer, soaking them in. It could be a while before he incited those sounds again — if ever. No matter the outcome, he would remember this feeling. Savoring it like a sliver of toffee on his tongue, he bowed to all three sections. On his final rise, a person's profile caught his eye.

His breath hitched.

Seated in the middle, the girl had the long ebony locks and olive skin of Lina Capello. It was a sight part of him always anticipated, mostly with dread.

Shan's periodic phone calls to her and her parents had connected them through the years, but he had yet to see the family since the winter he'd left. Two days after it all had come to a head, with Mr. Capello safely at home, he'd issued his apologies to everyone but Nick — between them there was nothing left to be said — and against Mrs. Capello's tender objections, Shan departed in time for the true family to celebrate Christmas together.

He had sworn to himself not to look back. But now his past was seated smack-dab in the center row.

That was his fear, anyhow, until the girl turned forward, and he realized once again he'd mistaken a face in the audience. Something that happened now and then, a trick of the eye, a haunting of conscience. Thankfully, this particular illusion caused less alarm than seeing Nick, or even Uncle Will.

Gathering himself, Shan hurried off the stage, anxious to outrun a life that never lurked far behind.

34

After the show, Bagley's reprimand was milder than anticipated. That wasn't to say it didn't entail screaming; there was plenty of that. The door of Shan's dressing room might as well have remained open given the way the director's voice carried.

But he made no mention of firing Shan, nor of docking his pay. He even reversed the billing changes in time for the midnight performance, though not without condition. "Don't you be thinking this is a damn reward. Pull something like that again, and I'll tan your hide before kicking it to the street. You got me?"

Secretly, he might have agreed that Paddy O'Hooligan's arrogance had needed to be tempered. More than that, however, he was likely just desperate to avoid a repeat of Paddy's ad-libbing.

Stripped of his brogue, Paddy had tried for a British accent that faded within a minute, the sole redeeming aspect of his bit. The worst being a string of knock-knock jokes fit for the birthday party of an eight-year-old. Laughs did arise from the audience, but mainly in response to clever slights from hecklers. At one point they rattled Paddy so much he forgot a punch line and pulled out a pocket-size comedians' book in search of the answer. This marked the singular instance of the crowd laughing with, versus at, him — until they realized he was truly scanning the pages, then once again he was the brunt of the joke.

Carl would have normally given him the hook, but the headliner up next couldn't find the oversize cork for her champagne number, and they needed to stall for time.

The second she was ready, Paddy scurried away with the look of a beaten pup. Shan almost felt sorry for the creep — but not quite. Besides, such lessons were essential for surviving the business. Shooting to be the top banana was all fine and good, but screw the wrong people and even the funniest comedian could find himself reduced to a candy pitchman, promoting the sales of penny treats at the start of the show.

Once Bagley had unloaded his moderate wrath on Shan, he'd wheeled and stormed out of the dressing room just as Carl entered. To cover a jawline burn from an old mishap with a stage light, the fellow always sported a scarf, indoors and out.

"This came for you during the show." He handed Shan an envelope. Notes from fans had been more common during his vaudeville days but still arrived every so often. "You sure do have that brogue down," Carl said with a smirk.

For an instant Shan wondered if his accent had come across as too authentic, raising suspicions of a long-buried history. But then the kid added, "Old Paddy had it comin', if you ask me." With that, he returned to the hall.

Shan sank onto his padded stool, its leather ripped at the seams. Harsh lightbulbs lined the mirror before him, deepening the tired shadows under his eyes. At twenty-eight, he was already battling some early gray hairs, wiry enough to defy his pomade. He drew a long breath. The smells of the room matched its look of a dusty attic, with a hodgepodge of costumes, walls weathered from the stories they could tell.

He turned his attention to the envelope, grateful tonight for an admiring boost. Yet what he found inside was a telegram. Every word — from the message to its sender — came as a shock.

EMERGENCY AT HOME =
PLEASE RETURN IMMEDIATELY =
LINA

Shan reread the wire, his mind abuzz. Was this the reason he'd imagined seeing her in the audience? A premonition of something to come?

They had chatted on the phone just days ago — on the first of June. It was his monthly check-in call, adhering to a promise he'd made to Mrs. Capello, which he had dutifully kept all these years.

He mentally reviewed the conversation. Lina, as she often did, had urged him to come home for a visit, but her tone suggested nothing unusual. "One of these days," he had said, his standard reply, and after her sigh she'd switched to a safer topic: this time about her latest story published in *Woman's Home Companion*. This only reinforced how well the Capellos were doing since he'd left. From what he had heard, unsolicited, Nick even joined them regularly for Sunday suppers.

Mrs. Capello had been next on the line. "Are you eating?" were her first words, as always; her last being, "Do not forget to eat." In between was an update on the neighbors, the garden, a charity event at church. Likewise, Mr. Capello's small talk centered on work and the weather and how the new president, FDR, would soon get the country back on its feet. "Any pretty girls in your show?" he had asked then, to which Shan answered, "A few." Still seeing no reason to inform the family about his venture into burlesque, he'd instead diverted to details of his upcoming stops. In closing, Mr. Capello added, "Mama says you must settle down soon." And Shan had agreed, with no plans to do so.

There had been nothing out of the ordinary. What could have possibly changed since then?

Shan gazed at the speckled mirror, struggling for an answer. Pop's health had been doing well, they'd all said. If he had taken a sudden turn, wouldn't Lina have wired as much? Perhaps it was something else, a topic she preferred not to put in writing.

His thoughts shuffled back to the days he and Mr. Capello used to spend together at the tracks. There was never cause for worry, with the man's motto of never risking more than he was willing to lose. Of course, that was before a quarter of the country lost their jobs. With fewer folks able to pay for Mr. Capello's services, how long could he and his wife have subsisted on trades of wine and paintings and shaves at the barber-shop? Maybe to get ahead, he had placed a large bet on a surefire horse that didn't come through. Or maybe it wasn't the tracks at all.

On the phone, when Shan had mentioned the Yankees losing to the Red Sox — a disastrous 0–6 that day — Mr. Capello brushed past the subject and wrapped up the call. The reaction seemed typical, as he despised when his favorite team failed to cinch a win. But was there more involved? Had the game cost him something greater than pride?

Until Shan knew, in spite of himself, he would not be able to rest.

The next day, midmorning light slipped through the hotel room curtains, never opened before ten due to Shan's late nightly shows. As he finished dressing, Kitty sat in bed enjoying her coffee and Parliament, her usual breakfast. A white sheet swathed her bare body from the chest down.

It always intrigued Shan that her flagrant immodesty onstage didn't extend to the bedroom. Proof that even showgirls were impersonators.

"How many years since you seen 'em?" she asked.

He was about to say six but caught his error. "Almost nine, I guess." Memories of the house scuffle, the blazing tree, the race to the hospital — they were still so vivid. It confounded him that so much time had passed.

Kitty set her mug on the night table and watched him pull a suitcase from the closet, several garments still inside. On the road, there was never a need to fully unpack.

"How long you reckon before you're back?"

He shrugged. "Not sure yet."

After he'd received the telegram, another phone call to Lina had yielded no details, just a plea for him to return, that she would explain in person. Her voice held such direness he couldn't help but agree.

"Ought to be soon, though," he added.

"It rightly better be." Kitty rolled onto her side, her right hand propping her head, her cigarette poised in the other. Her sandy-blond hair cascaded onto the pillow. "If I get too lonely, I'll have to find myself some company." She flashed a smile to soften her honesty.

The specifics of whose body kept her warm at night came a far second to merely having one there. This was no secret about Kitty — nor about Shan, in truth.

As with all the girls he'd shared flings with on his tours, a common emptiness had drawn them together with the force of a magnet. In the heat of sex, they achieved a semblance of being whole. And for a moment they could forget about the pieces hidden inside, too broken to ever be fixed.

"Then I guess I'd better hurry," Shan replied dryly, and proceeded to pack for his overnight train. The thought of the trip needled him with dread.

Once his suitcase was set — the rest he'd leave with Kitty — he shared the telegram with Bagley. The director agreed to the furlough, but with reluctance paired with a threat: while at home, if Shan got the notion to breach his contract by sneaking off to join another wheel, he'd sure as hell better hire a good lawyer.

Shan gave assurance he'd be back, not bothering to correct the reference to his "home."

Home wasn't Brooklyn anymore. It wasn't any particular place these days.

No, that wasn't true. His home was the road. Shan thought of this soon after, as he settled into the dining car of the train, its huffing and chugging providing the comfort of forward motion. This wasn't the first time he'd returned to New York; tours had dragged him through the state over the years, but always for quick stops and with a cast of performers that created a protective shield.

This time he was on his own.

"Sir, would you care for a cocktail?" the waiter asked.

Despite the repeal of Prohibition two years earlier, Shan drank only during nighttime hours; half a glass of whiskey served as a reliable sedative after midnight performances. And to this day, he still didn't smoke, not with a livelihood dependent on his voice.

But now, in light of tomorrow's destination, he decided the day called for an exception.

"Bourbon," he said. "Make it a double."

35

The din of locomotives and passengers, coming and going, swirled down the platforms of New York's Grand Central. Porters worked to maneuver trunks through the Saturday crowd, hindered by the clustering of blissful reunions. Over all of this, conductors bellowed their usual scripts of "all aboards" and "last calls."

Shan set down his luggage and scanned the surrounding faces. In the last photograph Lina had sent, she was just eighteen. His mind had preserved that image in a timeless tomb. It hadn't occurred to him how the additional years could have transformed her features.

Removing his fedora, he wiped his forehead with a pocket scarf. The morning air hinted at summer's coming humidity.

"Tommy," a woman's voice drifted from behind.

He turned but couldn't spot Lina. Then

his name came again and he startled at the caller. "Josie . . ."

She stood before him, clutching her pocketbook, her hands covered in ivory gloves. Her large-brimmed hat matched the black and white of her polka-dotted dress. Its moderately slender cut verified that her figure hadn't changed.

"Welcome back," she said. Her red lips stretched into a smile, as awkward as the light kiss she then placed on his cheek. When she lowered onto her heels, Shan bristled at the reenactment of an old scene.

This time he used his own handkerchief to erase any marks, and a pang of resentment surprised him. As if somehow she were to blame for all that had happened.

He looked around. "Lina was supposed to meet me. You haven't seen her, have you?"

"Actually . . . she's at home."

Shan realized then, though he should have right away: this encounter wasn't a coincidence.

Josie swiftly explained, "She thought it'd be all right if I came instead. Of course, she's over the moon about seeing ya. Your whole family is."

He arched a brow. "The *whole* family?"

Another discomfited smile. "Well — your folks."

Shan nodded, forbidding himself even an ounce of disappointment. "Figured as much."

And that was the truth. Less obvious was Josie's connection to Lina's message. From what little he'd been told, after Shan was gone Josie had continued working for Max, but her relationship with Nick had abruptly ended, which made her presence now all the more puzzling.

"Josie, it's nice to see you and all — but why are you here?" He rephrased, not intending to sound unkind. "Have you been told what's going on?"

After a pause, Josie glanced toward the station. "Why don't we go inside? Get a cup of joe at the Oyster Bar. Whaddya say?"

Her tone achieved casualness, but her preference to sit for the conversation only heightened Shan's apprehension. He gestured with his hat. "After you."

She led him through the station, neither of them speaking until they took their seats in the bustling restaurant. She'd requested a corner table with relative privacy. As soon as the waitress brought their coffees, Shan cut to the point.

"Josie, if you know what's brought me here, I wish you'd tell me. Lina wired about some emergency. But when I called —"

"It was me," Josie broke in. "The telegram. I sent it."

Shan sat back in his chair. Learning he'd been tricked made him even more wary.

"I just didn't know how else to get you to come. And Lina said it was okay to use her name —"

"Well, I'm here. Now tell me why."

She took a sip of coffee, her crinkled chin conveying a desire for something stronger. Finally she looked him in the eye. "It's Nick. I'm worried about him."

"Nick?"

"He's been in plenty of pickles before and always came out okay. But I really think he's in over his head this time."

Shan's resentment now felt justified. He had spent the entire train ride fretting over Mr. Capello's finances and well-being, even considering problems that might have befallen Lina and her mother. Instead, the "emergency" referred to an inevitable bind for a guy with a penchant for playing loose with the law.

As if reading the thought, Josie added, "Believe me, Tommy. He truly needs your help."

"And he told you that. Right?"

She gave a helpless shrug. "This is Nicky we're talkin' about. You know he won't ask for help from nobody."

"So why would he suddenly take it from me?"

"Because," she said, "you're his brother." Her reply was so matter-of-fact it seemed she'd forgotten what had split them all apart.

Shan shifted his gaze away. A couple of kids seated across the room were laughing between bites of custard. The warmth in their interaction underscored how opposite Shan and Nick's had been for years, even before their fallout.

Josie leaned forward, elbows on the table. "I'm no dummy, all right? With you and the family, I've always known there's more to it. That you were adopted or somethin'. But Nick cares about you. More than you know."

Her words, their undeniable sincerity, moved Shan unexpectedly. He felt the spark of old regrets, yet snuffed them out. While he couldn't discount the many years he'd thought of Nick as family, the guy had made it clear that Shan no longer held that title.

Besides, there was no guarantee Shan could help, assuming Nick allowed it. Who knew how deep a hole he'd dug for himself? If he and Max weren't bootlegging anymore, no doubt they had found some other lucrative scheme, and Shan knew all too well how

Nick treated warnings.

"Let me guess. The feds finally caught up with him."

She smiled wanly. "I wish that was all."

Curiosity trumped Shan's aversion to hearing more. "What, then?"

Josie gripped her cup on the table and lowered her voice. "At the club, word has it, some of the guys were caught skimming off the top. And that Nick was one of 'em."

"Stealing from Max?" Shan caught the spike in his volume. "Nick wouldn't be that stupid, would he?"

"Honestly? I don't know. Times have been tough. The liquor's still selling — all legit now. But the club's been slower, and folks got a lot less to gamble. Shop owners, I imagine they're hurtin' too. That means less dough all around."

"So he got desperate," Shan murmured. This, he hated to admit, was something he understood. "How much did he take?"

"I tried to find out more. Went to his place when he didn't come to work last week. Told him I was worried."

"And?"

"And he said he was fine. Wouldn't say nothin' else. But then, I'm not one he'd confide in . . . ever since . . ." She let the reference dangle, not needing to expound.

"All I can say is, he didn't look good, Tommy. As long as I've known him, I never seen him like that."

"Does the rest of the family know?"

"Just Lina. I told her all this, too. And she agreed you were the one to help."

Shan definitely didn't share their enthusiasm. But at least they hadn't burdened Nick's parents yet, Mr. Capello in particular.

"See, I was thinkin'," she went on, "you could go and talk to Max. He's always liked you a whole lot. I'm sure he'd listen, even work something out."

"Josie, I haven't seen the guy in almost a decade."

"But you could try, though. You could do that, couldn't ya?"

Regardless of history, Shan dreaded to imagine the worst. He assured himself that Max was a businessman; given Nick's long-standing relationship with him, surely the two would come to a sensible agreement.

Shan wanted to say this, but the plea in Josie's face impelled him to relent — as much as he was capable. "I'll think about it."

After a pause, she nodded. Her expression dimmed from disappointment.

Leaving his coffee untouched, Shan rose

and tossed two dimes onto the table. "I've got to visit the rest of the family, seeing as they're expecting me."

Thanks to Josie, as it turned out.

"Of course," she said, not meeting his eyes.

He grabbed his suitcase, battling a rise of guilt, and walked away. Before leaving the station, he would buy a return ticket to Pittsburgh. One night here would be more than enough. The Capellos were good people, no question. They just weren't a part of his world anymore, and he'd be wise not to forget that.

36

The welcome that waited at the Capellos' didn't meet Shan's expectations.

It far surpassed them.

Mere seconds after he'd knocked, Lina swung the door open. The force of her embrace caused him to drop his suitcase. Before he could catch his breath, Mrs. Capello nudged her way in with a stern chiding.

"What takes you so long to come home?" She held her fists on the hips of her apron, the joyous crinkles at her eyes betraying her. When Shan smiled, she cupped his face with ever-strong hands. Gray streaks through her bound hair attested to the passage of time.

Mr. Capello approached the entry in silence. His hair, too, had silvered, and his cheeks and middle had slimmed. A few of the lost pounds appeared to have transferred to his wife, but both exuded a healthful glow.

When Shan extended his hand, Mr. Capello ignored the offer. For the first time ever, he greeted Shan with a hug. It lasted but a moment, yet managed to weaken the defenses Shan had grown accustomed to upholding.

Mrs. Capello ushered him inside. "Come, rest," she said, closing the door. "Lina, help make lunch."

The two women — a description oddly befitting Lina now — headed for the kitchen. Not waiting for his wife's orders, Mr. Capello swooped up the luggage and shuffled up the stairs. He appeared stronger than ever.

Only then did Shan truly absorb his surroundings. The same davenport, sofa chair, and radio. Same dinner table and chairs. Yet it was the scents of meatballs and spices and simmering gravy that filled him with the greatest comfort. He'd forgotten just how much he had missed a home-cooked meal.

There was one change, however, to the room. The wallpaper had been replaced with a fresh design of tiny flowers in misty green. The wine stain was gone. Same for the singes left from the fire.

If a person didn't know better, he would be hard-pressed to believe anything but happiness had ever filled this home.

The afternoon passed with a feast of food and wine and words. At the table, Shan listened to Lina spill all the latest: who'd moved in and out of the area, which businesses had opened and closed, which teenage children had been disowned over one transgression or another, from eloping in secret to working as a taxi dancer for ten cents a twirl.

Mrs. Capello then spoke about the new variety of squash she'd planted, which apparently had earned a great deal of praise from other wives in the borough. She also described a recent date night with her husband at the Palace Theatre — among the last thriving stages for vaudevillians — as well as the latest films.

Naturally, this led to a debate with Lina over the correct names of the titles and starring actors. To bring this to an end, Mr. Capello diverted to the subject of popular radio programs. Many comics were not only salvaging their careers this way but actually finding profound success.

Mr. Capello proclaimed to Shan: "You

should be on these shows." As if it were that simple.

"We'll see, Pop. You never know."

Being a regular on the radio required laying down roots, an idea Shan had ruled out long ago. But here, now, sampling the comforts of a real home again, it seemed an option he just might consider.

Reality was, his current gig couldn't last forever. Politicians were cracking down on risqué entertainment, specifically Mayor LaGuardia. Plus the competition was growing fierce. While a nickel could buy a whole day of shows from the top balcony, skits on the airwaves came free of charge. And for those who could afford it, talkies were becoming the main draw.

But those thoughts could wait, for he could sense far greater concerns from Lina, her anxiousness growing for a private talk.

A neighbor came calling just then, bringing the meal to an end. Mr. Capello followed the man out to assist with a clogged drain. As Mrs. Capello cleared the dishes, Lina excused herself to help Shan settle.

And here it came.

Once they'd entered his bedroom — rather, the room that used to be his — she closed the door. "I'm guessing Josie told you everything," she blurted in a hush.

"She told me what she knew."

Lina waited for more, pressing him with those deep eyes of hers.

He lowered onto the desk chair. "As I said to Josie, even if I'm able to help, I don't know why you both think Nick would let me. Our relationship — it was bumpy even before."

Lina tsked, just like her mother. "That was stupid jealousy. It'd be different now."

"Jealousy?" He stared, incredulous.

Yeah, there was a time he might have harbored some envy over aspects of Nick's success. The luxuries of his lifestyle weren't exactly shabby. But those hadn't come until later.

"Is that what you thought?" he said. Then it dawned on him: "Because if you all think I went to Josie's that night to prove something, or to try to become more like him —"

Lina cut him off with a groan. "Not you, silly. I'm saying Nick was jealous."

After the initial shock subsided, Shan laughed. "Over what?"

Lina lifted her chin, taking this as a challenge. "Your grades, for one. Your diploma." She counted off on her fingers. "Your closeness with Pop, even working together. Then there was your fancy job onstage. For crying out loud, you'd entertain all their friends at parties. And all that time, Nick wanted Pop's approval more than anything. He finally thought he could get it by becoming some moneybags. Why do you think he went to work for Max in the first place?"

The unexpected recap sent Shan's mind reeling. Perhaps this was the real reason she and Josie had demanded he return, because they viewed him as the cause.

He stood up, defenses revived. "I had nothing to do with Nick's choices, and I still don't. He always hated school. And he sure as hell never wanted to lay pipes for a living."

"I know, you're right —"

"As for the club, he's the one who insisted we go there for a job, not me."

"Hold on a second. I never meant you were to blame." She raised her hands in a calming motion. "Please, just listen." She glanced at the door, reminding Shan they weren't alone. He felt heat creeping into his face.

He folded his arms and perched on the edge of the desk. Although he had plenty to add, he merely waited as Lina crossed the room.

She sat on the foot of Nick's old bed. Clasping her hands, she said, "Did my parents ever tell you about Tomasso?"

Shan was taken aback. How could this possibly relate? Wary of the detour, he shrugged. "A bit. When I first got here."

"Did you know he was Pop's favorite?"

Shan had to admit, he'd always sensed a special adoration from both parents, understandable given the circumstances. But he shook his head regardless.

"Parents will tell you they love their kids all the same. But even when I was a little girl, I knew that wasn't true. It wasn't Pop's fault. He and Tomasso just had a special bond. And it was even more that way after Tomasso got sick. That's when Nick figured out that bad attention was better than none at all."

Lina closed her eyes, just for a moment, and continued. "One night over in Siena, after Tomasso died, Nick got out of bed to pray. He must have been eleven back then. He thought I was asleep, but I heard him crying. He told God he wasn't truly glad Tomasso was gone, that he was just angry and sad when he'd said it, and he begged God for a second chance."

A memory rushed back to Shan. He'd been with the Capellos barely a few weeks when he and Nick discussed Tomasso's passing. There was something Nick had held back, and now Shan knew what it was.

"Don't you see?" Lina met his eyes. "When you showed up out of nowhere, needing a home and a family, even a name — you were his second chance. But then you and Pop got really close. Going on outings together, talking about baseball all the time. And the way you made him laugh . . ."

Shan recalled one of the few times Mr. Capello had spoken of the boy. The resulting revelation struck like a winter gale, stealing his breath. "Was just like Tomasso," he finished.

She nodded. "Exactly."

For the majority of Shan's life, he'd prided himself on his ability to read people, mimic them, identify their traits and quirks. But somehow he hadn't seen this — though it wasn't difficult to guess the reason.

Consciously or not, he had enjoyed the cozy spot he'd inherited in the Capello house, never affording much thought to what it might cost others. He'd been too preoccupied with how to keep what he had gained.

In that light, perhaps Shan deserved more blame than he'd realized.

37

The drive to Nick's apartment felt like a trip back in time. Little about the streets had been altered. Even the Model T truck Shan was steering hadn't changed. And yet, shaken by a fresh perspective, the life he'd spent here now appeared very different.

He parked in an open spot half a block from Nick's building. Early evening sunlight speckled the street, filtered by intermittent trees. A woman strolled past with a baby buggy. Shan watched her disappear around the corner as he took an opportunity to assemble his thoughts.

The first time he had run away from the Capellos, he'd been so angry at Nick. In truth, he'd been hurt. Nick had seemed determined to deflate any hope of finding Shan's American father. Finally Shan knew why: Nick didn't want to risk losing another brother.

For years Shan had struggled to forget

Nick's eyes and voice at the hospital, an icy message that said Shan wasn't good enough to be part of the family. Yet now Lina's explanation implied just the opposite. The incident with Josie had simply been the last straw. Another perceived attempt to covet something Nick held dear.

Maybe it was too late to make things right. Shan had no idea where to begin. But as Josie had said, he could at least try.

Just then, Nick emerged from the entrance, carrying a duffel bag.

Needing to catch him before he departed, Shan reached for the door handle. He was about to step out of the truck when three other men exited the building. Pockmarked cheeks gave the tall one away. Mel . . . no, Sal was his name. The fellow beside him had a stocky physique that also struck Shan as familiar. No doubt he was the same thug who had held up Mr. Carducci's store. The third guy was slim and wore a toothbrush mustache like Charlie Chaplin. Shan didn't recognize him but could surmise they all answered to the same boss.

This knowledge, paired with the way they were looking around, casing the area from beneath the brims of their hats, caused Shan to sink into his seat. Their black trench coats seemed odd in this weather until the long barrel of a gun peeked out from Sal's coat, draped like a cape. It was safe to assume he wasn't the only one armed.

The mustached one threw down his cigarette, not bothering to grind it out. Then he led the way to a parked Packard, where he took the wheel as Nick climbed inside with the others. The engine awoke with a soft growl. Seconds later, they pulled out and headed down the street, soon to vanish like the baby buggy, with no clue of a path.

Shan knew he ought to stay put. Still, worry and dark curiosity swirled over the bag, the guns, the suspicious manner. The more he knew about Nick's situation, the greater the chance he could help. With no time to debate, he eased the truck out and trailed at a distance.

Before long, they entered a tunnel that went on and on in an endless stretch. When Shan realized he was driving below the Hudson River, he felt the arched walls closing in around him. He gripped the steering wheel and tried not to imagine a leak of water bursting into a flood.

At the tunnel's end, the sky was a welcome sight. He refocused on the direction of the Packard, three motorcars ahead. They had arrived in New Jersey and were still rumbling along. How far could the men be going? Shan considered turning around but persisted a little longer, and soon the Packard pulled over.

Continuing past them, Shan again dropped down in his seat. He hoped he hadn't been spotted. At the next street, he turned left and cautiously circled the block. With the side of the Packard in clear view, he rolled to a stop behind a parked Chevy.

Shan peered through the windshield around the coupe. Nick's driver remained at the wheel, but the passengers were gone.

The sign on the brick building read: *Jersey City Savings Bank.*

Nick wouldn't. Would he?

There was no alarm ringing. Surely a teller would have tripped one by now, if there was trouble.

Maybe, on Max's behalf, Nick was just making a large deposit. This would explain the duffel. A few companions with concealed weapons might be a standard precaution. That was assuming they were even inside. Shan hadn't actually seen where they went. They could have entered another business, perhaps for a meeting of some sort.

Shan's desire to believe the scenario stood at odds with his gut.

"Come on, Nick," he whispered. "Get your ass out here." He scanned the area, feeling like Barsetti would show up at any moment. This time, Shan almost wished the agent were here, to step in before things went too far.

Then came a popping sound. Three more followed in quick succession, confirmed by passersby, whose attention snapped toward the bank before they scattered for safety.

"Oh, God," Shan said. His heart pounded. He gripped the door handle, vacillating. He stared at the doors, breath held, until they flung open.

Sal and the thug rushed out. They wore black handkerchiefs from the noses down, each wielding a Tommy gun. With Sal toting the bag, presumably filled with loot, they scrambled into the Packard.

They couldn't leave without Nick.

Shan's mind raced with possible reasons for the delay. Finally the alarm started to ring and the Packard shot away. They swerved around the block, leaving their fourth man behind. Cops would descend any minute.

"Goddamn it." Shan jumped out of the truck and bolted across the street, barely missing a collision with a taxi. The cabbie honked, but Shan didn't stop until he made it into the bank. About a dozen people lay facedown, hands covering their hats and heads. The few who dared to look up cowered when Shan shouted, "Nick!"

He continued farther in and balked at the discovery of a uniformed guard sprawled over white tiles. A red puddle spread around the revolver in his limp hand.

"Nick," Shan yelled louder, panic mounting.

He spied an open door that led to the back side of the tellers' cages, surely the bank safe too. Near the threshold, drops of blood created a trail. He followed them through the doorway and found Nick seated on the floor against a wall. Nick raised a pistol to take aim, and Shan threw his arms up.

"Stop, Nick! It's me."

Bewilderment swirled in Nick's eyes as he lowered the pistol. "Tommy . . ." Above the black handkerchief pooled at his chin, the edges of his mouth slid up. "What are . . . how'd you . . ." His voice sounded weary, his strength draining.

Inside the trench coat, Nick's left hand held the right side of his waist. Shan dropped to a knee and pulled back the coat. Blood covered the white fabric of Nick's shirt, seeping red between his fingers.

Shan's heart was beating like fists in his chest. He peeked around the corner. There were whispers and small movements among the would-be hostages. Their fear was fading, their confidence growing. A gentleman with the look of a bank manager was gesturing to a stout fellow in factory clothes.

In the distance a siren wailed.

Shan needed to stall just long enough to get Nick to safety. He nabbed the pistol and leapt to his feet, transforming into a man of far greater stature. "Stay down, all of you!" He waved the weapon in the direction of the people but pointed the barrel at the wall above them. Gasps arose as folks dropped back down.

A matronly woman in a pink hat clasped her hands in prayer. Beside her, a teenage boy squeezed his eyes shut, his body flat and stiffened as if to disappear into the floor.

Shan wished it were that easy.

He hastened over to Nick. "You hang on to me, all right?" He didn't wait for a reply before grabbing Nick around the back and maneuvering him to stand. Nick groaned and his right arm tightened over Shan's shoulder.

"Easy does it," Shan said, and guided Nick in an awkward shuffle toward the door. "Just keep your hand on that wound."

"Yeah . . . okay . . ." Nick spoke through labored breaths. "Guess I really . . . screwed things up. Didn't I?"

"And you just figured that out?"

Nick started to laugh, cut short by a sharp inhale from the pain.

Shan knew this was hardly the time for jokes, but the alternative was to fully face the severity of the situation. They were halfway to the door when Nick stumbled. Shan fought to regain their balance.

The siren grew louder. The cops were almost here.

"C'mon, we're nearly out," Shan urged, resuming their steps.

"I'm sorry . . . about everything . . ."

"Keep moving, damn it! Don't slow down."

" 'Bout Josie too . . . I was so stupid . . . letting her go." The emotion in Nick's tone impelled Shan to look over. In all of their years together, it was the first time he'd ever seen tears in Nick's eyes.

Then a shot blasted from behind and those same eyes widened to a bulge. Nick grunted and collapsed, taking Shan to the floor with him. Shan barely comprehended what had happened before he twisted back to look. The factory man stood near the dead guard, pointing a blood-smeared revolver in Shan's direction.

The world instantly slowed.

Shan watched the man's thumb ease down

on the hammer, a millimeter at a time. The cylinder gradually rotated, moving a bullet into place. The resulting click became the sole sound on earth. He curled a forefinger around the trigger, and Shan closed his eyes, bracing for impact. Another shot rang out.

But he felt nothing.

It occurred to him that this lack of pain was a benefit of death. Yet when he opened his eyes, the factory man lay on the ground, gripping his leg.

Shan's gaze fell to the pistol in his own hand. He dropped the weapon, shocked by the realization of what he had done.

The thought was eclipsed by the startling view of Nick.

Facedown. Eyes closed.

No sign of breathing.

"Oh, Jesus, no . . ." Shan shook him once, twice, to rouse him. But Nick's body had gone limp, turned heavy as stone. Shan scrambled to find a pulse, searching his neck, his wrists. Where was it, damn it?

"Don't do this," Shan ordered, wanting to shout, yet the emotion knotting his throat reduced the words to a rasp. A futile plea. For he already knew.

Nick was gone.

In that moment, everything that had

divided them — the years and wrongs, the differences and confusions — all of it melted away. And they were simply two friends made brothers by fate or God, both of them granted a second chance. And they'd failed.

"This is the police!"

The announcement drew Shan back to his surroundings. A sea of policemen and their cars filled the view through the glass doors. One of them held a megaphone.

"Drop your weapons and come out with your hands high!"

Shan glanced around in a haze. The bank manager had come to the factory man's aid. On one knee, he said to Shan, "Son, it's over. Don't make this harder than it needs to be."

The man was right. It was over — in more ways than Shan could possibly grasp at that moment.

Guided by a sense of floating outside his own body, he slowly rose, parting with Nick a final time, and raised his hands in surrender.

38

If there was a single element that carried Shan through the events after the robbery, it was his experience from performing. He was accustomed to the vulnerable nakedness of standing alone on a stage. From off nights in particular, when subjected to a cold crowd, he had gained a protective shell that kept reality at a distance.

For now, this included even the Capellos.

They did their best to support him through the trial, of course. Aside from helping him acquire a lawyer — the Italian son of old friends from their church — Lina and her parents sat vigilantly week after week in court. When escorted in, Shan would give a cursory nod in acknowledgment of their fretful greetings; he did the same after their encouraging words each time he was ushered out. All the same, he made a point of avoiding their faces, afraid his armor would shatter from the grief in their eyes. Or worse yet, gratitude for his attempt to help.

In a brief visit at the county jail where he was being held, Mr. Capello assured him that he and his wife had learned the truth from Lina, about rumors of a debt to Max, and that Shan wasn't to blame.

Shan didn't argue, despite knowing otherwise. The irony was, if he hadn't interfered, Clive Smead — the factory man, now on his way to a full recovery — might not have seen a reason to play the hero, instead leaving that role for the cops. In such a feeble state, Nick likely wouldn't have resisted.

If only Shan had ignored the telegram, stayed on the circuit, delayed his trip . . .

Worthless hypotheticals. There was no reversing the past.

He was put on trial for armed robbery of a bank, assault with a deadly weapon, and assault with the intent to kill. Although Shan wasn't innocent in the case, neither did he feel guilty of all those crimes. Nevertheless, his lawyer recommended they accept a plea bargain. And he wasn't the only one.

"Kid, you're not the one they're after," Agent Barsetti said through the bars of Shan's cell, prior to the first hearing. "For what it's worth, I don't believe you had anything to do with knocking off that bank. But my gut says you know who else was involved."

On his bunk, Shan sat with gaze fixed on the stained concrete floor. Whether Max had ordered the robbery as a means of repayment or his guys had pulled the job on their own, all paths led to Max Trevino, and Shan wasn't about to hand over a map.

Barsetti squatted to Shan's level, hands clasped, elbows on his thighs. "Tommy, look. I'm gonna be square with you. I never gave a shit about Trevino's booze. Hell, I was raised on more wine than milk myself." He paused, took a breath. "Thing is, my sister's son Vincent was a good kid. But he got mixed up with the wrong guys, like your brother. Wound up doing dirty work for Black Handers."

Recalling the ruthless extortionists known for "protective services" and kidnapping ransoms, Shan raised his eyes. He turned toward Barsetti, who then continued.

"Years ago, my sister came to me, asking for help. See, Vincent wanted out. But Trevino beat me to it — apparently he didn't like when competition invaded his turf. Vincent washed up in Newark Bay. We never found his missing pal, but I'd venture to guess he ain't on vacation. Point being, I promised my sister I'd do everything in my power to take down the son of a bitch responsible."

At last Shan understood Barsetti's true drive. For him, it was a personal matter.

But then, the same could be said for Shan. "Agent, I wish I could help you . . . I just can't."

Barsetti came back gruffly: "They're gonna put you away, kid. Use you as an example. You get that? We're talkin' hard time unless you give them what they want." He shook his head and glanced away. Part of his frustration at least seemed rooted in genuine concern for Shan. "Just throw 'em a bone, for Christ's sake. One name. Simple as that."

But he was wrong. Nothing was that easy.

The day after the arrest, a guard stopped by Shan's cell, said he wanted to make sure everything was comfortable. It felt oddly accommodating until the guard added that if Shan spotted any rats slinking around to feel free to give them a good stomp, that inmates tended to best handle those kinds of problems themselves.

The warning about snitches wasn't lost on Shan. He could have guessed who'd sent it even before seeing Max seated in a back row at the trial. Not that Shan needed any more incentive.

A plea bargain might land him a lighter sentence. But as a verifiable rat, he'd be putting his life in jeopardy, along with those of the Capellos. He decided to take his chances with the jury.

Shan did question that choice, however, when Clive Smead was rolled to the stand in a wheelchair, causing a few jurors to gasp. The bulky cast on the man's leg might have been standard for a wounded thigh, but the impression it made was not in Shan's favor.

Nor was the sight of the pistol Shan had used, held up by the prosecutor's gloved fingertips. While Shan was relieved to learn only one bullet had been fired from the handgun, absolving Nick of murder, the dried smear of Nick's blood on the handle still churned Shan's stomach.

That feeling continued when a mournful teller took the stand, describing the bank guard being murdered by the stocky thug. "His wife died years ago," she added, "so he'd spend every weekend doing projects around the community, or feeding pigeons at Central Park."

Again Shan clung to his armor. Without it, his want for justice surely would have broken him, causing him to spill it all.

Other witnesses from the bank testified,

most recounting their ordeal with intense passion. They each pointed at Shan to identify the man who had threatened them all by waving a gun their way, ordering them to stay down, although none could assuredly place him among the three original robbers.

Except for the matron. In a different pink hat, she adamantly claimed Shan had departed in his mask before returning for his brother.

Shan's first thought was that she'd been coerced. But her sincerity shone through; she truly believed her testimony. For this Shan couldn't blame her. Memory, after all, was funny that way. A person could convince himself of just about anything if he wanted to believe enough, especially when seeking comfort and security. And that was what his conviction meant to her: a major step toward restoration of her prior world, where a bad guy was caught and punished for his crimes.

The opportunity finally came for the defense to make its case.

Each of the Capellos sought to testify on Shan's behalf, but his lawyer urged them to refrain. As immediate family members of two accused bank robbers, he explained as delicately as possible, their tainted credibility would not benefit their cause. If anything, the fact that they'd permitted Shan to work at a questionable supper club at a young age might suggest that his parents had set the course for both sons' demise.

Instead the defense called upon Mr. Bagley. No doubt, the man was irritated to be summoned from his tour, though to his credit he hid it well. His testimony was to refute the allegation that Shan's plan of a mere daylong visit, after nine years away from his family, exhibited a premeditated effort to flee after the robbery. The prosecution had submitted Shan's return train ticket, found in his pocket during the arrest, as Exhibit C.

"I reminded him he had a contract to fulfill, so he'd better be back soon," Bagley affirmed, a mild paraphrasing of his stern legal threat. He went on to admit that Shan had cited a "family emergency" as his reason for the trip: a vague request with no specifics. Bagley was hardly the sort to care for anyone's personal details, yet the prosecutor skipped past that point and jumped at the chance to establish Shan's line of work, highlighting the immoral nature of burlesque as an apt reflection of his character. Photographs of the more industrious acts, including a hammock number starring Kitty Lovely — Shan's "nightly hotel companion" — further increased the jurors' looks of disdain.

By the time Bagley stepped down, Shan thought the only witness who could do more damage was Paddy O'Hooligan.

He was soon corrected.

Despite her bias as a longtime friend, Josie took the stand. She had a determination about her. The way she avoided Shan's eyes, he sensed guilt at the core of her mission, a duty to contain the fallout of a single telegram.

In her testimony, she verified that the gap between Shan's train arrival and visit with the Capellos wasn't spent scheming with criminals, but catching up with her over a cup of coffee.

"Just ask our waiter at the Oyster Bar, if you don't believe me." She exuded confidence and took great care not to delve into their actual talk at the restaurant, let alone Max's dealings. The girl was no dummy. She focused on Shan's strength of character: stellar grades and a clean record, working devotedly for his father, trading goods for customers who had fallen on hard times.

A couple of jurors even gave smiles of approval, all of which dissolved when the assistant DA got his turn at a cross-examination. Digging around into Josie's life had somehow uncovered her rocky past as a runaway, her tendency to "keep company with shady men" — a painful reference to the Jewish boy she had reportedly killed in an act of self-defense — and more recently her indiscretion with Shan.

"Well — yes, but we stopped right away," Josie asserted. "Tommy and I, we knew it was a mistake."

"Oh, certainly, Miss Penaro. I understand. And you were both sorry about it, I'm sure."

"That's right."

"Probably felt real guilty about it too."

"Yes. Of course we did."

"So guilty, in fact, that his brother, Tommy here, might feel obligated one day to make it up to him. Wouldn't you say?"

Shan's lawyer raised an objection, insisting Miss Penaro couldn't possibly be expected to testify what his client was or was not feeling. The judge sustained the motion and the prosecutor rested, but the damage was done. Shan could sense the collective conclusion solidifying among the jury: well intentioned or not, Tommy Capello had a motive.

And they found him guilty.

On all counts.

Before handing down the sentence, the judge asked if the defendant would care to speak. Shan managed to stand, fending off the pain of hearing Lina and her mother sniffling back tears. He apologized for wounding Mr. Smead. Never meaning to hurt anyone, he was only trying to help.

For this, he got twenty-five years.

More than two decades in a federal pen.

39

The judge sent him to Kansas.

At least Shan liked to think of it that way, conjuring a more pleasant image of fields and farmhouses than the reality of Leavenworth. More than once, restlessly dozing on his Army-style cot, he'd imagined himself on a Broadway stage in *The Wizard of Oz*. A few clicks of his heels and he would wake from the nightmare that had become his life. A life too grim to include others.

"You've got no business being in a place like this," he said to Lina a month into his sentence. In the visiting room, every chair was filled at the long chain of tables.

"I could say the same for you." She smiled with strained levity.

It had taken her a streetcar, two buses, and three days of train rides. Far too much to brave on her own. He was about to tell her so when she reached over the chin-high glass dividing them, seeking a connection.

Shan hesitated, afraid of jeopardizing the armor he needed now more than ever.

"Hands back!" a guard barked.

Lina pulled away. It was the only time she flinched in spite of her surroundings. The powdery scent of her perfume clashed with the room's stench of sweat and despair.

"How are Ma and Pop?" Shan diverted, part of him wishing he had taken her hand.

"They're doing all right." Her answer sounded genuine, for which he was grateful. "Of course, they'd be better if you were home."

Unlike Shan, she hadn't given up.

"We *can* still appeal this," she insisted, the same message from her letters.

"Lina, I told you. There's no point."

Even his lawyer had agreed that unless the faces of the accomplices were suddenly jogged from Shan's memory, the ruling was sure to stand. Besides, where injustice was concerned he was hardly unique. Every inmate at Leavenworth claimed he'd gotten a bum rap.

"Anyway," he told her, "it's not as bad here as you'd think."

At times that was true.

Other times, it was worse.

He spent his days surrounded by every form of criminal, from small-time to big.

Roughly three thousand, in fact — housed in a prison built for half as many. With just seventy guards, inmates had to look out for themselves.

The day after his visit with Lina, Shan was released from "A&O," the admissions and orientation cells reserved for new arrivals, and joined the general population. A fellow called "Mitty," built like a former lineman, invited him to share a cell. At first Shan was wary of any inmate seeking too close of a companion, but soon discovered the guy just craved fresh company. What's more, he had Italian roots. No different than in Brooklyn, guys here took care of their own.

Serving a ten-bit for racketeering along with some lesser offenses, Mitty would rattle on like a jalopy about old pals and sweethearts and fellow inmates of notoriety, but he was also generous with advice. He'd list off which meals, cons, guards — called "screws" or "hacks" — and work details to avoid. Otherwise, you followed the rules and stuck to the routine, always with ears and eyes open.

It helped when Shan picked up on the jargon. For some reason everything in the pen had a nickname. Shan's, for example, became "Monkey" — for one con anyhow.

It was Shan's second Saturday with the

population. On the recreation yard, a guy named "Pudge" used his heftier middle to bar Shan from passing. "I hear you was in the circus. Like one of those dancing monkeys. How 'bout you show us some of your tricks."

Shan felt stares stacking up around him. He shook his head. "It wasn't the circus."

He'd only meant to correct the misunderstanding, which must have evolved from the few tidbits he'd shared with Mitty, but the darkening of Pudge's eyes said that wasn't how it was received.

"You saying I'm a liar? Huh? That it?"

More stares, more tension. More inmates edging over. He could see them drooling for a fight, no doubt putting their bets on the challenger. While Shan might be quicker, Pudge's physique gave him an obvious upper hand.

Shan cut a glance toward the catwalk. The nearest guard held a rifle across his chest, his attention roaming elsewhere.

"What's wrong, Monkey?" Pudge sneered. "You all outta words? Maybe a few cracks to the skull will knock some outta ya."

Shan's stomach tightened, reverting to the bundle of knots that had only partly loosened since his first, endless night in prison. Reason and diplomacy held no value here.

Yet an alternative remained. A skill he had relied upon time and again for survival.

The men wanted a show. And Shan the monkey would oblige.

Crouching down, he battled back with the wild movements and "ooh-ooh" sounds of an ape. After all, any vaudeville acts starring animals — real ones, at least — had always been a hit.

Sudden confusion contorted Pudge's face. "Knock it off," he ordered, but his flustered words spurred chuckles among the incarcerated audience. When Shan pretended to eat a flea from Pudge's back, the laughter escalated. Goaded to anger, Pudge took a swing at Shan, whose squatting position made it easy to duck. Hecklers called out over a ragged rhythm of claps. Pudge appeared to gear up for a second strike, his thick neck reddening, but the alert sounded over the speaker.

Time to line up and return to their cells.

A guard hollered down from the catwalk. "You heard it! Fall in!" He drew down on his rifle, a warning Pudge heeded with reluctance.

In a comedic sketch, two contentious characters often shook on a truce, sometimes winding up pals. But that wasn't how real life worked, certainly not at Leaven-worth.

"Better watch yourself," Mitty told Shan as they made their way inside. "Jokes are nice and all, but only for so long. Take a beatin', they'll label you weak. Get pegged as a coward, and you're done for. And not just by Pudge."

Shan nodded, though he preferred an option that didn't require being pummeled.

As it turned out, there was nothing Pudge wanted to do more. By suppertime the next day, his thirst for revenge outweighed any threat of consequences. In the mess hall he marched over in front of everyone — surely that was the point — and tossed Shan from his seat. When Shan scrambled to stand, Pudge walloped him in the jaw and voices erupted through the room.

Shan's vision went hazy, yet still he detected eyes of judgment surrounding him. Heeding Mitty's warning, he summoned his strength and charged back, plowing Pudge into another table. Food splattered about, and a ricochet of punches flew between them. The blows to Shan's body no doubt caused more damage than the reverse. So much so, he felt relief when guards flattened them to the ground.

Shan, same as Pudge, was sent to solitary.

A barren single cell, the "hole" contained a sink-and-stool unit and nothing else. A mattress was provided in the evening, removed at dawn. The two meals a day were served cold in a loaf pan, piled up like pig slop. He was warned to finish every bite.

It wasn't a mansion, but in a distant life Shan had lived in a manner not much better. In a way, given the rare semblance of privacy, he welcomed the reprieve. He just wished the quiet hours didn't revive so many thoughts of Nick, of their last minutes together, of the Capellos losing another son.

Then again, what was Shan doing now if not atoning for it all?

By the third week in the hole, the sense of nostalgia and privacy had run its course. By the fourth week, Shan had recited every comedic act he'd ever performed at least fifty times. While this helped pass the hours, mostly he did it to keep from going mad. He was starting to doubt anything could prevent that when the cell door swung open.

His thirty days were up.

Upon his return to the general population, finally showered and shaven, he noticed small signs of approval. An acknowledging look, a flick of a nod. A hierarchy ruled Leavenworth, as it did throughout history wherever humans reigned. Although Shan was far from the top — such spots being reserved for the FBI's Most Wanted — he appreciated not scraping the bottom.

"Consider it an initiation," Mitty told him with a toothy grin.

Pudge had a different take. For him, the conflict was far from over. His steely glares made that abundantly clear.

Shan tried his damnedest to avoid crossing paths, a strategy that didn't always work. On several occasions, Pudge closed in on Shan with a spew of taunts, looking to finish the job he'd started. But before they could go to swings, a guard's presence cut the scraps short. Only twice did they make it to brawling. In both instances a couple of cons, including Mitty, were able to break up the fight before an approaching guard could intervene.

So far, Shan's injuries hadn't surpassed small cuts and hefty bruises, but it wasn't going to stay that way. Pudge's filed-down toothbrush, which Shan had barely dodged during the last scuffle, indicated as much.

Now seated in the library, watching Pudge enter the room, Shan was tempted to keep quiet. Instead he found himself declaring, "Ah, shit. Too bad we're fresh out of picture books." Though he didn't direct this straight at Pudge, the guy's flushed face said he understood the target, as did other cons, who snickered over their magazines. If not for the deputy warden popping in right then, nothing would have held Pudge back.

Really, Shan wasn't looking to make things worse. He'd just spent enough of his life in fear. In contrast to his days with Uncle Will, he now had the guts and ability to fight back.

To be fair, a portion of that courage did stem from knowing Pudge was serving time for money laundering and extortion, rather than first-degree murder. But as a bonus, so long as the rivalry continued, hopefully those convicted of the latter would show no interest in Shan.

Amazingly, now at the three-month mark, the whole situation had become endurable. The risks and rules, the guards and cons. Shan was reflecting on this thought when a letter arrived from Mrs. Capello. It was similar to all her others, full of kindness, concern, and updates of daily life. Yet in that moment, entombed in his cage of concrete and bars, something about her words seized him; it was the searing realization that this would be his life for the next fifteen to twenty-five years. What would be left of him when he was finally released?

He suppressed his anguish until Mitty departed with the majority of the other inmates for the weekly picture show in the auditorium. Then Shan sank into the corner of his cell and let his tears spill over. The wallowing didn't last. For here came Pudge, strolling right in, armed with more than a toothbrush.

"Lookee what we got here," he said, gripping a short steel pipe at his side. It was the leg of a cot, its wooden peg filed to a point. "You needin' your mama now? Huh, Monkey?"

Against the wall, Shan was trapped. A few guards and inmates no doubt remained in the vicinity, but none in immediate view. To survive he needed to get out.

He was scurrying to his feet when Pudge swung the spear like a bat. Shan threw his arms up and the metal slammed his left forearm. The stunning pain didn't stop him from going after the weapon. They fought for control, all four hands on the pipe, until Pudge kneed him in the stomach. The impact knocked Shan to the floor. Though curled up and gasping for breath, he saw that Pudge was determined to finally follow through with cracking his skull, or maybe driving a stake right through it.

Glimpsing the sink, Shan discovered his

only hope. He scrambled to reach under the bowl, where Mitty stored a shank in a narrow divot in the wall. As Pudge moved in, Shan pulled the blade loose and swiped wildly while rising. He sliced Pudge across the chest, sending the bastard stumbling backward. As he fell to the ground, his head hit the bunk, and the cot leg went rolling. His eyes had gone dazed. Blood seeped into his shirt.

The sight should have stalled Shan, even ceased him altogether. But in that moment, his despair turned to wrath in a way he'd thought would never happen again, and he found himself kicking Pudge's gut, harder and harder, fueled by a consuming fury. A black, sinister rage over everything he'd lost, the hurt he'd caused others, the choices that could never be reversed.

And suddenly it was over.

His memory of the fight ended there.

Shan awoke in the hole with pounding aches in his forearm and head. A solid, tender bump inches above his ear denoted a strike from a guard's billy club. Pudge would be punished too, Shan learned, but only after returning from the hospital ward. According to the inmate who delivered Shan's meals, the sum of the damage was a concussion, two broken ribs, and several stitches to the chest. His tone indicated that Shan should feel proud. Or at minimum, justified.

Shan didn't feel a thing — perhaps the scariest part of all.

A week later, stinking, bedraggled, and still beat up to hell, he was delivered to the deputy warden. The man didn't hide his agitation over Shan and Pudge's disruptions.

"As I understand things," he said, planted behind his desk, "you've become the primary instigator, suggesting your time in solitary is doing little good."

Shan grinned widely at the joke of it, which the deputy warden mistook for mocking. His eyes and voice tightened.

"Considering your possession of a knife and the condition Elmer was left in, I can only assume this won't be the last of your outbursts. The nature of your criminal conviction also speaks volumes."

On paper, Shan's robbery and attempted murder raps certainly topped Pudge's smaller ones. An ironic coup. But in that moment, all Shan could think about was Pudge's name being Elmer. The disparity, paired with sleep deprivation, actually made Shan laugh.

"All of this to say," the warden cut in

gruffly, "one of you needs a more suitable location."

There was no questioning which of the two he'd chosen.

40

They called it "Devil's Island."

Shan discovered why before even stepping foot on Alcatraz. He still recalled the day he was ferried over with the other new "fish" on the prison launch. Bound in handcuffs and leg irons, they'd rattled in their seats while cutting through the choppy bay. San Francisco had disappeared behind them, the fog creating a sense of being swallowed, forgotten.

Then up ahead, a guard tower had poked through the mottled grayness. A rocky shoreline had eased into view, followed by the formidable fortress, which appeared suspended in midair.

Cons considered this the end of the line. To Shan, that was precisely how it felt.

A former military prison, Alcatraz was intended to house the most incorrigible of the incorrigibles. Sometimes, word had it, a guard with a grudge was all it took to get slapped with a transfer to the Rock. But then, no cons here were angels. More than a handful of them were gangsters who'd made headlines for years, their convictions no small triumph for J. Edgar Hoover. And, of course, there were those deemed escape risks.

If Warden Johnston took pride in one aspect above all, it was the "escape-proof" title he had managed to maintain. Shan got this clear from the start. The man seemed to have thought of everything: constant standing counts, single cells with tool-proof bars, limited visitations through bulletproof glass, hawklike supervision — to the point of one guard for every three inmates. The strictness of his regimen was like no other. Rules dictated length of hair, how to eat, where to sit, when to shave, shit, and shower. Not even the way to wear a shirt was optional: only top button unfastened, sleeves always down.

"Abide by your handbooks there, and we'll all get along just fine," the warden announced during orientation. With the looks of a banker, he wore a suit and spectacles, his hair dove white. His manner seemed rather mild for a man controlling every facet of their lives, and that included their knowledge.

All current events were kept from prisoners through bans on radios and the censorship of mail, evidenced by marks in letters from the Capellos. Newspapers, too, were prohibited, as they featured ads that had supposedly facilitated escapes at other prisons, a tactic that would never have occurred to Shan.

Still, none of this had prevented "Dutch" Bowers from scaling a chain-link fence in the spring of '36. Assigned to incinerator detail, he'd been outside burning garbage. Shan had been on the island six months and was working nearby in the laundry. Through a barred window, he had watched the guy ignore warning shots from a tower guard. The next bullet sent Bowers plummeting seventy feet to his death on the jagged rocks below.

Warden Johnston called it an escape attempt, a cautionary tale for others with rabbit in their veins. Some inmates said Bowers had simply lost his marbles and was trying to feed the gulls. To Shan, it seemed a blatant act of suicide. Whatever the case, after a year at Alcatraz the fellow had hit his limit, and understandably so.

Sure, the confinement was no picnic, with a five-by-nine cell that seemed to shrink every day, the stench god-awful from a salt-water-filled john. The relentless monotony could test any man's endurance. But the real torture came from the "Rule of Silence."

Some softer guards looked the other way when it came to whispers here and there. Except for the yard and industry buildings, however, talking was prohibited. A rule that only heightened the feeling of isolation.

Many a night, struggling to sleep through inmates' snores and the bellowing foghorn, Shan lamented the absence of Mitty's company. Although Shan had forbidden the Capellos from ever making the trek, part of him regretted doing so. He missed their voices, their laughter. The sounds of his life had been reduced to cues from guards' whistles, shoes marching over tiers, the squawking of seagulls. Not to mention the thunderous rack of automated cell doors. At Alcatraz, one never had to ask why it was called the slammer.

But then January brought a change.

After more than a year of the same old grind, Shan digested the news with wary skepticism. The silence rule had been lifted — or rather, "relaxed" was the phrase Warden Johnston used. No singing or yelling would be tolerated, and definitely no whistling, but speaking in a respectful manner and at normal volume was allowed.

Rumors credited politicians and reporters for contending that severe rules at Alcatraz were causing insanity. The argument arose after an inmate chopped off his fingers with a hatchet. Doubtful cons claimed he'd faked the loony bit to earn a transfer to a cushy hospital. Either way, none of them were complaining. The result benefited them all.

At first Shan just listened to their abounding chatter. It seemed their stored-up tales couldn't pour out fast enough. For the curious types, the same went for questions.

One evening, from the next cell, a young, jovial con known as Digs said, "Capello, can I ask you something?"

"Why not. It's a free country." The irony seemed missed on the guy.

"Fellas here, they say you laid out some loudmouth at Leavenworth twice your size. Put him in the infirmary for months. That true?"

The account involving Pudge had apparently followed Shan and expanded along the way. At that point, he saw no upside to deflating the story.

"So they say," was his reply.

When first transferred, Shan had dreaded the possibility that Pudge might have pals on the Rock hankering for revenge. Or that a new initiation might land him in the morgue. This was, after all, Alcatraz. Readying himself, Shan had traded cigarettes for a shank made by a con in the blacksmith shop. Made of brass, the common weapon was somehow immune to the metal detectors, or "snitch boxes," and hid well in a sock.

Not once, though, had Shan needed to wield it. Perhaps the exaggerated tale, more than his grim stoicism, had forged a shield. A lone reason to be grateful to Pudge.

Under the altered rule, Shan was gradually finding his voice. He was never the type to beat his gums like Mitty, but neither did he wish to become so detached he'd take an axe to his own hand. Al Capone, once one of the most highly feared mobsters, served as another reminder.

Initially "Scarface" would shoot the breeze with other cons, strum his banjo during yard time. But these days, he spent many of those hours withdrawn in his cell, sometimes mumbling to no one. Which was exactly what he was doing now.

Shan caught a peek while on his way to the picture show. Held upstairs in the auditorium, it was a monthly event few cons missed, if only for a change of pace and scenery. For many, the actual film wasn't the attraction.

Requiring the chaplain's approval, the features invariably starred the likes of Shirley Temple and Buster Keaton over Jean Harlow and Clark Gable. No crime, no skin, no violence. But Shan didn't mind; they reminded him of his vaudeville days, a life outside of these walls. A time when he possessed not only freedom, but also a sense of control — over himself and the audience. He would pull their strings and make them laugh. Make them gasp or cheer.

He was remembering this as he watched *Our Relations* flicker on the screen, with Laurel and Hardy churning out their gags. A year or two after Shan moved to the States, he had seen Stan Laurel in a variety show in Manhattan. The guy's comedy sketch had been in the same vein as Shan's.

Boy, how different their lives had turned out.

The inmates broke into laughter, snagging Shan's attention. Laurel and Hardy were conspiring in a telephone booth when a drunken man squeezed in to answer a call. As he slurred over the phone, the comic duo tried to wrangle their way out. Their pushing and pulling toppled the whole booth, and the crowd howled again.

Shan was savoring that sound, even more

than the show, when the film halted. Stunned silence lasted only a moment before several in the room grumbled, "Not this again."

In the dimness, an older con in charge of the event scurried to the projector in the back of the room. Digs joined him as usual, ever handy with gadgets. Borrowing an officer's flashlight, they investigated the issue as others quietly chatted.

After ten or so minutes, "Ranger Roy" — the inmates' name for the well-liked lieutenant from Texas — made an announcement from the front. "Well, boys. Looks like we're not having luck this time. Reckon we'll have to wait till next month."

A sprinkling of boos surfaced, intermixed with orders that Digs hurry up and fix the dang thing. Some guy joked that he wanted his quarter back.

"Y'all hush down, now," Ranger Roy said.

Digs declared, "All we need is a screwdriver. Something's stuck in the part that feeds the reel."

Ranger Roy exhaled, dubious. Before he could refuse, Digs added, "In the meantime, Capello there can tell some jokes. Keep everyone entertained while we wait for the tool."

All attention cut to Shan. His muscles

stiffened, shackling him to his chair. He should have guessed that if his brawling tales had reached the cell house, other details would have too.

Several cons urged him to get up. A trickle of clapping swiftly gained momentum. Surely many in the group had no idea about Shan's history onstage. It was the threat of returning to their cells that made them instant fans.

Ranger Roy raised a brow at him, asking, *Well?*

As with everything in Alcatraz, there was little choice. Unless Shan wanted to make an enemy of every con in the room, he had better scrape together a few jokes and fast.

Nerves prickled his insides as he rose from his seat. A guy in his row directed him to the front, where white light illuminated the screen. Shan would have dismissed the suggestion except the walk gave him a chance to compile his thoughts.

Once there, he winced at the glare of the projector's beam, and it nearly caused him to stumble. Then it came to him.

Shan proceeded to stagger around, transforming into the drunk in the picture show. An inmate was quick to point this out, and curiosity turned to amusement. Slurring, Shan expressed his need to get home to his wife — after he remembered where he lived, that was — and if he had a wife!

Laughter in the room propelled him to continue. As he went to speak, he interjected a hiccup and started his sentence all over again. It doubled as a stall tactic to form the next joke, earning even greater laughs.

From his view in the spotlight, the faces in the shadows could have belonged to any audience, the auditorium to any cozy theater. And for a moment, Shan was just an entertainer.

But one who could bomb — with greater consequence — if he didn't keep it up.

He swiftly dismissed mimicking Laurel and Hardy; tackling them solo was a risk. Someone like Charlie Chaplin was safer, his famed Tramp character beloved by most. Hoping that held true in the pen, Shan switched to pantomime and straightened his invisible bow tie. Then he gave a signal to wait with his pointer finger and glanced around for a makeshift cane, but found none. Instead, drawing on the film *The Gold Rush,* he pulled off his shoe and reenacted the Tramp eating a boiled boot as if dining on barbecued ribs.

Some con yelled, "In the Atlanta pen, that's about how the mush tasted too!"

And they all laughed, including the guards.

Shan yanked off his second shoe. With a hand inserted into each, he pretended they were bread rolls and guided them in a dance as Chaplin once had. As the laughs continued, so did Shan's act. In the attic of his mind, an old trunk had opened. Characters returned to him like costumes mothballed for seasons. From memories of live shows and two-reel comedies, he became Groucho Marx with waggling brows and an imaginary cigar; Buster Keaton as a deadpanning cowboy.

By the time Digs proclaimed the projector had been fixed, Shan had forgotten his sole purpose of filling in. He took a bow and the room applauded, some fellows still chuckling. Shan reclaimed his seat in the sea of blue chambray shirts. Buzzing with an old familiar high, he found it difficult to focus on the film.

Afterward, when they were lined up to turn out, Shan was rewarded with compliments and pats on the back. But then, like every other con, he stood at his cell to be counted, and waited for the steel bars to slam.

41

A boyhood dream: Shan had finally made it to Broadway.

Just not the one he'd envisioned.

Broadway was the nickname for the main corridor between B and C blocks; it led to an area featuring a clock, suitably dubbed Times Square. When his chain had first arrived at Alcatraz, they were paraded down that thoroughfare in nothing but their birthday suits. The whole cell house had welcomed them with a rarely tolerated ruckus of hollers, wolf whistles, and tin cups clanking on bars.

Two years later Shan still lived there, on the bottom tier, known as "the flats." In addition to the extreme lack of privacy, the area was least desirable for the chill inherent in its long, slick stretch of cement — which made Ranger Roy's gift such a gem.

One night after Shan's impromptu act at the February picture show, the lieutenant caught Shan shivering too hard to sleep. Ranger Roy ordered a quiet guard known as "Yappy" to scrounge up a blanket thicker than standard issue. The task varied greatly from Yappy's usual deliveries of a few knocks to the head if an inmate was too disruptive, namely the loony ones, referred to as "bugs," who would otherwise make quacking sounds or repeat a single phrase for hours on end. Shan accepted the blanket with gratitude; it was the first time on the Rock he slept straight until morning.

Of course, this wasn't the sole reason he agreed to perform again. While a cruel jolt of reality would follow each sampling of his vaudevillian glory, any escape was better than none. On standby for projector glitches, he would also serve as a warm-up for the films.

Naturally, this required permission from Warden Johnston, who granted an allotment of ten minutes, no more. On the day he swung by for a personal look, this meant cutting Shan off mid-gag. The low lighting had prevented a gauge of the man's reactions, but they must have been favorable enough; soon after, Ranger Roy invited Shan to perform at the Officers' Club for the guards and their wives — "invited" being another word for "commanded." Really, how could he have declined?

In that regard, Pudge's crack about Shan being a dancing monkey wasn't too far off the mark. But at least Shan had new activities to occupy his thoughts.

Prior to the engagement, the deputy warden gave such a stern warning — as if any sane con would make trouble in that particular company — Shan could barely contain his nerves. But a few jokes in, laughter once more proved itself a universal need, as exhibited in any giggling baby. Incidentally, that was just how one heavyset wife sounded when she laughed to the point of tears. It appeared all residents on the island, even family members of the staff, craved a break from the norm.

Shan realized how comfortable he'd become when he nearly used the giggling woman as a spontaneous comedic target, a potential mistake. As was true when entertaining the cons, while mimicking or mocking, it was best not to offend people with the power to beat or stab you, or toss you in the hole.

The discretion paid off. Shan was asked to perform at the club twice more before being called to the warden's office. Though he was certain he'd done nothing wrong, the trip still made him question it until

Johnston stated his purpose. "I'll be hosting a birthday celebration for my wife next week, down at our house, and she'd very much like you to liven up the festivities."

Struck with as much surprise as relief, Shan tripped over his answer. "Y-yes, sir. Of course, sir. I'd be honored."

"Some very dignified friends will be coming from the mainland." Johnston removed his glasses from his mottled, blue-veined nose and wiped the lenses with his handkerchief. "Therefore, I'm confident I don't have to explain how important it is that you continue your model behavior."

He was right about that, and Shan didn't disappoint in any way.

In fact, promptly afterward, Mrs. Johnston made a point of finding him in the kitchen, where he was packing up to leave. By then, he had acquired a passable tuxedo made by cons in the tailor shop, with handy pockets for small props like a fan and harmonica. He'd even acquired a hooked cane and shoes with wooden taps, thanks to the carpenter and cobbler shops.

"That was lovely, just lovely," Mrs. Johnston said. She resembled one of his schoolmarms from Ireland, with her broad shoulders and glasses, her graying hair and downturned lips. Yet in contrast, she raised her lips pleasantly and shook his hand as she would any welcomed guest. For a moment, he almost forgot he'd been marched down from "up top."

In turn, Shan offered genuine compliments on her lavish home. Adorned with sleek, black-walnut furnishings created by inmates, the Spanish Mission–style mansion was said to contain an astounding fourteen rooms and scores of fireplaces. She smiled at his words but truly brightened when he lauded the Victorian garden in her side yard.

Soon they were discussing her blackberries and roses and poppies. Shan suggested red-hot pokers and snapdragons might do well in the seaside climate, as he recalled learning about their heartiness during the many hours he'd spent in the community garden in Brooklyn.

With his knowledge on the topic, Mrs. Johnston assumed he had been assigned to gardening detail. He told her he'd applied but was still on garbage duty. While he was grateful to have earned an outdoor job, growing plants would beat collecting trash any day.

"Well, perhaps we can do something about that," she said, just as Ranger Roy appeared to escort him back.

Mrs. Johnston proved true to her word.

Within days Shan received a work change. He was reassigned to a greenhouse on the east side of the island, down by the water tower. The improvements he made and hopeless plants he revived didn't go unnoticed. In fact, when the con assigned to the warden's garden and greenhouse shipped off to be paroled, his duties were transferred to Shan. This, in effect, promoted him to passman, one of the few handpicked cons who worked at the warden's residence. The other passmen primarily cleaned and cooked at the mansion. Shan obtained the rank faster than usual, thanks to his model behavior and uncommonly short criminal record. But mainly he credited a referral by Mrs. Johnston, even supported by the deputy warden and several guards. It was fascinating how easily humor fostered trust and likability.

Since his gardening work spanned the latter half of the day, starting at the warden's house and ending at the water tower, he served as a library orderly in the mornings. His literary knowledge often enabled him to match an inmate's tastes with a number of fitting books, a skill even public enemies like "Creepy" Karpis appreciated. As a perk, Shan had first pick of any new titles that arrived. By far the most popular books centered on lessons in bridge.

Inmates spent so many hours in their cells; aside from dreaming up escapes, the most common pastimes were smoking, reading, and playing games. Shan used his own tobacco rations solely for trade, exchanging hand-rolled smokes for a smuggled Hershey's bar or Jujubes. But with games as much as books, he was right in the thick of it.

After lockdown, he and Digs would often play checkers or chess from their respective cells, both with their own boards and pieces, calling out their moves. Bridge, though, was the cell house obsession. For many, that game became all they gabbed about, night and day. A caged man, more than anyone, needed a focal point to keep from going berserk.

Thanks to years of gaming strategies against Nick, Shan wound up winning three tournaments on the yard. There, cons were allowed to compete with specially marked wooden dominoes. Not only were they practical against the wind, but they also lacked the flammable coating found on playing cards.

As usual, nothing got past Warden Johnston.

Well . . . make that almost nothing.

42

"What's the hurry, Capello? You got a date?"

Shan stopped. He gripped the handle on the basket of tomatoes he'd emptied and turned back to Bert. The towheaded forger from Ohio stood in the warden's kitchen, wiping his hands on a dishcloth. The other passman, "Lefty," was distracted across the room.

Shan shrugged, trying to discern what Bert knew. "Just got a lot to get done."

"Plants aren't going nowhere, unless you're growing beanstalks." Bert's words were slightly garbled between bites of carrot. "I can whip you up a snack if you like."

The direction of the topic put Shan at ease. "I'm fine, thanks —"

"Shh," Lefty cut in. "I'm trying to listen here." In a white house jacket and trousers, a match to Bert's outfit, the counterfeiter from Boston had reddish-brown hair and a small scar on his chin. He was hunched over the kitchen table, cleaning. Or at least toweling the same spot over and over while leaning toward the swinging door to keep tabs on the Red Sox.

Every so often, Mrs. Johnston would just so happen to leave the radio on in the parlor at a volume that could reach the kitchen, particularly during a ballgame. Newspapers, likewise, were sometimes left lying around for quick perusal. The woman was nothing if not generous.

Shan was about to head out when he recognized a name.

"Here's Lazzeri, giving it another go," the broadcaster said. The Yankee slugger still ranked among Mr. Capello's favorites. "He's waiting for the pitch, looking confident now . . . here it comes . . . and it's a solid hit. A single over second."

"That's more like it." Bert slapped the counter. "DiMaggio's gonna pull this out. You watch."

Lefty hissed. "That rookie wop's just gotten lucky. I give him three seasons tops."

Shan envisioned Mr. Capello at home on the davenport, tuned in to the radio this very minute, saying, *Next week, you will see. With their Italian smarts, Lazzeri and DiMaggio — and Crosetti too — they will sweep the whole series.*

How Shan longed to share those conversations again.

As Bert and Lefty bickered over stats, Shan slipped out the door. He walked around the corner, a path he had been treading for the past five months. The sound of the waves and birds reminded him of Dunmore, as did the air, now cooling with summer long gone. Wispy clouds feathered the Friday afternoon sky.

Riding the salt-misted breeze, scents of chocolate and coffee wafted from factories in the city. Perhaps Shan had only imagined it, but the notion drew his gaze across the bay, to the sight that taunted every con on the Rock: civilization, just over a mile away.

On days like this, free of fog, it looked even closer. Impeding that short jaunt, of course, were treacherous currents, icy waters, and sharks desperate for a meal. Or so the rumors went. Johnston must have feared inmates would attempt to swim it regardless, since the prison showers were heated above normal to prevent cons from acclimating to the cold. At least that was the word on the hill.

Some fellas even claimed to hear ladies giggling from the yacht club. Shan had yet to catch it, but even now he heard plenty of laughter right here on the island. On the south end, below the warden's house, children were running about, antsy after the ferry ride back from school. They were strapping on roller skates and warming up for a ballgame. In lieu of cowboys and Indians, they played "guards and cons," taking turns locking one another up.

It was an odd scene, in light of their surroundings, but one that Shan would soon miss nonetheless.

He entered the greenhouse and closed the door, stepping down into the room. A lush spread of flowers — marigolds, daisies, freesias, and more — brightened the counters that ran both lengths of the walls. He set down the basket and wiped his hands on his coveralls. A stamp of *AZ-257* blared on the denim, a reminder of his identity.

From a nearby plant, he plucked a ripe cherry tomato and took it toward the supply cabinet. At the far corner, he lowered to a squat.

And there she appeared, like clockwork. Beneath the counter, curtained by hydrangea and stacks of clay pots, was Sadie Martin. She sat cross-legged in her rust-red dress and yellow cardigan. As usual, strands hung loose from her chestnut-brown ponytail, mussed from the school day and rides on the launch.

He held up the tomato before closing his hand around it. The ten-year-old waited, her hazel eyes glinting with interest. He waved his other fingers about, blew into his fist, and opened it to show an empty palm. It was the same trick he had used the first time they'd interacted — directly so, anyhow.

Back in May, he had detected her presence from the start but went about his business for weeks. Among the rules in "Old Seawater" Johnston's handbook was a strict ban on any contact with civilians on the island. This was rarely an issue, given the maze of fences, gates, and wires. But the girl evidently found ways to roam at will.

Shan had been determined not to jeopardize his good standing, his new detail most of all. Yet he could feel her curious eyes watching — the way Lina used to do — and one day she left a token.

Shells pasted together formed the shape of a person, eyes and mouth added with ink. The figure carried a basket, woven from weeds, making it clear the figure was Shan.

The next afternoon, he had heard her crawling back in. Always she would enter through a low, sliding panel used for water access. He was just heading out to report for his thirty-minute count — not even passmen had full free reign — but a thought came to him. He pulled from his denim pocket a hard-boiled egg saved for a snack. Below a small crack in the shell, he drew a face with potting soil and placed the egg outside of her hiding spot. When Shan returned from his count, Humpty-Dumpty had vanished, along with the girl.

For a time, they'd continued this way, furtively trading shell art — of animals and suns and flowers — for Shan's creative makings of fruit and rolls and leaves. Then one afternoon, he'd dug out some potatoes from beneath the counter, where he was growing them in a stack of tires. Practicing for the monthly picture show, he was juggling the vegetables when he glimpsed the girl leaning out for a peek. His awareness of an audience triggered the entertainer inside, and with little thought he transformed into a clumsy clown, nearly dropping the potatoes over and over until catching them with both hands and one under his chin. Though the girl disappeared into her haven, he'd heard her stifle a giggle.

Soon after, he couldn't say what emboldened him, exactly. Maybe it was the "relaxed" rules passmen enjoyed under Mrs. Johnston. Maybe it was the yearning to do anything that wasn't recorded, censored, or authorized. Or perhaps it was a familiarity he sensed in the girl, a loner type with defenses not easily lowered. Whatever the cause, he'd ventured to approach her with a snap pea, its texture and sweetness worthy of Mrs. Capello's approval. Too tentative to accept, however, the girl had withdrawn behind the pots, a fawn distrustful of a hunter offering berries.

Shan had been about to set down the gift, leaving it for her choosing, but reconsidered. Borrowing a trick from the circuits, he'd instead grandly displayed the snap pea and, with a sleight of hand, made it disappear. When she didn't respond, he'd yielded with a shrug. He had tried.

Yet once he'd stood up, she said in wonder, "Where did it go?"

Since then, her words had increased with each trick until far surpassing them. He'd made vegetables and flowers pop out of her ear, the air above her, even from her own hand.

This time, Shan continued to exhibit his empty palm, passing it before her eyes. He then swiped it over his mouth and pretended to chew on the cherry tomato. Through the months, Sadie had become harder to impress.

"I know you're not really eating it," she said.

He exaggerated a swallow and wiped his chin. "Now, why would you say that?"

She folded her arms, looking on the verge of a yawn.

"So where is it, then, smarty?"

She glanced at his hands, his coveralls, and pointed. "In one of your pockets."

He shook his head and turned his pockets inside out. "Got nothin' here."

She squinted, calculating.

"Or," he said, "did you mean yours?"

She hastened to investigate the pocket of her cardigan, from which she produced the tomato. A grin spread across her round face. "How'd you do that?" she said before plopping it into her mouth.

"Do what?" He shrugged and resumed his tasks.

It was a fitting place for magic. A separate world where earth and flowers scented the air, a house of colors and blooming and hope. And the plants agreed. Several were doing so well, they had outgrown their original pots. Shan needed to transfer them while he still had the chance.

It was already the start of October, and his assignment to the warden's garden would soon end for the year. Midsummer he'd been granted permission to expand his work to Saturdays, as there were always extra shrubs to trim or leaves to rake. But before long, his greenhouse duties would be reduced for the season, news he had yet to pass to Sadie. Though he dreaded another winter cooped up in the cell house, lately he was more concerned about leaving the girl on her own. From what he'd gathered, her initial reclusion seemed the result of her mother's death a year ago, which prompted the move to Alcatraz — maybe the same applied to the quietness of her father, Yappy. At any rate, Shan worried that the girl, with no sibling or friend to speak of, would quickly retract into herself.

"It's nice out there today," he told her, arranging pots on the counter for transplant. "You should be getting some fresh air, playing with other kids."

"It's too windy."

"Windy? You're on an island. That's not gonna change."

"Then why do *I* need to? I like it in here."

Shan sighed. Sadie was too clever for her own good.

"You know the last book you told me about?" she said.

With a garden trowel, Shan started loosening the first plant by its edges. "*Sense and*

Sensibility."

"I stopped reading it."

When he had mentioned his mam's favorite novel, which Lina equally adored, Sadie decided to borrow it from the school library. "I tried to tell you it'd be too hard," he reminded her.

"It wasn't that. It was just silly. Like *Little Women.*" Sadie was ripping dried leaves into little pieces. "All those girls care about are boys mooning over them, or what to wear to some dumb ball. It made me want to punch them in the nose."

Shan couldn't argue. His feelings over Jane Austen's stories hadn't been much different — though not to the point of punching.

"Anyway, I started a different one," she said. "*The Count of Monte Cristo.* Have you read it?"

He couldn't help but smile at the dark humor inherent in the question. "A long time ago," he said simply.

A novel about a wrongly convicted inmate who escapes from a heinous prison to lead a life of wealth and happiness, for some reason, wasn't on the approved list at the Alcatraz library.

"So far, it's pretty good. But . . ."

At her reluctance, he turned to her.

"What?"

"I'm at the part when Dantes and the priest are digging tunnels under the prison. All they've got are some tools made from candlesticks and stuff. How would that even be possible?"

Leave it to Sadie to think of this. Her own daring adventures — whether island exploring, shell collecting, or seawall climbing — were always evidenced on any limb not protected by her dresses. The girl was a future Nellie Bly, bound to circle the globe to defy the odds.

And she was right. At least at Alcatraz, if there were a way to dig a tunnel to freedom, an inmate would have done so by now.

"I guess that's why it's fiction," Shan said, and returned to his work. He preferred to dedicate his thoughts to something real rather than the impossible.

Just then, something moved in his periphery. Through the glass walls, a figure in denim approached. Shan signaled to Sadie and she ducked out of sight.

The door swung open.

It was Ralph Roe. Roughly Shan's age, with a mop of wavy brown hair, he was a bank robber essentially serving life. From their brief exchanges, Shan had picked up on a faint accent from the guy's Missourian roots.

"What can I do for you, Ralph?"

"Need an extra hose." Ralph held a shovel, both hands in gloves, supplies from his landscape detail. His face and coveralls were smudged with dirt.

"Sure thing. Give me minute, and I'll bring it to you."

"I'll get it."

Ralph stepped inside and Shan knew exactly where he was headed. The canvas hose sat coiled near the empty pots, a barricade for Sadie.

"You know," Shan said, trying to cut him off. "It'd be easier if I threw it in the cart for you."

"I'm fine." Ralph continued to the end with Shan on his heels.

"Really, it's no trouble."

Ignoring him, Ralph snatched up the hose, just as Shan realized Sadie was gone.

Slipped out like a mouse.

Shan pulled back casually. He gave Ralph ample room to pass, which the man did in a cooler manner than he used for others.

It was no secret the privileges of passmen were resented by many cons, worsened by suspicion given how much time they spent in the warden's home. Shan's bonus role as the "funnyman" afforded him leeway with most, but not all — Ralph being in the minority. This left Shan especially relieved over Sadie's clean getaway, for reasons other than a breach of the rules.

Rumors in the cell house spread much like gossip in the apartments of Dublin, where even "friendships" were twisted into something foul and dark. A convicted felon who enjoys the company of a ten-year-old girl?

Just imagine what they'd say.

43

At Alcatraz, it didn't seem possible for time to pass slower — until attending Sunday Mass.

Once more, slightly hunched in his vestments, Father Anthony droned even more than the former chaplain from St. Anne's. Worse yet, his aged warbling made his words even harder to absorb. If not for the responsorial psalms and having to rise repeatedly, Shan would be nodding off like Bert. In the row of chairs ahead, the guy's head kept falling forward before springing back up.

Shan suppressed a yawn and reviewed his missal. The typewritten program confirmed that they were about halfway through. As Father Anthony intoned the homily, Shan's attention drifted to the altar. The impressive wooden structure carved by inmates transformed the auditorium into a chapel replete with flowers, candlesticks, and a large cross.

Alternating with the Protestants, Catholic services were held every second and fourth Sunday. For a mere change of scenery, several cons had cited parents of differing faiths in order to attend every week. Yet even those inmates had gradually ceased coming to Mass.

Considering Shan's course in life, he couldn't say how he felt about God these days — so far, his almighty plan didn't rate a standing ovation — but Sunday services at least connected Shan to a waning sense of normalcy.

At long last, the priest prepared the Eucharist. Two altar boys assisted with the offering, including "Machine Gun" Kelly. Mass was the only time the con wasn't bragging about one caper or another — half of them baloney, according to others.

After the ringing of a holy bell, Communion and prayers, and more standing, sitting, and kneeling, the service came to an end. Father Anthony blessed and dismissed the congregation, launching a buzz of relief.

Shan blinked hard to rouse himself. He made his way to the end of the row, where he deposited his missal in a wastebasket.

Fellows mingled, in no hurry to turn out. Father Anthony was shaking hands, encouraging participation in his recent addition of post-service confession. In the corner, a four-paneled privacy screen, wood carved and painted white, shielded a pair of chairs not three yards from a guard. Nothing in Alcatraz was completely sacred.

Shan had almost managed to bypass the priest, but the holy man caught his gaze and extended a hand in greeting. "Peace be with you, my son."

Forcing a pleasant face, Shan said, "Also with you, Father."

The priest's grip, stronger than expected, lingered as he continued. "I noticed, after last Mass, you chose not to visit the confessional."

The observation did cause Shan a niggling of guilt, but it was of small consequence given the load he already carried. Besides, what would a Catholic do if he didn't suffer from guilt over one sin or another? He gently retracted his hand.

"I'm not quite up to it, Father. Maybe next time."

"I see." The priest's vocal quiver didn't hide his disappointment.

Shan yearned to escape the awkwardness mounting between them, but the crowd's movements held him there.

"Well, then, I urge you to take this with you." Father Anthony pressed a missal into

Shan's palm, his eyes firm amid his wrinkles. "Reread the Lord's message from the service, my son. Let it reach into your heart and provide salvation."

"Yes, Father." An ingrained placation since grade school.

Father Anthony smiled and moved on to another sinner.

At the door, a guard named Finley sniffed his nose in his usual rodent way. He ordered the inmates to line up and head out, with an exception. Those staying for confession were to quietly wait their turn in the front row. After all were finished, they, too, would return as a group.

Shan followed the procession out single file. He was nearing the stairs when the line congested a bit and his awareness stirred.

Something about Father Anthony unsettled him. The handshake, his eyes, his words. They were less insistent than pleading.

Shan opened the missal, which he'd planned to simply discard. In the top margin appeared a handwritten note.

Exod. 10:15 The great waters shall part and freedom will belong to thee.

Exodus . . . waters . . . freedom . . .

It couldn't really be a reference to — could it?

"Wake up, Groucho Marx," Bert called from the rear of the line.

Startled, Shan folded the page and glanced over his shoulder. Directly behind him stood an inmate named Ted Cole. His severely arched eyebrows and large nostrils from an upturned nose befit his sinister reputation.

Finley called out, "Quit holding things up, Capello. You're lagging!"

At the guard's order, Shan hurried down the steps to catch up. The prisoners were marched to their cells to obtain their wool coats. Shan hid the missal in his library book, stored on his wall shelf, before being ushered out to the yard.

Cons who hadn't gone to the Mass had been out here since breakfast. Much like kids from the parade ground, they passed the time with softball or horseshoes. Some played handball, the more dedicated ones trying to build up strength for a swim to freedom. Off to the side, a swarm of bridge players on low stools competed in heated matches.

"Capello," Digs hollered from among them. "You in?"

Shan struggled to focus, shook his head.

413

Digs swiveled back to deal more dominoes.

A burst of wind whipped at Shan's face, yet it was the priest's message that sent a shiver down his spine — though, really, it shouldn't have. Shan was jumping to conclusions. Father Anthony hardly seemed the type to conspire a daring prison break. The verse could have been a note to himself, transcribed for a future homily.

To be certain, he needed to clarify. And he knew just the person to help.

Shan strolled nice and easy through the jungle, a misnomer for the yard. They ought to call it the "zoo," with its concrete walls twenty feet high, topped with chain-link fences and barbwire. It made for a secure place to try like hell to tame animals captured in the wild.

From the perimeter catwalk, guards surveyed the herd, ready to subdue a periodic clash. Shan felt them watching now. Taking his time, he threaded his way to the pseudo-dugout, where Lefty did more griping than cheering for his team.

"Are you blind, dimwit? What the hell was that?" He spat and raked his fingers through his hair, creating spiky red tufts.

Shan sidled up next to him, hands in his coat pockets. Yappy stood high above, grasping his rifle, his features dark and angular. His attention was directed elsewhere, the way Shan regularly aimed to keep it. Whereas noisy disruptions in the cell house earned a couple of whacks to the noggin, consorting with the officer's kid would warrant far worse, if discovered.

"Hey, Lefty," Shan said. "I wanted to ask you . . ."

"Huh? How's that?" As the son of a Baptist minister, Lefty was known to be well versed in scripture, even if he didn't always apply it.

"At Mass today, I was trying to remember an old Bible verse my ma likes. I think it was Exodus, ten-fifteen. You know that one?"

"Chop, chop! Let's go, let's go!" Lefty clapped, urging on a teammate.

"Lefty?" Shan pressed.

"What? Oh. Ten-fifteen. Yeah. That's about, uh, the locusts, taking over Egypt. Gobbling everything up."

Locusts. And Egypt. Not great waters.

"You sure about that?"

Lefty turned to him and huffed a laugh. "Believe me. I'm sure," he said. Then he delved back into the game.

Thoughts spinning, Shan ambled away. A few months ago, Father Anthony had transferred from Leavenworth to replace Father Clark, adding a confessional two services back. Was Shan the reason why? This morning, was the priest shooting for a private talk? Was any of this possible?

The idea seemed ludicrous. Honestly, who would even have the power to manipulate such a thing?

Well — other than Max.

Shan supposed the man might have that kind of pull, certainly enough dough. With the value he placed on trust and loyalty, it wouldn't be completely outlandish to think Max might want to repay Shan for his silence in the courtroom.

But if that was the case, the numbers would have to signify something. Ten-fifteen.

A code? A time, a date?

It was a plot straight out of a picture show. He felt silly even entertaining the thought — before he remembered.

October the fifteenth. Ten-fifteen. The night of the warden's next party . . .

The event was less than a week away.

Once again, Johnston wished to exemplify his noble aim of rehabilitation over punishment. In doing so, he had scheduled Shan to perform. Or had someone else arranged that too? Many of the guests would be dignitaries, the type of powerful figures with whom Max Trevino would surely be acquainted.

If any of this had merit — which perhaps it didn't — more details were sure to come. But here was the real question: did Shan even want them?

Over meals, he'd heard about dozens of jailbreaks at other prisons. Some efforts were downright doomed from the start, while others were impressively resourceful. Many times they'd succeeded, if their boasts were to be believed. But the failures didn't evade consequence: beatings and months in the hole, sentences lengthened, elimination of all "good time" accumulated.

Or you could end up like Dutch Bowers, sprawled like seaweed on a rocky shore.

Shan surveyed his surroundings. His whole life had been spent on islands — first Ireland, then Long Island, now here. Though still no closer to paradise, Alcatraz wasn't the house of horrors the papers made it out to be. Dish out trouble, you'd get it right back and then some. But by keeping himself straight, Shan had built a tolerable existence. Over time, he had accepted his situation as reality and was sure he'd eventually come out the other end in one piece.

Granted, he had fleeting daydreams like

any other con, of scaling a fence or diving headfirst into the bay. But would such an attempt ever be worth the risk?

44

In the warden's greenhouse, Shan yanked more dead leaves from the pot of geraniums and pitched them at the floor. The plant was dying despite all his efforts. But that wasn't what bothered him most.

All night long he had dwelled on that priest and his scrawled note. Shan doubted he'd slept an hour. Four days remained until the party. Almost two weeks until the next service. At one or the other he would confirm if his notions of a plot were unfounded. Truth was, oddly enough, he'd been doing just fine before that damn message put ideas into his head.

"Mr. Capello." Sadie's voice stalled him. He had almost forgotten she was there, tucked away in her usual spot. She was absently fingering a design of dirt and bruises on her knees, looking at him with expectant eyes.

"What?"

"Well . . . do you?"

"Do I what?"

"Remember your mom?"

"Of course I do." If she was referring to his real one, his mam, that wasn't entirely true, which agitated him even more. He focused on removing more leaves.

"Like what?"

"What do you mean, 'like what'?"

"What do you remember?"

He knew it wasn't intended as a challenge, but he couldn't help feeling that way. "Lots of things, all right?"

A cold drop splashed his cheek, then his ear. He looked up and took one in the eye. Cursing under his breath, he rubbed his eyelid with the back of his hand. Dirt from his skin added to the assault, and he had to blink away the grime.

The overhead drip hose was leaking. A brilliant invention he had rigged himself.

He tramped over to the spigot and tightened the valve, but the light drips refused to stop. "Shitty goddamn thing," he hissed, as if that would help.

After several fuming breaths, he again recalled his visitor. The girl had fallen silent and retreated partially behind the pots. Worry filled her eyes, making him feel even worse.

This was one of her sadder days, when she missed her mother. Shan used to have those too. Normally he would cheer Sadie up with a magic trick or a juggling act or a witty joke, but he wasn't up for it. Another reason she ought to have a real friend.

He walked steadily toward her. Aware of her tentative demeanor, he stood back a ways. "Look, Sadie. It's just not a good day for me. Understand?"

She took this in and gave a nod, but the tension remained.

He glanced at the ceiling of dusty glass. Gray clouds were darkening the sky, assembling for rainfall. "You'd better get going if you want to stay dry. Mrs. Leonard will be expecting you soon, won't she?"

Sadie nodded again, this time with a grimace.

On weekdays, when her father's regular shift ended well into the evening, another guard's family in the neighboring apartment included Sadie for supper. Most meals were rubbery and overcooked, according to Sadie, though Shan suspected they simply couldn't compete with memories of her own mother's cooking.

"Okay, then," Shan said. "I need a tool to fix the thing, so . . . I'll see you later."

Not expecting a reply, he marched straight

outside and toward the house. Even the fresh salty air failed to lighten his mood. By the time he'd gone to the kitchen supply closet to retrieve a wrench from the toolbox — its contents accounted for daily — he realized the root of his frustration.

Years ago, he had made the mistake of relying on others to survive and swore he'd never let it happen again. A prison break of this magnitude would require inexplicable dependence on strangers and nameless people behind the scenes. The room for error enormous, the odds of failing high. And in the end, Shan would be the one to pay.

He did his best not to think of this, however, returning to the warden's greenhouse. There would be plenty of time to wrangle with his thoughts during the long night in his cell.

He was almost at the door when a voice hailed him from behind. "Hold up, Capello." It was Ralph Roe. How grand.

"What do you need?"

Ralph came within a few feet. He threw a glance over both shoulders before answering in a hushed voice. "My pal Ted and I, we got a proposition for ya."

The precautionary manner made Shan as uneasy as the mention of Ted Cole.

"What would that be?"

"See, we've been thinking it's about time we blow out of this joint. Figured the three of us, we could work together."

Although they had all been transferred on the same chain from Leavenworth, Shan seldom exchanged words with either of them. From what he'd heard of their history, he preferred it that way. They weren't just criminals who had knocked off banks and stores, even a Coca-Cola bottling plant; they would shoot it out with cops and take hostages. Plus, violence for Ted wasn't limited to the outside; he'd killed a cellmate at another pen, though allegedly in self-defense.

By stabbing the poor bastard twenty-seven times.

"I appreciate the offer," Shan said. "But honest, I just want to do my own time."

"Is that so?" Ralph rubbed his jaw with his gloved hand. " 'Cause that ain't how it seems to us."

"Oh? How you figure?"

"Gotta admit, for a while I had you pegged wrong. Staying out of the work strikes, getting all the privileges you do. Now I see how you've been biding your time. Finding ways to communicate and get what you need."

Shan went quiet, wondering where this

was going.

"Like at church, for example. Ted says you were carrying some special note yesterday. Made you pretty jumpy."

This was exactly what Shan didn't want. He waited to hear how much Ted had seen, but Ralph just smiled. It seemed he was testing him for a reaction, feeling out a hunch, and took Shan's silence for an admission.

Shan hurried to deny it. "That was nothing." He worked to level his voice. "There were some verses I liked. In the program. From the service."

"Relax, Capello. I'm a solid con, just like Ted. We ain't looking to stool on ya. We just want in on the plan. And you know from our history, we could be a real help."

The guy wasn't lying. Cons who had served with them at McAlester commended their past breakout schemes, Ted's in particular. A regular Houdini, he'd supposedly been smuggled out in a laundry bag, tried the same in a garbage can, and even sawed through bars with a razor.

Nevertheless, Shan wasn't interested.

"Look, I'm sure you've got fine ideas. But I'm not trying to beat the joint."

"Yeah? Then how come I'm not buying it?"

Shan deliberately held his gaze, as averting it could feed the guy's doubts. "Have you looked around? The place is escape proof."

"And Titanic was 'sink proof.' But look how well that worked out for those folks."

"Eh, Coe!" Finley appeared by the warden's house, a welcome interruption. "Stop loafing. Get back and finish up. Almost time to head in."

"Right away, Mr. Finley," Ralph hollered. "Just asking about treating the weeds." When Finley started back, Ralph whispered to Shan, "Like I was saying, everything's got a weak point. Hell, sometimes it can be the smallest thing." With that, he slid a look toward the greenhouse, at the lower sliding entry panel, smugness creeping over his face, before he turned and followed Finley's trail.

Ralph knew.

He knew about Sadie. That was what he meant about communicating, about using people for what he needed. Yet it wasn't his assumptions or knowledge that truly disturbed Shan; it was the view of Sadie as a negotiating chip. It was the chance Ralph could back up his threat, assigned to a detail that kept him outdoors. Not for much longer, but long enough.

Shan watched him walk away and his fists tightened. Until then he had forgotten the wrench in his hand. A good thing, or he might have had trouble fighting the impulse to lash out.

He stormed into the greenhouse and slammed the door.

The sound of a gasp startled him. For once, Sadie was outside of her cove, standing in plain sight. He'd thought she had gone home by now.

"You're leaving?" she said. Apprehension gripped her voice, her face. She wasn't referring to the workday.

"I don't know what you mean," he mumbled. "I'm not going anywhere."

"But I heard you. You and that man Ralph. Talking about your note and making plans to escape."

Holy God. He never should have talked to the girl. Not ever. For his own sake, yes — but for hers too.

"We're not doing anything like that. You just heard it wrong."

"But . . . that man, he said —"

"He didn't say any such thing." The words came out gruffer than intended. Shan realized this when she cowered. But her feet didn't budge.

"Sadie, you need to go."

Questions swirled in her eyes, darkened by doubt.

"Didn't you hear me?" Charged by emotion, he stomped forward. "I said beat it!"

Her face blanched. Like a spooked cat, she shot back to her refuge and scurried out the way she'd come.

Hands trembling, Shan closed his eyes. He cursed himself for creating this mess, or at least for not seeing it coming. Somehow, no matter his intentions, he wound up putting everyone around him in danger.

45

The line slithered like a snake through the grass, seeking out its next meal. In that way, Shan and the inmates surrounding him were no different. Just past noon, they each stepped through the snitch box, their concealed weapons skirting the alarm, and entered the mess hall.

"Good day, gentlemen." Warden Johnston nodded to the line, repeating the greeting at intervals.

Shan mumbled a courteous response and avoided eye contact, an effort to blend when he could.

Digs nudged him from behind. "How 'bout that. Gumbo and banana cake. Boy oh boy, I love that stuff."

Shan hadn't paid notice to the menu board, his priorities elsewhere. All morning, while cataloging books and censored magazines, he'd mulled over yesterday's events at the greenhouse and the conversation not meant for Sadie's ears, one he prayed she wouldn't share. Especially with her father.

Though she could rat on Shan based on spite or morality, he feared these less than her desire to keep him from leaving. That was why, right after mealtime, he would return to the warden's greenhouse, where he hoped she'd appear. He needed her to believe that she had simply misheard and to agree to steer clear of other cons. Then he would kindly send her off, as he should have months ago.

At the steam table, the aroma of food helped divert his attention. Lack of sleep over the past two nights had increased his appetite, and his stomach growled in anticipation.

Among the few benefits of living on the flats was being the first tier to turn out for chow. He appreciated this now as he dished shrimp gumbo and rice onto his metal tray. At any meal, you could take as much as you wanted, but waste a bite and you'd pay the price. Shan kept this in mind as he added buttered green beans and a piece of spiced banana pudding cake.

Tray filled, he walked to his assigned table. Afternoon light slanted through the windows and bounced off floors polished to a shine. Out of the corner of his eye, he caught sight of Ted and Ralph waiting in line, staring directly at him.

He ignored them as he settled on his bench seat. Upon the guard's whistle, he dug into his food. Across from him, Digs was less interested in the gumbo than in the rookie guard on his first chow duty. "Take a look at him, fellas. Nervous as a virgin on her wedding night."

Other cons at the table snickered. Shan glanced over to view the new officer, whose Adam's apple bobbed with a tight swallow. With a square face and medium build, he was far from scrawny. Yet who could blame him for being leery?

Guards, after all, weren't armed unless out of inmates' reach: behind the bars of catwalks and towers and gun galleries. So here the man was, overseeing a congregation of 250 criminals, with only his fists for defense. Though a wall of steel bars separated them from the kitchen area stocked with knives, cons still had utensils and hot coffee to boot. Some days even a nice, sharp T-bone from their steaks.

"Holy shit," Digs said suddenly, looking past Shan, all amusement gone.

Shan twisted around just in time to see an inmate from the line tackle Warden Johnston to the ground. Voices of shock, some of encouragement, surged through the room. Many craned their necks as the con kicked the warden in the stomach, the chest, the head.

It was "Whitey" Phillips. Another gem from Leavenworth who'd been on Shan's chain.

A window shattered two tables away. Not by a prisoner, as Shan first thought, but by an officer on the catwalk. It was Chandler, the guard who had killed Dutch Bowers. He shoved the muzzle of his rifle through the opening.

"Everyone down!" someone shouted. Half the room, including Shan, dropped to the floor, taking cover under the tables. The rest followed at the blast of a guard's whistle, so trained they'd become, like dogs on a stage.

Shan glimpsed two guards swooping into the fray, Yappy in the lead. He swung a leather sap at Whitey's back, causing the con to groan. A second swing, this time to the gut, doubled Whitey over. A third took him to the ground. The blows continued — *thud, thud, thud* — faster and harder. The guard's hat fell to the floor.

"The screws are gonna gas us for sure," Digs said through the din.

Shan looked up at the tear gas canisters lining the walls. The room was called the "gas chamber" for that reason, but he'd never truly feared they would be used until now.

More guards rushed to aid the warden, who had ceased to move.

"Hold your fire! Don't shoot!" one of them yelled. There were too many chances for a mistake.

All the while, Yappy pummeled away, his face flushed and teeth bared. His show of strength fulfilled the promise of his six-foot build. Whitey was curled up with his hands wrapping his head. Shan swore he heard a couple of bones crack.

"Fred, we got him." Ranger Roy tried to slow him down. "That's enough now."

But Yappy continued with no signs of relenting.

"Fred, stop!"

By then, Deputy Warden "Meathead" had arrived. He grabbed hold of Yappy's arm. After brief resistance, Yappy yielded and looked around as if suddenly aware of the other officers. Meathead patted him on the back, calming him or commending him. Likely both.

Then all of their attention shifted to carefully lifting Warden Johnston.

"Take him straight to the hospital," Meathead said.

"How 'bout this one?" Ranger Roy asked, indicating Whitey Phillips.

"Make sure the scum's alive; then we'll take care of him." Meathead turned to the room. "Show's over! Get back in your seats. Now!"

As the inmates obeyed, Shan watched Yappy wipe sweat from his brow and reset his hat. The place hadn't been this quiet in months.

Guards on mess-hall duty returned to their posts, the rookie clearly shaken up. Two others dragged Whitey, still unconscious, out of the room.

Shan looked at Digs. "What do you think they'll do to him?"

Digs shook his head. "Stupid bastard's going to the dungeon for good." He hurried to shovel down his banana cake before their twenty minutes of mealtime expired.

In the basement below A block, the dungeons were apparently as barbaric as they sounded. According to the few who'd done time in them, there was no light or bedding, no meals but bread and water. Just a bucket for a john. The area was damp and cold, magnified when the con was stripped bare. To top it off, since the cells had never been tool-proofed, the inmate had to be handcuffed to the bars. Some claimed standing up.

Only the worst offenses, however, would land a guy in the dungeon.

Like trying to escape.

Shan looked at his tray, having lost his appetite. He did his best to force the bites down until interrupted by an announcement. Inmates were to return to their cells as scheduled, where they would remain until supper.

All work details were suspended.

46

"Our plans are in the air, I'm afraid," Mrs. Johnston informed the passmen, worrying the pearls around her neck. It was the day after the mess hall attack. "Rescheduling the party might be difficult for the guests. But with my husband feeling under the weather, I do think it's best. We'll keep you all updated, so you can plan accordingly."

By "under the weather," she meant the warden preferred not to parade the success of his standing until his cuts and bruises had faded from the neck up. Shan surmised this even before Lefty and Bert expressed the thought once she had left the room.

In connection to the priest's note, assuming any link did exist, Shan didn't know whether he should feel disappointment or relief over the delay — unlike Sadie's absence, about which he felt both.

For the first Wednesday in months, she didn't make it to the greenhouse. Same for

Thursday. On Friday afternoon, in the warden's garden he heard schoolchildren pouring off the *McDowell.* He'd thought to offer a small wave, a peacemaking gesture to Sadie, but the residential apartments hindered his view, and he never saw her arrive.

Come Saturday she would be at home, her father typically off duty. Regardless, Shan left a note in her hiding spot. *I'm sorry,* it read. The only words fit to scribe.

After finishing at the second greenhouse, he headed out to be counted and escorted back to the cell house. In the distance, Ted and a line of other cons were returning from work in the Model Industries Building, three stories of various shops. The guy looked at Shan and sent a two-finger salute, his lips in a solid line. Less a greeting than a reminder.

And that reminder clenched Shan's jaw.

They'd leave her be, he assured himself. Even Ralph and Ted wouldn't dare harm the daughter of a guard. Certainly not after seeing what her father did to cons who stepped gravely out of line.

Then again, their pasts exemplified disregard for any obstacle in their way. Shan needed to convince them he had no plan in the works. Which, in fact, was the truth.

If there was any plan at all, it surely wasn't his.

On the rec yard the next afternoon, it took time to locate the duo. Cold wind and sprinkling rain turned every inmate into a twin: matching coats, collars up, caps low.

Ted and Ralph often loafed on the concrete steps with their Okie pals, like the notorious "Doc" Barker. But not today. When Shan recognized their profiles, he was thankful they were alone. Ted was leaning back against the concrete wall with Ralph standing nearby, both puffing on their cigarettes.

No guards within earshot.

Shoving his hands into his pockets, Shan made his way over. Ted appeared to announce the visitor to Ralph, who angled back with a look of intrigue.

By way of greeting, Shan said, "I want you to know I'm being square. If I was cooking something up, I'd tell you." When neither of them answered, Shan added, "So keep your hands off the girl, all right?"

Ted shook his head and spurted a dry laugh.

Shan straightened. He took a step closer. "I said, *all right*?"

Ted pushed off the wall and threw down

his cigarette. "Getting awfully protective over the kid of a goddamn screw, if you ask me."

Only a few feet separated them.

Shan glanced at Ted's hands. If the guy went to pull a weapon, would Shan have time to grab his own?

"Fellas." Ralph tugged on Ted's arm. A signal to stand down. "Let's not get riled up, huh? We're on the same team here." He sent a look toward the catwalk. The guard named Chandler was encroaching on their area, his beady eyes darting. A cleft in his chin emphasized his solid jaw.

Begrudgingly Ted backed away, prompting Shan to do the same. Ralph waited until Chandler was at a safe distance before continuing in a near whisper. "Here's the thing. Ted found a way down to the water, clean out of sight."

Ted gave Ralph a quizzical look at what he was divulging. But after a moment, he conceded with his silence. It was a trade of information.

"You got a plan up your sleeve," Ralph said, "you let us know. It's better if we all work together, see?" He took a drag off his cigarette, blew out the smoke. "On the other hand, we find out you're lying? We can make life hard for you, Capello. I don't think you'd want that. Do you?"

There was no real call for a reply. Ralph proved that by flicking away his cigarette and accompanying Ted toward the cell house. They joined the other cons retreating from the weather.

Craving a hefty distance, Shan waited a minute before trekking back inside. He didn't need guards, or anyone else, to think he was in cahoots with those creeps.

He was almost at his cell when the back of an officer winked through the bars.

Periodic shakedowns were standard in prison, but Shan's first thoughts were of Ralph and Ted. Planting contraband would be one way to make a con's life harder. Tipping off a guard, to ensure it was found, was another.

"Remain standing there," Yappy ordered upon noticing Shan. Not that he would have dared enter.

"Yes, sir."

This was the first time Yappy had tossed Shan's cell — which made him wonder if someone else was involved. Someone like Sadie.

As determined as a bloodhound, the guard examined every inch. He sifted through each rag, towel, and piece of folded clothing. He fingered through the shaving brush and pile of censored letters. There was nothing that warranted a write-up. Depending on the guard.

Circling the space, he eyed the few items posted on the walls: some photographs of the Capellos and a single postcard — from Kitty Lovely of all people, surely scrawled between shows and fresh companions on her tour. Then Yappy inspected the mattress, and Shan remembered. He'd stored a Bit-O-Honey bar through a small opening; though he had finished it the night before, he'd forgotten to discard the wrapper.

Appearing to miss it, Yappy moved on. He picked up a book from the shelf, giving the pages a hearty shake.

And the missal came fluttering down.

All sense of time vanished as Shan watched him flip it over. And back. Then Yappy opened the program and his eyes found the handwritten note.

Shan's pulse soared to an impossible speed, thundering in his ears. He had saved the thing in search of a second clue, a message in the typeset verses; as of yet he'd deciphered nothing. He should have ripped off the note and swallowed it, or flushed it down the toilet, buried it on the grounds.

But Yappy flung the paper aside. A lucky break, though he wasn't done.

Using a pen from his pocket, he leafed through the wastebasket, checked around the sink, the toilet. He paused, appearing satisfied, until noting an item he'd missed. A raincoat had slipped from a garment hook. He snatched it up, patted it down. Even before he pulled the item out, Shan's heart rose to his throat.

Yappy studied the craft made of shells, surprised, confounded. He pinned Shan with a hard gaze. "What's this?" His voice was low and rough, like metal scraping gravel.

Shan shook his head, stalling to collect the air he needed to speak. He forced a swallow while feigning an equally perplexed look. "Not sure, Mr. Martin. A butterfly, I'd guess. Might be a dragonfly."

It was a gift from Sadie that he'd once made disappear by sneaking it into his pocket. He had kept it in his cell for a time, envious of any creature with the freedom of flight. But he'd put it back in his coat with plans to store it in the greenhouse, in a jelly jar with the other shells . . .

"Where'd you get it?"

Shan's expression, of needing to give this some thought, was not a façade. "On the ground by the warden's house, I think. Figured Mrs. Johnston might like it. Just forgot to leave it with her."

For an infinite moment Yappy stared at Shan, as if seeking proof in the creases of his face. Shan implored his features not to tighten or twitch. He battled back memories of the officer beating Whitey to a pulp.

Once more Yappy regarded the shells. Enclosing them in a firm grip, he exited the cell in silence.

47

The announcement came Monday: the warden's party was back on. Postponed by a week, the event would take place in five days' time.

Until Shan knew more, he refused to obsess over something out of his control. He would stick to his routine, look out for only himself. What he should have done all along.

Since the cell shakedown, Yappy had said nothing more. A relief to Shan, but also a reminder of how careless he had been. Risking his privileges for magic tricks and trivial talks with a child. If he were punished for his actions, he alone would be to blame.

Sadie still remained out of sight, and he was grateful for it. To be safe, he buried his jar of shells along with any guilt at doing so. He had enough in his life to fret about, and she was no responsibility of his. She had a father who'd proven fully capable of protecting his own. If she roamed about the island, breaking more rules, that wasn't Shan's concern.

Besides, it was refreshing to complete his tasks in quiet for a change. More peaceful, more efficient.

He told himself this as the week rolled on, despite suspecting it was a lie.

Then Saturday arrived.

All day he trained his focus on his performance. Yet that evening, as he waited in the kitchen for his cue, he found it impossible to resist peeking past the swinging door. Men and women in their finery were transitioning from the dining room to the parlor, where a classical jazz trio continued to play. Shan caught whiffs of perfume and cologne. Their sweet and earthy scents competed with lingering spices from roasted pigeon and herbed potatoes.

Behind him, stewards followed Bert's orders by scrubbing counters and pans, cleaning dishes and glassware. Finally came a break in the music. Shan could hear someone making an announcement, and he visualized the guests taking their seats.

Seconds later Lefty swept in with a tray of dirty glassware. In passing, he flicked a nod at Shan. "You're on."

Shan shook out his hands. He confirmed

the placement of his toothbrush mustache, a tiny square black cloth adhered with corn syrup, and proceeded toward the parlor. The tuxedoed musicians strode past him without interest, just as they had during their last shared event. Their care lay only with their promised meals in the kitchen.

At Shan's appearance, the two dozen guests politely clapped from their chairs, aligned in tidy rows. Vases and paintings set a scene of grandeur, with elegant drapes meeting the polished hardwood floor.

As the applause waned, some whispered and shifted in their seats. Such discomfort was expected, even from the gentlemen. For they well understood — much like tenants in Dublin averse to seeing the homeless in their alley — often sheer luck alone prevented a reversal of roles. No doubt, more than a few here had achieved their powerful positions by bending some rules: through "grease money" or special favors or looking the other way.

Arguably one who appeared immune to the notion was the jolly man in the front row. Presumed to be the congressman, he had a beard and robustness resembling St. Nick's, his mood likely benefiting from the petite blonde at his right, a bit too young to be his wife. To his left sat the warden, who raised his chin, a signal for Shan to start. Mrs. Johnston gave an encouraging smile.

Showtime.

Shan straightened his bow tie in exaggerated form. At the flip of a switch, he transformed into the Tramp. The group was tentative to start, but with each gag the laughter grew and any discomfort crumbled away. He eventually moved on to singing and tapping. All the while, he couldn't help eyeing the crowd for an expression or demeanor out of the ordinary.

By the time his comical impressions were through, ending with that of a German beer vendor, nothing odd had alerted his senses.

The guests applauded and came to their feet, and Shan took his standard bows. The congressman was the first to approach. His face still flushed from his big-belly laughter, he shook hands with Shan, commending the performance. His companion shot Shan a timid smile before toddling away on her strappy heels, clinging to the arm of her date.

Warden Johnston followed. "Well done," he said, rewarding Shan with a pat to his upper arm. Other guests offered similar kind words. All within the norm. Nothing to raise a brow. Not even an intriguing wink.

And certainly no passage of a note.

When they had all dispersed to mingle before the ride to Van Ness Pier, Shan returned to the kitchen. He stood there, at a loss.

Bert was still directing traffic, storing leftover food. But overall, the chaos had calmed.

"Nice chops you got," said one of the musicians from the kitchen table. The trio was smoking and eating, their meals the same as the guests' but lacking presentation.

"Thanks," Shan said.

Just then, Lefty poked his head in. He informed the trio it was time to pack up, then disappeared to finish in the dining room. The performers, unlike Shan, would not be staying.

The musician who'd spoken to Shan was the first to rise. He wiped his chin with a linen napkin and tossed it aside. Lean and clean shaven, the fellow wore his hair as slick as his bearing. While the others gobbled their final bites, he grabbed an ashtray from the counter beside Shan and stubbed out his cigarette. "I hear you're real handy. Even take care of the greenhouse out there."

Shan went to answer but hesitated, struck by a sense of familiarity. "That's right."

"Hope you don't mind, but I took a peek.

Geraniums aren't looking so good. You ought to go down and check on 'em." The guy exhaled the last of the smoke in his lungs, and his voice dropped to a near whisper. "Tonight."

The intensity in the word matched the gleam in his eyes. An unmistakable order.

Shan edged out a nod.

The other musicians were collecting their coats and instrument cases, stored in a pile by the table. They thanked Bert for the food.

"Anytime, fellas," he called back, slinging a soiled dishcloth over his shoulder.

Before Shan could digest the scene, the trio had left in a flurry.

The greenhouse. *Tonight.*

Shan feared what other message he might find there, the events it could set in motion, the consequences he could face. But of course he had to go. He just wished he knew where he'd seen the musician before.

"Capello!"

He spun to find Bert staring with a curious look. "Is your hearing goin', or what?"

Shan forced a laugh. "Sorry. What were you saying?"

"You were looking kind of lost there. Making sure you're okay."

"Yeah, I was just thinking . . ." Shan stole a glance at the pendulum wall clock. Eight

448

forty-two. Eighteen minutes before he'd be escorted back. "I'm worried I left the drip hose on. If Ranger Roy gets here early, tell him I'll be back in a few."

48

In the greenhouse, Shan resorted to using a flashlight. He'd rigged a dangling light bulb for darker, foggier days, but its use tonight would project his every move to anyone outside.

Hunched low as a precaution, he went straight to the potted geraniums and examined them for a note. There was nothing. He riffled through the shriveled leaves that had fallen, dug through the soil, with the same result.

The message replayed in his ears. The geraniums weren't looking good, the guy had said; Shan ought to go down and check on them . . .

Go down.

He angled the light below the counter and discovered a large burlap bag he didn't recognize. After a glance over his shoulder, on the lookout for Ranger Roy's silhouette, he crouched and untied the bag. Inside was a foot-long tank. Silver and unmarked, it resembled a fire extinguisher, but with a dial-like valve and no hose. He had seen these before at drugstores, used by soda jerks to add bubbles and fizz to the drinks — but never with a compass on a long string looping its neck.

He opened the bag wider to reveal a pile of dark gray rubber. Layers of it. Beneath a thin, attached rope appeared a worn stamp barely legible: *U.S. Navy.* Tucked beside it were a short pole and paddle. The makings of an oar.

"Jesus, Mary, and Joseph . . ."

A raft. An actual raft, and the means to inflate it. But how did the guy smuggle it here? In a cello case, maybe.

Shan ran a hand over his face, trying to grasp the choice before him. A choice that would have to wait. He directed his light to the twin-bell alarm clock on the counter, which he relied upon for counts, and noted that fifteen minutes remained.

Scanning the room, he sought a safer place for the bag, at least until tomorrow.

Sadie's spot. It would have to do.

He fastened the burlap closed. Then he lugged it over to the corner and slid the pots out of the way. Two shimmering eyes made him jump back.

451

He snapped the flashlight forward and found Sadie, squinting against the beam, arms hugging her knees.

"My God," he exclaimed, "what are you —" He stopped, noting the tears streaking her cheeks. Her eyes were puffy, lips quivering. He lowered the light from her face.

"Sadie," he said gently. He reached for her, but she jerked away, clutching her hands to her chest. "Okay. It's okay." He displayed his palm, a show of reassurance.

Had his outburst caused her to feel this threatened, or was there something more?

Remembering the shelled butterfly confiscated by her father, Shan hoped she hadn't been punished for her wanderings.

He knelt down slowly, giving her space. "Honey, what happened?"

She inhaled a shaky breath. Her gaze remained on the floor. "I was only trying to help . . ."

Did she mean about his escape? About what she had overheard? He regretted having ever raised his voice. "I believe you," he said.

But her tears continued to fall. Below the short sleeves of her blouse, her bare arms shivered, more from fear, it seemed, than cold.

"Go on," he prodded. He was grimly

aware he didn't have much time. "You can tell me."

"I just . . ." She stifled a sob in her chest. "I want my mommy."

The desperation in her tone made his chest ache, a reverberating pain in the empty space his own mam had left behind. "I know, Sadie. And you'll be with her again, one day in heaven."

She shook her head and blurted, "She's alive."

Shan stared, bewildered. "I thought you said —"

"Daddy told me to say that, if people asked. To tell them she died. He said they'd say bad things if I didn't."

"So . . . where is your mother?"

"He would hurt her sometimes, when he was drinking. Not me, just her. When it got real bad, she went to find a new home in Kentucky, so we could live there. Just the two of us. She came to see me at school, on the playground. She said she got a job on a switchboard in a nice town, where there's a big river for picnics and swimming. I wanted to go with her, but she told me to be strong, that it would just be a little longer . . ." The memory played across Sadie's face and again her chin trembled.

"Then what happened?" Shan asked, still

stunned.

She raised her eyes to meet his. "Instead of walking to school one day, I was supposed to meet her. But Daddy heard us on the phone and pulled it out of the wall. Then he put all our things in the car and just kept driving." Her voice started to escalate. "I was crying, begging him to go back, till he got mad. Then he hit me. He said that if Mommy ever found us, he'd tell lies about her and she'd be locked up."

Shan swallowed his rising emotions, to an extent feeling just as helpless as Sadie. He wished he could say the truth would prevail. But he knew better. Even if a cop meant well, the lone fact that a wife had left her family would surely negate any reason behind her actions, no matter how justified.

"She doesn't know where I am," Sadie pressed on. "But I can find her. I know I can. That's why, if you're gonna go . . ."

Her voice broke, and suddenly Shan realized: "You want to go too."

He'd completely misunderstood. She wasn't scared he would leave; she was scared he would leave without her.

"Please," she begged, "take me with you."

What could he possibly say to that?

At his silence, she reached out and gripped his sleeve. "I can help us get away. Just tell

454

me what you need. *Please.*"

Only then did he notice the mark on the underside of her forearm. It was red and raw, as round as a pea. A burn he had seen before. From the end of a cigarette.

"Sadie," he said in a rasp. "Did your father do that?"

From the nearness of his fingers, she retracted her arm. Her eyes misted with more tears.

The answer was clear.

A rush of fury surged through Shan, a flood he could barely contain. His mind spun with memories of her past injuries — the ones he had seen. How many others had she hidden?

"So all those times you said you'd fallen down, or that you'd gotten hurt climbing, that's not what happened, is it?" He said this more to himself, already knowing the truth.

Hesitant, she shook her head, lowering her eyes in shame.

How had he missed it? All these months, the clues were there. He of all people should have noticed them. Perhaps, for many reasons, he hadn't wanted to.

The sound of distant voices jarred him. Ranger Roy could come looking any minute. And Shan still had to hide the raft.

"I have to get back. Can you go somewhere tonight? Until your father cools down."

Sadie wiped her cheeks. After a pause, she nodded. "The Leonards' — next door."

"Good. Go there now, and we'll talk again."

She looked reluctant to leave, understandably.

"You'll be all right. I promise."

The second the words left his mouth he wished he could take them back. Just look at his godforsaken life. Who the hell was he to promise anything?

49

Shan dreamt that night he'd been cast in a film. He arrived at the studio and recognized the set, a replica of his old street in Brooklyn. The director, Cecil B. DeMille, expressed relief at Shan's presence, referring to him as "Chinaman." This confused Shan until he realized he was dressed as an Oriental monk.

"Let's get rolling," DeMille said, and hollered through a megaphone, "Places, everyone!" As the crew hustled about, Shan panicked, as he couldn't recall his lines. "Action," he heard. Then a young actress entered the scene, pushing a squeaky flower cart over the fake cobblestones. She hit her mark, a lightly chalked *X* on the ground, and raised her sullen eyes. It was Sadie. Arms trembling, she handed him a white lily.

"Cut!" DeMille yelled.

Shan assumed he had made an error, that

he was supposed to decline the offering, and waited for a scolding.

"Where's his prop? Why can't anyone get Chinaman the right prop?"

"Got it, Mr. DeMille," said Carl, the stage manager from the burlesque circuit. It was a surprise to see him there, but before Shan could say as much, Carl shoved a stick into Shan's hand. The spotlight suddenly became blinding. When it dimmed, he discovered the setting had changed into a closet. In the corner, Sadie was balled up on the floor, covering her head, screaming for help. And the stick in Shan's hand was an axe.

"Now, strike her!" DeMille ordered — then Shan woke up.

Short of breath, he was covered in sweat and back in his cell. He lay awake the rest of the night, the disturbing image looping in his mind. He knew the original scene, from a film he'd watched as a kid at the Cohan Theatre. *Broken Blossoms* was the title, one he would never forget.

He didn't have to question why it now invaded his dreams. The link was crudely obvious. In the story, rage consumed a drunken man until he slaughtered his own daughter; even a monk seeking redemption couldn't save her. Though Shan told himself it was only make-believe, that they were actors on a screen, he knew the truth. Tragedies of the like happened all the time in various forms.

If Uncle Will hadn't died on that ship, Shan's fate could have been the same. Not just physically, but mentally, too, and over a stretch of years. A gradual chipping away, a beating down until there was nothing left to salvage.

Maybe it was meant to be, his meeting Sadie. Maybe it was his chance to do what the Capellos had done for him as a kid. All at once, he could make right what had gone so very wrong with Nick.

That was assuming, of course, the scheme could work. Getting down to the water was only half the challenge. From fishing outings as a child, he was well acquainted with rowing a boat, but could he do it fast enough? Tower guards were permitted to shoot anything within two hundred yards of the island. A raft would be a nice target. One, actually, that could sink Shan before it was even inflated.

At any moment, the burlap bag he'd tucked into Sadie's corner could be discovered, and every privilege he had earned would end. His warm-up acts and special shows, the hours in the greenhouse, his freedom outdoors. It would all be gone. And should he get caught in the act of escape? Even worse, with a guard's daughter in tow? He could add kidnapping to his record and another decade to his sentence.

But first would come the dungeon. Or segregation at best, where he would remain in a cell but for one hour a week. Once returned to his old block, he could face the barest existence for years to come.

Then there was Sadie. Imagine the punishment awaiting her at home — if she even survived the attempt.

Such prospects gnawed at his thoughts as he rose at the morning bell. The intensity notably grew during his trek to the chapel, where Father Anthony delivered another droning Mass. Shan managed to go through the motions: standing, sitting, standing, kneeling, mumbling the psalms. But he absorbed nothing of the service.

If only he could doubt Sadie's tale. Or if he'd never seen the extent of her father's temper. Then he could wash his hands of the whole damn thing. He could even give the bag to Ralph and Ted to use at their own peril.

Back during Shan's years on the road, he would have simply walked away. But now, unknowingly, Sadie had forced him to think of who he was before then: a boy on a ship determined to bring a lost little girl to her mother, whose tears of relief had over-flowed. It made him debate which fellow he wanted to be.

A swell of voices alerted him the service was over. Inmates were standing and gab-bing — for how long, Shan didn't know. Finley ordered those not staying for confession to line up at the door.

From the front of the chapel, Father Anthony sent Shan a pressing look.

Shan geared up while rising, and gave a nod. The priest smiled tightly before suppressing a cough. Clutching his Bible and rosary with knobby hands, he shuffled to his corner booth, forged from a privacy screen.

As guys lined up to exit — including Ted, fortunately — Shan sat down in the first row. The rookie guard hovered nearby. He ordered the con on the end to start. They totaled six in all.

One by one they visited the confessional, returning to their seats to do penance through prayers. A radiator clanked and hummed.

Shan was the last to enter.

Behind the screen, he took his seat across from the priest, their knees nearly touching. "Good morning, Father."

"Welcome, my son." Father Anthony coughed into his fist.

Shan waited to follow the man's lead.

"How long has it been since your last confession?"

"It's been . . . many years."

"I see." Father Anthony coughed with more force, further straining his voice. "And which sins do you wish to confess?"

Shan fumbled for an answer, suddenly questioning the priest's involvement. Before he could find any words, the man broke into a coughing fit. When he caught his breath, he rasped to the rookie guard, "Might I trouble you for a glass of water?"

Rookie easily agreed and strode toward the door.

In an instant, the priest recovered. He leaned toward Shan, whispering clearly but rushed. "Did you find the bag?"

"Yes, I — I did —"

"Then listen close and remember what I say. Behind the Model Industries Building, get past the gate and barbwire to reach the caves at the water. From the northern tip, it's a straight shot. Just follow the tide to Fort Point." Rookie was calling to another guard to help fetch some water as the priest charged on. "There's a beach landing. It's right under the south end of the Golden

Gate. You'll be driven to a safe place. Can you get away near nightfall?"

"I-I think so." Shan struggled to process the barrage of instructions. "It would . . . have to be before the final work count. I'd have thirty minutes."

The model building wasn't especially far from the lower greenhouse, but beyond Shan's usual area, and in view of at least two tower guards.

The priest cast a furtive glance past the screen before going on. "The tide will carry you, but stay on course and use the compass. If you stray too far, you'll be swept off to sea. Now, how soon?"

Shan had so many questions — of how the plan came about, how the priest was connected to all of this — but they would have to wait. "I'm not sure. I'll need a few days . . ." He thought of the coming week, leading to Halloween.

Rookie's footsteps were approaching.

Just then, it dawned on Shan how the festivities could help. "Saturday," he decided. Though circumstances obviously could change that.

With no time to respond, Father Anthony switched into his warbled voice. "I absolve you of your sins, in the name of the Father, and of the Son, and of the Holy Spirit." He made the sign of the cross, which Shan mirrored. "God bless you, my son. Go in peace."

50

A perpetual stream of nerves and second-guessing stretched the week interminably. Friday night was the longest of all. Shan tossed restlessly in his bunk as bouts of rain and wind alternated over the island. The foghorn moaned through the dark. For the hundredth time, the plan replayed in his head.

At the morning bell, he rose and followed the routine. He dressed and tidied his cell, ate and showered, and traded in his weekly laundry. All while hoping each step would be his last within the gray walls of Alcatraz.

Finally he was escorted through the thin afternoon fog, his cap lowered in the rain. When he entered the warden's greenhouse, his gaze went straight to the potato barrel, a habit now. On Monday, he'd added two tires from the rubber mat shop, where cons converted used tires into mats for the Navy. The expanded stack still held potatoes and dirt, but with the burlap bag at its core.

Though the barrel looked untouched since the prior day, he reached down into the soil regardless. He breathed easier at the ridged outline of the raft.

Now for the last component.

In Sadie's corner, he slid away the pots. There it was, just as she had promised. The large bundle was wrapped in brown paper. With hands dampened from rain, he moved it to the counter and untied the string. The hard-billed cap sat atop a small pile of folded garments: a uniform jacket with shirt and tie, finely pressed trousers, and a hooded raincoat.

"I know he won't notice," Sadie had said of her father's spare uniform. "He's got more." She'd volunteered the idea after confirming her conclusions ultimately were right: Shan was going to flee. He had wavered on the admission when she'd pressed the issue again, unrelenting, desperate, too wise not to know. In the end, torn by the girl's sufferings, Shan didn't have the heart to lie.

For days he scoured his brain for any other way to help her. After all, there was no guarantee they could find her mother. Or that her father would rest until Sadie was found.

But the fact remained: the girl didn't deserve to spend her life like an animal in a cage. Nor did Shan really, though he had forgotten for a time. Still, including her in the plan was ludicrous. The increased risks they would be taking. Maybe reporters were right about Alcatraz turning cons insane.

The faint giggles of children turned him.

Outside, excitement was brewing. The annual Halloween party drew every family on the island to an evening at the Officers' Club. In just hours, festive sounds were sure to distract the handful of guards on duty; the weekends always reduced a need for security. And who at the party, amid the chaos and cloaks of costumes, would notice one missing child?

Between regular counts, Shan made the few preparations he could, always mindful of the clock on the counter. Absently he cared for the plants. Yesterday in the warden's house, he had peeked at the *San Francisco Chronicle.* For an escape, the weekend projection of light rain and fog meant additional cover without obscuring the landing. Ideal conditions.

But as the hours eked by, he noted a warning in the clouds. The air smelled of electricity. Wind gusts rattled the walls. A storm was looming.

On the cusp of evening, he parked the pushcart just outside the door. An early darkness was setting in, accelerated by a dome of fog. The moon had vanished. Vessels would stay docked in these conditions, reducing his odds of being spotted in the bay. But would Fort Point be entirely shrouded by the time he shoved off? There was no way to know.

He loaded the cart with baskets of dangling bougainvillea. Unless searched, they would effectively hide the canvas tarp. He had obtained the material from the model shop, an aid for passage over the barbwire. Hopefully it would be enough.

Back inside, he returned to the stacked tires, garden trowel in hand. Sweat moistened his grip. This was it. Once he scooped out the dirt and retrieved the bag, there would be no going back. Already he felt perched on the edge of a cliff.

Suddenly a man shouted orders outside. "You two check the docks. We'll take the lighthouse." It was the voice of Warden Johnston, competing with rainfall and howling wind. "The rest of you spread out."

Shan strained to see through the water-streaked panes. He made out figures of off-duty guards and teenage sons. They were divvying up territory, organizing a hunt.

The white beam of a searchlight swept past the greenhouse. Over and over Shan had envisioned this happening — but only after he was gone. His pulse quickened and his lungs cinched. It all felt surreal; he was a fugitive on the run, the bandit in *Mark of Zorro*.

But then logic took hold. The search wasn't for him. He hadn't even left his detail, and they would certainly know where to find him. Could it be for another con? Had Ralph and Ted managed to break out of the cell house? The absence of a siren discounted the notion.

Raindrops pelted the ceiling, growing insistent. Tapping, tapping.

"Eh! Capello!"

His heart jumped. Leavenworth had taught him to stay keenly alert, a vital skill for survival, but somehow he'd missed the creak of the door.

He tightened his hold on the trowel before turning around. It was Finley, staring with his ferret-like eyes.

"Yeah, boss?"

"You seen a little girl pass by? Ten years old, light brown hair. About so high?"

Shan's stomach knotted. The reply had to sound natural, as steady as letting out fishing line. "No, sir. I'm afraid I haven't."

From the entry step, Finley scanned the area with an edge of discomfort. He wasn't a fan of the rare freedoms enjoyed by pass-men. "Aren't you about done here?"

"Sure am. Then I'll be heading to the lower greenhouse to finish up."

Finley lingered a bit — gauging, questioning — before he gave a small nod and turned to leave. When the door slammed, Shan's fingers tingled from adrenaline, tinged by fear. They weren't supposed to know she was missing — not yet. He hadn't figured on a search until his own absence triggered the alarm.

Once more, the potential consequences flickered through his mind. The dungeons, a beating, a bullet to the head. It wasn't too late to turn back. He could serve out his sentence by sticking to the grind, and one distant day walk out a free man.

But, no. No, it wasn't that easy. Not anymore. He recalled how Sadie had embraced him when he agreed to take her along, how she had cried as she whispered her thanks. And with that, any chance of reneging crumbled.

Through the fog, lightning cracked the sky. It cast an eerie blue glow over the warden's house, like a searchlight from above. The similarity conjured a thought.

They would be looking on the south end of the island, the civilian areas. The gymnasium, the parade grounds. They wouldn't suspect where she had gone.

They could do this.

The plan could still work.

So long as they never found the girl.

Shan transferred the cart. He reported for count. And now the minutes were ticking.

In the lower greenhouse, he turned on the overhead light bulb to prevent suspicion. The Powerhouse Tower guard wouldn't have a clear view into the room, but still Shan retreated to a back corner before removing and hiding his prison cap, coat, and coveralls. The guard uniform underneath, which he had donned an hour ago, was fully ready minus the raincoat and hat. He threw them both on.

The windows offered a faint reflection of his appearance. The whole uniform was a tad large, but he had no time to worry about that. He hurried back outside to the cart, set on the far side of the greenhouse. With no one in sight, he pulled out the burlap bag, now also concealing the tarp.

Steeling himself, he embarked on a walk guaranteed to be the longest of his life. The bag swayed in the wind, bumping hard against his leg. Though he assumed an air of authority, he kept his hat lowered under his hood, not unnatural given the weather. He fixed his gaze on the model building, his first destination. Thrashing waves echoed from the shore. The foghorn continued to moan.

From the Powerhouse Tower, the guard would have noticed his presence by now. More than eighty officers rotated shifts and stations every week. From a distance Shan's average build could fit one of many. He told himself this as he continued his strides, fighting the thought of a guard's finger on a trigger, taking easy aim.

Keep going. Walk with purpose. He was halfway there.

Cyclone wire and fencing waited ahead. The guard in the Model Tower, atop the industries building, was typically gone at this hour. But the officer in the Hill Tower stood at his post. His large shadow loomed above in the glass enclosure.

A gust of icy wind stalled Shan for a moment, causing him to gasp. Yet he forged on, determined not to stop. No longer an inmate, he was an officer assigned to drop off supplies.

Just fifty feet left now — and half as many

minutes. It took all his willpower not to break into a sprint. He could hear his own breathing, a hoarse rhythm in his ears.

The Hill Tower guard appeared to be facing the other way. Still no sign of an officer on the roof.

Shan briskly navigated his way to the fence behind the mat shop. There, he savored the reprieve from a tower guard's view. In seconds he found the locked gate through which cons discarded unneeded tire parts. It was the meeting spot he and Sadie had agreed upon. So where was the girl?

"Sadie," he whispered through the rain.

If she didn't show, would he be leaving without her?

She'd been so confident about reaching the place, having explored many areas deemed off-limits, though not always of her choosing. Since the warden prohibited booze, she'd explained, Yappy had occasionally tasked her with dumping the empties in the water out of sight. While he might not have specified how far, the bastard likely didn't care.

"Sadie," Shan called again a fraction louder.

A person approached from the dimness — not matching her likeness. Hunched in a winter coat, knickers exposed at the hem, the figure gave him pause. But once the kid got closer, Shan recognized her face, even before she removed her flat cap.

"It's a disguise," Sadie whispered. She shook her head to showcase her hair, hacked to a boy's length. "Like in *The Count of Monte Cristo.* They'll only be looking for a girl." Her conspiratorial smile almost made Shan forget the danger of their actions.

"You got the keys?" he pressed, setting down the bag.

"Right here." She scrambled to produce them from her pocket, and went to hand them over. But from anxiousness, or slickness from the rain, she let go too soon and the ring of keys dropped with a jangle.

They both froze. Alarm replaced the enthusiasm in Sadie's eyes.

But no guard shouted a warning. No shots were fired.

Shan snatched up Yappy's keys, raising them to the padlock on the gate. "Which one?"

She shook her head regretfully. She couldn't know them all.

He wasted no time before attempting the options. "Ah, come *on,*" he groaned after several failed.

Only four chances left. He shot a peek at the roof — no one there — and his thoughts whirled. Having considered this obstacle, he planned to use the air tank in his bag to bust the lock. Yet he couldn't be sure if rain and waves would hide the sound.

Another key slid in but wouldn't budge. Now three remained.

He tried again. It went in . . . and turned! The padlock released.

After another glance upward, he opened the gate and ushered Sadie through, tossing the lock into the withered weeds. He grabbed the bag and closed the gate behind them. Five rows of barbwire stood knee-high. Sadie looked up at him.

He retrieved the tarp and flung it over the rows. "Get on," he ordered in a hush, crouching down. She climbed onto his back and held tight to his neck. A deep blast of thunder shook the ground. Shan hugged the bulky bag to his chest and worked his way over the hurdles. He strained to keep his balance, refusing to envision the girl slipping off and tangling in the wires.

Once they had crossed, he set her down and yanked up the tarp, preventing a blaring trail. Now came the steep slope. Together, they negotiated the cliff, then strewn tire parts, to reach the water. Sadie made it look easier than it felt, traversing slick rubber and wet boulders. But then, she wasn't doing it while lugging a deflated raft.

Finally he and Sadie made it into a cave that extended far into an inky void. The air smelled of salt and decayed fish. Frigid water, ankle high, seeped into their shoes as they wove through piles of trash, tires, and debris. Waves broke on rocks bordering the entrance.

From this view, dense fog veiled the Golden Gate. Even buoys denoting the island's two-hundred-foot perimeter had disappeared. Until he and Sadie did the same, he prayed the uniform would once more shield him from a tower guard's aim.

Shan emptied the bag onto a heap of driftwood. Vision adjusting to the darkness, he united the raft with the valve of the tank. He gave it a crank and the air started to blow, feeding life into the rubber boat. A minute or two and they'd be on their way. But without notice, the whooshing of air waned and the raft swiftly died.

He turned the main valve of the tank as far as it would go, opening it full bore. But nothing came out. He shook the tank, terror rising in his chest. "Please, please no . . ." He tried again.

When he'd tested it days earlier, he had released just a whiff. Hadn't he closed the valve? Was there a slow leak? Had it been only partly filled from the start?

"What's wrong?" Sadie asked anxiously, hovering beside him.

At most, they had twenty minutes to spare. But they could do this.

He brought the valve of the raft to his mouth and blew out deep breaths. Faster, faster. The weight of the rubber slowed his efforts, but he kept going. Another breath, another. His lungs were burning, his brain turning lightheaded.

He patted the raft to gauge his progress. He wasn't filling it fast enough. How would they ever make it into the water in time?

Nights ago, he'd decided that if anything went terribly wrong, so long as they hadn't been discovered, they would sneak back up if they could. Try again another time, find a different way. He'd told Sadie and she had agreed, yet now he dreaded to deliver the news.

"I'm sorry, but we gotta go back."

Her lips pursed and her chin quivered. He wanted to comfort her — above all, to solve this — but the window of opportunity was closing. "We have to go now."

Sadie inhaled sharply, hands flying to her mouth. It was an expression of disappointment, he assumed, until she pointed toward the water. Shan turned just in time to catch a bright flash. He took it for lightning before it returned as a beam. A searchlight.

"Oh, God, no."

His absence shouldn't have been noticed yet. He had time left on his detail. Then he realized . . .

Still no alarm.

Suddenly a voice carried from outside. It was dim, but judging from Sadie's face, they had both heard it. Then louder. A man was calling her name. This meant Johnston had expanded the search. They were combing the entire island.

There was no escaping.

Shan would have to surrender — now as a kidnapper — or wait to be found. If his greenhouse chats with Sadie had risked foul and dark rumors, the fallout of this would be unimaginable. Not to mention what waited after Ted and Ralph learned of his deception.

And yet, from the sheer panic in Sadie's eyes, he feared even more the punishment she would face from her father. For bringing him shame, surely jeopardizing his career, how much more of her skin would he burn? How many hits could she endure before her body simply gave out?

Whether she had come voluntarily or not, Shan's crimes would be no different. His ending was sealed, but hers could be saved.

Shan leaned in and held her arms. "You tell them I forced you. Got it? That I threatened to hurt you, and your father, too, if you didn't help me. Do you hear?"

She nodded, her eyes rimmed with tears.

"Now, stay put." He rushed to the entrance of the cave, debating how best to surrender. Once they recognized him, the goon squad might descend with guns blazing, putting Sadie in equal danger.

He could always dive into the waves and ignore their warnings. Pull a Dutch Bowers. End it all right here. The idea gained appeal as he edged his head out and peered up the cliff. He expected guards to be working their way down, but no one was coming.

Again a voice called for Sadie. It traveled across the water, originating from the left. The silhouette of a rowboat carrying two people floated into view. One controlled the oars while the other held a flashlight, intermittently yelling, "Sadie!" Both were in guard uniforms and hats, topped with raincoats. Just like . . .

Shan.

The thought stopped him. In its wake an old memory slung back. Desperate to save himself and Nick, he'd once used the trick of a hat and a voice to become a ship steward. And the gamble had worked. The current stakes were inconceivably higher, but he glanced toward Sadie in the fuzzy blackness, and something in his gut, his heart, insisted he try.

An assessment of resources zipped through his mind, sprouting an idea.

"I think we still got a shot," he told her. "But we'd have to work fast."

The boat was closing in, likely with plans to pass by, but that was going to change. With supplies ready, Sadie crouched into hiding and Shan disguised his profile with his hood. He peered at the boat but still couldn't determine which guards were approaching. Hoping to high heaven they didn't include Ranger Roy, Shan transformed into the Southern lieutenant.

He cupped his mouth with one hand, further obscuring his face, as he stepped into view and hollered through the wind, "Fellas, over here! I need some help from y'all!" He motioned them closer, his heart thumping all the while. When the flashlight beamed toward his face, he angled away as if it were too bright.

"Who is that?" a guard shouted.

"It's Roy! Now, stop lollygagging and get over here. Found somethin' peculiar." Retreating into the shadows, Shan hugged the wall at the entrance. He waited, shank in hand.

If this didn't work, it would all be over.

Then came a *thunk* — the boat hitting rocks by the side of the cave. "Lieutenant? What is it?"

They were just outside. While searching for a civilian, they would be unarmed. Shan hoped.

He poked his head out just enough for a peek. "Y'all can tie up to that pile of tires there! But I need a hand from just one of ya. So hurry it up!"

If they hadn't heard him clearly and both came in at once, the odds of pulling this off could plummet.

The guards appeared to talk for a moment before one hopped out and quickly tied off the boat as ordered. Then he took the flashlight, leaving his pal behind, and scurried over a tire and some rocks.

The fact that it was Rookie was not a disappointment.

Shan moved a little farther in to assume his pose. His back to the entrance, hands on hips, he stared down at the raft. He heard the sloshing of Rookie's footsteps.

"What'd you find, Lieutenant?"

"Get a load of this," Shan said. "Reckon some inmates were fixin' to escape."

Rookie directed his flashlight at the ground and sidled up to Shan. "Well, how about that," he said in awe. "Who do you think —"

Shan stopped him with a blade to the neck. "Drop the light and put your hands behind your back." The guard bristled, and the flashlight fell into the water. "You keep silent, and my pal Ted Cole over there won't shoot the .45 he took off the Hill Tower guard. And trust me, he'd sure be happy to."

Rookie released a shaky breath and nodded. The guy was new to the gig, but not new enough to be unfamiliar with Ted's volatility.

In a minute tops, Shan had the guard seated behind a mound of tires with hands and feet bound with rope, gagged and blindfolded with strips of canvas. To support the ruse, Shan switched to the deeper, more sinister tone of Ted Cole. "Not a peep, you goddamn screw."

Rookie became a statue.

Shan salvaged the flashlight and scrambled back toward the entrance. Reverting to Ranger Roy, he would pull the same stunt in a flash. Only then did he consider that the second guard could be Yappy.

At the cave's edge, he was about to holler

regardless, yet caught himself. The boat was rocking, with no one aboard. Where the hell had he gone?

The answer came when the officer stepped from the side and stopped two feet away. It was Chandler, the guard with no reservations about shooting cons, as proven by the death of Bowers. The officer hedged, startled from recognition, and flicked a look at the shank in Shan's grip.

Though it was likely mere seconds, it felt far longer before Chandler lunged. All at once they were struggling for the weapon. Shan battled to hold on as he was slammed against the wall. The back of his skull met rock and his hat toppled forward. Chandler hammered at Shan's hand until the shank broke free. On reflex Shan reached out, but the blade disappeared with a splash.

He caught a glow in the water, from the flashlight now on the ground, before a fist struck his face. He'd barely registered the hit when another came to his gut. Trapped against the wall, he had to break loose.

Shan used every bit of his strength to push the guy back. He'd managed a few feet when Chandler lost his footing, taking them both to the slippery ground. The icy water stunned Shan momentarily; he recovered only to find Chandler scrambling for the shank.

In that instant, focused only on survival, Shan snatched the flashlight and swung it toward the guard, connecting with his head. The man collapsed.

Despite Shan's adrenaline, he registered fear about what he had done. But a quick check confirmed that Chandler was simply knocked out. With little time for relief, Shan heaved the guard to the side, enough to clear him from the water.

Shan was going to retrieve Sadie, but she was already at his side. He signaled for her to stay quiet. Then he snagged his hat, lifted her up, and carried her to the mouth of the cave. The searchlight was slanted away from the area. There were maybe five minutes to spare — their chances were minuscule. But at this point, hell, why not?

He untied the rope as Sadie climbed into the rowboat, and he after her. "Down on the floor," he told her. She obeyed without hesitation as he grabbed hold of the oars. Seated backward, he started rowing against the rain, the currents. Over his shoulder there was no destination to see, only a wall of fog.

The searchlight slid closer, closer. It moved over the black waves like an electric eel at the surface. Shan held his breath, clutching the oars, and the beam brushed right past them. After all, he was a guard. Or invisible.

That was certainly how he felt when the mist swallowed them up. He kept an ear out for proof that an inmate search had been launched. But due to the weather or a delay of discovery — the count perhaps disturbed by the hunt for Sadie — he heard no siren.

The boat picked up speed in the shipping channel, the outgoing tide sending them toward the Golden Gate. Southwest of the island, the red suspension bridge that he'd eyed for months, and with purposeful interest this past week, now lay in hiding.

Panic simmered in his gut as he recalled Father Anthony's words. Stray off course and they'd be swept off to sea. In this fog, they could very well be headed to Alaska.

Where was the damn bridge? Where was the mainland?

"Unbelievable," he muttered. He continued to row, scanning over his shoulder, his muscles burning. His damp body trembled from cold and adrenaline. "After all this, we can't even find the stupid landing?"

Sadie's face eased upward. Though there was probably little harm in her sitting now, he preferred to be careful, and to focus. He started to tell her to stay low when she interjected.

"Would this help?" She drew a necklace from under her coat collar. It was the compass, stored around her neck. The shock of it halted Shan.

"Actually, yeah." A laugh tumbled from his mouth. "It would."

Sadie grinned.

He directed her in holding the compass as he rowed. She displayed the wiggling needle, keeping as steady as possible.

The rain lightened to a sprinkle along the way, and thinning fog bettered visibility, but only in patches. At this speed, it couldn't be much farther. If they hadn't passed it already.

Maybe a large vessel in the Pacific would be willing to bring them aboard. Shan looked harmless, still in a uniform. Although why would he be out in this weather? It would be wise to create a plausible story just in case.

"There! There!" Sadie pointed.

Shan twisted around and spied a red tower of the monstrous bridge reaching for the sky, fading into the clouds. High above, haloed headlights projected from vehicles moving in both directions. Soft twinkling lights to his right marked the city. They were on the south side of the Golden Gate!

"Keep low," he told her.

Pulling back hard on the left oar, he cut the boat at an angle. Through the shadows came the outline of a sandy strip. He'd rejoice if not for fear of gliding right by.

As he neared the shore, a man emerged from the darkness. He rushed into the water and grabbed the bow. When he glanced up, Shan recognized his face beneath the rim of his hat. The musician from the party.

"It's you," Shan said, relieved.

The man scowled in return. "The plan," he said, "was to pop the raft, stuff it in the trunk. What am I supposed to do with this goddamn thing?"

Before Shan could answer, Sadie stood up in the boat. The musician snapped his gaze back to Shan, making clear the same question applied to her.

51

The only sounds in the Fordor Sedan came from the rumbling of its wheels. Even if the driver struck them as a conversationalist — which decidedly he did not — he'd already shared how he felt about their unplanned risks. The expletives he'd muttered while shoving the rowboat off with the tide were followed by several more as he hurled the oars in separately.

With no less warmth, he had hustled Shan and Sadie into the backseat. They were to remain on the floor, draped with a blanket for fear of roadblocks. Down that low, the air reeked of cigarettes and gasoline.

The drive had just begun when a police siren whizzed by. Sadie reached over to squeeze Shan's hand. Her palm was wrapped in a small bandage he hadn't noticed earlier. His thoughts shot to her son-of-a-bitch father, but this time, she said, the fault was hers. "I did it when I cut my hair," she whispered.

The guy was still a son of a bitch.

Soon their unseen surroundings quieted, and Sadie didn't look nearly as nervous as she should. Then again, she had endured much worse.

Shan ventured to ask the driver, "Where we headed?" They had been traveling for the better part of an hour. A peek through the back windows revealed little in the darkness.

"Away," the guy replied, and proceeded to smoke with the window barely cracked. "Keep covered."

Reluctant, Shan pulled the blanket back over, sensing even more familiarity. How did he know the guy?

He considered the man's bearing, hat pulled low, driving while puffing on a cigarette. And the image jogged a memory. Now Shan remembered. Without the toothbrush mustache, he was the getaway driver from the bank job. One of the robbers who'd left Nick to rot.

Shan feared what this could mean, especially for Sadie. There was no question how bastards like this treated liabilities.

A sharp turn changed the sound of the drive. The wheels were bumping over a dirt road. It then dawned on Shan how the blanket could have served another purpose: to keep him unaware of the destination. If so, it had worked. Shan had no inkling where they were.

The sedan stopped and the driver got out.

Sadie whispered, "Now what?"

Shan shook his head that he didn't know. He shoved his rain hood all the way down, straining to listen. From another peek, he detected only rural landscape.

Then the footsteps returned and the back door squeaked open. The blanket was yanked away. Shan's skin, warm and damp from breathing under cover, prickled from the cold.

"They're waitin'," the driver said flatly. "In there."

Shan unfolded from the car, back aching from the cramped quarters, jaw and gut sore from Chandler's fists. Sadie climbed out after him and adjusted her cap.

A barn lay ahead, outlined by moonlight pushing through the clouds. A crop covered the surrounding hills. Vines, Shan realized. This wasn't a farm, but a vineyard. The scent of fermenting grapes hung in the air.

Again Sadie held his hand. She knew something was off.

"It'll be okay." He forced a partial smile,

daunted by the unknown waiting inside. And yet, where else could they go?

He guided her forward. Every few steps he glanced back at the driver, now leaning against the car, keeping lookout. Shan had grown wary of having anyone behind him; even more so when that person was likely armed.

At the solid oak door, he steeled himself and raised his hand to knock. He got no further before the door swung open to a man boasting a wide grin.

"Hell, look at this," the fellow said. "Two years in the pen, and the place turned you into a copper." His pencil mustache and light hair, slightly shaggy, didn't match his voice. A voice Shan knew almost as well as he knew his own.

He peered into the guy's eyes to confirm the impossible, and what he found nearly buckled his knees. Standing before him, alive and well, was Nick Capello.

The discovery stunned Shan to silence.

With a heavy sigh, Nick put a hand on Shan's shoulder. "Gotta admit, I was starting to get nervous. Been pacing for hours and . . ." The rest fell off when Sadie caught his eye.

"Sweetheart, close the door," a woman called out. Josie's voice.

Stepping back, Nick ushered them in and locked the door. A lantern glowed yellow on a table in the room. It threw shadows across wine barrels aligned in rows.

Shan struggled to grasp the world he had entered, a place where Nick was walking, talking, and breathing. Nick. The friend he had lost.

"But — you were — I thought —"

Nick smiled at Shan's battle for words.

Before Shan could try again, Josie appeared and said, "Now, who've we got here?" Her attention rested on the child clinging to his side.

Nick, too, looked in want of an explanation.

Shan scrounged for an answer through his tangle of thoughts. "This is . . . Sadie. She needed to come too."

"Oh," Josie said, surprised. "I thought she was a —" She cut herself off, an effort not to offend.

"It's a disguise," Sadie volunteered. Her tone was quiet but lined with pride.

"Well, you sure had me fooled," Josie said. "And trust me, I know my disguises."

Indeed she did. Josie was barely recognizable, with her platinum curls dyed black, shortened to just below the ears. In place of a sparkly, curve-hugging number, a cream cardigan layered a simple peach housedress. Likewise, Nick sported a workingman's shirt, brown woolen trousers, and dusty boots. A far cry from the fancy suit he'd been wearing when Shan last saw him.

On the day he'd died.

Shan was still straining to comprehend. "In the bank, I thought you were . . ."

"Shot to hell and hauled away?" Nick said.

"This," Josie said, "sounds like boring grownup talk. Sadie, honey, you got a little time to spare. How 'bout we get ourselves a drink. Some grape juice, maybe. You hungry?"

Sadie looked up at Shan, gauging the offer.

"She's an old friend, Sadie. You'll be all right."

Relaxing, Sadie released Shan's hand and accepted Josie's. The two trod past the barrels and into another room, with Josie making conversation all the way. The gal always did have a talent for lowering people's guards.

"Come on and take a load off." Nick motioned to the right with his chin. "You gotta be beat."

As though following a ghost, Shan trailed him to the table. Made from the lid of a barrel, the furnishing was flanked by two ladder-back chairs. Beside the lantern waited a bottle of red wine with a pair of long-stemmed glasses.

"Here, have a seat," Nick said, and worked to remove the cork. But Shan remained standing.

Nick proceeded to pour for them both. "We've been hunkered down here all day. Friends said we could help ourselves, but honestly my gut's been twisted." He shook his head and let out a breath. "You're here now, though, ain't ya," he said, and raised his glass in a toast.

Part of Shan wanted to jump in and celebrate. But his startle was now morphing into a sense of betrayal. The grief and guilt he had harbored all this time couldn't be so easily shed.

"You had a funeral." Not a recollection. An accusation.

Nick's eyes dimmed, revealing his aware-ness that he had this coming. He lowered his glass and gave a small shrug. "They switched me for a John Doe. Guy had no one to claim him." He raised a palm as if swearing in court: "A stroke. I had nothin' to do with it."

The alternative hadn't crossed Shan's mind, though at this point it should have. "Did Ma and Pop know? And Lina?"

"Nah. Not at first," Nick said, assuring Shan he wasn't the only one duped. "The undertaker told them a closed casket was best, 'cause of my wounds. If there'd been another way, trust me I would've done it. But first, I was out of sorts, trying to recover. Then with the heat from the feds, I didn't want to put my family in a tough spot. Not like I did you." His voice thickened, as if by his own layer of guilt. He cleared his throat, washed it down with wine. "Of course, they were real happy when they found out the truth. And they'll be even happier when they hear about you now."

Shan had to remind himself he was free at the moment. He was grateful for that. But then, he never would have been imprisoned if it weren't for Nick.

He pulled off his guard hat. "What were you thinking, stealing from Max anyway?"

Nick eyed him. "You really thought I was that dumb?" He smiled and reclined on his chair.

Right at that moment, Shan realized he didn't know a thing. But he did deserve to understand the reason he'd spent two years behind bars. "Why the robbery, then?"

As Nick took a sip of wine, Shan opted to sit after all. He could tell this wasn't going to be a simple story.

"It was Sal and Vito," Nick explained. "For years, they were in charge of collecting tax from shopkeepers. Protection, you know, by Max. Come to find out, the two of 'em kept hiking the prices, pocketing the difference. Shopkeepers were afraid to complain, so the tax kept going up."

It didn't take much for Shan to imagine the scenario, having survived it firsthand.

"Finally Max hears what's going on. Along with a rumor that they're working on some racket with a wiseguy in Jersey. So Max confronts Sal and Vito. They come clean about the shops, full of sorrys, swearing to repay double, but they deny the rest. Max doesn't buy it. But he wants proof before doing anything drastic. Also he wants to know who this wiseguy is. So that's where me and Jimmy — my pal out there — came in."

Shan glanced toward the door. He had forgotten the driver was outside. Of course, clearer in his mind was watching the "pal" leave Nick at the bank in a pool of blood. "And then?"

"And then," Nick said, "we put out a leak that I've been called out for skimming off the back room. Then I go to Sal, tell him I'm desperate for cash and how I'm fed up with Max and his small-time thinkin'. I tell him me and Jimmy got a lead on a hot deal in Pittsburgh, but that Max wasn't up for the risk."

Nick rested an elbow on the table and swirled his wine a bit. "Pretty soon, Sal comes back and says he's got a solid connection who wants to meet. Some banker in Jersey, crooked as a fishhook. So we all drive together. Sal has Jimmy pull over and wait. Says too many people will make the banker jittery."

"Let me guess," Shan said. "There was no deal."

"There was no connection. Not there anyway. They put on scarves, stuff one in my hand, and draw their guns. Sal hollers for everybody to get down. Says he'll start shooting if anyone trips the alarm. By then, Vito nabbed the guard's pistol, and Sal's telling me to put on the mask. What was I supposed to do?"

"How about make a break for it? Get back to the car."

"Because I was guilty just being there," Nick said, and Shan had to acknowledge the hard truth in that; the past two years were solid proof. "Anyway, Sal starts stuffing cash in a sack, tells me how he and Vito have alibis in place. That if I don't want to take the rap for this, I'm gonna convince Max they're not doing side deals. Make sure they're back in his good graces before the boss sends a torpedo their way."

"So . . . you refused," Shan guessed, a reason they would have left him behind.

"Nah. I lied and told him I'd do it — if we got right the hell out of there. But Vito doesn't wanna go without cracking the vault. We start arguing, and shots blast our way. Guard must've been packing another gun. He hits me with a slug before Vito takes him out. Then comes the siren, and off they go."

"Including Jimmy," Shan reminded him.

Nick raised a shoulder. "They told him I was dead. Can't blame the guy, what with cops closing in. Even so," he pointed out, "I'd say he's made up for it."

Shan thought of the smuggled raft, the escort here. He supposed he couldn't disagree. He set his hat on the table and rolled the stem of his glass between his fingers. "So, how the hell did you make it out alive?"

"I nearly didn't," Nick said. "If the coroner hadn't noticed my pinkie movin' — or didn't have the smarts to call Max — I'd have been done for. But now look, huh? Just like you, I got another start. And with Josie too." He gazed across the room where she'd disappeared, and his eyes softened. "We're living in Wyoming now. Nice small town. Lots of good folks there."

Shan remembered Nick's last words at the robbery, his deep regrets over losing Josie. He just hoped that clarity wouldn't fade. "I assume this means you've gone straight."

Nick just looked at him. "I'm a pipe fitter at an oil refinery. Can't get much straighter than that."

Shan noticed a touch of grit under Nick's nails and felt some pleasure at the irony. Finally he took a drink of his wine, savoring the indulgence he'd missed — a blend of blackberries and pepper — but also listening for wheels on the driveway. He wished there were windows, to keep an eye out for headlights.

"I know what you gotta be thinkin'," Nick said after a pause. "It's not fair to her, having to start all over. I realize that. I just . . . I couldn't let her go again." There was a raw sincerity in his tone that Shan found refreshing, even comforting.

"Yeah, well. Doing what's right and what makes sense aren't always the same thing."

Nick smiled a little.

It seemed to Shan that Josie had never loved Nick for all the glitz and glamour; she'd loved him in spite of it. Something

Nick, too, appeared to have realized.

About to take another sip, Nick hesitated. "Speaking of girls, what's the story with the kid?"

Shan didn't have the time or energy to spin a tale. And since they seemed to be spilling all . . .

"She's the daughter of a prison guard."

In the midst of a swallow, Nick spit part of it out. He set down his glass, wiping his mouth. "Christ."

"She needed to get away, so she can live with her mom. For good reason."

"I would hope," Nick said. "When you meeting this woman?"

"As soon as we can."

"You don't have anything set?"

"She's in Kentucky, some town by a big river. Works on a switchboard. There can't be all that many. And Sadie knows a few more details. We'll find her before long."

"Wait," Nick said. "You plan to just traipse around with this kid, knocking on doors?" He shook his head, bewildered. "You realize you'll be in every major paper in the country, right? Make that both of you now."

Shan downed a gulp of wine. It wasn't an ideal plan, but what were the choices?

"I'll . . . get a disguise," he said.

"No. No way. Do you know the headache,

not to mention the dough, it cost me to get you out of that hellhole?" Nick leaned on the table toward him. "In four months, I got everything set up at Leavenworth. Two guards, the chaplain, a surefire plan. Even a cellmate to make sure you didn't go and die before I could bust you out. Then what do you do? You get yourself transferred to the most secure prison in the damn country."

Shan stared at him, dumbfounded. His thoughts drifted back to Mitty, a friendly cellmate eager to help. And the chaplain, Father Anthony.

"Almost two years it took me to finagle this," Nick charged on. "That jazz group had to be personally requested *twice* by congressmen. And that's not including the favors to get that priest transferred to Alcatraz. So I don't know how you're gonna get this girl to her mother, but unless you both want a trip right back to that island, I strongly suggest —"

"I'll do it." Josie's voice abruptly turned Shan and Nick. She stood halfway across the room, a protective arm around Sadie.

Shan put down his glass, noting the worry in the girl's face. He rose and made his way over. He didn't have to wonder how long they'd been listening.

When he reached them, Josie said, "Sadie

explained everything. You were right to bring her, Tommy." Her resolve made clear Sadie's sufferings had struck a personal chord. Yet Josie seemed to have forgotten her own predicament.

"You're not supposed to be drawing any attention," Shan told her.

"And I won't. Fact is, I'm the only person in the room who's got nobody looking for 'em."

Oddly she was right about that. Still, how could Shan possibly walk away, leave the girl with virtual strangers?

Appearing to understand, Josie eased down to Sadie's level and spoke in a gentle voice. "Sweetie, can I ask you somethin'?"

Sadie pursed her lips, stained purple, waiting.

"Now, I know we just met. And it can be real scary to venture out with folks you don't know. But if you'll let me, I'll do everything in my power to get you back to your mama. I swear on my life, we won't rest till we find her." Josie used a thumb to brush crumbs from Sadie's cheek. "Could you trust me enough to do that?"

For several seconds Sadie peered into Josie's eyes, as if seeking evidence for an honest answer. Then she looked up at Shan in silent debate.

Shan wanted to say he would join them, that he would help deliver her to her mother firsthand. He wanted so desperately to be there when the two embraced, assuring him of the happy ending Sadie deserved. But he also knew his presence would only jeopardize the chance of that ever happening.

Siding with logic, against the pull of his heart, he gave Sadie a nod — a pledge that she could believe his friend.

With a look of understanding Sadie returned to Josie, and she agreed.

Just then, someone pounded at the door.

The room halted.

"Time to beat it outta here," the voice said, muffled through the wood.

Nick's shoulders lowered. He called back, "All right, Jimmy. Warm up the car."

Josie smiled at Shan, a sign that she would make good on her word. He already knew she would. But at this very moment, it shrank to the smallest of his worries.

Slow with reluctance, for a final time he lowered onto one knee before Sadie. Emotion billowed inside as he realized that while he just might have saved this little girl — this brave adventurer capable of conquering the world — she had managed, in more ways than one, to save him right back.

"You're gonna be okay now," he said, his

voice turning hoarse.

She nodded and offered a wisp of a smile. Somehow she was the one giving the real reassurance.

Not ready to leave, he tapped the compass around her neck. "You keep that, all right? So whenever you feel lost, and you think there's no way out, you just remember this day."

At this, her chin crinkled and her eyes went glossy with tears. Shan resisted a rush of his own. He had far more to say, but aware he'd choke on the words, he just lifted his hands and said, "Come here, smarty."

Sadie leapt forward and threw her arms around him. He felt moisture from her tears on his cheek, and the soft patter of her heart. "I won't ever forget you," she whispered.

Needless to say, he felt exactly the same about her.

A quarter of the moon now shone over the vineyard, lighting a path to the sedan. Behind the steering wheel, Jimmy puffed away, anxious to leave. Warmth lingered through Shan's sleeves from his farewell hug with Sadie, then Josie.

"This is for you," Nick said, handing him a travel bag as they walked.

"What is it?"

"Some money, new ID, books from Lina. A change of clothes. You can put them on during the drive. You got a long road ahead."

Shan pulled out the envelope, thick with cash, far more than he would have expected. "Nick — this is too much."

"Don't worry. It's fine."

"But you and Josie are gonna need that. Especially now, with Sadie."

Nick hedged, looking away, not answering.

It wasn't from him, Shan realized. "I take it this is from Max, huh?"

At the car, Nick hitched his hands on his hips. "Look. Max helped plenty, pulling strings and all. But this — he didn't want me to say, but this is from Pop."

"Pop?" Shan said.

"Apparently he keeps a hefty stash for a rainy day. Must've pinched pennies here and there for years."

Shan recalled the morning he'd first trailed Mr. Capello to the tracks, how the activity had become their special secret. Maybe it still was.

"Now, remember," Nick said, opening the back door. "When Jimmy gets you to your next stop, you lay low. I mean, not even showing your mug in the window for at least a month. You got that?"

"I got it." Shan tossed the bag into the backseat, which rumbled from the idling motor. "And, *you* remember. If anything goes wrong with Sadie —"

"You'll hear about it," Nick stressed. "But hell, after pulling off tonight? Finding this mom will be a walk in the park."

Jimmy urged over his shoulder, "You want any chance of crossing state lines, we gotta go."

Shan stood at the open door, not wanting to climb in. "Well . . . I guess this is good-bye."

"For now," Nick asserted, his words underscored by his signature smirk. Then he drew Shan into a hug. "You're my brother," he said near his ear. "We'll meet up again."

Then Shan got into the sedan and shut the door. He raised a hand as they pulled away and Nick's silhouette faded into the darkness.

Bumping along the dirt road, Shan opened the bag. A small pouch lay in an upturned fedora. He shook out its contents of spectacles, a fake mustache, even his old sixpence. It wasn't a wild guess that he'd need any luck it possessed.

He set the items aside. Packed below a

black suit and wingtips were books that had once belonged to his mother, except for one. *The Man in the Iron Mask.* He opened the cover and read the inscription: *I was wrong. Life is full of second chances. — Josie*

Shan surely hoped to prove the theory.

He noticed a document peeking from the pages. A new identity for a new start. He unfolded the paper and only then did his tears start to fall. For the name Nick had chosen wasn't that of a stranger. It was Shanley Keagan, a name he'd spent more than half his life earning back.

52

It was official: Tommy Capello was dead.

At a press conference three days after the escape, Warden Johnston proclaimed the news. "After an extremely thorough investigation," the papers quoted, "we have every reason to believe the prisoner drowned. The U.S. Coast Guard has located the rowboat the inmate acquired by force. It was badly damaged and upended from the storm. There is no evidence to suggest a landing in the surrounding areas, and no cars were reported stolen within forty-eight hours of the attempted escape. The dense fog and strong currents would have made it almost impossible for anyone but a highly trained seaman to navigate the boat effectively. As a precaution, however, we will continue our search efforts, working closely with local authorities and the FBI to ensure the citizens of San Francisco are safe."

In the end, Shan supposed, Alcatraz's

escape-proof title remained moderately intact, since no fleeing prisoner had made it out alive. A distinction that brought comfort to many.

Even more than residents on the mainland, civilians on the Rock were desperate for an assurance of security. And they soon received it with little help from the warden. Aside from a few initial articles questioning a connection between the prison break and Sadie Martin's disappearance, journalists were quick to uncover a darker story of an alcoholic guard whose violent tantrums could have led to the death of his young daughter.

"I tried to look out for her as often as I could," their neighbor, Mrs. Leonard, lamented to the papers. "Being next door, we knew things weren't right for some time, but we never dreamt it would come to this."

The woman had reportedly visited Sadie's apartment, intending to offer her help in preparing for the Halloween party, but the girl had gone missing. Not unusual, in and of itself. But a bloodied shirt in her room — from cutting her own hair, Shan would guess — had raised grave concern. When immediately questioned, her intoxicated father had flared with anger, spurring the warden to launch an immediate search.

Island investigators further concluded that the distraction of the girl's disappearance, coupled with heavy fog, had provided a clear opportunity for Tommy Capello's escape.

Escape, of course, being a relative term.

Seven weeks had passed since the breakout and still Shan remained in hiding, confined to a remote log cabin in Oregon. He'd received no word about Sadie — a good sign really. By now, he had faith the girl had been reunited with her mother. If not, he knew Nick wouldn't give up until he reached the goal. Shan just wished he, too, had a worthwhile mission. Other than waiting.

He'd reread each of his books four times and played countless rounds of cards. Always solitaire. His host was a reclusive lumberjack whose range of preferred vocabulary was as wide as his menu, which consisted of five dishes. Shan had yet to learn his name and relation to Nick; it went without saying that ignorance would benefit them both.

Fortunately, outdoor sounds — twigs snapping, branches rustling — had lost their initial impact, and Shan no longer imagined G-men stalking behind trees, closing in for the kill. On the downside, the isolation had grown wearing. Although there were no steel bars, some days it seemed they were there but simply invisible.

It was another Monday afternoon — or was it Wednesday? Shan sat at the small hand-carved table, eating beef stew yet again. He had to confess, he did miss the food at Alcatraz, if nothing else. The wood-stove crackled and raindrops streaked the room's lone window. Another gray overcast sky. He slurped more stew and wiped his short beard with his sleeve. Every day he hoped the all-clear sign Jimmy had promised would arrive before Shan became as grizzly as the lumberjack.

Right then, as if conjured by the thought, the man plodded into the house, bringing the smell of dampened trees. Back from a periodic trip to town, he closed the door with his boot and set down a sack from the store, a newspaper and magazine poking from inside. He hung his raincoat on a wall hook made from an antler.

Greetings were wasted, Shan had learned, met with silence or a grunt. He didn't bother now, partly due to his own sour mood. He just returned to forcing down his meal.

The man pulled an envelope from a back pocket of his coveralls. He ripped it open and slid out cash that he briskly counted.

From the bottom of the pile, he unfolded a single sheet of newspaper. The top half of a front page, it appeared. After a glance, he tossed the clipping over to Shan.

The headline shouted in bold letters.

TWO MORE ESCAPE ALCATRAZ IN FOG

Shan perked in his seat. He dove into the article.

On December sixteenth, Ralph Roe and Theodore Cole, after weeks of secretive sawing, broke through a window sash in the Model Industries Building. They kicked out two glass panes to reach the ledge. Using a wrench, they removed the padlock of a gate used for discarding tires and proceeded to the rocky shore with empty five-gallon oil cans, intended for floatation. At his request, Roe had recently transferred to work in the mat shop beside longtime friend Cole. The felons had likely been inspired to swim from the northern tip of the island after the escape of Tommy Capello. As with the previous incident, Roe and Cole were presumed to have drowned in the fast-moving tide, though searches would continue with the aid of revenue cutters, Coast Guard vessels, and police craft.

Shan paused in his reading. He noticed an indention from handwritten letters on the other side of the paper. He flipped it over. *Bon voyage,* it said in pencil over newsprint.

This was the sign. The message he'd been waiting for. A smile stretched his mouth and a laugh bubbled out of him. The lumberjack frowned, not understanding. But Shan did. With Roe and Cole taking priority, the case of Tommy Capello would fall to the back of the files. Shan was finally able to leave.

Just to be certain, he continued through the article. It went on to describe a history of the criminal acts committed by the two felons. What followed were snippets related to Alcatraz: an inmate strike that had been subdued in the fall; injuries Warden Johnston had incurred months ago from an attack by disgruntled prisoner Burton "Whitey" Phillips.

Shan was skimming to the bottom, expecting a standard history of the island as a military fort, when a name stopped him cold. *Fred Martin,* it read, *the former Alcatraz guard who was relieved of duty following the disappearance of his ten-year-old daughter, died in the midst of a police investigation in November. Police claim Martin was intoxicated when he drove off the Pleasant Valley Bridge.*

It is unclear whether the act was deliberate or accidental.

Shan read the summary again and sank into his seat, the last of his worries melting away.

Wherever she was now, Sadie, too, was free.

53

Beneath the cloudy winter sky, greeters swarmed passengers at Dún Laoghaire. Daylight at the Dublin port was fading fast. The air carried a chill, but Shan didn't bother to fasten his overcoat. He hurried through the crowd, antsy from the ten-day crossing and limited in time. If he wanted to reunite with the Maguires today, he had to reach the shop before it closed.

He waved his hat to hail a taxi, and off he went.

On the streets appeared far fewer horse-drawn wagons than when he had left, and the gas fumes and city grime varied little from conditions in New York. Perhaps that was why Ireland didn't feel as foreign as he'd expected.

At the familiar intersection on Kerry Street, he rushed to stop the driver, the order coming out brusque.

"Bloody Yanks," the cabbie muttered in reply.

Shan refrained from correcting him, not quite knowing which nationality to claim. He simply paid a bit extra before resetting his hat. Then he climbed out with his travel bag, returning with little more than what he'd taken all those years ago.

He waited for folks on the sidewalk to pass, their brogues like an old lullaby in his ears. When he stepped through the door of Maguire & Co., the fragrances of teas and sweets were much like he remembered. For an instant he was again the eleven-year-old boy who'd found sanctuary within these walls. But then he noted how those walls had changed. An apricot hue had replaced the dark brown paint, and shelves had been rearranged. Books were now in the corner by a pair of cushioned chairs. Displays of merchandise, no longer in rows, zigzagged through the room.

"Sir, I'm afraid we're about to close," a woman said with a gentle lilt. "Can I help ye find somethin'?" She was feather dusting a table nearby. In her midtwenties, she had long red wavy hair and a pencil tucked behind her ear. She wore a white apron over a russet dress that highlighted her matching eyes.

Shan was surprised by the addition of an employee.

"I'm looking for Mr. Maguire."

The girl stopped dusting. "I'm sorry," she said regretfully. "But Mr. Maguire isn't around anymore."

Shan shot a glance at the counter. He found a vacancy where the kind man should have been standing. Just like that, the world went still. Shan should have considered the possibility, given the passage of decades, but he hadn't brought himself to imagine.

"Sir?" Concern lined her brow. "Are you all right?"

Shan's mouth had gone dry. He pushed out the words. "I knew him. As a boy."

She nodded, waiting for him to go on.

Images of a heart attack, like the one suffered by Mr. Capello, followed by painful bedridden days, flashed through Shan's mind. "What happened to him?"

She stared for a moment before her eyes widened. "Heavens me, I didn't mean —" Her full lips burst into a smile. "I just meant he's retired, so he only comes in now and then."

"Ah, thank God," Shan said, and heaved a sigh.

The girl strove for a serious face, but a giggle slipped out. She covered her mouth and shook her head. "I'm sorry. It's not funny at all."

Shan felt such relief he couldn't help but laugh too.

"Now that I've scared the wits out of ye," she said, extending her hand. "I'm Caitlín, Mr. Maguire's niece."

He accepted her handshake, and slowly the pieces moved into place. "Wait. I remember you. You visited a few times when you were little."

"It would've been every day if my family hadn't lived so far off."

"You were from . . . Kilkenny?"

"Castlecomer. My mam's convinced I only attended university here to be closer to the shop." Caitlín shrugged. "She was right, mind you. Just don't tell her I said so."

Shan couldn't believe this was the same small lass who used to skip around the candy bins, singing tunes off-key. Her ruffled dresses perpetually bore drool from toffees she would eat one after the other.

"Mind if I let go now?" she asked.

Shan didn't realize he was still shaking her hand. He relinquished his grip and felt a flush in his neck he hadn't experienced in years.

She gently bit her lower lip, amused.

"About the Maguires," he said, the reason

he'd come. "Any idea where I might find them?"

"Aye. And I just might be able to tell ye if I know who you are."

"Sorry," he said. "Of course. I'm Shan Keagan." He was still growing accustomed to using the name again.

Caitlín fell silent. Her mouth gaped. Now she was the one struggling to speak. "I . . . didn't recognize . . ." Gradually the shock in her eyes softened, and her smile returned. "Give me a minute to lock up."

Upon their reunion, unlike the day Shan had departed from Ireland, Mr. Maguire made no effort to hide his emotions. His tears rolled as freely as did those from his wife. The couple took turns enveloping him with hugs and exclamations of joy.

Caitlín, who'd eagerly swept him across town, interrupted to take Shan's hat and coat. She hung them on hooks in the entry of the Maguires' charming two-story cottage.

"I can hardly believe it." Mr. Maguire shook his head. "Shanley Keagan. Here under me very own roof." The man's sweater was no less taut around his belly than it once had been, while the wrinkles on his face had doubled. His hair, all silvered now, formed a thin wreath.

"I just wish it hadn't taken me so long," Shan said.

Mr. Maguire chuckled. "Would ye listen to the lad. Talkin' like a real American."

"And so grown up, he is." Mrs. Maguire held her fists to the hips of her housedress. Her hair, too, had gone pure gray, still pinned in a low bun. "How about some supper, now? You must be famished after such a journey."

"I'd love nothing more," Shan said, an honest answer. Between the cabin's limited menu and unimpressive ship food, it was hard to recall his last enjoyable meal.

"I'll get started straightaway," Mrs. Maguire said. "In the meanwhile, Caitlín can show you up to her old room, where you're welcome to stay as long as you please."

"Aye," Caitlín said. "But first, I'll be showing him to the bath."

Shan glanced down at his suit, his tie and shirt stained, his shoes in dire need of a polish. Second class was a great improvement over the accommodations of his original voyage, but his wardrobe options were still minimal. "Am I that bad?"

"Not at all," Caitlín replied. "You're actually worse."

Though they all laughed at this, Shan

recognized her lack of exaggeration when he stood before the bathroom mirror. His mustache and beard were far overdue for a trim. Then again, here, so far from America, neither would be necessary.

He found scissors and a shaving kit in the mounted cabinet. As steaming water filled the claw-footed tub, he shed the remnants of his disguise.

Over supper, it was as if Shan's personal "Rule of Silence" had been lifted. All it took was a little whiskey and Mr. Maguire asking about America, and Shan's stories poured out like a river. He began with Uncle Will dying on the ship, and the Italian family that welcomed him in. Of course, he said nothing of a borrowed name. Nor of the obstacle now keeping him from the Capellos, only that he direly longed to reunite with them someday.

Next came his vaudeville tours, the excitement and gruel of them, and even a mention of his time in burlesque. Though Caitlín didn't bat an eye, a slight blush did color her cheeks. Not surprisingly, Mr. Maguire got a good chuckle over the tale of Paddy O'Hooligan and could hardly believe Shan had performed with such legends as George Cohan, Steve Porter, and his favorite Billy Murray.

Shan also spoke of his years in plumbing, including a few of Mr. Capello's humorous anecdotes. And he talked about gardening — without specifics of location — and how he'd gained a true passion for the craft.

"Why, with all those experiences," Mrs. Maguire remarked, "you're sure to have your pick of jobs whenever you're settled."

"You know, you're probably right," Shan said. For years, his primary goal had been survival, with not much thought beyond it.

Once they had finished their meals — a delicious plateful of sausages, beets, and buttered potatoes — an awkward quiet amassed over the room. Something was not being said. Perhaps Shan's talk of burlesque, or of the pipe clogged from a mistress's stocking, had caused offense, after all.

"You'll have to pardon all my blabbing," he said. "I've obviously been cooped up on a ship too long."

"Not a bit, lad," Mr. Maguire said. "Your tales are far more interesting than ours."

Shan nodded, though out of the corner of his eye he caught Mrs. Maguire and Caitlín sharing an odd look. Before he could define it, Mr. Maguire brought the meal to a close and suggested Shan retire for the night.

It was a clear cue. Shan thanked them for

the hospitality and bid good night to Caitlín before she headed for her flat. Yet hours later, as he lay in bed, the exchange continued to trouble him. Something wasn't right. Unable to sleep, he decided to fetch a glass of water. He crept into the dark hall, careful not to wake the couple while passing their bedroom, and heard them engaged in conversation. The intensity of their voices drew his ear.

"We have to say something to him," Mrs. Maguire was saying. "I won't be able to keep pretending. Truth is truth."

"I know, Nora. I know," her husband said. "I'm just not sure how to phrase it."

"Well, if you don't say it, I will."

"Aye. All right. Just give me the night to think it over, will ye."

"Fine. You have until tomorrow."

They knew.

For weeks, Shan's photograph had been plastered across America. Maybe somehow the news had traveled. Maybe he'd shared too much at supper, clues that solidified the connection. He rubbed his bare cheek, wishing he hadn't felt safe enough to shave away his cover.

He should go. In the morning, he would rise early and gather his sparse belongings.

He would seek another refuge, once more without a home.

54

A note of thanks waited on the pillow. When the couple awoke and saw no sign of Shan, they would peek into his room and read his genial words. Relief would overcome them, as any needed confrontation would have left with Shan.

He skulked into the hall, travel bag in hand. Thankfully the Maguires' bedroom door remained closed. Shan had slept longer than he'd planned, but dawn had barely broken. There was still a chance for a clean getaway.

He navigated the stairs with care. On the third step down, the wood creaked from his weight, and he cringed. He had just reached the bottom when a rustling came from his left.

Mr. Maguire sat at the dinner table, gazing out the window. The start of daylight brushed a soft glow over his features. When Shan took another step, the man turned.

"Shanley," he said. "Could you not sleep well either, lad?"

"Not really," Shan said, which was true.

"Would you care for warm milk?" Mr. Maguire raised his ceramic mug. "Usually does the trick for me."

Shan went to decline, but Mr. Maguire gave him a bewildered look. "Leaving so soon, are ye?"

Shan glanced down at his travel bag. "I have some things to do yet, and didn't want to wake you."

Mr. Maguire sighed, contemplating. "Well, then. I suppose now's the time we'd better have a chat."

Shan wavered, certain this wasn't necessary.

"Please." Mr. Maguire gestured to the chair across from him.

The man had always given so much. How could Shan not honor the request?

He set down his bag and plodded his way over. The second he took a seat, Mr. Maguire leaned forward with clasped hands on the table.

"I'm not sure at all the best way to say this. So I'm just going to come right out with it."

Hopefully, the pain would lessen for them both if the discussion passed quickly.

"Shanley," he began, and hesitated. "You have a second father. He was a sailor from America."

Taken aback by the unexpected course, Shan stared at him.

"I understand this must come as a great shock."

The only shocking part was Mr. Maguire's knowledge of this.

"John Lewis," Shan supplied.

"You knew? So your mother told ye?"

Shan shook his head. "I found a letter. It was from him to Mam. In one of her books."

Mr. Maguire picked up his mug and sat back, appearing relieved. But Shan leaned forward in turn, anxious to know where the conversation was leading, and how the Maguires had come to uncover any of this. He had never shared a word with them on the topic, not wanting to risk shaming his mam's memory in the eyes of others.

Could Uncle Will have spilled the tale after a few too many pints? Or maybe he'd confided in Doc O'Halloran during a visit to the flat. It didn't take long for gossip, Shan had learned, to make the rounds on an island.

"Do you know anything more than that?" he asked, equally wary and hopeful.

After a sip of milk, Mr. Maguire said, "I

can only tell you what I've heard."

Shan was glad he had already taken a seat. On the verge of the unknown, he braced himself before signaling with a nod.

"In that case, here's my understanding . . ." Mr. Maguire geared up, setting down his cup. "When your mother was nineteen, she was in Liverpool on a mission with the church and met a special fellow. They apparently fell in love instantly and spent every spare moment together. On the morning she was to return home, the sailor proposed marriage. He had no idea how they'd manage, just that he couldn't bear not seeing her again. Your mother accepted, and after telling her parents the news, she would come right back to marry. Then John would arrange for her to join him in America once he shipped home.

"Sadly, as feared, her parents heartily protested. She ran back to the sailor anyway, only to discover his crew had shipped out. John tried his best to find her, having no address to speak of. But after several months and telegrams from various ports, he located the church she'd traveled with. He mailed her a letter with hopes of reuniting, yet heard nothing. He wrote many more, but all were ignored. Still serving in the Navy, what could he do? Though heartbroken, he eventually gave up."

"His final letter," Shan chimed in, "that was the one I'd found." At last he could understand how the sailor's words on the page fit into their story. "Please, keep going."

"You see, months before, your mother came to suspect she was in the family way. Shunned by her parents, she had no money or home. When the doctor confirmed her condition, she wept from despair. It seemed the sailor was gone for good. But the doctor — never married and many years older than her — gave her another option. An offer that provided security for her and, most of all, her child."

"It was me," Shan thought aloud. Finally he comprehended the choice his mother had made, and he loved her all the more. But he was also stricken by the tragedy of it all. "So the sailor never knew any of this?"

"Not until many years later, when he received a letter."

"A letter? From whom?"

"Your mother," Mr. Maguire said. "She wrote it when she was suffering from the consumption. Certain you'd be orphaned soon, she reached out to John, confessing the whole lot. She wanted him to know you were his son."

"He knows I exist?" Shan said, stupefied.

"After saving up a good sum, he came looking for ye. Searched high and low, town after town. Even had your photograph from your mother."

Shan took a moment to digest the blistering revelation. He had to remind himself to breathe. "When?"

"About six months after you left for America."

The irony was enough to make Shan burst into tears — or laughter.

"We told him we knew you but had no inkling when we'd hear word. He stayed in Dublin, waiting for a postcard, a telegram. Anything. He'd come around sometimes, just to hear stories about you and your love of records and music."

"That's how you learned all of this," Shan realized.

"Aye. Then after a while, he knew he ought to move on with his life. He married and had children. A boy and a girl."

Shan gazed out the window, orange and pink lighting the sky. By a cruel twist of fate, John Lewis was probably living in Brooklyn now. One of the many places Shan wouldn't be able to visit for years to come. "Where did he go?" he dared ask.

"He never left, lad. He's here. In Dublin."

Shan's face snapped back to him, and his throat tightened. "What?" he rasped.

"Works at Trinity College. A music professor, he is."

A thousand thoughts raced and tumbled through Shan's mind. The sailor — his father — was alive. And here. And he'd wanted Shan in his life. All that time they had been searching for each other, they'd have likely crossed paths if just one of them had stayed put.

Shan registered a gentle hand patting his arm. He looked back at Mr. Maguire, who smiled gingerly. "As I said, I know this must be quite a shock. There's no rush at all. But if ever you're ready, Caitlín would be glad to take you to meet him."

For Shan, there was no question of *if*.

"How is now?"

The music building on campus didn't open for hours yet. But the minute it did, Shan followed Caitlín inside. As they walked, her flared green dress swished beneath her winter coat.

"He's got a half-past-eight class every mornin'," she explained, guiding Shan through the empty halls. "If his routine hasn't changed, he'll be settling into his office first."

Shan nodded, his nerves suddenly buzzing. After several turns, Caitlín stopped before an office door. The room appeared dark, but she peeked through the glass pane. She even tried the knob. Locked.

In the distance, footsteps echoed. They were gaining volume, coming closer.

Shan removed his hat and smoothed his hair, styled with tonic, and straightened his tie. Though sized perfectly, his suit felt confining.

"You look handsome," Caitlín said, and squeezed his hand.

It was silly to fret about his appearance, really, but he couldn't help himself. The academic surroundings of brick walls, polished tiled floors, and fancy display cases added to the sense that he was preparing for an exam.

The footfalls continued to approach. From around the corner some thirty feet away, a suited man appeared wearing thick glasses and a long beard. He walked with the aid of a cane.

Shan looked at Caitlín, who shook her head. It wasn't him.

"He'll be here," she whispered.

Once the bearded man passed, Shan started to pace. He rubbed the sixpence in his trouser pocket, the coin as smooth as silk, trying to envision his father.

Father. Would Shan call him that? Or was "Professor Lewis" more appropriate? The man was still a stranger.

Either way, if he didn't arrive soon, there would be no time to talk before class. A meeting at the end of the day would be more practical.

"Come over and sit beside me," Caitlín said. She had taken a seat on a bench across the hall.

Fussing wouldn't speed up the process.

He sat down next to her, clutching his hat. On the way here, he'd grown excited over not only meeting his father, but also having two siblings. But now doubts were filtering in. The man had moved on with his life, Mr. Maguire had said. Established his own family. Why would he want another grown son complicating the situation?

Shan could write a letter first, to give the man time to absorb the shock.

Caitlín broke into the thought. "You know what the middle initial stands for, don't ye?"

She was clearly trying to distract him. He followed the direction of her finger to the stenciled letters on the door: *John S. Lewis.*

He shook his head, not in the mind-set to guess.

"It's for Shanley," she said, a point of assurance. He noticed she smelled of lavender. Together with her smile, it managed to bring him comfort.

"Caitlín?" a man's voice came from the side. "What a lovely surprise."

"Hello, Professor," she replied, rising.

Though she didn't state his name, Shan knew it was him. His features, while aged by decades, matched those on the sailor's photo ingrained in Shan's mind. The downturned eyes, the thin lips. His uniform long gone, he now wore a brown suit and tweed overcoat. He removed his brimmed hat while greeting Caitlín, revealing wavy black hair like Shan's.

"What can I do for you?" the man said to her brightly.

Caitlín glanced at Shan, waiting for him to stand and answer. But his legs had turned to stone and his mouth refused to cooperate. All notions of what to say in this moment had slipped out of reach.

"I've brought someone to see ye," she supplied. "A person you've been waiting to meet for a very long time."

"Is that so?" John looked over, interest piqued.

Mustering the courage, Shan finally came to his feet and said, "My name is Shan."

He got no further before the man's expression changed. Like shadows from passing clouds, the expressions on his face moved from curiosity to recognition. Disbelief. Then joy. His jaw trembled and his eyes moistened as he stared at Shan, a mirror of his youth. A past that had haunted him with longing and hope, love and loss. A portion of himself always missing in his depths.

Just as it was for Shan.

Overwhelmed by the journeys that had delivered them here, they both stood unmoving, paralyzed by emotion, until Shan drew a breath and took the first step.

AUTHOR'S NOTE

I was searching online one day when I happened across an intriguing documentary titled *Children of Alcatraz*. The compilation of interviews featured people who had grown up on Alcatraz Island as children of the prison staff, some even claiming to have secretly befriended notorious inmates despite rules to prevent any contact. By the end of the video, I knew I had a story to tell, one of a hardened prisoner whose acquaintance with the young daughter of a guard would ultimately change both of their lives.

When I began to research Alcatraz, I was particularly surprised to learn about an inmate named Elliot Michener. As an entrusted passman, he had been assigned to work in the warden's mansion, where he later built and tended a greenhouse, and was even granted special permission to work outdoors seven days a week under limited supervision. The paradoxical setting fascinated me: one of a colorful, peaceful haven meant for nurturing and growth, set next to a bleak concrete prison where lives often withered. During a night tour on Alcatraz, surrounded by the steel bars and cold gray walls of a cell, I gained a sense of appreciation for the cherished respite found in that greenhouse.

It was on this trip that I became enthralled with numerous escape attempts outside of the widely known Great Escape of 1962. I was amazed to discover how many had occurred in broad daylight, some without even the cover of fog. Two cases that especially piqued my interest took place below the Model Industries Building, including that of Ralph Roe and Theodore Cole. Although their bodies were never found, and various reports of sightings filtered in for years afterward, the two were soon presumed to have drowned. Similarly, Floyd Hamilton, the driver for Bonnie and Clyde commonly dubbed "Pretty Boy" Floyd, was also pronounced drowned after an extensive search failed to find him hiding in a stack of discarded tires in one of the island caves. He surrendered two days later, propelled by an onslaught of hunger, frigid temperatures, and snapping crabs.

In another attempt, using inflated rubber gloves for floatation, John Paul Scott managed to swim across the bay, nearly reaching fog-enshrouded Fort Point before he clung to a rock for fear of being swept off to sea. Battered and in shock from the cold, he was treated in a mainland hospital before being returned to Alcatraz. Other true accounts that influenced my story were tales of inmate performances in plays and bands at various U.S. penitentiaries, as well as internal corruption that infested the ranks of guards, chaplains, and even wardens.

While I made great efforts to stay true to history, conflicting research materials occasionally forced me to choose the most likely among them. The notable liberties I consciously took for storytelling purposes involved the following: inmate number AZ-257 was actually assigned to Rudolph "Jack" Hensley; the "Rule of Silence" was relaxed late, not early, in 1937; in the early prison years, movie showings under Warden Johnston were limited to holidays and special occasions, later to become monthly events; and, to my knowledge, Ralph Roe's landscape detail prior to working in the mat shop is fictional.

In addition, Burton "Whitey" Phillips's assault on Warden Johnston in the mess hall occurred a few weeks earlier while prisoners were in line to exit; to subdue the attack, Whitey was tackled by officer Joseph Steere and knocked out with a billy club by Lieutenant Culver. As for duties at the warden's residence: it was the wife of Warden Madigan (Johnston's successor) who was said to have left the radio on and newspapers lying around, and the warden's greenhouse was actually built and tended by Elliot Michener many years later. The lower, rose-terrace greenhouse, however, did stand during the story's timeline and was cared for by inmates.

For information about Alcatraz, I relied heavily on the following books: *Alcatraz: The Definitive History of the Penitentiary Years* by Michael Esslinger; *Alcatraz: The Gangster Years* by David Ward with Gene Kassebaum; *Guarding the Rock* by Ernest Lageson Sr. and Ernest Lageson; and from inmates' perspectives: *Alcatraz: The True End of the Line* by Darwin E. Coon and *On the Rock* by Alvin Karpis. The documentary I found most intriguing was National Geographic's *Alcatraz Breakout: New Evidence*, featuring a U.S. marshal who uncovered evidence strongly suggesting that the inmates known for the Great Escape actually succeeded in crossing the bay, though we will likely never know for sure.

To learn more about vaudeville and burlesque, respectively, I highly recommend the documentaries *Pioneers of Primetime* and *Behind the Burly Q: The Story of Burlesque in America.* From creative ways strip acts evaded decency laws to chorus line girls blowing bubbles for bathtub routines, the tales included in these videos — as was the case for much of my research for this novel — often left me saying, "You just can't make this stuff up."

Please turn the page
for a very special Q&A
with Kristina McMorris.

Who or what was your greatest inspiration when creating Shanley Keagan?

My late maternal grandfather's roots all trace back to Ireland. Since he and I were very close, I've always had a special fondness for all things Irish, most of all his limericks, which never failed to make me laugh. My visits there only solidified how much I enjoyed the music, the people, and of course the breathtaking landscape.

Still, when I set out to write a 1930s story about a guy from Brooklyn caught in a web of crime that leads to Alcatraz, I assumed he'd be Italian American. But while imagining his history, I pictured him on a ship and realized he was an immigrant from Ireland. You see, my grandfather was dark Irish with an olive complexion, brown eyes, and wavy black hair. Growing up, I often heard my mother say how her dad was easily mistaken for an Italian. Fortunately, that memory came back at just the right time.

Were there other characters in the story that were influenced by real people?

For creating the Capellos, historical memoirs about Italian immigrant families in New York were tremendously helpful. But also, during my college years, I was fortunate enough to live in Florence, leaving me with a lifelong passion for Italy (and not just for their amazing food and wine!). So, Mr. and Mrs. Capello were largely shaped by people I met there. At a friend's house in Genoa, I remember we'd barely finished eating and her mother was already gearing up to cook the next meal, always insisting that we weren't eating enough.

I also drew on a lifetime of experiences with my father. Although he emigrated from Kyoto, many of his traits seem to parallel those of a typical Italian immigrant father, such as his passion for family, his determination (okay, stubbornness), his heavy accent even after four decades in the States, and his deep pride in being American. In fact, much like Shan's reaction upon seeing the Statue of Liberty, my father still speaks about how, back in Japan, his chest would tighten every time he heard "The Star-Spangled Banner." And like Mr. Capello, my father still has a penchant for practicing English words over and over (every so often, we make him say "aluminum" just for fun).

Which historical facts surprised you most while researching for this book?
The first one that comes to mind is "Machine Gun" Kelly serving as an altar boy at Alcatraz. The irony still makes me smile —

as do many tales from the burlesque circuits, and the creative use of teacups during Prohibition. On a more sobering note, I was astounded to learn about the "Rule of Silence," which many claim was one of the greatest hardships at Alcatraz, along with the monotony. I also had no idea that Al Capone had literally gone insane during his time there, due to the onset of paresis from syphilis. And I was equally surprised by all of the ways inmates were able to create and hide weapons while imprisoned, and even skirt the metal detectors!

Were there other interesting true accounts that didn't make it into the final draft?
There were definitely some entertaining facts I wanted to include but held back for the sake of story. I recall two that involved Capone at Alcatraz: the first was a formal reprimand he received in the mess hall for not eating the outside edges of his cake, since wasting was forbidden; and how he would subscribe to magazines that were later passed around to his approved list of fellow inmates, sometimes scratching their names off in retaliation for one grudge or another — while in the past, he would have likely settled the score with a bullet.

Other tidbits that didn't make the final cut included the fact that families could pay to watch baseball games in public stands at the Leavenworth penitentiary; that at one time, corruption at the Atlanta penitentiary enabled inmates to live in a luxurious hotel near the prison rather than in the cell house; and that notable escape attempts at Alcatraz had relied upon secret help from up to twenty prisoners. On a separate note, I was also amazed by the dark nature of such silent films as *Broken Blossoms,* in contrast to popular lighthearted features starring the likes of Charlie Chaplin.

What proved to be the most important or rewarding part of your research?
Aside from interviewing people and hearing their stories firsthand, I love hands-on research the most. For previous novels, my favorite experiences were a ride on a restored B-17 and a pilgrimage at Manzanar War Relocation Camp. For *The Edge of Lost,* it was undoubtedly my night tour at Alcatraz. Later, while writing scenes set in the mess hall or cellblock or on the docks, I was able to close my eyes and recall the gas canisters on the walls and the thunderous sound of the prison doors slamming shut.

Had you planned the major plots twists at the end of the story when you first set out to write the book?

I'm typically such a plotter, since my novels are usually set during World War II and therefore are heavily dictated by a historical timeline. In this case, I had a strong sense of the plotline, but at least half the story unfolded in a different way than I'd first envisioned. This included the major twists toward the end of the book. Since I personally didn't see them coming, hopefully most readers won't either!

What was your greatest challenge in writing *The Edge of Lost*?

I admit, I spent an embarrassing number of hours just sitting in a chair, staring at a map of Alcatraz Island, feeling like an inmate trying to conjure a way to escape with only the tools and resources a prisoner could have possibly acquired at the time. On some days, it was enough to make me batty.

Also, as I mentioned, the 1940s was my usual comfort zone when it came to historical writing, so tackling the '20s and '30s was a bit daunting, especially when combined with multiple ethnicities and cultures spanning from vaudeville to Alcatraz. I care so much about accuracy that it was easy to obsess about the tiniest details — only to cut them later when storytelling took priority. I'd venture to guess every historical novelist knows exactly what I'm talking about. But then, I suppose that's why writers tend to keep chocolate and wine on hand. In my case, a nice Italian red.

■ ■ ■ ■

A READING GROUP GUIDE: THE EDGE OF LOST

KRISTINA MCMORRIS

■ ■ ■ ■

ABOUT THIS GUIDE

The suggested questions are included to enhance your group's reading of Kristina McMorris's *The Edge of Lost.*

DISCUSSION QUESTIONS

1. Love, forgiveness, redemption, loyalty, and sacrifice are among the most prominent elements in the book. In your opinion, what was the main theme of the story?

2. At a young age, Shan learned to quickly adapt to his surroundings, much like a chameleon. How did this ability both help and hinder his personal growth?

3. Who were your favorite and least favorite characters, and why? Were there any you disliked at first but grew to care for later? If so, what altered your opinion?

4. Early on, Shan became dependent on humor to survive and later recognized how trust and likability are often cultivated through making people laugh. Discuss how different each segment of his life would have been without this skill.

5. From Uncle Will's exchanges with Doc O'Halloran, Shan observed, "When a person had something you needed, it was best to show you were worthy." How did this belief translate into Shan's relationships with each member of the Capello family?

6. From Irish pubs to Bronx supper clubs, and burlesque shows to prison cells, *The Edge of Lost* features several diverse parts of history. Did you learn something new from the story? What was the most interesting?

7. In recalling his late parents, "Shan felt the weight of their absence, as heavy as stone on his chest." How did this traumatic childhood loss influence his future choices?

8. Not only Shan, but Mr. Capello, Nick, and Josie all sought a form of redemption. Do you think each one fully achieved that? Is it possible to right a wrong with an unrelated act?

9. In hindsight, much of life could be viewed as ripples set into motion by a handful of pivotal events. How different would Shan's

life have been if he had never left Ireland? How would this have affected the lives of the other major characters?

10. The deeply held secrets of many characters were revealed throughout the story. Do you agree with their reasons for keeping those secrets? Is withholding the truth the same as lying? Is it always best to be forthcoming?

11. In an effort to help others, Shan chose to enter the scene of the robbery and later to escape with Sadie. Would you have done the same in both situations? If not, why?

12. How do you imagine Shan's life five years after the end of the story? Do you think he ever reunites with the Capellos?

13. Though alluded to, Sadie's outcome was never fully depicted. Do you think she ever found her mother? If not, where do you picture her?

14. How did you interpret the cover art of *The Edge of Lost* when you first began reading the story? Has your view changed since finishing the book?

The employees of Thorndike Press hope you have enjoyed this Large Print book. All our Thorndike, Wheeler, and Kennebec Large Print titles are designed for easy reading, and all our books are made to last. Other Thorndike Press Large Print books are available at your library, through selected bookstores, or directly from us.

For information about titles, please call:
(800) 223-1244

or visit our Web site at:
http://gale.cengage.com/thorndike

To share your comments, please write:
Publisher
Thorndike Press
10 Water St., Suite 310
Waterville, ME 04901